Acclaim for Lindsay Harrel

THE JOY OF FALLING

"In *The Joy of Falling*, Harrel beautifully connects with us as she takes us to the hard places of grief—the doubt, the fear, the sadness. Then, with sensitivity and hope, she walks us back out to the dawn on the other side—to joy! Touching, true and full of sensory detail, this book enchants."

—Katherine Reay, bestselling author of *Dear Mr. Knightley* and *The Printed Letter Bookshop*

"What started as a story about a race turned into a deeply moving novel about recovering from grief and finding joy not just at the end but in the middle of the process. Full of powerful truths, *The Joy of Falling* is a beautifully written novel that made me laugh, made me cry, and has all the feels of a book you want to read over and over. Highly recommended!"

—Susan May Warren, *USA TODAY* bestselling, RITA award-winning author of *The Way of the Brave*

THE SECRETS OF PAPER AND INK

"Harrel unspools a gentle, captivating narrative about women who unknowingly discover their strengths and fortitude. As they learn to let go of the heartbreaks of life, they find joy, enlightenment, and romance along the way."

—*Shelf Awareness*

"This is a charming story of female strength, friendship, and forgiveness."

—

"Harrel delivers a wonderfully unexpected and skillfully executed adventure of love, loss, and healing. The ebb and flow of perspectives between two modern-day women and the life of a mysterious Victorian woman mesmerizes and captivates. While each woman's life is individually compelling, when intricately stitched together into the same tapestry, the result is unforgettable and breathtaking. Book lovers will be right at home in (or perhaps envious of) the quaint and cozy Cornwall bookstore and intrigued by the historical journal's mystery. The author champions the soothing balm of friendship and community, all while exuding a spiritual strength, hope, and irrefutable faith-based identity in the face of brokenness, desperation, and betrayal."

–Hope by the Book, Gold Star Review

"This book interlaces the voices and time periods of the women as they rotate narrating chapters, creating an engaging story perfect for readers who enjoy strong women of faith, budding romantic relationships, and historical and contemporary English settings."

–Booklist

". . . uplifting tale . . . a charming story about finding one's voice after letting go of the past."

–Publishers Weekly

"A historical mystery and sweet modern-day story entwine to offer a message of healing, hope, and second chances set in charming Cornwall."

–Rachel Linden, bestselling author
of *The Enlightenment of Bees*

"In a delightful weaving of past and present, Lindsay Harrel creates authentic characters around a moving story that both inspires and encourages. *The Secrets of Paper and Ink* is about broken people, second chances, hope, and—my personal favorite—the incredible power of story."

–Heidi Chiavaroli, Carol award-winning author
of *Freedom's Ring* and *The Hidden Side*

"In *The Secrets of Paper and Ink*, Lindsay Harrel explores the power of love—and how it influences us to make choices that bless others, as well as ourselves. Or sometimes, we can do just the opposite and make choices that harm us and others—all the while calling it love. Harrel pens an honest, true-to-life novel that's woven through with the Truth that offers hope when our decisions—or the decisions of the ones we love—wreck our dreams for happily ever after."

–Beth K. Vogt, Christy Award-winning author

THE HEART BETWEEN US

"A bucket list from the diary of an organ donor sparks a healing journey for two sisters in this poignant tale from Harrel . . . [*The Heart Between Us*], with many descriptions of delicious foods and famous landmarks from around the globe, will please readers of travel fiction looking for an inspirational story."

–Publishers Weekly

"Narration by both Meg and Crystal, full of emotion and soul-searching, will resonate with anyone who has struggled to see another point of view. Both characters are drawn as independent and persistent, occasionally to their detriment, but not too stubborn to get past stumbling blocks. Harrel's (*One More Song to Sing*, 2016) second novel is a charmingly gentle read that will please those who enjoy faith-based, hopeful fiction with a delightfully positive tone."

–Booklist

"Harrel's second book is a well-crafted, compelling story about love, hope, relationships, family importance, and God's trustworthiness."

–CBA Market

"Lindsay Harrel has penned a charming story that is sure to touch the hearts of her readers. Through the stories of Megan and her sister Crystal, readers get a glimpse of adventure, restoration, conquered fears, and realized dreams. Lindsay will no doubt win readers with this heartfelt story."

—Lauren K. Denton, *USA TODAY* bestselling author
of *The Hideaway* and *Hurricane Season*

"A sweet story of sisterhood, familial bonds, sacrificial love, and finding your own identity amidst the storms of life. Poignant with tender moments, as well as laughter, *The Heart Between Us* is a touching novel that is sure to please."

—Catherine West, author of *The Memory
of You* and *Where Hope Begins*

"I love this story of facing our fears. Harrel pens a clever, well-written love story between two sisters, the men in their lives and the dreams of a heart donor. Life is more fleeting than we know and this timeless story reminds us to love well."

—Rachel Hauck, *New York Times* bestselling author

"*The Heart Between Us* is an absolute gem of a story. The intriguing premise drew me in from the start, but it was the authentic characters and their relatable struggles that kept me reading. I especially loved getting to travel vicariously through Megan and Crystal! A heart-tugging, not-to-be-missed book from an author who belongs on your keeper shelf."

—Melissa Tagg, author of the Walker Family series

"Lindsay Harrel has given readers an engaging story about stepping past fear and finding adventure in the unexpected. *The Heart Between Us* is sure to become a fan favorite!"

—Katie Ganshert, award-winning author of *Life After*

The
Joy
of
Falling

ALSO BY LINDSAY HARREL

The Heart Between Us

The Secrets of Paper and Ink

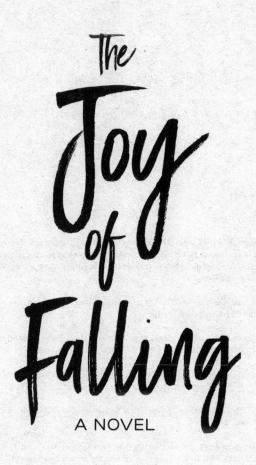

The Joy of Falling

A NOVEL

LINDSAY HARREL

THOMAS NELSON

Since 1798

The Joy of Falling

© 2020 Lindsay Harrel

All rights reserved. No portion of this book may be reproduced, stored in a retrieval system, or transmitted in any form or by any means—electronic, mechanical, photocopy, recording, scanning, or other—except for brief quotations in critical reviews or articles, without the prior written permission of the publisher.

Published in Nashville, Tennessee, by Thomas Nelson. Thomas Nelson is a registered trademark of HarperCollins Christian Publishing, Inc.

Published in association with the Books & Such Literary Management, 52 Mission Circle, Suite 122, PMB 170, Santa Rosa, California 95409-5370, www.booksandsuch.com.

Thomas Nelson titles may be purchased in bulk for educational, business, fund-raising, or sales promotional use. For information, please email SpecialMarkets@ThomasNelson.com.

Quote from C. S. Lewis, *A Grief Observed* (New York: HarperOne), 2015. First published 1961 by Faber and Faber.

Scripture quotations are taken from the Holy Bible, New International Version®, NIV®. Copyright © 1973, 1978, 1984, 2011 by Biblica, Inc.® Used by permission of Zondervan. All rights reserved worldwide. www.Zondervan.com. The "NIV" and "New International Version" are trademarks registered in the United States Patent and Trademark Office by Biblica, Inc.®

Publisher's Note: This novel is a work of fiction. Names, characters, places, and incidents are either products of the author's imagination or used fictitiously. All characters are fictional, and any similarity to people living or dead is purely coincidental.

ISBN 978-0-7852-3000-7 (trade paper)
ISBN 978-0-7852-3002-1 (e-book)
ISBN 978-0-7852-3001-4 (downloadable audio)

Library of Congress Cataloging-in-Publication Data

CIP data is available upon request.

Printed in the United States of America
20 21 22 23 24 LSC 10 9 8 7 6 5 4 3 2 1

Once upon a time, color had dominated Eva Jamison's days.

Now she stared at a white wall, with nothing but a black computer screen, a pen holder, and a stapler decorating her tiny world. Flat off-white fixtures overhead fed canned fluorescent light to the open room where her desk was squeezed in with ten others. The single window in the space—located about as far from Eva's desk as possible—gave a view not of Central Park but the side of another gray building.

But it wasn't the Manhattan Heart Center's fault that it was an artist's nightmare, with its minimalist black furniture, drab olive carpet, and tacky motivational posters.

No, the problem was her. She didn't belong here.

And yet this was the only place she wanted to be.

"Eva."

She startled. The center's director, Maryanne, stood next to Eva's desk, wisps of graying hair falling from her bun.

"Oh, hi. What's up?"

"I need those reports for my one o'clock." Maryanne checked her teal watch, which clashed horribly with her fuzzy red short-sleeved sweater—an interesting choice given the cloying end-of-August humidity outside. "Did you send them?"

Reports? . . . Which reports? Eva's cheeks burned. "Um . . . I thought so." She turned back to her computer and navigated to her woeful to-do list. Found the item Maryanne referenced.

Not checked as complete. Ugh.

"I'm sorry, Maryanne. I was working on it yesterday and got distracted. I'll get on it right away."

Maryanne rubbed the corner of her right eye, clearly suppressing a sigh. "No, it's fine. Send Jerry what you have and he'll help me finish."

"I don't mind. Really." She was supposed to meet her best friend, Kimberly Jensen, for lunch in a few minutes, but she'd understand if Eva needed to reschedule.

"No, no. We've got it."

In other words, Eva had failed. Again. Last week's debacle—in which Eva had accidentally sent an internal message to all donors—had upended what little confidence she'd gained at her job.

If she were a paid employee, Eva surely would have been fired by now.

But the nonprofit center couldn't afford to turn away volnteers, even ones so ill-suited to administrative work as Eva Jamison.

"I really am sorry."

"Why don't you take your lunch break? In fact, why not just take the rest of the day off? We'll see you tomorrow, fresh and ready to go." Maryanne's tone indicated wishful thinking rather than certainty that any improvement in Eva's work would ever occur.

As Maryanne walked away, Eva locked her computer and snagged her phone to text Kimberly. Like always, the photo on her screen sent a jolt to her heart: Eva in a gorgeous A-line dress on a beach in Hawaii, her self-made bouquet of orange roses, cymbidium orchids, bird-of-paradise, and red ginger dangling from one hand as the other embraced her new husband.

They'd looked so different—Brent with blond curls and skin that tanned only after burning a few times in early summer, Eva with dark eyes and long brown hair. But their hearts were the same.

He'd been her inspiration. Her muse. Her joy.

All that was gone now.

Everything was gray.

Eva sent a text, grabbed her purse, and hurried down the hallway.

"I have to redo everything Eva touches." Her coworker Valerie's voice drifted from the break room. "It's ridiculous."

Eva ground to a stop outside the door. She told her feet to move, but they wouldn't.

"I'll admit, she's not very good at remembering the details. But she's very sweet and friendly."

Thank you, Susan. The fiftysomething woman had been kind to Eva since her first day here six months ago.

"But we need someone who is also competent enough to follow simple directions. It's not like the stuff Maryanne gives her is difficult."

"Her husband and brother-in-law died in a horrific accident. She's still grieving."

"Oh, sure, bring up the dead husband," Valerie huffed. "We've all had tragedy. My husband left me, but do you see me unable to do the simplest of tasks? No. And I didn't get one cent out of my ex. Brent left Eva richer than God."

Eva nearly protested out loud. Sure, No Frills Fitness—the string of high-end gyms and yoga studios that Brent co-owned with his best friend, Marc—had done well in the last three years. But other than taking out enough to pay the rent on her Brooklyn apartment and other basic living expenses, Eva had most of it tied up in investments and savings.

Money had never mattered to her or Brent. It had only been a means to live out the adventures of life.

"That's enough."

"What? I wish she'd just leave us a sizable donation and take her attempts to help far, far away."

Eva had considered doing that, but being here, in a place that had meant a lot to her husband, made her feel closer to him somehow.

Susan's audible sigh met Eva's ears. "I feel bad for her. You can tell she just wants to make a difference. I only wish there was a kind way to tell her that her efforts are making more work for the rest of us."

Tears welled in Eva's eyes as she strode out of there, nearly stumbling across the freshly waxed epoxy floors in the center's lobby. When she exited the building, a wave of oppressive heat smacked her in the face. Yesterday's thunderstorm had left the air charged with moisture, and the eighty-degree temperature felt more like one hundred. Thankfully, the jaunt to the restaurant where Kimberly waited was a short one. After five minutes, Eva had managed to wipe away evidence of her cry session before walking into the trendy vegan place.

Or so she thought.

As Eva approached her friend, who sat in a corner booth studying the menu, Kimberly's head popped up and her eyes narrowed. "What's wrong?"

"Nothing, nothing. I'm fine." Eva leaned over to give Kim a hug, then slid into the booth opposite her.

Kimberly's brown hair had been pulled into a smart knot on the top of her head, accentuating her long neck. Her couture white blouse and diamond climber earrings evidenced her growing success as a wedding coordinator. "You forget I've known you since we were scrawny thirteen-year-old wannabes. I can tell when you've done some makeup patching. So spill."

"You're bossy."

"And you love me for it."

Her friend, who'd attended college in NYC and started her event-planning business after graduation, was the whole reason Eva had come here from Portland seven years ago at the age of twenty-three. When she'd called Eva about an acquaintance looking to hire an apprentice in his florist shop, Eva jumped at the chance to learn more about a career where she could put her creative tendencies to use. It definitely beat waiting tables and teaching drawing to a handful of students around town.

Despite the protests of her engineer mom and professor father—neither of whom understood their artsy daughter with no interest in college—Eva left home in a matter of days and moved in with Kimberly. They'd worked together on countless weddings since then, Eva always being Kim's florist of choice.

But that all stopped just over fifteen months ago. May 19 of last year had changed everything.

Kim set her menu down and drummed her French-tipped nails on the distressed wooden table. "Let's order and you can tell me what *is* going on, because there's something. And then I have some exciting news to share with you."

"Oh, what's up?"

"Nuh-uh." She waved the waitress over. "You first. After we order."

"I don't know what I want yet. What are you getting?"

"Santa Fe salad. But choose your own meal . . . the way you used to."

"Fine." Eva closed her eyes, lifted her finger in the air, twirled it a bit, and planted it firmly on the plastic menu. Her eyes opened, and she glanced down. "Eggplant caponata with sun-dried pesto crostini, it is."

They placed their order with the server, and then Eva sighed and told Kimberly what she'd overheard in the lunchroom, feeling no need to hold back any details. After all, Kim and Brent's mom,

Sherry, were the two reasons Eva wasn't still glued to her bed day in and day out, her apartment scattered with half-eaten salads and empty pint containers of Halo Top ice cream. When they'd seen her uncharacteristic listlessness, they'd helped her realize her need for therapy.

Her therapist, Charlotte, had recommended Eva find something productive to do with her days that would make her feel close to her husband—which in turn would hopefully make her feel like herself again. Thus, she'd landed at the heart center, a place that had become near and dear to Brent after his father died of a heart attack.

The waiter delivered their lunch as Eva finished the story about her coworkers.

Barely noticing the food's arrival, Kimberly slammed her fist on the table. The ice in their water glasses shook. "Those . . . I can't even . . . Argh!" She sat back against the black cushioned booth and folded her arms across her chest, fire in her eyes. "I want to march right up to those women and give them a piece of my mind."

Her loyalty warmed Eva's heart. "They're right, though. I'm awful at the job. But I am determined to get better. Maybe I can check out a book that'll help—there has to be an *Administrative Assisting for Dummies* or something like that." She picked up her fork and poked at the whole-grain bread topped with eggplant, olives, and capers. The fresh scent of roasted garlic aioli tickled her nose. "Enough about me. What's your great news?"

Kimberly dug into her salad. "I just secured the Carlton wedding."

"Congrats. That's amazing!" Jessica Carlton was the youngest daughter of business tycoon and billionaire Louise Carlton and her senator husband. "This will be huge for your business."

"Yeah, I'm thrilled." Her friend paused, tilting her head and studying Eva. "There's more. They saw your work in some magazine spread from early last year and specifically requested you for the flowers."

Oh. Eva swallowed a gulp. "I . . ."

"I know you've taken some time off, and I'd never push you if you're not ready." Kimberly paused. "The actual wedding isn't until the beginning of next June, if that helps. Although if you *were* ready to get back to it, I definitely have other events I could use you on in the meantime."

Something deep inside Eva roared to life at the suggestion, craving the process of creating, the merging of her soul with the world.

But with Brent gone . . .

The roar became a mew, then all was silent.

"I don't know, Kim. It's just hard, you know? Designing for weddings, when . . . Well, I'll have to think about it." But she already knew she'd be saying no.

"All right. Just let me know your decision in the next few weeks, if possible." Kimberly poked at a tomato on her plate. "Evie, I just can't help but feel like you're wasting your talent in a place where you're not appreciated—and doing something that's not you. Brent would want you to be happy, doing what you're passionate about."

"I know. But artists have to pull inspiration from a well deep inside—and mine is drained. Bone dry. When I met Brent, it was like meeting the other half of my soul. His courage and the way he lived life inspired me to be better. To be more creative."

Eva smoothed her finger down the side of her glass, making a trail in the condensation.

"But now I have nothing to give, Kim. Life has no color." Her hand thudded to the table. "And I'm afraid it never will again."

જ

For the first time in years, things were going according to plan.

Angela Jamison hustled inside Philip's Place, praying Juliet would forgive Angela's first-time tardiness in picking up her children. Her eyes roamed the waiting room and spotted her oldest daughter sitting underneath a framed photo of a golden retriever snuggling with a child. Lilly and Zach were likely in the counseling center's playroom, though the whole place seemed eerily quiet.

Kylee hunched over her phone, fingers flying across the screen. A goofy grin split the fifteen-year-old's face—evidence that she did smile on occasion, even if it was never directed at her mother.

Angela advanced and touched Kylee on the shoulder, causing her daughter to nearly drop her phone.

Upon seeing Angela, her features tightened. "Hey."

"Hi, sweetie. Did you have a good session today?"

Silence. "Sure."

Angela bit the inside of her cheek. "Where are your brother and sister?"

"Back there somewhere. Waiting for you." Accusation laced her tone.

"I'm sorry I'm late. But I have some good news. Great, actually."

Kylee stood and snatched the keys from Angela's hand. "I'll be in the car."

"I was hoping you'd go"—the door shut—"get your siblings." Angela blew out a breath and unclenched her fists. *Buck up, Angela.* She pasted a smile on her face and wandered into the bowels of the facility. Was this how children felt when heading into the principal's office? "Hello."

"We're back here," Juliet called from her office.

Angela crossed the large central room filled with toy bins and tables, each of which housed a different craft—from coloring to clay, paper doll making to beads. She reached Juliet's door, the scent of lavender greeting her as she entered.

Seven-year-old Lilly lay curled up on the red couch asleep, her head resting on Juliet's lap, and ten-year-old Zach sat in the La-Z-Boy tucked in the corner, reading his latest library book.

Juliet looked up. "Hey, Angela." The mom of two, who couldn't have been much older than Angela's thirty-six years, stroked Lilly's long brown hair.

Something twisted in Angela's gut at the sight. "I'm very sorry I'm so late. I texted Kylee . . ." The excuse seemed insufficient now. Yes, a promotion was a big deal, especially in Angela's world. After Wes died, she'd transitioned from homeschooling her children to working forty-five hours during the week as a realty office receptionist and fifteen hours at a local spa's front desk on the weekend. But as her military father had always said, punctuality was tantamount to godliness—one of the only lessons he'd intentionally taught her before shipping her off to live with her aunt in California.

"It's fine. My husband is taking the boys to a Friday night movie, so I'd planned to catch up on work anyway. I hope everything's okay."

"Oh yes. More than." Angela moved toward Zach, who hadn't yet acknowledged her. "Hey, bud." She squatted down to his level and placed a hand over his book.

He glanced up, his already big blue eyes made larger by the lenses in his glasses. "Oh, hi, Mom."

"How was your time at group?" That's what they called the two hours they spent here every Friday afternoon. *Group.*

Whatever they called it, this place was a godsend. When her sweet Lilly had gotten into a fight, Zach had received his first F, and Kylee had stopped communicating with her beyond complaints and eye rolls, Angela had been at a loss. Punishment hadn't seemed quite right, even though their behaviors warranted that. The school counselor had suggested Philip's Place, which hosted weekly grief support for the whole family. They split up into different age groups and used storytelling, art, music, play, and talking to process their grief together.

All three of the kids had fallen in love with their time here, and they were usually enthusiastic when she asked how their day had gone.

Zach rubbed his fingers along the edge of the comic book's glossy pages. "It was fine."

It was clear that was all she was going to get from him, at least for now. "Awesome." She forced cheer into her voice. "Kylee's waiting in the car if you want to join her. I'll grab Lil and meet you there."

"Cool." He snagged his backpack and book, his chicken legs lumbering out of the office.

"Sorry for the trouble. It won't happen again." Angela moved to pick up Lilly, but Juliet's hand shot out to touch Angela's arm.

"Angela, would you mind sitting for a minute? I'd like to talk to you."

Oh no. Here it came. Was the counseling center finally going to begin charging for the group sessions? For the five or so months the kids had been attending, group had been free. But what if the gravy train was about to come to a grinding halt? How would she ever manage to pay for it? Her new promotion came with a raise, but she'd hoped—

"Angela?" Juliet lowered her voice.

"Sorry." She perched on the edge of the brown seat Zach had vacated. "What is it?"

"First, we really miss you around here."

"Oh. Thank you." How could Juliet miss her? She didn't even know Angela, who'd only attended two group sessions months ago. "I wish I could make it more often, but you know. Work."

No, that wasn't the only reason, but she wasn't admitting the other to a therapist. Because only one emotion had overtaken

Angela when she'd listened to the other members go on about how much they missed their spouses.

Rage.

Rage at the senselessness of Wes's death. At his choices leading up to it. At him.

But what good did all of that anger do? Wes was gone, and sitting around talking about it wouldn't change that. Not for her, at least. Besides, she was too busy making sure her kids had the things they needed, since it was now all on her shoulders. Yes, Eva and Sherry had offered to lend her money, but Angela had to show her children how to survive when tragedy hit.

That strength was the only thing holding them together fifteen months later.

"I understand." Juliet's fingers stilled in their steady movement across Lilly's head. "Have you ever explained to your kids why you aren't here?" Her words gentled, as if she sensed that giving Angela one more thing to manage would break her.

"They know I have to work." Angela hesitated. "Why do you ask?"

"During our full-group sharing time today, your children expressed concern that you are distant and don't seem to care about your husband's death."

Angela shot out of her chair. "That's not true at all." Oops. She hadn't meant to raise her voice. Fortunately—or maybe unfortunately—Lilly didn't stir.

"Angela, I'm not accusing you." Juliet talked as if she were addressing a wounded animal that might strike at any moment. "I'm merely telling you that when children don't have all the information, they still process things as if they do—and they make assumptions if they aren't told what they need to know. I'd encourage you to consider how you talk about Wes and invite your kids to share anything they're thinking with you."

The counselor glanced down at Lilly, then back at Angela. "And consider trying to make it to group, even if it's just once a month. During the half hour when we are all together, many children feel more supported when their caregiver is with them."

Perhaps Angela could get Sherry to attend with the kids. She already depended on her mother-in-law much more than Sherry liked to babysit, but . . .

As if sensing Angela's train of thought, Juliet made eye contact with her for several moments before speaking again. "They need *you*, Angela. You're their mother. I know you're hurting too—"

"I'm fine, actually. Doing better than ever. Just got a promotion." Angela fiddled with the wedding ring on the chain around her neck. It hadn't fit her finger since she'd had Lilly, and she'd never bothered to have it resized. "So now I'm going to have even more time with them. We're going to get through this, together."

"I can tell you're a survivor. But there's more to grief than surviving. Someday you're going to thrive."

"Of course we will." And this promotion was just the start they needed. "Thank you for your concern, Juliet. My children are blessed to have you in their corner." Angela meant it, however stale she sounded.

"We love having them here."

The unspoken words hung between them—*and we'd love to have you here too.*

"I'd better get going." Waking Lilly, Angela whisked her to the car, climbed in, pulled away from the counseling center, and headed toward their home in Queens.

"Where are we going?" Kylee asked. "I'm spending the night at Becky's."

"Yeah, and we're going to Grandma's, right?" Zach called from the back seat.

"Actually, I wanted to share some good news with you guys. I got a promotion." She waited for their enthusiasm, but silence met her announcement. "So that means I can quit my weekend job, and you don't have to spend the night with someone else on Fridays anymore. How about we grab a pizza and have movie night to celebrate? That'd be fun, right?"

"But, Mo-om! Grandma said she'd make Mickey pancakes in the morning." Lilly's yelp resounded in Angela's ears despite the air whistling loudly through the vents of the old car.

"I can make pancakes at home. We used to do that a lot, remember?"

"Grandma's are better. She uses chocolate chips for eyes and the smile."

"I can try that."

"I want Grandma's."

Angela couldn't see Lilly but could hear the pout in her voice.

"I'm with Lilly on this one," Kylee said. "Besides, Becky and I are going running with the team tomorrow."

The high school cross-country team met occasionally throughout the summer to keep in shape. She secretly loved the fact her daughter had latched onto Angela's sport of choice, even if Angela hadn't run in many years.

"I'll take you over in the morning."

"You never change plans. Besides, don't you have to give notice at your job or something?"

Kylee was right about both things, of course. But just this once, Angela had wanted to do something spontaneous. To celebrate the one piece of good news they'd had in a long time.

Angela sighed and rubbed her nose. "Zach, what do you want to do?"

"He's reading again, Mom," Lilly piped up. "But he told me earlier he couldn't wait to show Grandma his latest book about bugs."

An ache spread. Angela had been so sure that this promotion was the first step to getting her family back the way it was supposed to be. Once upon a time they'd enjoyed each other's company. They'd learned together. Laughed together. Had fun together.

And then Wes had decided all of that wasn't enough.

Her hands began to tremble.

"Fine." Angela swerved around the corner and pressed her foot on the gas, pointing the car in the direction she did every Friday night. Sherry's house first. Then on to Becky's.

Then she'd go home, indulge in her nightly treadmill-and-*Grey's Anatomy* routine, shower, and collapse in bed.

Alone.

2

Somehow Eva had managed to stay the course at work for the last week without royally screwing up.

Her step had an extra skip as she walked toward Maryanne's office for their 9 a.m. Friday meeting. She was even five minutes early.

Kimberly's pep talk last Friday had infused Eva with enough vigor to ignore Valerie and Susan's comments—even to treat them with extra kindness. You caught more flies with honey, right? And she'd found a new app to help her better stay on task.

Her phone vibrated in the back pocket of her jeans. Pulling it out, she glanced at the number. Strange. The caller ID indicated an international call from Unknown. After Brent died, Eva had arranged for his calls to be forwarded to her phone, and he had several international contacts who might be trying to reach him.

Probably a sales call, but curiosity got the better of her. She veered off course and headed toward the break room, which was likely empty by now. "Hello?" Stepping into the black-and-white room with three small round tables and a few kitchen appliances that looked older than she, Eva slid into one of the hard chairs at the farthest table.

"Good day." A pleasant-sounding British woman spoke on the other side of the phone. "I'm looking for Brent Jamison."

Would Eva ever get used to the way hearing someone ask to speak with him sliced at her insides and robbed her of her breath?

She found her voice. "Who's this?"

"Tina Landry with Ultimate Race Adventures. I need to speak with Mr. Jamison."

"Oh, well—"

"Is this not the number for Brent Jamison? I apologize if I've made an error."

"Yes. This is his wife."

"Ah, wonderful. Would you please have him call me as soon as possible? It's quite urgent. We have not yet received the balance for his team's entry fee into the New Zealand race this March. If it's not paid by September 12—which is only eight days away, mind you, dear—his team will have to forfeit their spot, along with the thirty-four-hundred-pound deposit. Oh, and I also need to know the name of the specific charity they'll be raising money for."

Eva's brain blurred around the edges at the woman's rapid speech. "I'm sorry, I don't understand." Eva stared at the vending machine, the only place in the room with any color thanks to Doritos, Skittles, Laffy Taffy, and the like.

"I sent him several emails and never received a reply." Tina paused. "Will you please have him call me so we can work this out?"

Eva heard herself agreeing. It was easier than speaking the truth to a complete stranger.

"And would you happen to have the contact information for the other participants, Wesley Jamison and Marco Cinelli? For some reason that is missing from the application."

"Marc?" What did he know about all of this?

"Yes, dear. Oh well, that's all right. I can ask your husband for the information when he calls me back. Cheerio."

The call ended, and Eva bent forward, placing her head on the table. Why hadn't she told Tina Landry that she wouldn't be getting a phone call back from Brent? Had she wanted to spare the woman the embarrassment of asking to speak with a dead man?

Or maybe she'd simply frozen, the awareness of her reality flattening her once again.

She inhaled deeply. Counted to ten. Tried to breathe normally as Charlotte had taught her to do in moments like these, when her emotions crashed over her in waves. Some days doused her with water so heavy she could only dog-paddle through, her head dipping under more times than she could count. Her lungs burned as if she were drowning. Her blood alternated between hot and cold; her heart sped up; her head pounded and then felt fuzzy and light.

Gradually, her heartbeat slowed and her mind functioned once more. Replaying the conversation, Eva decided it was the mention of New Zealand that had sent her into a tailspin. Going there had been on her and Brent's bucket list.

They'd had so many plans. But because of one freak accident and the loyalty between brothers, her adventures with her husband were over.

Okay, Eva. Back to work. She had a meeting to get to, and now she was late. Hoisting herself from the chair, she hurried from the break room and toward Maryanne's office, trying to forget the conversation with Tina Landry.

Trying . . . and failing.

One detail nagged her. Tina had mentioned Marc. Maybe he'd want to know about this so he could pay the money and still participate in the race. Other than the occasional yoga class and phone call to chat about essential business operations that he wanted her to weigh in on, she hadn't talked to him much over the last several months. That was probably her fault.

She, Brent, and Marc had hung out together so often that Brent had taken to calling them the *Tre Amici*—an Italian spin on the "Three Amigos" and a nod to Marc's roots. But without her husband

17

as the glue, she'd allowed herself to drift away from one of the only people who connected her to him. That was just plain wrong. And now Marc deserved to have the option to run the race without Brent and Wes. But calling out of the blue just to ask him about this wasn't right.

As she careened into Maryanne's office, Eva sent him a text, asking him if he'd like to meet and catch up.

"Sorry I'm late." She shoved her phone into her back pocket and took one look at her boss before dread pummeled her in the stomach. "What's wrong?"

3

Few places reminded her more of Brent than the Saturday-morning farmers' market.

Eva soaked in the colors, smells, and sounds of life teeming around her. Even at eight thirty, the large parking lot hosted thousands of New Yorkers hunting for everything from fruits and vegetables to heritage meats, plants, textiles, fresh-baked breads, pickles, syrup, wine, and more. Children darted in and out of the white tents, chasing one another and laughing, absorbing the last moments of summer freedom before a new school year began on Tuesday.

Here, for a few hours, Eva was transported back to a time when she and Brent would peruse piles of produce in a rainbow of colors, daring each other to try at least one new food every time. They'd spend the morning selecting the plumpest bell peppers and the best-looking bundles of spinach and asparagus, plus whatever else looked enticing, and they'd take it all home for brunch. They had such fun exploring different foods—and many an experiment had ended with breakfast unfinished and forgotten as one flirty kiss led to more.

Eva averted her gaze and hurried past a booth of fresh-cut flowers, zigzagging toward a booth from a local farm that always had the juiciest berries. She greeted the tall man and snagged a carton of especially large strawberries.

"Let me get that."

She turned, and Marco Cinelli stood next to her, his deep brown eyes filled with compassion. His light-scruff beard tickled her cheek as he leaned down to give her a quick hug.

"Hey, Marc." He'd responded to her text yesterday in a matter of minutes, saying he would meet her wherever she wanted today. "Thanks for coming."

"Of course." Marc paid the vendor for the berries. "It's been too long. How are things? How's work going?"

As they wandered the booths, Eva fiddled with the top of the paper bag holding her strawberries. "Considering I nearly got fired from my volunteer position yesterday, just dandy." Maryanne had expressed concern that several coworkers weren't happy with Eva's work. She knew a week of not screwing up didn't really negate all the times she'd been bad at her job, but the words hurt nonetheless.

"I'm sorry, Eva." He ran a hand through his short brown hair. "You know you always have a place at the business if you want one."

"Thanks." Months ago, when Charlotte had suggested she do something productive to honor Brent's memory, she'd considered working at No Frills Fitness's main office, but the thought of trying to replace her husband at the job he'd loved . . . no way. "I'll stick it out. Brent was all about perseverance, so I will be too."

They stopped at a vendor to sample a slice of honey beer bread slathered with butter. The crispy crust gave way to a soft, chewy inside filled with flavor—a nice blend of savory and sweet. "Mmm."

"Holy cow, that's amazing."

The vendor, wearing a tight and rather low-cut shirt, eyed Marc. "I can share the recipe if you want."

His eyebrows rose. "That's a tempting offer, but I don't have much time to bake these days."

"Give me your number. I'd be happy to give you another sample sometime." Her voice dripped with attempted seduction.

Eva turned her face away, biting her lip to keep from guffawing, but not before she caught the surprise in Marc's eyes. The pretty young thing shouldn't waste her time. Marc had always been committed to his job first, and he liked nice girls anyway, not ones who salivated over him as if he were a tasty cut of meat. His last girlfriend, Katrina, had been poised, lovely, and warm, but they'd gone their separate ways over a year ago when she'd received a job offer in Paris she couldn't refuse.

"Oh, well . . ."

Eva slipped her arm through Marc's and tugged. "Let's go find that Italian beef you love so much."

"Right." He thanked the woman for the sample and let Eva lead him away. "Thanks for the assist."

"No problem." It took her a moment to realize she still grasped Marc's arm. The warmth of his body close to hers comforted her.

Alarmed, she released her hold, and they continued shopping and chatting. After they'd gathered an assortment of cherries and peaches, Gouda cheese, and bread, they left the market and walked in the direction of a small park.

Marc sat under a large London plane tree, a cross between a sycamore and an oriental plane tree. The shade offered a welcome respite from the increasing heat of the day.

Eva lowered herself beside him and leaned against the tree's white-and-gray trunk. "That was fun." She reached into her bag and pulled out a few peaches, tossing one to Marc.

He settled into the trunk space beside her, their shoulders skimming each other. "I usually go by myself, so I'm in and out in twenty minutes. I tend to stick to the same few booths. But I noticed a lot more when I was with you."

Eva's fingers rotated the peach in her hand, stroking the fuzzy exterior. "That's how it was when I was with him." Her voice grew quiet. An intense longing flared inside her.

She took a bite of her peach. The juice filled every crevice of her mouth, the sweet flesh making her feel alive, even if just for a few moments.

Exhaling, she finally brought up the reason she'd asked him to meet. "I wanted to talk to you about something."

He polished off the rest of his peach and set the pit on the ground between them. "Okay, shoot."

She removed her steel water bottle from her purse. "Yesterday I got a phone call from a woman in England about some race Brent signed up for in New Zealand. She said you and Wes were his teammates. I was a little thrown off at first and didn't ask many questions." She took a sip of water. "So it's what? A marathon? A really expensive one?"

He rubbed the back of his neck. "It's an ultra-marathon, actually. One hundred fifty-five miles across New Zealand. Runners have to complete the race in increments over seven days. You can walk it, but of course Brent wanted to run the whole thing. We signed up a week before . . ."

"Why didn't he mention it to me?"

Marc's right thumb massaged circles into his left palm. "He was going to surprise you. Said you guys wanted to do New Zealand together, and he was going to make plans to stay for a few weeks afterward to sightsee."

That man . . . always full of surprises.

Eva rallied her spirits before she could sink into the emotion threatening to topple her. "It seems like a shame to let the spots go to waste. Why don't you still run it?"

"We signed up as a team because all the individual spots were taken. It's a miracle we even snagged a team spot. This marathon fills up years in advance, and it's only in New Zealand every twenty years. But we decided we'd rather do it as a team anyway. We'd have to rely on each other to make it through, to run faster, to be better." Marc coughed. "I have no desire to run it on my own."

Eva leaned closer to him. "I get that."

"I miss him every day."

"Me too."

"I was supposed to be with them that day." He punched his palm. "If I hadn't gotten that stomach bug . . ."

Eva reached for his hands to still them. "I know what you're thinking. But you might have ended up down there without enough oxygen too."

He stared at her hands on top of his, a far-off look in his eyes. "If I'd been there, I could have gone for help when Wes got his foot stuck in that rotten board. It might have made a difference."

From what authorities told the family afterward, in addition to exerting all his energy trying to free his brother from the collapsed ruins of the underwater shipwreck, Brent had likely succumbed to nitrogen narcosis, which could lead to dizziness, anxiety, and unconsciousness.

"We don't know that. You can't dwell on the what-ifs."

"And yet I do . . . all the time."

"I know. Me too."

Marc was quiet for a moment. "I think I held him back. In the business, I mean. He was such a dreamer, the king of big moves, and I was always limiting his potential. Worried that moving too fast would sink our shot at success."

Marc had come from a very poor Italian immigrant family. His parents moved to New York a month before he was born and had struggled to find decent jobs, finally landing positions as a grocery clerk and a housemaid. Last year he'd purchased them a comfortable home in a family suburb not far outside the city and given them enough to live on for retirement.

Many men would have let prosperity like he'd experienced change him. Instead, he'd used his wealth and influence to make others' lives better.

Eva squeezed his hands. "He never saw it like that. You guys complemented each other really well." Brent had been the idea man, Marc the numbers and business guy. They'd respected each other's gifts and used them to build a business that focused not on making a quick buck but on helping individuals get healthy and heal holistically.

"Yeah, well, he sure knew how to take life by the reins."

Eva smiled and pulled her hands back into her lap. "Brent was always that way, even before his dad died."

Unlike Wes. Before a heart attack had taken Roy Jamison at age fifty-eight, Wes hadn't put much stock in his health or what it meant to "truly live"—his words. But their father's death had really pushed Wes to evaluate the meaning of life and do all he could to live it to the fullest.

"And he saw the spiritual, a purpose, in everything. It's why he wanted to run this race in particular. Not only because it was somewhere the two of you dreamed of going, but also because the money runners raise in pledges goes toward the heart charity of their choice." Marc's voice cracked. "He actually had the goal of raising a million dollars for the Manhattan Heart Center. And you know what? If anyone could do that, it would have been him."

"That's for sure." A million dollars would have been nothing for Brent Jamison. People loved to open their wallets for a good cause if he was the one involved. She'd seen it happen time and time again when he'd given speeches at the heart center's fund-raisers.

A million dollars raised to honor his dad. An ultra-marathon across New Zealand—something that would have taken lots of training and preparation, that would have pushed Brent to the brink of what he thought he could do physically.

What an accomplishment that would have been.

4

Today had to be perfect. They needed to make at least one good memory before the summer officially ended tomorrow.

While *Wild Kratts* blared from the den, Angela finished slicing an onion, piling it onto a large platter next to pickles, tomatoes, and lettuce. From the backyard, the smell of freshly grilling burgers wafted into the tiny kitchen. Just a few more minutes and they'd be ready for lunch. As Angela pulled potato salad, Jell-O, and macaroni salad from the refrigerator, she ran through her mental checklist.

"Mom." Kylee popped her head into the kitchen. Even in a pair of running shorts and a Nike T-shirt, her blonde hair pulled back into a ponytail, it was very obvious how her lean body was growing more womanly every day. "When are Grandma and Aunt Eva going to be here?"

"Soon, hon. Hey, can you toss the salad for me? There's a kit in the fridge."

"Okay." Kylee headed across the room, opened the fridge, dug around in the vegetable drawer, and emerged with the kit. "I have a question." At the counter she ripped open the plastic bag and dumped the loose lettuce into a mixing bowl.

"Hold that thought, sweetie." Angela ran outside, pulled the burgers from the grill, and came back in. "Go ahead." She placed the platter of burgers in the microwave to keep warm.

Kylee dropped croutons into the salad. "Liam wants me to come over tomorrow after practice. He doesn't live very far, and his mom said I could stay for dinner afterward."

"Who is Liam?"

That earned her an eye roll. "Liam Bradford. We've gone to church together for, like, ever."

"Right." They'd attended a large church, so it was easy to forget people sometimes. Then again, several class members had followed up when Angela quit attending after Wes died. Now that she was leaving her second job, would the kids expect her to start going with them and Sherry again? The thought left a bitter taste in her mouth.

"So, can I go?" Kylee turned to her, eyes expectant.

Angela cleared her throat, studying her daughter. She copped an attitude more often than not lately, but she'd never done anything truly rebellious. Still, the thought of her hanging out with a boy one-on-one . . . "I'm not sure that's a good idea."

"Why not?" Kylee's lips twisted into an ugly frown.

"You're too young to date." Angela hated how strict she sounded. But she didn't know how this mom-of-a-teenager thing was supposed to go. Her mom had died when she was young, and Aunt Deborah had worked eighty-hour weeks, leaving Angela to her own devices much of the time.

"Liam is just a friend, Mom." Even so, Kylee's cheeks grew pink.

"Then someday I'd love to have him over for dinner so I can get to know him better." That was a good compromise, wasn't it?

Her daughter's face brightened as she poured the dressing over the salad. It fell from the package in ribbons. "How about tomorrow? We can just hang out here instead."

"I have to work late tomorrow night, honey. Remember? This promotion is a good thing, but there's a lot to learn."

"So, basically I'm stuck at Grandma's after practice. Again."

Her daughter jabbed the salad with a large spoon, mixing the contents together. "Dad would let me go."

"Watch your tone." Gripping the counter with both hands, Angela exhaled. Hard. "Who knows what your father would have done? He's not here to tell us, is he?" Her words boomeranged and smacked her in the face.

Oh no. The rage had just slipped out, not meant for any ears but her own.

Her daughter's face crumpled.

"I'm sorry, Kylee. I didn't . . ." Angela rubbed her forehead. Tears should have been stinging her eyes. But they weren't.

They hadn't fallen at all since the moment she'd learned Wes wouldn't be coming home.

"I hate you." The words hissed from her daughter's lips as she tossed the spoon into the bowl and fled from the room.

Wonderful. The "perfect" day, ruined. Sounded about right.

Just then the doorbell rang. Lovely timing.

Angela walked down the hallway, glanced through the peephole, and opened the door. "Hey, Eva. Come on in."

Her sister-in-law was a knockout in a yellow-and-gray striped romper with short bell sleeves. "Thanks for having me over, Angela." On her arm she clutched an oversized handbag that probably cost more than Angela made in a month.

Eva leaned in for a hug at the same moment Angela turned to walk back toward the kitchen. Angela stopped midturn and tossed an awkward one-armed squeeze across Eva's shoulders, releasing her quickly.

"Sherry isn't here yet, but the kids are around somewhere."

Angela and Eva hardly ever had occasion to be all alone. The only things they really had in common were that they'd been married to brothers, that they'd lost those brothers in the same awful way, and that they both cared for their mother-in-law. Between the two of them, they always made sure Sherry had somewhere to spend every holiday—thus a Labor Day BBQ at Angela's today.

As they passed by the den, Lilly's squeals deafened Angela.

"Aunt Eva!" Her youngest raced from the room and threw her arms around Eva's legs.

"Lil!" Eva bent in half to hug her niece, long hair falling forward in luscious waves.

Lilly untangled herself. "Are you still gonna teach me how to draw fairy princesses today?"

"Uh, yeah. Obviously. Fairy princesses are my favorite."

"Mine too. And I told Alicia Bluth that I'd come back from summer break knowing how to draw them better than she does, so we might have to practice all day."

"I'm here until your mom kicks me out. Alicia Bluth will wish she'd never messed with you."

Lilly grinned. "Oh, I'm gonna tell Kylee you're here!" She skipped down the hallway.

Eva peered into the den. "Zach Attack! How's it going, dude?"

Angela watched from the doorway as Eva approached her son, who sat engrossed in the TV show. But as soon as Eva got close, he flipped off the television and grinned at his aunt. "Want to hear about centipedes, Aunt Eva?"

Eva's laugh trickled through the air like a graceful melody. She plopped down on the couch. "Who wouldn't, Zacharoo?"

"I'll get my new library book." He leapt up and raced from the room.

"Bud, make sure your room is clean before Grandma gets here. Tell Lilly the same, please."

Groans followed Angela's request.

Angela sank onto the opposite end of the couch, allowing an audible sigh of relief to escape. It felt good to sit.

"Is there anything I can do to help with lunch?" Eva turned her knees toward Angela and crossed her legs, accentuating her gorgeous beaded sandals and manicured toes.

Tugging at her mustard-stained T-shirt that always seemed to show off her I've-had-babies pooch when she sat, Angela clasped a throw pillow to her abdomen. "It's all ready, actually."

"Great."

Angela played with the golden tassel on the pillow, which had already been old when she and Wes purchased it fourteen years ago for their first real home. Even though her in-laws had been wonderful—allowing Wes and Angela to live with them for nearly two years while Wes finished school and Angela cared for Kylee— they'd been so excited to finally have a space of their own.

"So." Eva played with her oversized hoop earring. "I got this call on Friday. Did you know that Brent and Wes signed up to run an ultra-marathon in New Zealand this spring?"

"No." Of course Wes hadn't mentioned the race. He probably knew how upset she'd be that he was running off to explore and play, leaving her to run the household by herself for the thousandth time.

Angela stuffed the thoughts down deep. She couldn't let herself have any more emotional outbursts, which meant she needed to be better about disguising her feelings. As far as her children were concerned, things between their parents had been wonderful. They didn't have to know about the fights, the tears, the fact they couldn't seem to get on the same page.

It didn't matter anymore. Wes was gone, and they'd never reach a resolution to their issues now. The best thing Angela could do was forget about them, put on a happy face, and move on.

"Aunt Eva, you're here!" Kylee's joyous exclamation filled the room as she rushed in and dropped into the chair where Zach had been sitting.

Her children's reactions to their aunt made sense. Eva was

cool, fun, spunky, free-spirited—basically everything Angela was not. Angela was the one who had to say no to their whims. The responsible one.

Eva only had to look after herself. Plus, she could literally afford to do whatever she wanted with her time.

"Good to see you, girl." Eva reached across the divide and squeezed Kylee's hand.

"What were you saying to Mom about an ultra-marathon?"

"Oh, I was just telling her that your dad and Uncle Brent signed up to run one in New Zealand."

"Really?"

Angela shifted in her seat.

"Yeah, I got a call from some woman. She had no idea that Brent . . ." She swallowed, her eyes pooling with tears.

Kylee leaned toward her aunt, gripping her hand in both of her own. "*You* should do it."

"Do what?" Eva squinted at her niece.

Yes, what was her daughter talking about?

"Run the race in his place. You know, like in memory of him or something. I dunno. Lots of people have done stuff like that. Like, there was this mom who ran the London Marathon in memory of her daughter who died of cancer. The daughter was sick for twenty-six weeks, so the mom ran a mile for every week her daughter lived after her diagnosis."

Angela stared at Kylee, who had just said more in the last minute than she had in the last month. Revealed more, anyway. "Why did you happen to read about that?"

Avoiding Angela's gaze, Kylee shrank back in her seat a bit. "I thought about doing something like that in memory of Dad."

Oh, sweet girl. Angela's heart twisted, and she longed to cross the room, gather her daughter in her arms, and cry with her.

But the thought of Kylee, stiff and unresponsive at her offer of comfort, kept her still. She didn't want to make her daughter uncomfortable, especially in front of Eva.

"That is the best idea in the world, Kylee. Get over here."

Without hesitation, Kylee moved to the couch, allowing Eva to embrace and snuggle her close. The sound of quiet crying rose to meet the silence in the den.

And Angela, sitting not five feet away, stood and snuck into the kitchen to pour the drinks for lunch.

5

Her niece was a genius.

"You *should do it*." Eva couldn't get Kylee's words from last night out of her head as she emerged from the subway stop nearest the heart center and crossed the street with hundreds of other New Yorkers on their way to another day of work.

Something about the day felt new, the air laden with possibility. A hint of saffron and cinnamon tingled Eva's nose as she strode past a local Indian eatery, a bakery, and a trendy independent bookstore all packed together on one street corner.

Kylee might not have meant for Eva to take her suggestion seriously, but something about it resonated deep.

Because it was a chance to feel closer to Brent in an even bigger way than volunteering at his favorite charity. To honor his legacy. And maybe to rediscover the color of life that had vanished with his absence.

As Marc said, Brent had been the king of big moves. He'd have completely supported this one.

Heading toward her destination, Eva found the number she needed in her phone.

"Ultimate Race Adventures, Tina speaking."

"Hi, Tina, this is Eva Jamison. Brent Jamison's wife."

"Oh, hello, dear. I still haven't heard from your husband."

"No." Eva inhaled as she navigated the crowded sidewalk. She turned down a quieter street. "And you won't. You see, he died about fifteen months ago."

Tina gasped. "I'm terribly sorry. If I'd known—"

"Please don't feel bad."

Rustling papers filled the background through the receiver. "Well, dear, it's highly unusual, but I can see about getting you a refund on his deposit. I cannot promise it, but—"

"Actually, I'd like to ask you something else."

"All right."

Eva stopped two blocks from the heart center. In front of her loomed a large cast-iron gate with a rustic hand-carved sign for East Side Garden. She drew in a shaky breath. "I wanted to see if it was possible . . . to run in his place."

"Oh my. Well . . . normally we don't allow that sort of thing, you understand. But perhaps . . ." Tina paused. "Could I place you on hold while I discuss this with my supervisor?"

"Of course."

As Tina clicked off and elevator music looped onto the line, Eva reached out to touch the garden's sign. A tremor ran up her arm. She'd discovered the free-to-the-public garden with thousands of gorgeous blooms in the heart of Manhattan when she'd first moved here. Back then, the garden had become a sanctuary from the smog of the city and the noise of life whenever she could sneak away from work.

It's where Brent had taken her six years ago and proposed.

And Eva hadn't set a foot inside since he'd died.

Peeking through the garden gate, her eyes located the stone bench where Brent had surprised her with a diamond that gorgeous May day, when the primroses were in bloom, their orange, purple, pink, blue, and red petals turned to the sun.

She'd thought it a sign, given the most common meaning of primroses: "I can't live without you."

Now these primroses—*their* primroses—lay dormant.

Some primroses bloomed twice in one year. Would these? Or would they keep their color tucked out of sight through autumn and the long winter ahead?

Eva's chest physically ached as she sucked in quick breaths.

What was she doing? She had somewhere to be. And it wasn't here. Turning abruptly, she scurried toward the heart center.

"Ms. Jamison?" Tina Landry's voice interrupted her thoughts.

"Yes, I'm here." The words punctuated the air in a desperation Eva hadn't meant to convey.

"We are very pleased to allow you to run in your husband's stead."

Light from the sun bounced off the windows of a high-rise. "Oh, that's wonderful."

"So long as your husband's teammates are amenable to the change, that is."

"What? Oh, well . . ." Ugh, she hadn't even thought about that aspect of the race, or to explain the full circumstances to Ms. Landry. "You see, my brother-in-law, Wes, died the same day as my husband."

"Oh goodness. I'm very sorry." Tina clucked her tongue. "I don't see why we wouldn't also make an exception for a close relative who wanted to run in his stead."

Kylee *had* said she'd wanted to run a race for her dad, but 155 miles would be too much for a teen.

Hmm. What about Angela? She used to run, right? Her sister-in-law may not show much emotion, but last night Eva had glimpsed the same hopelessness in Angela's eyes that Eva saw so often in her own reflection. Perhaps running this race would be good for both of them.

"I'll have to ask. If I can't find someone, can I still run the race on my own?"

"I wish I could make an exception for that, but we have very strict rules about allowing participants to switch from team to individual entrants, and a team must consist of at least three people. Now, if you started off as a team and one person was forced to quit during the race, that's different. But we only have a certain number of individual and team starting spots—and as of now, they're all full."

Eva clenched her phone. "All right. Thank you so much for this opportunity. I'll have to get back to you."

"Please remember that the deadline to pay the balance due on the account is this Saturday. After that, we will have to give the team's spot to the first alternates."

"I understand. And thank you again."

Eva arrived at the heart center, and her eyes followed the white concrete walls up, up, up toward the cloudless sky. Should she just go inside, forget this whole thing? It's not like doing the race would be easy. Eva was a yogi and enjoyed a hard-won spin class, but she'd never run long distances. Three, four miles tops at a time.

Images of gorgeous New Zealand flashed through her mind: the snowcapped peaks, the azure lakes, the green hills, the orange sun bringing all the flora and fauna to life.

Wild country brimming with possibility. Growth. Newness. Color.

A place she'd wanted to experience with Brent. Maybe there she'd finally sense him with her again.

Eva called Angela.

When her sister-in-law answered, Eva launched into a quick explanation of her phone call with Tina. She finished talking. And waited. But only silence met her.

"Angela? You there?"

Finally, a laugh that was far more caustic than happy puffed across the phone line. "So you want *us* to run an ultra-marathon.

One hundred and something miles. Halfway around the world. Six months from now. You're crazy."

Hurt bloomed in Eva's heart. "I don't think it's so crazy. And yes, you, me, and Marc." She hadn't even asked Marc, but knew he'd be up for it. It was for Brent, after all.

"Eva, I haven't run in years. That's a lot of work even for someone who is in the best running shape of their life."

"You might be surprised how quickly it comes back. Also, we don't have to actually run. Just walk twentysomething miles a day. You could do that. Don't you already walk a bunch on your treadmill? We can add in some cross-training, jog a little, whatever. We'll train together. It doesn't matter how fast we get there. The race wouldn't be about winning. Besides, Marc and I would be there to help you. We'd work as a team."

Eva, you're rambling. She clamped her mouth shut.

"Look, this is a fine idea for you if that's what you want, but you don't need me. I'm working forty-plus hours a week. I can't be away from work or my kids for two weeks. I already ask Sherry to watch them far too often. And what about the money? I'm sure it costs thousands of dollars to fly over there, stay somewhere for the first few nights. And what's the entry fee?"

"Money is no object. I'll cover all the expenses." Eva waved her hand in the air.

"Must be nice." Angela's words had an edge to them. "I'm sorry, Eva. That wasn't kind. It's a very generous offer, but it just won't work for me right now. I wish you the best of luck, though."

"You say I don't need you, but actually, I do."

"What do you mean?"

"They were registered as a team. There have to be three people to make a team, and the race organizers will only allow us to sub in a family member."

A groan filtered across the line. "I'm sorry, Eva. I just . . . can't."

6

Finally. A Friday night when Angela didn't have to rush to bed thanks to an early Saturday shift at the spa. It had been two weeks since she'd given her notice, and now they could begin to find their new normal as a family.

She pulled zucchini bread from Sherry's oven. "Perfect." The loaf was just wet enough on top that it was sure to be decadent throughout. She placed it on the counter to cool next to several loaves of banana bread and cookies Sherry had made earlier in the day.

Her mother-in-law looked up from the German chocolate cake she was making and turned off the handheld mixer. "Smells divine."

At only sixty years young, Sherry was average in height and weight with more gray than blonde up top. But despite losing both of her sons, and her husband a few years before that, somehow she radiated peace and kindness. And Angela was the beneficiary much more often than she deserved. She wouldn't have survived without Sherry and her willingness to keep the kids when Angela had to work on the weekends or after school hours.

Angela allowed a smile to settle on her lips. When had the gesture become so foreign? "Just like you taught me."

When she and Wes first married, Angela had known nothing about homemaking. But Sherry had shown her young daughter-in-law the ropes—not only in how to make bread rise, but in how to raise a baby.

Once she'd finished mixing her cake, Sherry poured it into a greased cake pan. "The kiddos will probably want dessert soon." They'd already eaten dinner by the time Angela arrived to pick them up. Work had run over again today, and Sherry had offered to snag the kids from group and feed them her famous lasagna.

"Zach mentioned needing some of your cookies." All three kids were watching old home videos of Wes and Brent in the living room. Angela had hated to pull them away when she'd arrived, so she had gladly complied when Sherry asked for some baking assistance. "Should I take them some?"

"If you'd like. But there's something I'd like to talk about first, if you don't mind." Her mother-in-law adjusted the temperature on the oven and slid in her cake.

"Of course." Angela snagged a few cookies off the counter and sat at the table. "Is everything all right?"

"Oh yes." Sherry poured two glasses of milk and set one in front of Angela, then joined her. "Eva called last night." A pause. "She told me you still haven't decided about the ultra-marathon."

Oh, Eva. She'd been so persistent since her initial call on Tuesday, even after Angela's firm no—make that nos. Her sister-in-law just couldn't understand why Angela wouldn't consider the race. But that shouldn't surprise Angela. The two of them lived very different lives.

Angela bit into a cookie and took a large gulp of milk. "I *have* decided. I told her no. Several times."

"That's certainly your right. But I'm curious why you shot the idea down so soundly."

What was Sherry getting at? It wasn't like her to butt into Angela's business. "You know how crazy life is for me. It's getting a little more manageable now that I don't have two jobs, but I've got new responsibilities because of the promotion, and those come with a learning curve. I can't add in something like training for a race, not to mention leaving the kids for several weeks to go halfway across the world. Life would spin completely out of control."

Silence ensued as Sherry's face tightened. "And control is something you feel you have currently?"

The woman had a point. "No, but it's something to strive for. Obviously there are some things I can't control, one of them being the hours I have to work to keep us afloat. My children lost their father, and I'm gone enough from them already. We have to make time together a priority, and I can't do that if I'm flitting off to run all the time. And for what? Something that's not going to bring their dad back. But me—I'm flesh and bone. I'm still here. And they need me."

"Yes, you're here physically." Sherry placed her hand over her own heart. "But what about in here? Angela, forgive me for saying so, but I think your children feel like they lost both of you when Wesley died."

The remains of her cookie crumbled in Angela's hand. First Juliet. Now Sherry. Did the whole world think she was a bad mother? Yes, sixteen years ago she'd seriously considered whether she wanted to sacrifice her dreams and plans on the altar of motherhood, but she'd tried to dedicate herself to the job as fully as possible once Kylee arrived.

"They said that?"

"Not in so many words."

Using her napkin, Angela scrubbed at the smushed chocolate on her hand. How had she tried so hard and still failed to be what her children needed? "I don't know what else to do."

Sherry got up and sliced a piece of the banana bread, then worked a knife full of butter across it, back and forth, slow, methodical. "Do you remember when I went on that retreat to Canada all by myself a few months after Roy died?" She plated the slice and reached for another.

"Yes."

Sherry had gone to the same place where she and her husband had honeymooned thirty-five years before. She'd been lost in her grief, and Angela and Wes hadn't known how to help her.

"I came back a changed woman. Met God there in a way I didn't expect." She returned to the table and slid one of the plates of butter-slathered bread in front of Angela, then sat again with her own plate. "I didn't come back all better. When you've known great loss, grief never goes away. Yes, it will lessen, and it won't be this pulse always beating quite so strongly in time with your heart. But it changes you, becomes part of who you are, the way you function."

Had losing Wes really changed Angela? Sure, it had acutely changed her circumstances. But the change inside of her? That had been happening long before she got the worst call of her life. "I'm glad that trip was beneficial to you, Sherry. But I'm not quite sure what it has to do with me."

"I suppose I just wanted to communicate that, for me, it took something drastic to help me shake off the funk I was feeling. To embrace the new order of things, a world in which I didn't necessarily have control. Receiving that truth changed my perspective. About life. Death. Even about my husband."

Surely Sherry didn't know of the conflict Angela felt deep inside. The ache. The wondering. The anger. All the emotions swirling together. The ones she never let through to the surface—because if she did, she feared the volcano that might erupt and the damage those emotions could do.

She'd already seen the results of the tiny fissure she'd allowed to develop earlier this week when she'd yelled at Kylee.

"Did you . . ." Angela couldn't form the words. The heat from the stove seemed to reach across the room and suffocate her. "Did you find that you understood Roy more? After—" The last word broke.

Sherry's eyes crinkled with compassion. "For me, there was freedom in giving myself permission to explore all of my emotions, no matter how guilty they made me feel—and no matter how scary they were to face."

"I—"

"I'm not saying that doing this marathon will ultimately help you do any of that. But what I *am* saying is that you will never be able to help your children heal until you show them how." Grabbing hold of Angela's hand, Sherry squeezed. "You will never experience the full joy of life until you face the sadness, the anger, and the grief head-on. This I know."

Angela's throat grew thick. She placed her hand on Sherry's, patted it. "Thanks, Sherry. I'll think about it."

"Don't think too long, dear. Eva told me the deadline to finalize the registration and pay is tomorrow."

Oy, the money. That was another reason to say no to the marathon. Eva had offered to pay for the entire trip, but that wasn't right, even if she had plenty of money.

"I'm going to deliver those cookies to the kids now." Angela plopped a few cookies on a platter and walked down the hallway toward the living room—and stopped at the sight in front of her. All three of her kids cuddled together on the sofa, watching images flit across the screen. A young Brent was hanging upside down from a tree, trying to coax his older brother to climb up. Wes looked like he wanted to, but just shook his head and kicked at a rock.

Why couldn't he have remained that cautious boy forever?

"Hey, guys. I brought cookies."

Their stares remained riveted on the screen.

Upon closer inspection, Angela saw tears streaming down Kylee's face. Her daughter finally turned and looked at Angela. Something in her eyes caused a shiver to course through Angela.

In that gaze flowed a mixture of emotions—blame, longing, deep sadness, hopelessness.

And in it, Kylee seemed to be asking for help.

But Angela didn't know what she could do to relieve the pain.

Sherry's words flitted back to her. *"You will never be able to help your children heal until you show them how."*

What did healing look like, for Angela?

The screen caught her eyes again. In this movie, young Wes cradled an injured baby bird in his small hands. He talked to it sweetly, gently, coaxing it back to life.

Now *this* boy . . . She remembered him. Remembered how he'd been with her. How they'd been together.

Where had everything gone wrong?

Maybe if she could finally understand the changes in Wes during those last years of his life, she could let him go. Move on. Heal. Become more than this shell of a person with all the plans in the world but no real connection to it.

She owed the children huddled on the couch that much.

Planning hadn't gotten her any closer to what she really wanted. What she—what they—really needed. Maybe it was time to take a page from Eva's playbook and try impulsiveness on for a change.

"Guys." Angela strode forward, set the cookies on the coffee table, picked up the TV remote, and paused the video.

Three sets of eyes focused on her.

She nearly bit the words back, but they tumbled free from her lips. "What would you think about me doing the ultra-marathon with Aunt Eva?"

7

Nothing could have prepared Eva for the call she'd received from Angela last night. Her sister-in-law was in.

And Eva couldn't wait to start preparing.

But first—coffee.

She studied the menu at Starbucks and ordered a pumpkin spice latte, as the weather had blessedly dipped into the seventies this week. Once she'd retrieved her drink, Eva headed to the table where her sister-in-law and Marc were already chatting in the back corner of the small café.

Norah Jones serenaded the crowded room from speakers hidden overhead, competing with the sound of blenders and grinders erupting from behind the counter. The powerful fragrance of ground coffee beans infused a sense of calm in her. When Eva was excited, it was difficult to focus on the details of what needed to be accomplished. Thankfully, Marc and Angela both had heads for planning, as evidenced by the notebooks and pens each had brought to the meeting.

She slid into the seat next to Marc, who was already taking notes. Even though it was Saturday, he wore a black polo and dark blue jeans—not the jogging pants and T-shirt Brent would have opted for when he was away from the office.

"You ready?" He took a sip of his drink.

"Let me guess. Hot chocolate?" The man was obsessed with the stuff no matter the time of year.

"You know it."

She laughed. "I'm ready, but you sure I can't get you a real drink first?" Teasing Marc felt good. Their time at the farmers' market last weekend had done wonders to ease the awkwardness of being together without Brent.

"Only if it would taste as amazing as this."

"Most grown-ups think coffee does." Eva had never been much of a coffee drinker until Brent had dared her to try his favorite Cuban roast—and it was all over from there. Together they became coffee connoisseurs, buying the latest and greatest espresso machine and French presses and trying a variety of local roasts until they found their favorites.

Angela cleared her throat. "I told Kylee I'd be home in about an hour so she could go running with her team."

"All right, let's get started then." Marc tapped his pen against his notebook and turned to Eva. "Where would you like to begin?" He'd been so willing to agree to all of this, to see her vision.

She took a swig of her latte, dotting her tongue with subtle spice. "I was hoping someone with more organizational sense might lead the meeting."

Marc studied her for a moment, then nodded. "I think it's important to establish our goals for this event up front. What does each of us want, and how can we help each other achieve that? Also, we should chat about any concerns we have or challenges we foresee. Finally, we need to talk equipment, training strategy, and our schedules."

See? Definitely a good idea for him to be in charge.

"Why don't you go first, Eva?"

"All I know is I'm going to be on that plane to New Zealand and run my heart out for Brent." She pulled at the corner of the brown cardboard sleeve ringing her cup. "The rest doesn't matter."

Angela snorted. At Eva's sharp glance, her eyes went wide. "Oh, you're serious."

"Well, yeah. I know there's obviously a lot to arrange, but I'm just stating my goals. Like Marc asked." She emphasized those last three words. Angela might think she was some brainless ninny, but she was just looking at the big picture. She and Brent had both been that way, always pushing each other to new heights. "Go big or go bigger." That had been their motto. "Anyway, I'm flexible on the details."

"Apparently." Angela pushed her shoulder-length blonde hair back from her face and grasped her notebook with two hands while she studied what she'd written. "My goal is simply to finish. I propose we walk the whole thing. I don't think running is realistic at this point in the game, and I don't want us to be disappointed."

"But don't you think the guys would have run it?"

At Eva's question, Angela pursed her lips for a moment before erasing the emotion from her face. "Perhaps, but they had run a few marathons—well, this would have been Wes's first one, but Brent had already run a few with you, right, Marc?" At Marc's nod, she continued. "I haven't had a chance to research exactly how much time training will take each week, but I don't want this thing to take over my life."

"But—"

"Eva, I'm sorry. Weren't you the one who told me we could walk the whole thing?"

Yeah, but she'd been trying to get Angela to agree, sure that once she considered it, she'd want to do more than that. Still, it wasn't fair of Eva to suggest it as a possibility and then quibble about it later. "You're right. If we need to walk the whole thing, that's fine. Or maybe we can try running some of it?"

"Whatever we do, we have to stick together, ladies. And I mean that literally. Since we're a team, we can't be separated by more than fifty feet the entire race. So how about we just see how training goes? Does that seem fair?" Poor Marc was playing referee. That shouldn't have to be his role.

"Of course." Eva forced brightness into her voice. Fake it till you make it, right? She needed to stay positive—otherwise they'd never survive the next six months. She didn't want to give Angela any excuse to quit before then.

Marc spoke up again. "I can be in charge of gathering our equipment if you'd like. I took a quick look at what's required, and the first priority is getting the backpacks. Walking without one is obviously a lot easier than with, especially once it's loaded down, so we'll want to train with them on as much as we can."

At their nods of agreement, he glanced at his notes once more. "Before we talk details regarding our training schedule, we should discuss gaining pledges. We technically don't have to do this—it's not required—but I do think it would be awesome if we could wrangle at least a few thousand in pledges to donate to the Manhattan Heart Center."

"Brent wanted to raise a million." Eva leaned forward, nearly knocking over her latte in her eagerness. "I say we do the same."

Angela took a bite of the muffin in front of her and chased it with a swallow of her coffee. "How do you propose we do that?"

Aha! The one detail Eva had managed to work out before arriving this morning. "After I called Tina Landry and paid the balance, I chatted with Kimberly about doing a fund-raising gala. Between Brent's contacts in the heart community and Kim's contacts in the event-planning world, she thinks we can pull it off in about six weeks."

"Really?" Angela's tone showcased her doubt.

"Yeah, apparently there's a great venue in Brooklyn that just became available on October 24—one of her brides caught her fiancé cheating on her—and Kim thinks she can convince the owner and all or most of the vendors to donate their services that night to the event."

"Why would they do that?"

Marc cut in. "It's good PR. Plus, I'm guessing Kim has some sway in that community."

"Oh yeah. She's one of the most sought-after wedding planners in the city right now. So if vendors can get on her good side by doing her a favor and come out smelling like a rose for helping charity, well, it's a no-brainer." Eva glanced at Marc, who looked at her with something like admiration in his eyes.

A flash of heat hit her middle.

What in the world?

"Sounds like that's settled then." Angela's pen jiggled against the notebook in front of her. "Was there anything else, or can we move on to training? What are you envisioning? That's my biggest concern due to the time constraints and my own abilities. I haven't exactly had the time or opportunity to stay in the best of shape the last several years." She tugged at her blouse as if it didn't fit right.

Obviously Angela was a very capable person, and she struck Eva as fairly confident in most things. She was tall and strong, with striking brown eyes and hair that sparkled golden in the summertime—definitely no need for self-consciousness. Why then did she hide her body under clothes at least one size too big for her?

Marc jotted something in his notebook, then looked up at Angela. "You walk regularly on your treadmill, right?"

"Yes, but just as stress relief. I watch TV and use it as a way to unwind since I'm sitting all day at work."

"How many miles would you say you currently do?"

Angela shrugged. "I usually just walk for an hour and a half—long enough for two episodes. Maybe five miles a day?"

"If you're doing it every day, that means you're hitting thirty to thirty-five miles a week, which is a great base, especially if our intention is to walk much of the course. Now you can start adding in cross-training—hiking, cycling, weight lifting, et cetera—a few times a week."

"I'm going to have trouble finding time for that." Angela chewed her lip as she wrote in her notebook. "I'll squeeze it in when I can, I guess."

According to Angela, she had a long way to go. Would she be able to push herself enough alone? "I'm more than happy to come train with you after work. My schedule's fairly flexible." She could cut back hours at the heart center if she needed to. Her coworkers would probably throw a party in celebration of the occasion.

"Sure, maybe." Angela focused on Marc. "So how much do we need to work up to?"

"Ideally, each week you'll have two days of cross-training, two days when you walk or jog six to twelve miles, and one big day when you eventually walk or jog twenty to forty miles."

Angela choked mid-drink and dribbled coffee on the table in front of her.

"You all right?" Eva handed her a napkin.

"Yeah. Sure." Her sister-in-law's reply sputtered out like her coffee had. She avoided eye contact with Eva and Marc as she wiped up the mess.

"I know it sounds overwhelming, but we are already behind. Most people recommend training for seven to eight months. We have to build endurance, enough to walk consistently day after day, mile after mile. Of course, on that long training day, we can start out with shorter distances and work our way up. So a base of ten miles would be good, then add on two to three miles a week to give our bodies time to adjust and strengthen." He turned to Eva. "If you want, I have a buddy who specializes in this type of personal training. I can ask him to draw up a detailed plan for each of us to follow and see if he has time to work with us weekly as well."

"Great idea."

"I can't afford to pay him," Angela said.

"I've got it covered." Eva smiled.

"I don't think we should add on any unnecessary costs at this point." Her sister-in-law's voice tensed.

Eva didn't want to rock the boat, so she held in a sigh of exasperation. "Well, even if he just creates a training plan, that would be pretty helpful."

Marc's eyes ping-ponged between the two women. "Agreed. I think it's something simple we can do to lessen our disadvantage. It's too bad we can't go out to New Zealand early. The terrain there won't be all flat like it is here, so getting to practice in the actual race environment would be a great advantage." He snapped his fingers as if an idea had just come to him. "Oh, another advantage . . . Maybe we can participate in a marathon a couple of months before the ultra. That would give us a smaller goal to train for and help us gauge how well we're doing, which would allow us to adjust our training if need be."

"Brilliant." Eva clapped.

"I guess . . ." Jaw tight, Angela stared down at her notebook.

A single word written on the page glared up at Eva: *How?*

It had been circled so many times, it appeared a thick Sharpie had made the marks instead of a regular pen.

Doubts crashed into Eva's resolve, but she tamped them down. Impulsive or not, this decision felt right deep in her bones. Sure, it would come with challenges, but what didn't?

The next several months would be a test in patience and staying the course. If Eva didn't remain confident, Angela never would.

But in the end, all of this angst would be worth it. Eva just knew it.

8

The first day of training dawned bright and cheery.

Angela was not amused by nature's attempt at convincing her this was a good idea.

Light filtered through the trees of Central Park where she waited for Eva and Marc near the reservoir. The nearly one hundred acres of water stretched across the park, granting gorgeous views of the city skyline beyond the four-foot-high fence with cast-iron ornamentation that wrapped along the path.

The air still shimmered with a crispness common in the not-quite-but-almost-autumn mornings. Though it was early and a Sunday, lots of joggers and walkers passed Angela on the running track. Each one appeared relaxed, happy, self-assured.

If Angela reached deep into her memory, she could almost conjure the ghost of those feelings associated with running.

But in the here and now, all she saw was the impossibility of it. What had she been thinking to agree to this?

"Angela! Hey, sorry I'm late." Eva approached, her lithe body clothed in stretchy black pants, a tight-fitting bright blue tank top, and a black jacket that paired nicely with her tan skin. A matching blue headband kept her side-swept bangs out of her face.

"No problem." Angela should have spent the time stretching, but instead she'd only dawdled. She folded her arm across her chest, feeling the tightness in her shoulder blades. "Though I expected Marc already."

"Didn't you get his text? His uncle is in town, and his parents wanted him to attend their church and do lunch today as a family."

Well, they couldn't expect him to drop all of his weekend plans just because Angela had decided to come on board at the last minute. With his busy schedule, it was a miracle he'd found time to attend their strategy meeting yesterday.

"Okay. How do you want to do this then? Should we set a goal? Marc said to do six to twelve miles a few times a week. The loop around the reservoir is about one and a half miles, so we could plan to do that four or five times."

"Perfect." Eva placed one leg on a bench and leaned into a perky stretch. "Since that's all we're doing, maybe we could try to run today."

"Eva, we discussed that." Though there was nothing in her stomach, Angela was sure she might be sick. Walk six miles . . . sure. But running was a different beast.

"I know, I know, but maybe we could just try? It might be nice not to be in very last place, you know?" Eva switched legs. "We've totally got this."

Maybe *Eva* had this. Once, Angela could have said that too. She'd originally joined cross-country to add a sport to her college applications, since the best schools wanted to see diverse interests. But immediately she'd known there was something different about running compared with debate team, or science club, or the literary magazine. When she ran she forgot all the rest. Somehow it became about more than beating her opponents.

After that, it was the one thing she'd done for the pure thrill of it. She wasn't the best, and for some reason, that hadn't bothered her.

But that was then. This was now. Adult Angela carried a lot more weight—literally and figuratively—than teenage Angela ever had.

If her sister-in-law thought she could just change their goals, snap her fingers, and make Angela's athletic abilities magically increase, well, she unfortunately had a big surprise coming.

"Come on, Ang. Positive thinking, babe." Wes's voice appeared in her mind out of nowhere, slapping her in the chest. It was the same voice that had assured her everything would be all right a few hours after she'd first seen the plus sign on the pregnancy test sixteen years ago, unmarried and a sophomore in college.

Positive thinking. Yes, she *could* do this. Though it didn't feel like it, she was the same woman who had landed a full scholarship to UCLA, who had managed to get the only A in her freshman calculus class, who had given birth without an epidural three times.

If she wanted something—really wanted something—she could get it with a little elbow grease and a heart of steel.

And that was the problem, wasn't it? She oscillated between being excited for what this challenge could mean for her family and giving up completely at the ridiculous notion that anything could ever change in her life.

"All right. Let's do this. I can't promise I'll be fast or that I'll be able to run the whole way, but I'll try."

"Great." Her sister-in-law studied her for a moment. "So what pace do you want to aim for?"

"I don't know." *How about a mile an hour?* "I guess you can just set the pace and I'll do my best to keep up." It might burn a little, but she could handle pain. And it wasn't like she'd never run before. It just had been awhile.

"Okay." For the first time Eva's tone sounded doubtful, but her sister-in-law led them onto the crushed-gravel track.

A few runners passed, and a slight breeze tousled Angela's hair. Birds tweeted in trees throughout the park.

Her sister-in-law started jogging and Angela followed suit, starting the timer on her watch so she'd get a general idea of pacing.

The shuffle of their feet on the track drowned out the distant sound of rumbling planes overhead.

Eva called out greetings to other runners and walkers, her breathing easy and light.

This wasn't so bad. Eva was clearly holding back, but Angela couldn't go any faster. Still, she was holding her own. She was doing this. Her goal was to walk the ultra-marathon and finish, but maybe with six months of training she could actually run some of it.

Then the slow burn in her side began. Her legs shook; her lungs constricted. Angela tried to remember running advice from her sports days—breathe in through the nose, out through the mouth—and ignore the ache spreading through her whole body.

The lower part of the sleeve on her oversized T-shirt rubbed. Oy. How many times had she become raw under her arms and between her thighs when running in high school? The unpleasant parts of the sport flooded back to her. The blisters. The chafing. The black toenails—although her coach had always said losing a toenail was a badge of honor, the sign a runner had persevered.

But right now all of that sounded painful and purposeless. How had she ever actually enjoyed this?

How much longer? Angela glanced at her watch and saw 16:24 glaring back at her. Seriously? It felt as though they'd been going for hours, not sixteen minutes, and according to her GPS, they'd only jogged a little more than a mile.

One. Stinking. Mile.

And in six months' time she had to somehow walk or run 155?

Angela slowed to a walk, holding the stitch in her side that could no longer be ignored.

Eva stopped. "You okay?"

"Just a little pain I've got to work out. Maybe I started too quickly. Need to warm up more." How embarrassing for Eva to know just how pathetic Angela was.

"Should we stop?"

Yes. That's what Angela wanted to say. But if she quit after the first day of training, how could she face her children—especially Kylee, who had thrown her arms around Angela in a triumphant hug after she'd announced her intentions to run the ultra?

"No." She wouldn't stop. But she did need to do this at her own pace. "I'll be fine. Why don't you go on ahead, though? I'll catch up soon." She infused her voice with as much assurance as possible.

Her tone clearly didn't convince Eva, but her sister-in-law shrugged and started running ahead.

One foot in front of the other. That's how Angela was going to accomplish this.

She inhaled and started jogging again.

9

Yoga did not solve all problems, but Eva hoped this time it would.

She desperately needed a temporary reprieve from the discouragement and irritation warring for prominence in her heart, not to mention the stretch her body craved after nearly three weeks of training for the ultra-marathon.

Her shoes crunched orange and yellow leaves that had fallen to the ground as she approached the front door of No Frills Fitness's Broadway location. She entered and, instead of the smell of sweat and stinky shoes, a sweet rush of eucalyptus and lavender essential oils greeted her. Beyoncé sang from somewhere above, an upbeat tune about making sure your man treated you right, that was interrupted occasionally by the clanging of weights and underscored by the whir of machines and chatter from the smattering of patrons here for a midday Friday workout.

The college student behind the receptionist's desk smiled. "Hey, Eva. You here for class?" She eyed the yoga mat stashed under Eva's arm.

"I sure am, Tonya."

"Awesome. It's taught by a probationary instructor."

"Yeah, Marc asked me to come try her out to see whether we should hire her permanently." It was a small way Eva could help out here. And now that she'd cut back her hours at the heart center to spend more time training, she was a bit more available.

She'd hoped to have more joint training sessions with Angela built into her schedule but . . .

No. Dwelling on the negative did no good. She needed to sweat out the toxins trying to overtake her since training had begun.

Eva walked to the yoga room and peeked inside. A petite red-head chatted with a few gym regulars at the front of the class. No Marc. He was supposed to join her if he could, but maybe something had come up.

Classes always filled quickly, so Eva rolled out her mat, then slid off her coat and hung it on a peg in the back of the room. This wasn't a hot yoga class, but the room still felt warm compared with the sixty-degree weather outside.

As she peeled off her shoes and socks, Eva couldn't help grimacing. Blisters had recently formed on the back of each foot thanks to her extra running efforts, and she'd covered them with moleskin and gauze. Still, they burned.

Did her efforts or her pain really matter? If everyone on the team wasn't as dedicated . . .

No. Focus.

A few women greeted Eva before the instructor spoke. "Hello, class. For those who don't know me, I'm Kendra. Today we are going to work toward a peaceful space where each person can find what he or she came looking for. Please join me."

As Kendra lowered the lights and lit a few candles around the classroom, Eva sat on her mat. She needed the peace that Kendra spoke of, especially today as she wrestled the emotions that training for this ultra-marathon had brought to the surface.

Soft music with a variety of synthesizer textures filtered through the room. Kendra led them in opening stretches.

"Hey."

Eva glanced up to find Marc sliding a mat in next to hers. His muscled arms flexed in his orange ventilation tank as he settled onto his mat.

"You're late. I didn't think that happened." Eva whispered so as not to disturb their classmates.

"A call with one of the potential new investors ran over."

This was the first time she'd seen him in two weeks, as he'd been traveling to explore expansion opportunities in other cities and meeting with investors there.

As Kendra led them through warm-ups, they lay down. Eva pulled her knees into her chest and curled forward, pressing her spine into the mat, focusing on feeling in sync with her body. *Ouch.* Her muscles ached in ways they never had before, a surprise given how often Eva worked out. But Marc and Angela both had warned her that running long distances would do that to her. She had worked up to five miles of running plus five miles of walking so far on her long-distance day.

Who knew where Angela was in her training. She hadn't met up with Eva again since that first day in Central Park nearly three weeks ago.

They rocked into a boat pose, which required class members to balance on their sitting bones with legs elongated in the air, making a V shape with their bodies.

"Extend into the full pose. Good. Lift the gaze, lift the chest, and hold."

This pose challenged the abs and hip flexors—the entire body's core, really—and Eva never had difficulty with it. But today her muscles screamed at her, as did her mind.

This isn't going to work.

You're going to fail Brent.

Happiness was a once-in-a-lifetime thing for you.

Eva's body trembled as she struggled to hold the pose.

"What's eating you?"

She glanced over at Marc, his arms and legs perfectly straight and lengthened, his feet pointed. Though he looked at the ceiling, his brow furrowed as he whispered, "Eva?"

"I—"

"All right, now we'll move into a plank position." Kendra's soothing voice floated across the room to the back.

Eva and Marc followed the others in the class, first into a normal plank and then into more difficult side planks, where their bodies turned and balanced on one hand as the other side lifted. A burning bled through Eva's whole body, worse than usual. Sweat dripped from her brow onto the mat, plopping in three successive droplets.

Kendra called out pose after pose—from cobra to downward-facing dog to full fold uttanasana—and Eva's body protested with each movement. Despite the instructor's encouragement to focus on breathing and let go of negative energy, Eva felt her muscles tightening and tensing.

"Is it the instructor or is something else going on? How's the planning for the gala coming along?"

Eva nearly stumbled from her eagle pose as Marc's words hissed across the space between them. Yoga often allowed her to escape the world, but how had she forgotten Marc was next to her?

Turning to look at him, her breath caught at the concern in his eyes. It was a balm to her spirit, seeing how much he worried for her. How much he cared.

Yes, she had people in her life who loved her. Her parents and sister, who did their best to support her from across the country, even though they had no clue how. Kimberly. Sherry.

But there was something altogether different in Marc's gaze. Eva couldn't put her finger on what it was, but it caused a tingle to rush down her spine.

"So?" His eyebrows lifted as he effortlessly performed the star and goddess poses.

Eva couldn't help but admire his athleticism. Many men wouldn't be caught dead in a yoga classroom, but Marc owned the experience. As had Brent.

The thought sent a tremor through her legs as she lifted her heels and dropped her hips. "The gala arrangements are going well. Kimberly has it all figured out, and we have an amazing guest list so far. That's not the issue. I'm just . . . frustrated."

The music switched to soft piano songs, and Kendra invited them into the cool-down phase.

Eva moved her mat a bit closer to Marc's and sighed as she lay flat on her back, heels planted on the mat, pressing her hips to the sky as she elongated her back and tried desperately to breathe steadily. "Training is harder than I thought it would be. And Angela . . . well, I think we overdid it that first day." She told Marc about how her sister-in-law had lagged behind Eva for the final three laps around the path, and Eva had walked the final two laps with her after completing the loop four times at a jog. "I don't think Angela is taking this whole thing as seriously as I am."

"What makes you say that?"

"Every day for the last three weeks I've invited her to go running with me, and every day she's declined. She claims she's too busy with the kids . . ."

"I've got more than just myself to worry about, Eva. You don't understand."

Maybe she really was too busy. Angela was right. Eva didn't know what it was like—even if sometimes she dreamed about how that might be.

"So she hasn't trained at all?"

"She has, I think. Just not with me. So I have no clue how far she's gone or how fast or anything like that."

"Don't worry so much. She doesn't seem like the type to commit to something without thinking it through."

"You're right. I just have so much riding on this." *I have everything riding on this.*

"We all do."

As Eva lifted her right leg across her body and touched her knee to the mat, she considered Marc's words. She'd taken his participation as a given, but why *had* he agreed to it? Was it for Brent?

Or was it for Eva?

And why this little trip in her heart that sent her blood racing at the thought that it might be the latter?

She flattened her whole body on the mat, spreading her arms outward, her legs stretched straight in front of her, allowing herself to be completely still. Her breathing at this point should have been relaxed, steady.

Instead, Eva gulped in air like she'd just run a quick mile.

"Stay here for as long as you need to, class. Thank you for joining me on our journey today."

Other classmates rose and rolled up their mats. Someone blew out the candles, and overhead the lights flickered on. Pachelbel's "Canon in D" ended abruptly.

"Eva, I know you're frustrated with Angela." Marc's gentle voice intruded on her thoughts. "But we're a team. And as a team, we have to support each other."

She struggled to sit up, as if a brick sat on her chest. "I do support her. I know this is hard for her. That's why I want to train with her. To encourage her. To motivate her. It's hard to do it by yourself." *Especially if you had to be convinced to do this whole thing in the first place.*

Of course she was grateful to Angela for agreeing to the race—whatever her sister-in-law's actual reasons.

"You're going to have to let Angela set the pace, you know." Marc paused. "Whether you like it or not, you need her."

10

Kimberly had outdone herself.

Eva balanced on her stilettos, gawking at the two gorgeous French Renaissance–style ballrooms her best friend had utterly transformed into a casino royale. Marble columns met the garlands of floral moldings ringing the ceiling. A chandelier high above them hung nearly as wide as the room itself—and that was big enough to fit thirty ten-top tables plus a stage where Eva would speak in a few short hours and urge donors to pledge their money to a great cause.

Guests had begun to arrive moments earlier, milling about in the room adjacent to this one, where casino tables featured everything from poker to blackjack, roulette, and more.

"What do you think?" Kimberly sidled up next to Eva, holding her phone, which Eva knew from experience was how she kept track of her to-do list during events. Her friend looked amazing in a shimmery black mermaid gown that hugged her hips and puddled at the ground. Kim's long hair had been slicked back dramatically, and her eye makeup was on point.

"I can't believe you pulled this off in six weeks." Eva's eyes probably resembled an owl's as she took in the opulence, how the candle sconces along the wall flickered and hummed, how the oil paintings in gilt frames and antique brass statues accented the grandeur of this palatial venue.

"Most of it was already planned for the wedding that was

canceled. Other than the last-minute advertising and contacting donors—which you and the heart center took care of—it merely required a bit of finagling to get all the services donated."

"Was that part difficult?"

"Some vendors were resistant at first." Kim flashed her straight teeth that were all too white for someone who drank so much coffee and diet soda. "But when I reminded them I'd soon be recommending vendors for the Carlton wedding, well . . ." She glanced down at her phone, which had lit up with a call. "Sorry, I've got to take this. Remember to mingle and urge people to locate the pledge table at the middle of the room to get more chips or enter the raffle."

"Will do. Thanks, Kim."

At three hundred dollars a head and approximately four hundred guests in attendance tonight, they'd already raised more than one-tenth of their goal. But it would be up to her, Marc, and Angela to schmooze and urge people to open their wallets even more. They figured the best way to raise the money was for guests to pledge on a per-mile basis.

If they convinced even three hundred to pledge twenty dollars a mile, they'd have more than enough to reach their goal of $1 million. But to add in some extra incentives, Kim had organized a few amazing raffle prizes, such as lunch with Senator Elliott Carlton and an exclusive dinner party for six hosted by Theodore Maine, an executive chef from one of the city's top restaurants.

Kimberly's staff bustled about, prepping the last-minute details of the dinner and seating arrangements. Classy lounge music filtered through the wide double doors from the next room over. Hopefully Marc and Angela were already in there, chatting up the donors and making connections.

Eva took a deep breath. Time to make Brent's dream a reality—the next step of it, anyway.

She strode into the room, which was bursting with life at every turn. Women in dazzling dresses and men in tuxedos stood around the roulette wheel, some groaning and some cheering as it spun and the ball landed. A table full of blackjack players snuck looks at their hands, serious concentration fixed on their faces while their dates looked on.

Roaming members of the catering staff offered glasses of champagne and wine. Eva took a glass of red off a tray carried by a young female server with a nose ring as she passed by.

Cupping the bottom of the glass in one hand, she allowed the strong scent to embolden her. She continued scanning the crowd but caught no sign of either of her partners in crime just yet.

"Eva!"

She turned to find Maryanne at her elbow. Despite her unusual taste in clothing, Eva's boss glowed in her soft yellow gown, a genuine grin playing across her features as she leaned down to offer a hug. She'd been out of town on vacation the last two weeks and had flown back early to be here tonight.

"Hi, Maryanne. So glad you could make it." Eva pulled back from the hug and offered the woman a smile in return. "Thank you again for agreeing to speak. I'm sure nothing will inspire people to give more than hearing from the director of the center we are donating tonight's proceeds to."

"That's where you're wrong, hon." Maryanne snagged a flute of champagne from a passing tray. "I believe it will be your speech that will guarantee your success tonight. I have no doubt that you will speak from the heart, and that hearing your story will move people to action."

Eva pressed the glass to her lips and drank to keep from bursting into tears at Maryanne's sweet words. The wine went down a mixture of sour and sweet—just like this whole thing. "That is nice of you to say. I'm just grateful that all of these important people were willing to pay so much for a ticket and happened to be available." Several people who were here had canceled other plans to attend. Others sent in donations. It was more than Eva could have hoped for.

"That is all a credit to your husband, and you too." Maryanne gestured around her. "Brent was beloved in the heart community."

"Thank you for saying that. And for putting up with this crazy scheme of mine."

"Are you kidding? Thank *you* for all you're doing to help our organization thrive. Hundreds more people will have access to education and preventive care because of this generous gift."

"I hope we can raise the million Brent wanted. I guess I'd better go mingle before dinner. I'll see you later." Eva left Maryanne's side with a renewed sense of confidence. This was where she was meant to be, what she was meant to be doing. She may have doubted Angela's commitment and abilities, but her sister-in-law had said nothing more about her own doubts. And even though they hadn't talked in a few weeks beyond a handful of texts, each one briefer than the last, Eva had to assume that Angela would reach out if she needed help. Eventually they'd land on the same page, right?

She approached the nearest table and introduced herself to those there. After half an hour of making the rounds and encouraging people to enjoy themselves, Eva finally located Marc and Angela. She excused herself from her present company and made her way across the room, grimacing at how her heels rubbed the spots on her feet that were sore thanks to six weeks of training.

Marc spotted her and waved. Was it her imagination, or did his eyes skim over her ever so briefly? It had been so long since she'd dressed up—he likely just wasn't used to her wearing more than yoga pants and a tank.

But tonight she'd wanted to stand out, to at least embody colorful hope despite the doubts she'd experienced since they'd started this journey. So when Kimberly had dragged her shopping and Eva had seen the bright red cape-back lace halter gown with the deep V neckline on the rack at Neiman Marcus, she'd put aside her fears and grabbed it without even trying it on.

Seems it had been the perfect choice.

At last, Eva reached Angela and Marc. "Finally found you guys."

Marc looked handsome as always in his tuxedo. He'd left a bit of a five o'clock shadow on his chin and jaw, cutting a nice blend of classy and rugged. Leaning in, he kissed her on the cheek. "You look beautiful." He pulled away before she could figure out his cologne, but whatever it was left her with an odd feeling in the pit of her stomach.

Her smile wavered, but she pushed through the nerves. "Thanks. You don't look so bad yourself." She turned to face her sister-in-law. "And you look lovely too, Angela."

Angela sported the pale green empire-waisted bridesmaid dress she'd worn to Eva's wedding five years ago. Her hair hung in simple ringlets around her shoulders. She looked gorgeous—perhaps more toned from her training?—and yet a certain cloud hung over her. Makeup couldn't cover the dark bags under her eyes. "Thanks." Her back was as straight as a stick, and her voice even stiffer. She stared at the ground.

"Where's Kylee?" Her oldest niece had begged to come, but Eva hadn't caught a glimpse of her yet.

"Somewhere." The response was as flat—and distant—as the first.

Eva held in a sigh. She'd so hoped that doing this race would bring her and Angela closer together, help her understand her sister-in-law better. But despite Marc's gentle admonishment at the end of their yoga class three weeks ago, and Eva's willingness to try again, apparently Angela felt differently.

Eva turned back to Marc. "Has anyone said they were going to make a decent-sized pledge?"

"Definitely. Although after the program, I'm sure even more people will flood to the booth to donate." Marc checked the Rolex he saved for special occasions. "Speaking of, it's almost time for dinner now."

"Eva." Angela's head popped up suddenly. "We need to talk."

Uh-oh. What was that about?

"Sure—"

"All right, everyone." Kim's voice came over the speaker system as the music dimmed. "I know you're all having a blast, but it's dinnertime! Don't worry, though. Once we've eaten and heard a bit from our speakers, you will have several more hours to enjoy the casino entertainment, as well as time to place your pledges and enter to win one of our amazing raffle prizes. Please proceed into the dining room and find your name on the seating chart. Bon appétit."

Eva hooked her arms through Marc's and Angela's. "Sorry, Angela, we'll have to chat afterward. For now, let's go raise a million dollars for our men."

*   *   *

She had to tell Eva. Now.

But every time she tried, Angela lost her nerve.

She sat there at the fancy table staring at the stage as Eva talked about Brent, his passions, and his legacy. The four-foot centerpiece bursting with exotic flowers and beads blocked part of her view, but she could hear the conviction, the wavering emotion, in her sister-in-law's voice.

Why couldn't Angela feel that way? Instead of dread, guilt, and the ever-present anger she tried to stuff away, why couldn't she focus on the excitement of making something good out of Wes's death?

Maybe if she—like Eva—had the time and energy to do so,

and no children to worry about feeding and keeping clothed and housed . . .

Angela's eyes drifted to Kylee, who bit her lip and gripped her fine linen napkin as she watched her aunt. Her oldest daughter had seemed to blossom overnight thanks to the on-clearance dress they'd found her. The way she'd curled her hair and dabbed lipstick and blush on, she was no longer a little girl playing dress-up with Angela's old clothes and makeup.

She was a girl on the verge of womanhood, and the idea shot fear right through Angela's already-full heart.

Eva concluded her speech to thundering applause, and the speaker portion of the night ended. Then they were all swept up in a surge of guests rushing from the room to place pledges and continue playing at the casino tables. Before Angela could grab Eva—she needed to end this charade *now*—her sister-in-law disappeared into the crowd, presumably to mingle and gather even more support for her cause.

A cause Angela didn't know if she could stand behind anymore. Not because she didn't believe in it, but because it was slowly killing her.

With every hour that passed at the gala, she felt the noose tighten more and more. As the money flowed in from donors, they were in this. They were committed. And yet Angela didn't know how she was going to survive another day of this training schedule, much less four and a half more months.

Angela maneuvered through the organized chaos, feeling like she had a cold—her ears felt stuffed with cotton, her throat raw from swallowing the remorse and dread that kept bubbling up, her eyes glazed with fatigue. The muted sounds of laughter, flying dice, applause, and music dazed her as she wandered, seeking out Eva. Seeking and never finding. What a metaphor for her life.

Okay, now she was just tired, thinking in riddles, her mind

giving in to the tiredness her entire body had felt for weeks—a new level of weariness she hadn't experienced in a long time. And all of it due to training multiple hours a day after working and caring for her children.

She wasn't going to find Eva in this madness. Angela snatched the heels off her feet and walked toward the edge of the room where she located a few high-back stuffed chairs that looked less than inviting. She sank into one of the chairs, and the muscles in her body groaned and her knees crackled. Her stiff fingers released the shoes, and her head thunked against the headrest. The room faded as she closed her eyes.

"Angela?" A gentle touch to her shoulder jolted her awake. She blinked, her mascara clumping her top and bottom eyelashes together. Her nose and eyes felt as if they'd been exposed to a blast of desert wind, and her head ached. Had she fallen asleep right there in the middle of a party?

She quickly realized the party was over. The music had ended, and Kimberly's crew was whisking away empty glasses and plates. The casino rentals staff folded tables.

Eva lowered herself into the chair next to Angela. "Sorry to wake you. But it's time to head home."

"I went looking for you, and when I didn't see you, I just . . ." A muscle spasmed in Angela's middle back. "Where's Kylee?"

"I think she's chatting Kim's ear off in the kitchen." Eva laughed. "Guess what, Angela? We did it. We raised a million dollars. Well, more than that, actually. Between initial ticket sales, raffle purchases, and pledges, once the race is complete we'll have made 1.2 million dollars for the Manhattan Heart Center." Tears glistened in the corners of Eva's eyes as she reached for Angela's hand. "Brent and Wes would be really proud."

Angela stared at Eva's hand in hers. Now was the time for her to be truthful. She hated to do it, but what choice did she have? She couldn't go on as she had been. But how to word it in a way that wouldn't break Eva's heart, her spirit?

"Eva, I can't do this anymore." Ugh. Couldn't she have come up with a better way of saying it than *that*? And why did her voice always sound so void of emotion?

But that was the result of being so drop-dead tired that you fell asleep in the middle of a casino room. Her brain just plain didn't work anymore.

"Can't do what?" Eva's pretty eyes narrowed in confusion, her bow-shaped lips pursing into a frown.

Even though she and Eva were nothing alike, Angela never wanted to see her in pain. Angela sighed. "I wanted to tell you earlier, but there wasn't a chance. The last six weeks have been pure pandemonium for me. My house is in shambles, I feed my family complete junk, and I never see my kids anymore, all because of the extra time that training for this race is taking."

This whole race was supposed to be for the kids, but how were things going to improve if they never had quality family time and Angela never had a chance to truly focus on healing? She'd been foolish to think that impulsively jumping on board with Eva's plan would result in anything other than complete tumult.

She continued her explanation, hoping Eva would understand, even if she couldn't relate. "And it's not just that my life is falling apart around me. I'm exhausted. I forgot how taxing running so much could be." Not that she always ran when she was training. But it made sense to try to get her mileage in faster, which meant upping her pace. "I actually fell asleep at work yesterday and missed a really important call we'd been waiting for. My boss was so upset that I'm shocked she didn't fire me. That was the last straw for me."

Eva withdrew her hand from Angela's arm. "But I can't do this without you. I told you that. And what about tonight, all the money we raised?"

"I know, I know. And I'm sorry. But I can't lose my job, Eva. And my kids deserve more than I'm able to give them. Before this race came up, we were struggling, I'll admit. But we're worse off now. I just don't have the time or energy to give to this anymore."

Her sister-in-law stared at the ground for several moments. Then her head popped up and she looked at Angela directly, her face brightening. "What if we didn't wait until March to go?"

"What?"

"Like, what if we went to New Zealand before the race? We could leave whenever you wanted. Rent a house there. We could really focus on training. Learn the lay of the land. Bask in the gorgeous New Zealand weather. It's going to be summer there soon, you know."

There she went again with her dreaming, floating around above reality. "Eva, what are you talking about? I have to work. The kids have school. And I would never leave them for that amount of time. Aren't you listening?"

"Don't you miss homeschooling?"

"Of course."

"What if it was an option?"

Didn't Eva understand how painful her questions were? "Again I ask, what are you talking about?"

Eva leaned forward. "Angela, you know Brent left me a lot of money, and the business is really profitable." Her features hardened into determination. "We have to find a way to get through this. Maybe what we all need is to step out of this winter of our lives and into the bright light of summer."

"Oh, Eva." What a dreamer.

"I can tell you think I'm crazy, but we could do it. I'll pay for everything. Quit your job—I'm sure you can find something similar when you return, but if not, come work for Marc at one of our gyms."

"I don't know . . ." Angela's head spun with all that Eva's suggestions entailed. The impossibility of it all.

And yet a tiny what-if burrowed into her heart.

"And Sherry could come and help with the kids when we're out training. We can go whenever you want. Next week. Next month."

Could she really take her children out of school and away from all they knew—the house where they'd lived with their father—for months on end? And could Angela really make herself beholden to Eva financially like that? Paying for her to do the race was one thing. But to allow her sister-in-law to fund an entire trip for the whole family for several months . . . that was different.

All of it—the race included—was just far too disruptive. Angela had to put her foot down before Eva's train of good intentions ran all of their lives off the track.

"I'm sorry, Eva. I have to quit. Maybe they'll let you do the race without me if you explain the situation." Angela grimaced as her head pounded. She blew out a steadying breath. It was the right decision.

"You're quitting? Really?"

Of course. She couldn't find her daughter all evening, and she'd chosen this moment to show up.

Kylee stomped toward them, her face a mask of rage.

"Hon—"

"No, Mom, just . . . stop. I mean, I guess I shouldn't be surprised. You quit on Dad too."

The words caused a physical throb to spread through Angela's entire body. "Excuse me?"

Wes had been the one to quit on *them*, not the other way around. Who had taken care of the children while her husband had flitted off to seek out danger? Who had wiped her kids' eyes and calmed their nightmares when Wes had landed himself in the hospital with broken ribs after a rappelling adventure gone awry—a whole year before he died in a stupid accident that could have been avoided if he'd only listened to her pleas for him to stop?

"Nothing. I just thought you were finally going to show the world—show us—that Dad meant something to you. But I guess that's too hard for you, right?"

"Kylee." Eva spoke her niece's name gently. "Be kind. Your mother has her reasons."

Surprisingly, Kylee didn't crumple into a heap and lean into Eva. Her lower lip trembled as she pasted on a defiant look and folded her arms across her chest. "Don't defend her, Aunt Eva."

How could she get through to her daughter? Hadn't Kylee noticed the strain that training had taken on their family already? "I loved your father, but . . ." No, she wouldn't say what she really wanted to. Wes had been Kylee's world, and Angela wouldn't ruin her image of her hero. She steeled herself against the indignation and other emotions threatening to tumble out. "We can discuss this later, when you've calmed down."

"I'll never calm down. Want to know why? Because I don't want to be anything like you." Kylee whirled on her heel and ran from the room.

Angela sunk back into the chair, her chest heaving.

Eva stayed beside her, quiet.

What was the right thing to do? Angela was living trapped perpetually on an elevator. But no matter what floor she chose to exit on, something unpleasant awaited her. And as evidenced by the last year and a half, waiting on the elevator for a better floor to open up wasn't a real choice either. Neither was staying stagnant, allowing a tiny space to suffocate her slowly.

"If you find that something you're doing isn't working, change course."

She recognized the voice in her head immediately. Her high school cross-country coach, Bryan Simmonds, had been a bedrock of encouragement and leadership, never steering her wrong as she sought to become better at the sport. Why were his words returning to her now? Maybe because she'd finally started running again—could that have knocked the memory loose?

He'd said more than that, though, hadn't he? Angela focused, trying to dredge up the reminder of that day long ago when she'd become frustrated over not being as fast as she wanted—when her small world had seemed to spin out of control.

What else had he said? Oh yes . . .

"Switch up your breathing, get a new pair of shoes, do something different. It just might be the difference between surviving the race and conquering it."

Could it be that the choices before her weren't as cut-and-dry as she'd believed? That it didn't have to be "do the race" or "don't do the race"? Maybe Eva was onto something. Perhaps time away from work and the familiar would somehow put things back together.

All Angela knew was that in this moment—with her daughter hating her, her sister-in-law disappointed in her, and a community of people who'd given money and would feel betrayed if she quit—maybe it was time to become a conqueror.

And the first conquest would be her own pride.

She glanced up at her sister-in-law, biting her lip so hard she tasted blood. "When do you propose we leave?"

Eva had read that New Zealand was a land of contradictions. It was one reason Brent had always wanted to visit. Rugged mountain ranges coexisted with glaciers, sandy beaches, fjords, volcanic plateaus, fertile farmland, and subtropical forest. The wind blew westerly in some months, but now and then an easterly wind took over.

It was a land of mystery and—some would say—magic. Of exquisite beauty.

And maybe, if their hearts were willing, it could become a place of healing.

Nearly three months after she'd received the initial phone call from Tina Landry, Eva removed her eye mask, flinching for a moment at the bright lights of the airplane. The captain had just asked them to prepare for landing in Queenstown, New Zealand, after a flight from Auckland—and before that, two other really long flights that totaled nearly twenty-four hours of travel. Then, once they'd landed, they would still have a bit of a drive to their final destination of Wanaka.

Next to Eva, Sherry read a book, the picture of calm. On Sherry's other side, Kylee sat with her earbuds in and eyes closed. Lilly chattered with Angela across the aisle, her excited voice rising and lowering, existing in a vacuum created by the plane's white noise, while Zach zeroed in on his tablet.

Sherry glanced at Eva. "Did you sleep well, dear?"

"I guess so." Eva maneuvered her neck to the left, then right, stretching the taut muscles. She'd never been able to sleep on airplanes, but given her utter exhaustion and the cottony feeling in her mouth, she must have done so. Her face felt like dirt clung to every pore. Eva ran her hand through her hair and tried to breathe through the mixture of thrill and nerves building in her stomach.

She'd kept busy the last five weeks as she and Angela prepared for the trip—finding a real estate agent in New Zealand to arrange for a short-term rental, booking flights, working with Marc's personal assistant to schedule his visit around the holidays to run a marathon that was happening in New Zealand in January, and transitioning her work at the heart center to other coworkers. Eva had wanted to outsource all of the planning to a concierge service, but Angela insisted they handle everything themselves so they would know it had been done correctly.

Since Eva didn't thrive in the details, she'd helped by watching the kids and bringing meals over to Angela's whenever her sister-in-law would let her. It was very obvious Angela had difficulty accepting help—or maybe she just didn't want to spend more time with Eva than necessary.

The three team members had also managed to squeeze in a few training sessions together. Eva and Marc had allowed Angela to set the pace, which meant they mostly walked—and this was more difficult for Eva than she'd wanted to admit.

During her own training sessions, she'd begun to crave the adrenaline of running and the way an ache built in her lungs, how stitches fisted her sides with a vice grip, how her thighs itched minutes into a run, how her muscles burned slow and long.

Some might call such a craving masochistic, but for Eva the physical pain was welcome relief from what pummeled her heart almost daily.

Regardless of not quite being on the same page regarding training, all of the plans for getting out here early had come together beautifully, and being here now should allow Angela the break she needed to focus more on training. Maybe she'd even be more open to running.

Eva slid her tray table into its locked position and pushed up the window shade next to her. Clouds surrounded them—white, downy ones, not dark ones like they'd left at home. Here they resembled thick batting used in quilts and pillows, creating a blanket of fluff below the plane, striking against the pure blue sky above them.

She squinted. Was it her imagination or were those snowcapped mountain peaks rising from the clouds?

Yes. Amazing.

What other beauties would they see while they were here?

Suddenly the world outside the plane was obscured in white as they descended through the cloud cover. Could the pilot see in this?

Instead of inciting fear, the question caused her dormant sense of adventure to leap to life.

As they dropped from the clouds, she was rewarded with a heart-stopping view as a green valley opened up, surrounded by the mountains they'd just seen from above. The plane approached the runway, a placid and beautiful lake in the distance.

It was December 1, and everything at home had begun to ice over, become frigid, and die. But here, life bloomed.

"Wow."

"Wow is right." Sherry angled for a view.

From her spot across the aisle, Lilly exclaimed over everything she saw.

Eva peeked at Angela, whose eyes remained fixed on the airplane seat in front of her. Was she regretting her decision to come? Even though she and Eva had spent more time talking in the last month, Angela had been all business. The crack in her emotions that Eva had glimpsed at the gala had been patched over—as if it had never existed at all. And during training they never spoke except to communicate regarding pacing.

But they were here now, and maybe all of that would change.

୧

Angela had never seen such beauty, and she'd grown up along the gorgeous Southern California coast.

She stepped onto the porch of the house on Lake Wanaka that had come available at the last minute. They'd been able to sublet it for four months—a miracle at this time of year—and it fit their needs perfectly. The wood creaked beneath her bare feet as she walked to the banister and took in the scenery: the rippling rolls of the lake's gentle waves, the pine trees towering above her, the mountains that jutted from the earth, big and strong and overwhelming in their beauty. How strange that back home people were preparing for the first major winter storm of the season, while here they jet-boated and cycled.

The little town of Wanaka was just a short walk down the lakeside path, but they hadn't had a chance to explore it yet. Yesterday they'd crashed as soon as they'd arrived at the house. Jet lag had invited Angela to sleep for thirteen hours straight, and the kids were still tucked away in their second-story rooms despite the late morning hour.

"You ready?" Eva's voice broke through the solitude.

"For what?" Angela racked her brain but couldn't remember today's schedule. Despite sleeping the night away, she'd woken mind-tired—Wes had haunted her dreams for the first time in months. Of course, her weariness was more than that. Between all the hours she'd spent training, packing, planning school curriculum, working, arranging for house sitters, and everything else that came with being away for four months, she was more than a little exhausted physically, mentally, and emotionally.

Eva approached, wearing her designer running gear. "For our first day of training here."

Ugh.

They'd found a few times to train together in New York in November, and each time Eva barely seemed to break a sweat after miles of activity. It wasn't a competition, true. But being the one who slowed the team down . . . that rankled. No matter how much Angela improved, she sensed it might not be enough for Eva, who still had her heart set on running the entire ultra-marathon.

"I need to change."

"No problem. Once you do, there's a path that goes past town and winds around the lake. I was thinking we could do about nine miles. That would take us past town, and then when we reach half-way we could just come back."

At this point in her training, nine miles of walking was nothing. In fact, on Angela's long training day each week, she'd worked up to about fourteen or fifteen miles.

Okay, well, not *nothing*. Whenever she increased her mileage and the incline on her treadmill, her body protested. At first it had taken the form of blisters on her feet, tiny irritants that made every step she took more annoying than the last. Lately her hips had started protesting after long or faster walks.

But despite the unpleasantries, she'd grown more used to the exercise. Not that she'd ever fully get rid of the "mom bod," but she'd even lost some weight and gained muscle.

Still, the supposed positive effects of increased exercise, like better sleep and a boost in her mood, had all been canceled out by the anxiety that weighed heavily on her mind: Was she right in dragging her kids here and doing this?

Angela turned from the lake. "I'll be right back." She left Eva standing on the porch and headed to her room, then dug into the depths of her suitcase until she emerged with a worn pair of workout pants and a vacation Bible school volunteer T-shirt from five years ago. She got dressed and headed back downstairs.

In the kitchen Sherry flipped pancakes over the stove as Angela stopped to pull a water bottle from the fridge. "Headed for a walk?"

"Yes. Do you mind staying with the kids?"

When she'd told the children about her decision to come here early and have them complete the rest of their schooling for the semester online, Zach and Lilly had cheered. Kylee, however, acted offended at the thought of being forced to leave her friends for several months—apparently she hadn't overheard that part of her and Eva's conversation at the gala. Despite her poor attitude, Angela had indulged her daughter's desire to finish out the cross-country season before they left.

"Of course not. That's what I'm here for."

"Thanks, Sherry." Opening the back door, she found Eva doing some sort of yoga pose, face turned toward the sun.

Eva unfolded herself. "Do you want to try running again?" Her face was a mix of hopefulness and timidity.

Everything in Angela wanted to yell "No!" at her sister-in-law for the thousandth time. Because she didn't want to run ever again.

It had been her thing in high school, yes, but she was a different person now. Back then she'd had dreams, plans for the future that looked nothing like the life she had today. Not that she hadn't ended up loving the life she'd fallen into—before Wes had gone and died, of course—but the girl who ran was someone who never failed at anything. Someone who was going to become a successful doctor and not let anything stand in her way of a well-positioned life. Someone who didn't need anyone else in order to prevail.

But she wasn't that girl anymore. Somewhere along the way,

Angela Jamison had become a woman—one whose dreams had been pushed aside because she'd lost sight of the prize.

Because she'd fallen in love.

Angela sighed. "Let's just see how it goes, all right?"

"Okay. Sure." The light in Eva's eyes flickered, but her sister-in-law smiled anyway. How did she do that? Even in the worst circumstances, Eva seemed determined to keep faith in the mission.

They loaded their packs onto their backs—since they hadn't purchased all of their supplies yet, about twenty pounds of bottled water and heavy books filled the bags now—and Eva led the way down the porch steps onto the lakeside path. Settling into a nice rhythm, they walked.

Long golden reeds rustled near the water, and seagulls cawed in the distance closer to town. Cyclists shouted hello as they whizzed by, and other pedestrians nodded greetings. Friendly place, this.

As a group of moms with strollers fast-walked past them, Angela noticed Eva's clenched fists at her side, the way she gnawed at her lip. It was clear she wanted to bolt.

"You can go ahead." Angela made the same offer she had during their first training session over two months ago.

"No, we should stay together." Eva smiled again, but this time it seemed tighter, as if forced.

Well, she'd tried.

They continued on in silence. Angela breathed in the fresh pine scent surrounding her. The path weaved along the lakeside, a canopy of tree branches above them and then nothing but stark sky.

Her body started to relax into the cadence of the wind sweeping across the lake, the crunch of pebbles beneath her feet, the feel of the sun's warmth on her face as it rose higher in the sky. And slowly she began to increase her pace. At first, unintentionally. The beauty that surrounded her reminded her so much of California—not because it was exactly the same, but because she hadn't really been in nature like this since then. New York City held its own appeal for some, but she and Wes had only moved there initially for the free lodging his parents offered during their first few years of marriage.

Before she knew it, Angela started running.

And oh, the freedom that rolled over her as she flew down the path, legs pumping like a gazelle, the breeze whispering through her hair, the adrenaline washing over her in waves. She hadn't felt this way running back home.

In fact, when was the last time she'd felt this way at all?

A vision tugged at Angela's memory, foggy at first. But as she moved along the path next to Lake Wanaka, it morphed into a full-blown movie reel in her mind.

It was second semester of freshman year. She'd been running on campus, just for fun—with her full load of premed classes, she no longer had time for non-career-related extracurriculars—and suddenly a guy she recognized from her biology class joined her. Angela averted her eyes and kept her head down.

"Hi." She'd never seen him running this route before. "Mind if I join you?"

Angela pursed her lips and increased her speed. "Actually—"

"I'm Wes Jamison." The wiry man kept pace with her despite his poor running form. "We have bio together."

Couldn't a girl go for a run without getting hit on? Angela pulled up short under a towering tree. "Look, I'm sure you're very nice and everything, but I don't date, okay?" Even if she had time, the two dates she'd been on in her lifetime hadn't gone well. Her aunt always said men were intimidated by an intelligent woman, but who knew if that was the reason.

And that was fine with her, really. To become a doctor, she'd have to stay focused. Men only complicated things.

Instead of frowning and walking away, a slow grin spread

like molasses across Wes's face. It was a nice smile—not like the kind guys wore when they leered or when they thought they were all that and a bag of chips. No, this smile lit something deep in the pit of Angela's stomach.

He seemed like the good, stable, guy-next-door type. The kind of guy who wouldn't want anything to do with awkward, serious Angela Ladd.

"Well, that's okay. I wasn't looking for a date."

"You weren't?" Why the disappointment flooding her heart? Angela's toes curled in her shoes, itching to run again. "Why did you stop me then?"

"Technically I didn't stop you. I just asked to join you." He nudged her with his elbow.

Angela stiffened at the contact. "Well—"

"Relax, I'm teasing you. I tried to grab you after class yesterday, but you left really quickly. And then, just now, I was sitting over there studying when I saw you running past. So I thought I'd try again."

"Why did you want to talk to me?"

He flicked his fingers through his short blond curls, scratching the base of his head where his head met his hairline. "Uh, okay, well, you're really smart and I thought maybe we could be lab partners. I asked Professor Higgins if I could switch, because the girl I'm paired with right now is so clueless. And I noticed you don't have a partner." Wes shrugged. "So if you're open to partnering up, maybe we could try it out."

Just like his smile, he seemed totally sincere in his request. "Sorry, but I work better alone."

He studied her for a moment. "Maybe you do. Maybe you don't. Why not try working with me and see?"

Angela couldn't help but gawk at him. "I—"

"Don't answer now if your answer is going to be no." There

was that beaming again. Why did it affect her so much? "If you decide to be my partner, just come sit by me tomorrow in class. If not, no hard feelings."

What a strange guy. "Okay."

Wes turned to leave but stopped, looking over his shoulder. "I do hope you say yes, though."

Seventeen years later, Angela sucked in air and slowed her pace again, snapping the cap off her water and sipping the cold liquid. Her heart bumped wildly against her chest—whether from the physical exertion or the memory, who could say?

That one day had forever altered the trajectory of Angela's life. What if she'd just kept on running? Hadn't slipped into a seat next to him in class the next day?

Would she take it all back?

No.

The answer thrummed through her entire body, and relief chased it.

She may have a lot of complicated feelings where Wes and their life together were concerned, but at least she knew that much.

And for now—for this moment—that was enough.

12

Eva had to get out of here.

Slowly she rose from the overstuffed gray chair situated by a large picture window.

Angela stood next to the floor-to-ceiling stone fireplace, fingertips splayed across her forehead, eyes slightly closed. "Kylee, for the last time, just because we're in a small town doesn't mean you can run off with the first people you meet."

Eva took another step, praying Sherry or one of the other kids would walk in and save her from the awkward drama playing out in front of her.

"Mom, all I want to do is meet them for ice cream in town. It's bad enough you took me away from all of my actual friends. Now you're also going to keep me from making new ones? Like, really?"

"Stop overreacting. I simply said you needed to invite them here so I can get to know them first."

Almost to the kitchen . . . Eva's foot hit the leg of a chair, and she winced at the loud thump.

Angela and Kylee looked up at the noise. Angela's face turned white—maybe she'd forgotten Eva was there.

What could Eva say? "I'm going to walk into town." Yes, that would be just the break she needed. She couldn't handle much more of this tension—they'd been here a week and already she'd been witness to one too many arguments. "You want to come with, Kylee?"

"Yes!" Kylee ran toward the stairs. "Be down in three."

"Sorry. I guess I should have asked you first."

"It's fine." Angela leaned her head against the window. "Seems I can't do anything right these days. Sorry to argue in front of you."

Most of the time her sister-in-law struck her as strong, unbreakable even, but then she'd show tiny chinks in the armor she put on every day to protect herself from . . . well, from what, Eva wasn't sure.

Eva retraced her steps until she stood next to Angela. "I fought a lot with my mom as a teenager. I'm sure you did too. It's kind of par for the course, you know?"

"My mom died when I was young. I hardly remember her. And my aunt was almost never home."

"Oh." Eva had known that, right? She had a vague memory of Brent telling her something to that effect. "Well, believe me. It's normal." She wanted to reach out to squeeze Angela's arm, but Angela also wasn't the overly affectionate type—toward Eva, at least.

"Thanks." But Angela didn't look like she believed Eva. Eva couldn't blame her. She couldn't imagine how hard it would be to love a child and have so much friction.

Couldn't imagine it, and now she'd never experience it. If only she and Brent hadn't decided to wait to have children. Of course, then she'd be a single mom with fatherless children. Like Angela.

Still . . . at least Angela had people to come home to every night.

"Ready, Aunt Eva?"

Eva turned to find her niece changed into a pair of shorts that showed off her strong legs and a cute ruffled top with polka dots. "Yep."

After a quick bye to and from Angela, Eva and Kylee left the house and started down the path that would get them into town in five minutes.

Eva and her niece walked in silence for a few minutes, and Eva's spirit leaned into the chorus of nature singing all around her.

And then there were the colors—the blues of the water, the vivid greens of the leaves, the white dotting the sky, and the brown mountains in the distance. It all made her fingertips tingle with the desire to create.

An inkling of hope, at last.

But she could sense that Kylee was not quite so calm. Her feet stomped more with every step, and her hands clenched and un-clenched at her sides. Poor girl. She'd experienced so much loss at such a tender age. Distraction. That's what she needed. "You want to shop a little?"

Kylee grinned. "Yeah?" But then her lips changed direction. "I don't have money."

"I've got you covered." Eva laughed at her niece's squeal of delight.

Music and laughter indicated they'd reached the edge of town. As they made their way up the beach, Eva took it all in. There were several grassy areas lining the promenade, and groups of young people played Frisbee and sat on picnic blankets eating ice cream. A man fed a woman a fancy chocolate truffle. Just up the way, a street artist had strung a low tightrope between two trees and walked it while juggling several brightly colored balls. Tourists relaxed on benches lining the path. Families walked by with strollers and dogs on leashes. The smell of roasted coffee drifted from a shop on one corner of the main street lined with boutiques and cafés, res-taurants, and pubs of every sort.

"New Zealand is pretty cool, huh?" Eva hip-bumped Kylee.

Kylee eyed a group of teenage boys throwing back sodas and teasing one another. She quirked a smile. "It's okay, I guess."

"So maybe you could give your mom a bit of a break about bringing you here?" Eva tried to say it casually as they stepped into a souvenir shop filled with sheepskin slippers, jams, Manuka honey, and mini collectible figurines from The Lord of the Rings movies.

Kylee pushed some hangers aside as she browsed a rack of New Zealand souvenir T-shirts. "I guess."

They looked around a few more stores before landing on the stoop of a florist's shop. Eva fully intended to walk on by, but the front window display stopped her.

Primroses. A whole arrangement of them. But they weren't even native to this region.

Brent would have said it was a sign. Of what, Eva wasn't sure. But in this moment, she felt him here.

"We should get some flowers for Grandma." Kylee turned expectant eyes toward her aunt.

Sherry *had* given up the next four months of her life to help Angela with the kids. Flowers weren't much, but her mother-in-law might appreciate the small token of gratitude.

"Okay." Eva's hands trembled as she pushed open the door.

The familiar smell of perfumed bliss overtook her. Like artwork on a life-sized canvas, splashes of color from lilies, pansies, orchids, cyclamen, bromeliads, and more accented the gorgeous shop, which was surprisingly devoid of Christmas decor except for garland and some prominently displayed arrangements boasting red blooms.

Several customers milled about, dampening the strands of classical music feathering from the radio on the desk.

"Hello." A thin brunette with high cheekbones looked up from a large floral arrangement near the checkout desk. "Let me know if you need any help." The woman's British accent lilted in the shop and—along with her slacks, blouse, and the strand of pearls around her throat—gave the fortysomething woman a very prim and proper air. She turned her attention back to her arrangement.

"Thanks." A variety of scents rose from the flowers set in vases along the wall of the shop. The honey-and-mint smell of freesias, the addicting bitter orange of daffodils, the syrupy sweetness of hyacinths—each one was intoxicating in its own way.

"We're looking for flowers for my grandma. My aunt is a very talented florist."

Eva cringed at the praise and prayed the woman would ignore Kylee.

But she looked up again and floated toward them, full of natural grace. "You don't say. It's always lovely to meet a fellow flower artist." The florist clapped, a huge grin lighting up her face and softening her features. "How long will you be in town?"

"Till the end of March, actually."

"Splendid, splendid." The shop owner tilted her head. "If you ever want to chat flowers, I'd love nothing more. I get so inspired by others' ideas. I'm Joanne, by the way."

"I'm Eva and this is Kylee. And that would be fun."

Liar. Because what inspiration could she offer? She'd quit because once Brent died, all her creativity had oozed like Jell-O down a storm drain. That, and she couldn't take being around other people whose happy endings were just beginning.

Another customer approached Joanne.

"I'll leave you to peruse then. Give a shout if you need anything." Joanne turned to the waiting customer and followed her across the room.

The woman gone, Eva allowed the tears she'd held at bay to finally fall as she pulled a pink rose to her nose.

"You cry a lot, Aunt Eva." Kylee's words were tinged with sadness.

She'd nearly forgotten her niece was there. Eva drew her nose away from the rose's heady smell. "I'm definitely more emotional than most, I guess." She tugged her niece into a side hug, praying that wasn't the wrong move.

But Kylee snuggled in, resting her head against Eva's shoulder.

It took Eva a moment to form the words in her heart. "You know, when you've loved deeply and lost deeply, it's okay to feel deeply."

Sure, some people like her parents expressed concern that she still cried so much, as though there was a time limit on grief. But how was she supposed to move on from a love so great it had formed the very person she was? Though growing up she'd always felt like a bit of a square peg in a round hole, Brent had understood her, had given her a place to belong.

And without him, how could she ever be happy again? Yeah, she may be able to snatch pieces of color and pull bits of happiness into her world now and again, but all color eventually faded.

Every rose eventually wilted.

"Sometimes I wonder if my mom really loved my dad."

Whoa. A heavy thought for someone so young. "Why do you say that?"

Kylee took a white rose petal between her fingers, stroking her thumb and forefinger across the silky surface. "I haven't seen her cry since Dad died. Not even at the funeral. And they fought a lot before he died."

"Oh, hon." A few of her tears soaked into Kylee's hair. "Every couple fights. Even me and Uncle Brent."

"Really?"

True, it had been rare, but then again, they'd been so alike. What did they have to fight about? "Yeah, and we all grieve differently. Your mom has had to be so strong for all of you. To be honest, I don't know if she's really had a chance to grieve."

Kylee pulled away, her nose scrunched. "It's been a year and a half."

Eva considered her answer before continuing. "Sometimes our feelings might not be in sync with the passage of time. One day can seem like a thousand years when you're without someone you love. Other times a day passes without notice."

The rose petal tore off in Kylee's fingers. Her hand stilled, and she swallowed hard. "I miss her. My mom, I mean. The mom she used to be."

"I know, sweetie." Eva plucked the damaged rose from its bucket, intent on adding it to the bouquet for Sherry. "When some people have so much grief inside of them, it's hard to figure out how to release it. And it's easy for the rest of us to only see the prickles—the thorns—that happen as a result. But don't forget there's a rose there too. You sometimes just have to wait for it to bloom."

13

Her family was all together, and no one was fighting.

Was Angela dreaming?

"Cool, Mom, look at that!" Zach ran toward the restored stone-and-wood huts of the Chinese miners' settlement on the edge of historic Arrowtown, a village located about an hour from Wanaka.

Lilly followed hot on his heels. "Wait for me!"

"You guys, watch where you're going." Though they'd come first thing in the morning, a large crowd of tourists already joined them in their quest for history. Angela sped up her pace, leaving Sherry and Kylee to meander the dirt path. Finally, she caught up to the younger kids where they circled a tiny hut established during the 1860s Otago Gold Rush.

Not far behind them bubbled Bush Creek, a tributary off the Arrow River. As with every part of this beautiful country she'd seen in the week and a half since they'd arrived, swaying trees surrounded the settlement—everything from willow to poplar and hawthorn. The sun sparkled bright, not a cloud in the sky. It was supposed to reach seventy-five degrees Fahrenheit, making it a perfect day for running, but Angela had bailed on Eva at the last minute this morning. Her excuse had been preparing for the field trip, but to tell the truth, lactic acid stiffened her legs thanks to the way she'd started pushing herself this last week.

While waiting for Kylee and Sherry to catch up, Angela studied the pamphlet she'd received from the visitor center in the main part of Arrowtown. "According to this, migrants from China constructed the huts and stores with a variety of materials, including mud brick, corrugated iron, mortared stone, canvas, and wood."

"Sweet." Zach examined the hut in front of them from all angles. "How many people lived in them?"

As Sherry and Kylee joined them, Angela thumbed through the pamphlet again. "Looks like anywhere from two to six per house. And it was probably only men who lived here, since they were mining for gold and working their claims, though approximately seventy percent of them were married."

Kylee's eyes scanned her own pamphlet. "Sad."

Huh. Angela had expected complete boredom on Kylee's part, and yet, ever since her walk with Eva into town earlier this week, she'd been almost pleasant. Angela would have to ask Eva her secret.

"Why didn't they live with their wives?" Lilly's rumpled nose accentuated a spray of freckles across the arch. She fiddled with the wedding ring on her grandma's right hand.

Sherry squatted down to Lilly's level. "They probably had to work and send money home to their families. It would have been hard and very expensive to move everyone here."

"Yeah, it says here that China was having a difficult time, so they came here to try to get wealthy." Kylee lowered the pamphlet, frowning.

What was her daughter thinking? If only Angela could see into her brain. But asking might disrupt the tender bridge being built between them.

Zach darted inside one of the huts, then emerged. "No way would I want to live in one of those. I'd have taken my chances in China, thanks."

How wonderful to see her children exploring and learning again.

She'd missed homeschooling more than she'd ever allowed herself to admit. "Bud, if you were responsible for a family, you would do whatever it took to protect them."

It took a moment for the words she'd spoken to leave her mouth and find their way into her heart. A sudden pang crushed her chest, and she blinked to keep a flash of hotness behind her eyes.

Because Wes . . . he hadn't. He'd . . .

Angela breathed in sharply, then exhaled. No. She wouldn't re-visit that thought, because she'd already determined to move on, to make this trip about being a family again. And she couldn't do that if she was always thinking bad things about her husband—things that made her want to curse his name. Things that would hurt her children.

Thankfully, no one seemed to notice her reaction. They toured the rest of the buildings, including the store of a respected com-munity leader, and ate a picnic lunch near the creek. The kids begged for some ice cream, so they walked back into the adorable town and strolled down Buckingham Street, where they passed several small heritage buildings and miners' cottages, as well as classy galleries, shops, cafés, restaurants, and a delicious-smelling fudge shop—all framed along the main tree-lined avenue.

The children ran ahead and hopped into a line forming out-side a walk-up window. When they were next in line, Sherry took the younger kids to save seats at a table that had just become free several feet away.

A boy who looked about seventeen or eighteen worked the coun-ter, and his eyes immediately flew to Kylee. "Hi." He ran a hand through his shoulder-length hair. "How ya going?"

"Uh, hi." Kylee bit her bottom lip, and her cheeks reddened.

Uh-oh. Angela stepped forward. "Can we get five one-scoop cups of your hokeypokey ice cream, please?" The words came out sharper than she'd intended.

Next to her, Kylee tensed.

"Yeah, no worries." The kid started scooping the vanilla ice cream with bits of honeycomb in it. "I've not seen you before. Are you just visiting?" He directed the question at Kylee.

"We are." Her daughter fiddled with her hair. "For four months, though."

More than friendly interest lit in the boy's eyes. "Where are you from?"

Hurry it up, bucko—and stop looking at my daughter like that. That's what Angela wanted to say, but she held her tongue.

"New York." Kylee traced a *K* on the wooden counter. "You?"

He laughed. "Up north originally, but here now."

"Cool. We're staying in Wanaka."

Angela cleared her throat. This random boy did not need to know anything else about her fifteen-year-old daughter. She snatched the three already scooped cups of ice cream and pushed them toward Kylee. "Hon, can you please take these to the table?"

If glares could flatten, Angela would be a pancake, but her daughter did as she asked.

Angela paid for the ice cream and thanked the boy, who kept making eyes at Kylee until they left. Her daughter was quiet the rest of the way back to the house, and Angela couldn't help but wonder if the tiny bridge of trust between them had crumbled at her feet.

ↄ

Why was it so difficult to go in? It was only a shop, after all.

Eva stood outside Joanne's Flowers for ten minutes at least. It was nearly dinnertime and she needed to get back soon. The entire walk into town she'd tried to talk herself out of coming, but the flowers inside had issued a siren call—and she was helpless to ignore it.

Blowing out a breath, Eva finally made her way into the shop. Despite there being less than two weeks until Christmas, the place was empty of customers.

Eva took in details she'd missed on her first visit to the boutique with Kylee. Wooden crates of varying sizes displayed an assortment of blooms, each housed in a glass vase. A vintage serving cart exhibited clay pots in earthy tones and charming polka-dotted jars perfect for growing windowsill herbs. From the ceiling hung antique pendant lights that resembled delicate vines ending with a glass shade in the shape of a flower. Floral supplies overflowed shelves and bookcases that lined the tan brick walls.

And the blooms themselves . . . they almost seemed to be waving at her, welcoming her home.

"Hullo," a voice called from the back of the shop. "Be right there."

"Take your time." Eva wandered the rows of flowers, running the tips of her fingers across petals of every shape, size, and color.

She closed her eyes, imagining how it had felt to weave together an arrangement from scratch. Each type of bloom added its own unique something to a bouquet. Just being among them brought back the rush, the satisfaction Eva had felt in making something beautiful for a bride's big day.

A clatter of heels sounded on the terrazzo, and Joanne appeared. "How can I—" As the older woman's eyes alighted on Eva, her lips curved. "I was hoping you'd come back."

"Nice to see you again."

"Did your mother-in-law enjoy the bouquet last week?"

"She did, thank you."

Joanne came closer, considering her. "What can I do for you today?"

Eva turned her eye to the flowers, drinking in the beauty, holding back tears. "Um . . . I just . . ."

As if sensing she needed time, Joanne walked to the front door, flipped the sign to Closed, snagged a basket, and returned to Eva.

"I didn't realize you were closing. I can go."

Waving her words away, Joanne nudged the basket into Eva's hands. "Would you like to help me select the best blooms for an order I just received? I need roses, pohutukawa, hydrangeas, and freesias. Red ones, of course. Christmas and all that."

"Oh. Sure." Eva grasped the handle of the wire basket. "Wait, which one is the poo-hoo-too . . ."

"Pohutukawa. That one." Joanne indicated a grouping of bright red blooms whose hundreds of slender petals protruded from the flower head, giving the appearance of prickly fuzz. "Part of the myrtle family. The pohutukawa is considered New Zealand's Christmas tree. You should see one covered with these, all in full bloom. Absolutely marvelous."

"I can imagine." Eva perused the options and selected a few of the strongest flowers. Why this woman was trusting her to do this, who could say? But handling the blossoms felt like the most natural thing in the world.

"So, what brings you to our fair island for four months?"

Talking about Brent while handling flowers . . . that also felt natural and right. "I'm part of a team running the ultra-marathon here in March." She launched into an explanation of the purpose behind their trip.

Joanne worked alongside her in quiet, listening. Then she placed a hand on Eva's back. "That is quite the tale. I'm sorry for your loss."

Such a simple thing for someone to say. Yet so often, when people learned of Eva's tragedy, they said nothing. Or worse, platitudes rolled off their tongue. Offering condolences without trying to make it better . . . *that* was the right way to comfort people who were grieving.

And often those who knew what to say had experienced grief themselves.

"I really appreciate you saying that." Eva plucked a final pohutukawa bloom from the bucket in front of her, lifting it to her nose. Hmm. No real scent. "What about you? You don't sound like you're native to New Zealand."

"No, I'm from a tiny town on the Cornish coast of England called Port Willis. But I've been in Wanaka nearly twenty years now."

"What led you to move all the way here?"

Indicating that Eva should follow, Joanne headed to the back of the store. "My first husband, Ian, and I divorced. I have two boys, and the divorce occurred when Neil, my youngest, was two." They slipped through the doorway separating the main floor from the workroom. "The whole thing left me so devastated I moved us here, where we didn't know a single soul."

"Why here?"

Joanne set the flower basket on the top of a round worktable strewn with all kinds of Christmas baubles used to make arrangements more festive. "Would you believe I saw it featured in a magazine? I am not the type to make drastic moves, but I was quite desperate at the time to create a new life for myself and my boys."

"That must have taken incredible bravery."

"Or incredible idiocy." The shop owner chuckled as she selected a flower box from a shelving unit on the wall. "I had no one to help me with the children while I opened my business. They spent every morning, afternoon, and evening here playing amongst the flowers. Until I met Graeme, that is."

"Who's Graeme?"

"My neighbor first. Now, my husband."

"Ah." Eva slid into a folding chair next to the worktable. "And how long did it take before he swept you off your feet?"

"Eighteen years."

"Really?" Friends-to-lovers stories were some of her favorites, even though it hadn't happened that way for her and Brent.

"Yes. We've been married for eight months." Joanne pulled her phone from the pocket of her black slacks, clicked the screen a few times, and walked toward Eva, phone extended. On the screen was a fancied-up Joanne in a gorgeous wedding dress with full lace sleeves and a long train, a handsome groom beside her. His salt-and-pepper hair looked distinguished, as it always did on a man.

"You look beautiful." The couple stared at each other, smiles stretching across their faces, wrinkles crinkling the corners of their eyes. "And so happy."

Slipping the phone back into her pocket, Joanne snagged some silver ribbon from her decor stash. "We *are* happy."

What a blessed woman to have such a second chance.

Joanne watched Eva for a few moments. "Excuse me." With a quick turn, she was out of the room before Eva could acknowledge her words.

Eva placed her hand on the basket of flowers, feeling the ridges of the stems, the crisp coolness from the water that had bolstered their life over the last several days. And then a hidden thorn pricked her, and reality nudged her back as she stared at the spot on her thumb now beading with the tiniest drop of blood.

Hissing, she popped the tip of her finger in her mouth, and the contact burned.

Joanne flitted back just as quickly as she'd left, her fist clutching something small. "Here." The kind brunette pressed a hard, cold object into Eva's hand.

A key. "What's this?"

"That opens the back door. You are welcome here anytime, my dear. Day or night."

"But . . . you don't even know me."

"I know enough. We are kindred spirits, as they say." Joanne cupped Eva's cheek gently, as a mother or kind aunt might. "Whenever you need a break from life, from the sadness, from the memories, you may come here and enjoy the flowers—nature's promise to you that life will one day bloom again."

14

Where in the world were Marc and Eva? Had they forgotten about the reporter?

Angela bustled around the kitchen, shoving dirty lunch plates and cups into the dishwasher, starting a cycle, and snatching a rag to wipe down the table. A reporter had called Eva a week or so after getting her information from the organization putting on the ultra-marathon. They wanted Simon King to do a feature article on them in their quarterly magazine, *Worldwide Runners*. So they'd set up an interview today—in two minutes, to be exact—and Marc and Eva hadn't returned from a morning bike ride in the countryside surrounding Wanaka.

Marc had arrived late the night before. He planned to stay about three weeks to train and run the full marathon with the women on January 9 in preparation for the ultra-marathon in March.

It had been Eva's idea to meet here for the interview in the first place. She'd thought being at the house would make the interview cozier and a lot quieter than any public place. This morning Angela had asked Sherry to take the kids into town for some ice cream so they wouldn't be a distraction.

Her nerves tingled. Why was she so on edge? It was just a little interview.

The doorbell rang just as she was putting on a pot of coffee.

She'd meant to change clothes before the interview, but her yoga pants and Wanaka T-shirt would have to do. After peeking in the hallway mirror to ensure her hair wasn't a total disaster, Angela opened the door.

"Hello." The brown-haired man standing on the front porch smiled, his straight teeth gleaming at her. He was on the tall-but-not-too-tall side, with an athletic build, but not overly muscled. With brown slacks, a white button-up shirt rolled to mid-arm, and a messenger bag slung across his chest, he looked professional and casual all at once. He seemed not much older than her—perhaps around forty. "I'm Simon."

"Angela Jamison." She shook his hand. "Come on in." Moving aside to allow him entry, she then closed the door and led the way to the kitchen. "I apologize, but my sister-in-law and our other team-mate haven't returned from a bike ride yet. I'm sure they'll be here soon. Would you like some coffee while we wait?"

"That'd be great, thanks." Simon pointed to the modern black table for six, his accent confirming he was a New Zealander. "Are we doing the interview here?"

"If that's all right." Angela reached for two oversized mugs and poured some java, setting one in front of Simon, who'd pulled a notebook, pen, and small recorder from his bag. "Here you go. Cream, sugar?"

"Black is perfect." He took a sip, the high temperature of the liquid not even fazing him.

Angela slid into the seat across from Simon, her own mug cradled between her hands. "Do you have fun plans for Christmas and New Year's?"

"Yeah, but I've still got loads to do. My kids are excited, though. I'm knackered just thinking about it."

She joined his laughter. "I can relate."

"You have kids?"

"Three." She drummed her fingers along the edge of the mug, waiting a few moments before speaking again. "I'm not sure why Eva arranged to do this right before Christmas. I'm sure it could have waited until after the holidays."

"It was my fault. My editor wants the piece as soon as possible, and I was flat tack all last week."

She stared at him blankly. The local slang still left her flummoxed half the time.

"Sorry. Just means I was busy." There was that smile again, those extremely white teeth. Against his tan skin, his grin was dazzling. Little laugh lines crinkled around his eyes and mouth, proof that he spent more time with the smile on his face than without it.

And now it felt warm in here. Angela stood and walked to the sliding-glass patio door. She opened it and slid the screen door into its place, allowing a breeze to waft inside. Better.

Angela peeked at her phone once more. No texts or missed calls. "I tried calling Eva to see where she is but haven't heard back. I hope we don't have to wait long."

"You and I can start now, and I'll finish the interview once she arrives. Do you mind if I record?"

"No, of course not." She took her seat again and folded her hands around her mug.

He clicked on the recorder. "I know the basics of why you're here, but why don't you tell me in your own words?"

She should have waited for Eva. Running this race was her idea in the first place. "I'm not quite sure where to start."

"I've found the beginning works quite nicely."

"Oh. Right. Of course."

The twinkle in his dark brown eyes gave her pause. He was teasing her.

That earned him a tiny smirk. "You're funny." Angela took a sip of coffee. "Well, uh, a little over a year and a half ago, my husband,

Wes Jamison, and his younger brother, Brent, went scuba diving, as they often did, but this was their first time exploring a shipwreck. It was off the East Coast of the United States. My husband's foot went through some rotted boards and he got stuck." Was she giving too much detail? "From what the authorities surmise, Brent tried to free him, he wasn't able to, and both ran out of oxygen. And died."

How many times had she had to say that—that her husband was dead?

Normally when she spoke the words out loud, they sounded so cold, so matter-of-fact. Today, though, her voice held a slight tremble. Strange. Although maybe not, considering how many emotions had started rising to the surface every time she ran. Every step was a painful one, slicing through her body—and it wasn't just a physical pain, although, sure, that was there too.

No, this pain was deeper, something she felt in her bones. Something she hadn't allowed herself to feel in a long time.

Simon cleared his throat. Oh. She'd quit talking.

"In September, Eva found out that our husbands and their friend Marc Cinelli had signed up to compete as a team in the New Zealand Ultimate Race Adventures' ultra-marathon." She laid out the rest of the events as simply as possible. "And that's how we came to be here."

"Amazing story. Tell me, why did you decide to come out here early?" Simon tapped his pen against the mug. The metallic *plink, plink, plink* blended with the whir of the dishwasher.

How much should she tell this stranger? "It's complicated."

Simon looked up from his notes, studied her, nodded. "Life always is, isn't it?" He drained the rest of his coffee, seeming to consider his next words. "How old are your kids?"

Whew. Neutral territory—no emotions involved. "Lilly is seven, Zach is ten, and Kylee is fifteen."

"I've got an eleven-year-old boy and a thirteen-year-old girl. Benjamin and Ella."

"Does your daughter hate your guts too?" Angela covered her mouth with a hand. Oops. "Just kidding, of course." Swigging her drink, Angela coughed as she caught some too quickly in her throat.

Simon chuckled. "Having a teenager in the house can be challenging."

"That's one word for it." Ever since the incident with the ice-cream server in Arrowtown, Kylee had only spoken to Angela when absolutely necessary, which had made homeschooling oh so fun. Of course, at her age, Kylee usually did much of her work online up in her room, with Angela reviewing it at the end of the week.

"And single parenting is hard."

"It sure is." Wait, was he asking or stating the fact from experience? A fleeting look and she saw his ring finger was bare. Divorced? Widowed? Never married? But that was none of her business. She hardly knew this man, and she certainly didn't need to know his life story—even if she was telling him hers. "But we do what we have to for our kids. I only pray that I don't screw them up too badly on my own."

Oy. It was true, but did she really want that ending up in a magazine article? Why was she being so loose with her speech? Sure, Simon was easy to talk to, with his relaxed mannerisms and relatable eyes and . . .

She squeezed out a guffaw, as if she'd been joking. "But seriously, my kids truly are wonderful. They've handled all of this better than I have." Again, too much information.

His eyebrows knit together, and he reached forward to turn off the recorder. "I know what you mean. Kids are resilient. When my wife died of cancer three years ago, I was a wreck. My children saved me. Truly."

Angela's mouth formed an O, and she had the urge to reach for his hand. The admission sat there between them. How should she respond?

"Mom!" Zach burst through the kitchen door and skidded to a halt. "Who's that?" His eyes swung between Simon and Angela; they widened, then narrowed in suspicion.

"This is Mr. King. He's a reporter doing a story about the marathon."

"Oh." Her son grabbed a banana out of the fruit basket. "Cool."

The rest of the house was quiet. "Zach, where are your sisters and Grandma?"

"Lilly wanted to fly her kite, so Grandma's watching from the dock."

"What about Kylee?"

He shrugged as he bit into the banana. "As soon as we got back, Grandma took Lilly to the dock and Kylee said she was going out."

"What?" Angela turned her whole body, and her knee knocked against the table leg with the abrupt movement. "Where?"

Zach shrank back a bit. "I dunno. Probably the coffee shop. She saw Daisy there on our way home."

"Oh." The next-door neighbor, Daisy, had befriended Kylee and introduced her to others their age in the area. The coffee shop was only a few minutes' walk, and so far Wanaka had proven itself to be a small, peaceful town. *There's no need to worry, Angela.* "Thanks, bud."

He stuffed the rest of the banana into his mouth, tossed the peel into the trash, and left.

Angela directed her attention back to Simon. "Sorry about that."

Kylee would be fine, right? Yes. Fine.

So long as she used good judgment—exactly the thing Angela hadn't done herself.

"Not a problem. You ready to resume?"

"Yes, absolutely." Because the sooner they finished, the sooner she could go check on Kylee.

Where was Eva when she needed her?

15

Christmas Eve in New Zealand sure looked different to Eva than it did back home.

Daisy's parents, Jim and Fiona, had invited the entire Jamison clan over for lunch. A cloudless sky overhead guaranteed another gorgeous day, and the sun warmed Eva's cheeks where she stood in their neighbors' backyard, making her grateful once again she was missing one of the worst winters in New York history. Not only was the holiday weather opposite here, but instead of a turkey roasted in the oven, Jim had thrown venison and shrimp on the barbecue, and Fiona had laid out a spread of cold desserts—from pavlova to cheesecake to fruit salad—in the place of hot pies on the table. The combination of aromas nearly enticed Eva to forgo her manners and dig in before it was all ready.

Laughter rang out from the Adirondack chairs on Jim and Fiona's back porch where Kylee and Daisy were on their phones, exclaiming over some heartthrob or other. Zach and Lilly kicked a soccer ball with Marc. Sherry helped Fiona set the long picnic table with plastic plates and silverware.

Eva's heart swelled. A wonderful day of togetherness lay ahead.

But wait. Where was Angela?

Eva scanned the yard. Finally, she spied her sister-in-law on the Jamisons' dock. What was she doing down there? Hopefully she wasn't still upset that Eva had put her in an awkward position with the reporter yesterday. Marc had gotten a flat tire on their bike ride and it had taken them longer than anticipated to get home for the interview. Add to that the fact Eva's phone hadn't had service, and it had been the perfect storm.

Eva walked over to the neighbors' yard and up the path to the dock, then stood next to Angela, whose legs dangled over the side as she stared off at the mountains that were farther away than they seemed. "Am I disturbing you?" Not waiting for an invitation that would never come, she lowered herself next to her sister-in-law.

Angela's gaze swung to meet Eva's briefly before she turned back to the mountains. "Oh. Hey, Eva." Her cheeks had reddened slightly, though from the cool breeze or some emotion, who could tell. "Is it time to eat?"

Well, she was talking to her. That was a good sign. "Almost." Eva slid off her sandals and dipped one toe in the water, then quickly withdrew it. The locals had said the lake remained frigid year-round—around fifty degrees Fahrenheit, if memory served—but every day she still tested it.

Brent probably would have gone for a swim by now regardless of the temperature. Eva laughed at the thought.

"What?"

"Nothing." Bringing up Brent or Wes only ever seemed to gain her a cool look from Angela. Even after spending nearly a month together in close quarters, this woman remained a mystery in so many ways. There were times Eva would spy a wistful something in her sister-in-law's eyes, but her words and actions never seemed to follow suit. How could Eva get her to open up?

Guess she'd try the direct approach and see what happened. "So, how are you feeling today?" Being Christmas Eve, did Angela ache with missing her husband like Eva did? Had the past weeks been a blessing to her as they had to Eva, bolstering her lonely spirit and imbuing a tiny taste of color back into her life?

At the shuttering of Angela's eyes, Eva knew she'd chosen the wrong words. "How are you feeling about the upcoming marathon, I mean." There. Hopefully a safer topic, considering how much Angela had seemed to improve in their short time here. Of course, the bodily side effects were still obnoxious—adding uphill trail running to their repertoire had resulted in some nasty aches for both of them, but that would hopefully resolve soon. As their mileage increased every day, Eva actually found herself struggling more than Angela, whose cross-country experience surely was an advantage.

Not that she'd said as much. Whenever Eva tried to spark conversation during training, Angela kept her answers short.

Her sister-in-law kicked her feet a bit as she studied the water beneath them. "Thanks to last Saturday's training session, we know we can at least walk twenty miles in one day. So after a few more weeks, hopefully we'll be able to do twenty-six on race day."

"Right." Eva paused. "But how do you *feel* about it?" Would her sister-in-law humor her with an answer?

"It'll be a good chance to see how we're really doing. Just like Marc said during our very first strategy meeting."

Was Angela being intentionally vague, or did she honestly think she was answering Eva's question? "Yeah, that'll be good. But are you, like, nervous or anything?"

"It does no good to be nervous."

"That might be true, but I can't always stop myself from feeling that way."

"Sure you can. Simply school yourself not to."

"How?" Was that why Angela often seemed so devoid of emotion regarding the deaths of their husbands? Did she tell herself not to grieve, so she just . . . didn't?

"When a negative thought or feeling comes, put it in a box in your mind. Tell yourself that box is sealed, that opening it will destroy everything you're working toward." Her voice had gentled slightly, as if talking to a child.

And maybe that's how she saw Eva. But just because Eva was six years younger and not a mother didn't mean she was incompetent or less than. She'd loved and lost, just as Angela had. And unlike Angela, Eva had gone to therapy. She knew the method Angela described would only lead to eventual heartache.

But how to explain that in a way that brought them closer together—that didn't divide them further?

Zach and Lilly's squeals of delight drifted across the yard along with the luscious smells of lunch, a reminder that Eva didn't have much time before she and Angela would be called away.

"I agree that repeatedly remaining in a state of fear and worry is not good for you. There's evidence that thinking the same negative thoughts over and over again forms a permanent pathway in your brain, and those kinds of thoughts can create actual toxins in your body." Brent had loved studying how the mind and body were connected, and he'd often shared his findings with Eva.

Eva tugged at a strand of hair that had fallen over the front of her shoulder. "But I think you're doing yourself a disservice never to consider why you're having those thoughts in the first place. Because how will you ever change your patterns if you don't address the underlying issue? And when it comes to grief, you can't just ignore it. It won't stay stuffed away in some box in your mind forever. Eventually it'll find a way out."

Nothing but a slight clenching in Angela's jaw showed she'd even heard her.

Maybe putting herself out there first would give Angela the nudge she needed to be vulnerable as well. "Well, I for one *am* nervous. Because what if we can't do it? The marathon, I mean. I know we still have a few more months to train for the ultra. I should look at the positives, and I do, most of the time. But I guess I just don't know what I'd do if we failed. What does life look like afterward if we can't do this and do it well?"

A tiny pinprick of burning nipped at her scalp where she pulled on her hair. She released the strand. "I don't even know what I want beyond all of this. I can't let myself look that far down the road. So I focus on the next thing, and right now, that's the marathon. I think our training is going well enough, though, don't you?"

Oh man, she'd rambled good and long that time. But once she'd started talking, her thoughts had just boiled over like water left too long on the burner.

"It's fine, I guess." Angela swallowed hard. "I've . . . enjoyed running again."

Victory! It wasn't much, but it was something. An opening.

Before Eva could ask Angela what she enjoyed about it, Lilly careened down the path. "Mom! Aunt Eva! Food's ready!"

"Thanks, baby. We'll be right there." Angela stood and turned to follow her daughter, who was already scampering back toward the neighbors' yard.

Then she stopped for a moment, pivoted, and offered Eva a hand up.

16

Today was going to be a New Year's Eve to remember.

"You guys excited?" Eva squeezed Lilly's shoulders. Her young niece stood between Eva and Kylee, springing on her tiptoes and trying to see around the people in front of them in line for the Queenstown Skyline Gondola. They'd been waiting for thirty minutes already at the base of Bob's Peak, but that wasn't surprising for one in the afternoon on a holiday.

Lilly tucked her hand inside Kylee's. "Yeah!"

Kylee stared at the mountains rising around them, a tiny grin flickering across her lips. It warmed Eva's heart to see her niece taking a little pleasure in her surroundings after moping around for weeks. In fact, she'd been pleasant all day during their trek into Queenstown—first for breakfast, then while they wandered the shops. Tonight they planned to stay for a New Year's Eve bash with live music, food, and fireworks along the lakefront.

But before the party, Eva had arranged for a fun adventure at the top of Bob's Peak, and her lips nearly burst at holding in the secret. It would be a nice reward for making it through the holidays intact. Distracted as they were by new surroundings, Christmas Day hadn't been as difficult as last year, but they'd all struggled through the week in some form or another. Would the holidays ever feel truly happy again after losing people they loved?

Finally, they stepped into the building where they'd load onto the gondola—one step closer to Eva's surprise. She hoped it would be the perfect way to ring in a new year as a stronger, more joyful family unit. It was just too bad Sherry wasn't here, but she hadn't slept well the last few nights and had opted to stay home alone and enjoy the quiet.

"I've read that the Skyline Gondola is the steepest cable car lift in the whole Southern Hemisphere." Zach pulled on the sleeves of his jacket, which Eva had insisted he wear. According to the woman at the information center she'd spoken with yesterday, warm outerwear was a must since they were headed to the peak of a small mountain, where the climate was a bit unpredictable.

"My little encyclopedia." Angela ruffled Zach's hair and laughed as he ducked from her grasp.

It was good to see her sister-in-law smile, since she'd been pretty quiet all week. Eva had hoped their training sessions would be a bit livelier after their chat on the dock, but Angela seemed to be more determined than ever to keep to herself.

Or maybe she was just finally dealing with her emotions and didn't have the words to express them.

"I read that there's a two-hundred-and-twenty-degree panoramic view of Coronet Peak, Queenstown, and . . . what's the other one?" Marc stroked his short beard in an exaggerated display, slapping on an over-the-top confused look.

"The Remarkables! Oh, and Walter and Cecil Peaks too." Zach grinned at knowing more than Marc.

Marc winked at Eva over her nephew's head. Her stomach flipped.

The last week and a half with Marc had been wonderful. In between the hours he spent working, they'd talked about ideas for the business, toured the countryside, and taken selfie videos dedicated to Brent. Of course, they'd also strategized about the big race, poring over maps of the area and trying to guess the exact route, which wouldn't be publicized until the ultra-marathon had begun.

It was strange—Eva had been friends with Marc for years, but she'd never spent this many consistent days in his company. A few times she'd detected a confusing undercurrent between them, something she'd never noticed before. It was probably just her imagination, a combination of nerves and excitement over what was to come first with the marathon and then the ultra-marathon.

She hoped so, anyway.

Angela pointed. "Oh, look. We're next."

The people directly in front of them loaded into a cable car.

As the next car entered the building, Angela and the children got ready to step in. Only four people could fit on a gondola, so they left Eva and Marc to catch the following one. Normally they would have been paired with the next two people in line, but there were several groups of families behind them who wanted to ride together, so that left Eva and Marc with their own ride to the top.

When the door of their gondola slid open, Marc climbed in after Eva, taking the seat opposite her. The doors shut, and the gondola gave a little jolt as it started to rise.

Windows surrounded them, giving them a view of everything below—Lake Wakatipu spreading out one side, the trees stretching so high it seemed they could reach out and touch the tops, the mountains peaking in their majesty.

Marc's cologne drifted across the enclosed space, bringing hints of tarragon and spicy cinnamon to her nose. So different from Brent's everyday cologne, which contained a blend of apple and lime, with undercurrents of vanilla, rum, and leather.

Still, she couldn't deny the allure of Marc's scent. He smelled like he was going to a black-tie affair, but it didn't seem pretentious on him.

"Eva?"

"Hmm?" Oh man, why had she spent the better part of a minute thinking about Marc's cologne?

"I asked how you think training is going." His eyes were quite serious, almost concerned, as he leaned forward on his bench, forearms flat against the tops of his legs.

"Okay, I guess. I'm not sure how Angela feels about it, though."

"Have you asked her?"

With a tug on her long sleeves, Eva frowned. "Yes. And I thought we were getting somewhere, but she doesn't seem to want to connect in the same way I do."

"I'm proud of you for trying." He straightened. "Brent would be proud of you too."

"I hope so." Tears welled in her eyes. Ugh, would she ever stop crying when she heard his name?

Where had that thought come from? Ever since he'd died, she'd embraced every tear as a sign that she really and truly loved him, that the depths of her emotions couldn't be measured. There was a kind of pride in carrying a torch for someone who no longer could.

So why did she suddenly feel like the weight of the torch was too much?

No. She had to remain strong in her resolve, keep welcoming the tears, do everything she could to live life the way Brent would have. To grasp at the straws of happiness left to her and weave them together into something beautiful. Somehow.

"I know he would. And whether she understands it or not, Angela needs you."

"Sometimes I find that hard to believe." Eva tucked a strand of her long hair behind her ear.

Marc's eyes followed the motion as he waited for her to elaborate. Why did his gaze suddenly unnerve her?

She bit the inside of her cheek and looked out the window, taking in the panorama of nature around them. "I keep reaching out, but we aren't really any closer than we were three or four months ago when all of this began. And we should be, right?"

"I don't know. There seems to be less strain between you guys than, say, at that first strategy meeting. I'm guessing all of this is just a lot for her to deal with."

"I just wish she'd . . . I don't know, come to realize what Brent and Wes knew about life, what they taught me. But she doesn't seem inspired by their zest for adventure. In fact, she seems to despise it. I don't understand her."

"Give her time. Maybe being here will give her a new perspective on all of that."

And hopefully Eva's surprise would be a start. "You're right." Her eyes connected with his once again.

His hadn't moved. They remain fixed . . . on her. "New perspectives can be frightening." Marc's voice sounded so tentative, with a hint of longing, and her soul recognized something in his tone.

An emotion welled up inside her chest—one she couldn't quite define, that felt both thrilling and dangerous. It was the same feeling she always got at the start of something new. The fear of failure and the unknown played chicken with a deep knowing that the risk was worth it.

She swallowed hard. "They can."

"But that doesn't mean we shouldn't try them out, does it?"

What was he really asking her?

The gondola stopped and the door slid open. When an attendant stuck his arm in and helped her from the cable car, Eva couldn't help but breathe easier. Because the way their conversation had been going . . . she wasn't ready to go down that road. But maybe she was way overthinking things. Which she probably was.

From up here, the town seemed even smaller than normal, especially when compared with the view of Manhattan as they'd taken off from JFK Airport at the start of their adventure. Angela and the kids leaned against a railing not too far away, exclaiming over the views.

Her sister-in-law turned. "Thanks, Eva. That was really nice."

"It was pretty awesome, wasn't it?" And hopefully they'd all think her surprise was just as wonderful. "Let's go this way."

"What's over there?" Zach squinted.

"Just a little something I've arranged." She led them a short distance down the path, toward steps that went up to a platform that jutted out over the trees.

If Wes and Brent had been on this trip with them, they'd have made sure the kids and Angela and Eva did something adventurous.

"We're here."

Angela did a double take as she saw the sign for Zip Line Encounters. "What are you talking about?"

"I've set up a zip-lining tour for all of us. Get ready to see New Zealand in a whole new way."

⁓

What was Eva thinking?

But she wasn't, as usual.

Granted, that was not the most gracious thought, but really. Her sister-in-law stood beaming at her like a kid who had just earned perfect grades on a report card, completely oblivious to the feelings rising inside Angela. Clearly her intentions were good, but why hadn't she bothered checking with Angela first?

The thought of her children dangling over the city, the zip line snapping, them plummeting down, down, down . . .

"When a negative thought or feeling comes, put it in a box in your mind. Tell yourself that box is sealed, that opening it will destroy everything you're working toward."

The words she'd spoken to Eva a week ago taunted her. She'd

need a concrete bunker for all the emotions roiling through her at the moment.

"I don't think this is a good idea." Somehow she managed to keep her voice steady. A small miracle.

"It'll be fine, Mom." Why couldn't Kylee ever look that excited over something Angela suggested? Her daughter took the few steps up to the platform where a few zip-line employees prepared harnesses for two twentysomething women. "I've always wanted to go zip-lining."

"Kylee, wait."

"Yeah, Mom. This is so cool." Zach raced behind his sister.

Marc looked between Eva and Angela, and it appeared as though he might say something. But Lilly grabbed his hand and dragged him away, leaving Angela alone with her sister-in-law.

Eva's face was a combination of confusion and hurt. "What's wrong?"

Angela took a deep breath and crossed her arms. "I'm just not sure my children are ready for this. You should have asked me, Eva."

A cry of glee rent the air. Angela's head jerked toward the zip line in time to see one of the twentysomethings fly down the line. The woman let go and hung upside down as she raced along the tree line, her feet in the air, arms waving.

A shudder ran up Angela's spine.

Her sister-in-law's mouth opened, closed. "I didn't . . . I just thought that if Brent and Wes were here, they'd want us all to experience something like this. And if you're worried about Lilly, she can go tandem with a guide. It's all perfectly safe."

Perfectly safe. Angela had heard those words before . . .

"Hey." Wes leaned against the living room doorjamb, hands tucked into his pockets.

Angela looked up from her hands-and-knees position. She'd

just tucked two-year-old Lilly into bed and was searching under the couch for Paci the Bear, whom she'd promised to find before tomorrow. "You're finally home. Rough day at work?" Wes's job as a social worker often required long hours and a lot of heart— the latter of which her husband had in spades.

"Yeah. And Mom called. The headstone for Dad's grave finally arrived."

Angela stood and walked to her husband, wrapping her arms around his stomach, which softly bulged over the waistband of his khakis. His pregnancy sympathy weight, he called it. Two years later and it had become a permanent feature. She didn't care, though, considering her own extra twenty pounds. "I'm sorry. That must have been difficult." She planted a kiss on his lips.

He pecked her briefly, but his thoughts seemed elsewhere. Still, she allowed herself the luxury of being held. Since his father's death a month before, he'd been busy checking on his mom and helping her with finances and such; plus there was always some crisis at work. She'd had to hold down the fort at home even more than usual, but she didn't mind doing her part. Sherry was family, and she was alone now. Angela couldn't imagine how that must feel.

Wes's arms squeezed and released her. He took her hand in his and played with the ring on her finger. It was simple, a gold band with a half-karat diamond, but he'd been so proud to present it to her on their fifth wedding anniversary after saving a little from every paycheck. "So, Brent asked me to go climbing with him this weekend."

"At the gym? You should go." Wes could use an outlet for all of his stress.

"Actually, he suggested the Adirondacks. Make it a whole weekend trip."

"Oh." Angela bit her bottom lip. That would leave her alone all weekend with the kids, and there was the church-wide BBQ on Saturday. It was always difficult to keep track of everyone by herself, but she could manage if Wes needed her to. "All right."

"Really? You're okay with that?"

"Yes." She rose on her tiptoes and kissed him again. "So long as you come back to me in one piece." She laughed the comment off, but part of her meant it. Brent was known to pull some crazy stunts—had been doing it his whole life. Still, Wes always knew how to rein in his little brother.

Her husband gathered her back into his arms. "Of course. It's all perfectly safe."

Angela's hand trembled at the memory. Wes had been wrong. Living Brent's lifestyle came with taking chances—and Wes had bought into it. Of course, most of the time things were safe. But why take the chance when you didn't have to?

"I'm sorry, Eva. The answer is no."

"But—"

"Hey, Mom. Look!" Lilly's voice cut through the strain.

Angela turned her attention back to the tree house, and her heart nearly leapt from her chest. Zach had a harness fastened to him, and the guide squatted at his level, giving him instructions. Her son nodded, concentration visible on his face. Then the guide stood and slipped a helmet onto Zach's head.

She raced toward the platform. "Wait! Stop!"

The guide looked up, confused. "What's the problem?"

Angela grabbed Zach and hauled him toward the stairs, away from the edge. A gasp flew from her mouth at seeing how high up they were. "Don't you need some sort of waiver or permission slip to allow children to zip-line?"

"I slipped away during breakfast to sign the waivers at the main office in town." Eva's voice spoke up behind her, quieter than usual. "I didn't know you'd have a problem with it."

Angela tried closing her eyes, but all she saw was red. Finally, she faced her sister-in-law again. "Can we talk?" After ensuring Marc was watching the kids, Angela led Eva back down the stairs and up the path where no one could overhear.

"Eva, I know you mean well, but these aren't your kids. They're mine. *My* responsibility. Do you understand what that means?" Her words chafed, leaving her throat raw.

"I just wanted to help." And there was the telltale tremble in Eva's voice. The woman's shoulders slumped and she chewed her thumbnail. A tear trickled down her cheek.

Great. Now Angela looked like the big bad wolf blowing down a little piggy's house. She rubbed her nose. "I know you're trying. And you're a fun and wonderful aunt. But you just don't seem to get the fact that my number one priority is keeping my kids safe and protected. And when you go against me like this, I end up looking like a stick-in-the-mud to my kids." Of course, it went deeper than that, but Angela didn't want to explore those thoughts at the moment.

"I'm sorry." Eva visibly folded in on herself, her hands rubbing her upper arms as if she were freezing.

Angela's maternal instinct had her reaching for her sister-in-law. But no. Eva must know she was serious. If they were going to live together in close quarters for another three months and have any chance at successfully completing this ultra-marathon, Eva had to know where she stood.

Otherwise, all of this might just fall apart—if it hadn't already.

17

Eva glanced at the clock. It read 2:37 a.m.—a new year.

Another year without Brent. Without a purpose beyond this race.

The whole house echoed the silence. Everything had been quiet for hours once they'd returned home from the botched zip-line attempt. They'd skipped the New Year's Eve party in Queenstown and had driven straight home, retreating to their rooms after a quick dinner. Apparently no one cared about ringing in the New Year together anymore.

Well, that wasn't true. Marc had offered a walk, but she'd refused, claiming she wouldn't be very good company. It's not like he hadn't seen her vulnerable many times before, so why was this different?

Eva slid from beneath her comforter. Her feet padded along the wooden floors of the hallway, down the stairs, and into the kitchen. The moonlight streaked in through the windows, leaving patterns on the countertops and floors. She pulled a glass from the cabinet and poured herself a cup of coconut milk. Then she rummaged in a ceramic jar for one of Sherry's cherry chip cookies.

She dunked the cookie into the milk and took a bite. The tart cherry flavor danced on the tip of her tongue. Amazing. The best part about all of this training? She'd burn this cookie off tomorrow when she went running with Marc and Angela. After over a week of training with all three of them, they'd started to find a rhythm. The upcoming marathon would give them some sort of measure for how they'd do in a competitive race environment.

Maybe it would even help Angela figure out why she was really there. Because Eva couldn't figure it out for the life of her. If nothing else, the events of this afternoon proved that they were not necessarily here for the same reasons.

She polished off the cookie and drained the last of the milk. As she headed back toward the stairs, something on the deck outside caught her eye. Someone was sitting in one of the chairs. A short someone, so it wasn't Marc. Eva slid open the back door, cinching her robe tighter around her at the sudden chill. She stepped out to find Sherry gazing across the lake, which was dotted with lights that appeared to pirouette across the undulating water. The sky was a blank artist's canvas if she ever saw one, speckled with brilliant gold and white paint. And though the mountains were barely visible in the dark, Eva sensed them rising around them, strong and steady. Ever present.

Sinking into the seat next to her mother-in-law, she laid her head on Sherry's shoulder.

Sherry didn't say a word, but her arm slid up and under Eva's chin, patting her cheek.

"Couldn't sleep again?" Now that Brent wasn't here to take care of his mother, it fell to her and Angela. But Sherry could never be a burden—she was the only part of Brent that Eva had left. Besides that, her mother-in-law was so consumed with serving everyone that she tended to let her own health fall last on the priority list.

"Something like that. I was getting a glass of water in the kitchen and couldn't pass up this opportunity."

"Opportunity?" Eva snuggled closer to Sherry, who smelled of flour and sugar.

"To worship. The Creator has done beautiful work here, hasn't he?"

A chorus of cicadas seemed to sing in agreement, growing louder, then softer again.

Nature had always been a draw to an artist like Eva, but though she'd grown up going to church with her family and believed in God, she'd not thought much lately about his creative heart. The concept put a small smile on her face. "He sure has."

If only she could create something so beautiful—even half as much. A quarter. But she feared her days of creating were gone forever.

"What's on your mind, sweet girl?" Sherry's hand squeezed Eva's knee. "Are you thinking about today? I hope you don't blame yourself. Your intentions were good. Angela will see that in time."

"I do feel like I keep messing things up without meaning to. Even begging her to come to New Zealand. Maybe that was a mistake."

"Personally, I don't think it was. It is good for Angela to finally slow down enough to confront her grief. It's been looking for her for a long while now, and she's been running. Be patient with her. Love her anyway. I know you will. You have a kind spirit, Eva."

A tear trailed down Eva's nose, hanging on to the edge for a moment and then falling onto her mouth, salt tingeing her lips. "Thank you for saying that, Sherry." She sighed. "But good intentions or not, I just don't know what to do next. Brent always knew what to do."

A bird cawed in the distance, and it sounded like a mixture between a small dog yipping and a cat meowing. The wildlife was so different in New Zealand.

Sherry remained quiet for a time. "I understand feeling lost when the love of your life is gone. I certainly was."

"It's more than that, though." How could Eva put the utter devastation, the hole in her life, the loss of herself into words? Eva sat up, pulled her legs onto the chair, and hugged her knees. "Did I ever tell you that I knew he was the one for me the first day we met?"

"Really?"

"Yeah, and it wasn't just the fact my breath hitched when his gaze first caught mine or how handsome he was. I could just sense a zest for life pulsing from his being. It was like he knew a secret the world didn't, and he wanted to share it with whoever would listen."

Eva closed her eyes for a moment, relishing the memory. She'd headed into her yoga class, and when she'd emerged sweaty and invigorated, she'd bumped into Brent. He'd steadied her—his hands clutching her upper arms—and stared deep into Eva's eyes. She couldn't even remember if he said anything out loud or if his soul simply spoke to hers.

All she knew was that evening she rushed home and in a daze threw together the most brilliant wedding bouquets she'd ever created.

Her eyes opened again. "He changed everything for me, Sherry. Once I met him, life burst with more color, more energy, more . . . everything." Dare she say the rest? "Now I can see the rest of my life yawning before me. And it's not good, not like it was. I . . . I'm afraid I'll never be truly happy again."

Sherry twisted in her chair to face Eva. Even in the dark, Eva could glimpse the depth of her mother-in-law's compassion. "I am so glad my boy knew so much love from you. But happiness is fleeting." She patted Eva's knee. "It's a feeling, an emotion, and when we have it, things are good. But it can go away just like that. Don't aim for happiness. You'll only be disappointed by life and people if you do."

A sob bubbled in Eva's throat. "So what do I aim for instead?"

"Joy, my dear girl. Aim for joy."

What was the difference? "I don't understand."

"Joy isn't based on emotion. It's there no matter what's going on in your life. You can have joy even when the world is falling apart."

"How?" Something deep and desperate inside of her reached for the answer. "How can I have joy when my soul mate is dead? When I have nothing but his memory left?"

"Because joy isn't dependent on you or even the good things in life, like a wonderful husband. It's dependent on God, and on you being reconciled with him. It's rooted in a deep knowing that no matter what happens in this life, you have someone you can hold on to even when you're drowning."

Sherry had often talked about her faith, and she'd clung to it in the hard times. It was a nice thought, that God might care, but he wasn't here to speak words of love to her. He'd never held her in the late-morning hours and stroked her hair when she was sad. He'd never sat back and clapped, whistling in admiration when she'd stayed up all night creating the perfect bouquet.

That had all been Brent. A physical person she could grasp and hold and kiss and love.

She missed that. Needed that. Needed him.

A deep sigh expelled from her chest, and she imagined it pushing out across the water, disappearing and lingering all at the same time.

18

Finally, something was going right.

Angela bent over just outside the rental house, hands on her knees as she sucked in large gulps of air. She checked her watch and pumped her fist. "Yes!"

Marc and Eva ran up behind her. Once again they'd let her set the pace, and in the last moments of their run, she'd surged ahead, moved by something deliciously familiar.

Her inner athlete reemerging at last.

Marc whooped. "Nice work, Angela! That was your first ten-minute mile. Incredible progress." He held up his hand for a high five.

She slapped his palm. "Thanks. It feels good." Even though her muscles and lungs burned, there was something rewarding about the feeling. The weather this evening had turned slightly cold, and as she leaned into a lunge, she started to feel the prickles on her skin, her sweat evaporating.

Eva smiled, though it didn't reach her eyes. "Great job." She hadn't been the same since the zip-line incident two days ago, and a flat voice had replaced her normally bubbly one.

Angela should reach out, say something comforting. But fear tugged on her vocal cords anytime she attempted it. If she wasn't 100 percent firm with Eva, her sister-in-law was liable to pull another crazy stunt.

And Angela had had enough crazy stunts pulled around her.

If she'd put her foot down with Wes . . .

No. She wouldn't go there. Right now she would allow herself to feel good about something, even if it was the fact she'd run the last three miles of their course today without stopping. Okay, jogged. But still. It was something.

"Thanks. You too."

They finished stretching and walked into the house, immediately met with the delicious enticement of Sherry's famous lasagna. Her mother-in-law stood at the counter slicing tomatoes.

"Something smells amazing." Marc headed to the sink and washed his hands, rubbing them dry on a dish towel. "How can I help?"

Eva followed suit. "Yes, what can we do?"

Sherry shooed them away. "Have a glass of wine on the deck. I'll let you know when dinner is ready. Probably another fifteen minutes."

"Forget wine. There's enough time for a hot chocolate." Marc elbowed Eva, who rolled her eyes and groaned. "All right, wine it is."

As Marc pulled a few glasses from the cupboard, a grin stretching across his face, Eva selected a red wine.

Angela took the opportunity to approach Sherry.

"You are amazing." She gave Sherry a squeeze on the shoulders, which was met with a look of surprise. Sherry quickly covered her reaction.

Clearing her throat, Angela leaned against the counter. "Are the kids in their rooms? I'll have them come set the table."

"Zach and Lilly are, but Kylee asked to go to Alistair's with Daisy for a quick coffee. I know you've let her go before, so I said it would be fine. I hope that's all right."

"Yes, of course." It wasn't easy to let her teenager have her freedom, but after being here a month, Angela had begun to feel much more comfortable about letting her do some things on her own in the small town. Besides, she'd grown tired of fighting with Kylee.

She had to remind herself frequently that her daughter had never done anything to prove that she wasn't worthy of trust. "I'll call her to let her know dinner will be ready soon."

The call went to voice mail. Hmm. Her daughter's phone was an appendage, never more than an arm's reach away. Perhaps the coffee shop was louder than usual. Sometimes they had live music going on the weekends.

Angela headed upstairs and rushed through a shower in two minutes, dressing in a comfortable pair of leggings and an oversized tunic. When she rejoined Sherry in the kitchen, Kylee still hadn't returned, and another call went to voice mail. "I'm going to walk to Alistair's to grab Kylee. If dinner is ready and everyone else is hungry, don't wait. We'll be back soon enough."

A brisk five-minute walk and she arrived at the classy coffee shop. Entering, she took quick inventory. Patrons swarmed the counter and the seating area was packed, but the girls weren't there.

A chill ran up Angela's spine. *Where are they?*

Despite the many customers waiting to order, Angela approached the barista at the counter, who was patiently standing by for the portly gentleman at the front of the line to tell her what he wanted. Her name tag reminded Angela her name was Vange. "Excuse me."

The young girl with a lip ring and spiked hair turned her direction. "Angela, right? How are you?"

"I'm okay. Listen, have you seen my daughter Kylee? She was supposed to be here." Angela pinched the skin between her thumb and forefinger.

Vange's eyebrow rose, and she pointed. "She's right there."

Relief flooded Angela's whole body, and her gaze followed Vange's finger—until her eyes landed on a couple making out on a chair near the front door.

"Oh, sorry, I think you're thinking of someone else. I'm talking about Kylee. She comes here with Daisy Hogan all the time."

The woman's eyes oozed sympathy. "I've seen them here together before, but lately she's been in here with that bloke."

It can't be her. But upon closer inspection, the girl who sat on the guy's lap was wearing a bright pink sweatshirt with turquoise stripes. Kylee had one just like it. Still, her daughter didn't know any guys here and—

The couple came up for air, and the girl leaned her forehead against the guy's, giggling.

No. "Kylee Lynn Jamison." The shout echoed across the small café as Angela charged toward her daughter. She'd barely breathed out the first syllable when Kylee jerked her head back and met Angela's gaze, her eyes wide, lips pressed hard against each other. The guy poked his head around Kylee's body, and Angela recognized the teenage boy from the ice-cream place in Arrowtown.

"What do you think you're doing?" Had that screech of a voice come from her? Sure, maybe she was overreacting. But then again, this was the kind of behavior that led to mistakes Kylee wouldn't be able to take back. The kind that could derail her future.

The murmur of others at the surrounding tables swelled, and Angela felt a million eyes on her. How embarrassing. But she stiffened her back. Who cared? After March, she'd never see these people again, but Kylee would always be her daughter.

"Mom." The single word hissed out through Kylee's teeth. The fear in her eyes had been replaced with something much darker. "Don't freak out."

"Don't freak out? Excuse me, missy"—ugh, had she actually just said that?—"but I have every right to freak out." She pulled her daughter off the guy's lap. "And you. How old are you, anyway? Did you know she's only fifteen?"

The boy flipped his hair over his shoulder and stood, hands lifted. "I don't want any trouble." He snatched up his jacket and left the shop.

Kylee jerked from Angela's grasp. "Why did you do that? Now he'll never ask me out again." Her daughter sniffed and smeared a falling tear from her cheek. "I hate you."

Angela rubbed her temples. "There are so many things wrong with what you just said, and we will address them. But not here. I came to get you for dinner. Let's go."

"Gladly." Her daughter spun on her heel and stormed from the shop.

With a quick inhale of breath, Angela sped after Kylee, not looking at anyone else. Well, she wouldn't be coming back here, that was for sure—

"Angela?"

She fixed a smile to her face and turned to find Simon King behind her. Lovely. "Hi." *Please don't add this to the article.* "How are you?"

He cocked his head and took a sip of his drink. "Better than you, it appears." His wristwatch glinted under the coffee shop lights.

"Ah, you heard that, did you?"

A grin teased his lips. "Difficult not to."

Angela closed her eyes briefly and blew out a groan. "I told you my daughter hated my guts. There's your proof."

"Any teenager caught pashing in public by her mum would react much the same. Welcome to the Hated Parents Club." He raised his cup as if in a toast.

She huffed out a staccato laugh. Joking about it with someone else felt kind of nice. "Well, thanks." Angela glanced back toward the door. "I guess I'd better make sure she actually goes home and doesn't run away."

"Would you be keen to commiserate over dinner sometime?"

Was he asking her on a date? Or just being kind? "That's sweet, but I'm very busy with marathon training and homeschooling."

Something like disappointment flashed in his eyes. "If you

change your mind, I'd love to show you more of our town. Get your mind off of teen troubles."

She considered him. Perhaps it would be nice to get advice from someone who knew what it was like to single-parent after the death of a spouse. Just as friends, of course. "On second thought, I might be able to find time in my schedule."

19

Sometimes after a bad dream a girl just needed an immediate video chat with her best friend. Thankfully, the crazy time difference meant Eva's middle of the night was Kimberly's morning.

"It sounds as if you're making progress training for both of your races." From her place in bed, Kimberly raised an oversized purple mug to her lips with one hand and kept her phone positioned in front of her with the other. Her hair was pulled back in a messy ponytail, face void of makeup, thick-rimmed glasses resting on her nose. What an awesome bestie. She'd been up late last night throwing a fiftieth birthday bash for some celebrity and didn't have to be anywhere until later today, but she'd still answered Eva's call. "How do you feel about that?"

"I feel good . . . most of the time. It's getting harder the more mileage we add. My body is used to exercise, but running long distances takes a lot more stamina." Computer balanced on her lap, Eva leaned back against her bed's gray upholstered paneled headboard, which was plush and button-tufted. She ran her fingers over the black-and-white, diamond-patterned silk duvet. "And I've been struggling a bit with the mental side of things. Not just with the running, though that's there too. Lately I'm just filled with doubt."

The dream tonight hadn't helped matters.

"Doubt about what?" Kim took another sip.

"Everything. My relationship with Angela." *And Marc.* She pushed aside the thought. "My future. Whether we'll really be able to accomplish our goals here."

Kimberly set down her mug and adjusted her glasses. "So what happens if you don't accomplish your goal?"

Honestly? She had no clue. Even though she'd feared the possibility, Eva couldn't imagine what life looked like after the race—failure or not. Would she return to the heart center? Or what about being a wedding florist again? She'd already turned Kim down on the Carlton wedding, but her friend would accept her back into the fold for other events, no questions asked. And she'd taken baby steps by visiting Joanne a few times a week in her florist shop in town. Being around the flowers—and the sweet florist, who was quickly becoming a close friend—brought a calm she couldn't explain.

But when she tried to picture herself creating again, a colorless void stared back at her.

Flickers of the dream she'd had an hour ago flashed in her mind once more.

"Girl, I can see the emotions warring on your face. You called me in the middle of your night. What's going on?"

Eva snatched a strand of her hair, rubbing it between her thumb and forefinger. "I'm just confused."

"About?" Kim's lips curved into an encouraging smile.

Eva let go of her hair. "I had a dream about Brent last night."

"That's not new, is it?"

"Not necessarily. I have them now and again. But this one just . . . it felt so . . ."

"Real?"

"Yes and no." She'd have to explain. After all, it's why she'd called Kim in the first place. "I was walking with Marc down by the lake, having fun, laughing—forgetting for a moment that I was supposed to be grieving. And then Brent appeared, glancing back and forth between us." His eyes had not been the kind ones she remembered. They'd flashed with something like jealousy. Which was ridiculous.

"How did you feel when you woke up?"

Her heart had pounded, guilt trapping her lungs and forcing her outside into the cold air to take in deep gulps of air. "Like I'd been caught doing something I shouldn't."

"And what's that?"

Tears welled in her eyes and her throat swelled. "Being happy. But it doesn't make sense. Because Brent would want me to be happy. I know that. And I know I never really will be without him." The echo of her conversation with Sherry several nights ago reverberated in Eva's head. But no matter what Sherry said, Eva couldn't picture a life separate from Brent, even though it had been her reality for a year and a half.

Maybe that's why she had so much trouble discerning what to do next. He wasn't here to give his input, so she'd been left to figure out a way to keep him close.

"Evie, you talk a lot about what Brent would have wanted. What do *you* want?"

"I don't know."

"The very fact you upended your life to move to a whole new country for a few months tells me you want to move forward, but you're afraid to. Why?" Kim frowned, her brow wrinkled. "You can't stay stuck in limbo forever."

If anyone else said those words to her—her parents, for instance—Eva would have declared they didn't understand and found a way to get off the phone pronto. But Kim knew her, accepted her, loved her for who she was. She'd been the only one before Brent who ever really had.

And that meant Eva had to consider what she said, as difficult as it was to hear.

It took her a moment. "Maybe . . . maybe I'm afraid of what moving forward really means. Does it mean letting Brent slip away? If I keep doing things for him, to honor him, maybe I don't have to really say goodbye." Her lips quivered. "And I don't have to figure out who I am without him."

"Ah, Evie. I'm so sorry, friend. I wish I knew the answer." A pause. "But what I do know is this. You are the same strong, free-spirited, amazingly kind, and creatively talented woman you have always been. Brent didn't change that about you, and neither did his death."

Aaaaand there came the tears rolling down Eva's cheeks. "Thanks, Kim. I don't deserve you."

"Hold that thought, because I've got one more question. And it's one you're probably not going to like."

Figured. "Okay."

"In the dream you were laughing and having fun with Marc. Do you think you would have felt guilty over being happy if you'd been doing the same with Angela or Sherry?"

So Kim had caught that, huh? Leave it to her best friend to ferret out the heart of the matter.

The truth—that Eva was developing feelings for Marc.

She fisted her duvet cover, bunching the material in her hands. "Ugh. Why did you have to ask me that?"

What kind of person was she? Here she was in New Zealand, for Brent—a man who had loved her with everything he had—and she was thinking about another man. At least on a subconscious level, if not a conscious one.

Eva couldn't deny it any longer.

But accepting it and acting on it were two different matters. Just because she could finally acknowledge that she was attracted to Marc and liked being in his company didn't mean she had to do something about it.

She simply had to remind herself why she was here—and that was *not* to fall in love with her husband's best friend.

☙

Angela had to keep reminding herself that this was not a date. Because if it had been a date, it would have been going very well—and she could not afford that, emotionally speaking.

"This looks like a nice spot." Simon unfurled a soft blue blanket onto the grass near Rotary Playground. A huge tree created an awning of leaves and branches over them, blocking out the evening sun. Not twenty feet away, the water of Roys Bay lapped against the lakefront, and the peaks of Mount Aspiring National Park framed the postcard-worthy scene.

She lowered herself onto the blanket and rummaged in the picnic basket Simon had brought. "Ooo, what do we have here?" When they'd made plans at the coffee shop, she'd offered to bring her own dinner, but Simon wouldn't hear of it. To make it very clear that this wasn't a date, Angela had offered to buy dessert on their walk back to the house, where Simon had picked her up a few hours ago.

He'd first walked her through town and told her all about the history of Wanaka, what had changed in the last few decades, what hadn't. He knew all kinds of facts about his hometown that she wouldn't be able to find on the internet, and pride shone in every syllable.

At times Angela missed the warmth and beauty of California, but she'd never really considered it home, just the state where her aunt lived. Where her father had sent her. Before that, she didn't remember much, but she knew they'd moved a few times thanks to her dad's military career.

Then she and Wes had moved to New York after they married,

and while it held sentimental value because of her life with him and the kids, she'd never taken the same delight in it as Simon clearly did in Wanaka.

Angela and Simon ended their tour here in a park on the outskirts of town. Children shouted as they played on the yellow swing set, and the few brown-slatted picnic tables were occupied. Still, there was something intimate about the setting.

Simon sat next to her and pointed to the various containers Angela had pulled from the basket. "Fig, mozzarella, and prosciutto salad, roast turkey sandwiches with homemade apple butter and cheddar, and a walnut, chocolate, and pear tart."

Her eyes widened and she whistled. "Fancy." A man who could cook and who looked as good as he did in his jeans and rolled button-up shirt was a dangerous combination. Good thing she wasn't looking to start a relationship with anyone anytime soon—if ever again. "But I said I'd take care of dessert."

He shrugged. "There was a new recipe I wanted to try."

"Where did you learn to cook like this?" Angela handed him the containers and then got out a few plates and forks.

Opening the first plastic tub, Simon scooped some salad onto their plates. "I started taking cooking classes with the kids after Sarah died. It was something we could do together, and it was necessary since I could only make frozen pizzas and peanut butter sandwiches." From the second tub, he pulled two sandwiches wrapped in deli paper and tied with twine.

"I'm not used to such fine food." Angela unwrapped her sandwich and took a bite of the thick, rustic crust. "This is delicious. Thank you for treating me. It must have been a lot of work."

He smiled. "Ella helped."

His daughter hadn't minded packing a dinner so her dad could spend time with a woman who wasn't her mom? But perhaps Simon had reassured Ella this wasn't a date. "Sometimes it's like pulling teeth to get Kylee's help in the kitchen. She hasn't even spoken one word to me since Saturday night."

Simon took a bite and chewed, his gaze thoughtful. "Have you tried talking to her?"

"Of course, but she just ignores me." A drop of apple butter fell from the sandwich onto her jeans, and she rubbed it away with a napkin. "I just don't know how to do this, and I hate feeling helpless. But there's no Parenting 101, and even if there was, I'm not sure it'd cover how to walk your kids through the loss of a parent."

"It's definitely the hardest thing I've ever done."

"How do you do it?"

"One day at a time, I guess. Just when I think I've made progress, something new comes up and I have to navigate rough waters."

"I know what you mean."

Silence descended for a few moments while they both ate.

Then Simon polished off the rest of his sandwich and snagged the tarts from the basket. "Look, I'm no expert, but maybe you could find some special way to connect with your daughter. The cooking class started off as a way to learn how to cook, but it gave us time together and something to accomplish. Maybe you could ask your daughter to train with you. Does she like running?"

Huh. "Yes, actually. She's very into it. But I'm not sure she'd say yes to running with me." She bit into a tart and groaned as the flavors melded.

Simon's eyes showcased his pleasure at her appreciation. "It doesn't hurt to ask. Don't you have that marathon coming up?"

The tart turned sour. "This weekend, actually." It had snuck up on them all.

A few kids threw Frisbees along the water's edge. The discs zinged through the air one moment and caught the wind the next, floating as if weightless.

Angela's emotions did the same thing, angling toward hope,

then crashing into a darkness she'd rather not examine. Would the marathon be a disaster or help them feel that the ultra was more than just a pipe dream?

"Maybe see if she wants to do it with you. If it wouldn't interfere with your group dynamic, that is."

Would her daughter say yes? Maybe Kylee would like to accompany Angela, even just as a pacer or for moral support. Why hadn't Angela thought of that before?

As she considered the possibilities, they both finished their dessert and the breeze rustled the empty plates. Simon tossed them into a nearby trash can. "Would you like to stay here or walk a bit more?"

"The food was so rich that a walk sounds like a wise idea."

After throwing on a light brown jacket, he helped her to her feet, and the moment their hands touched, her fingers tingled. Her brain warned her even as her heart leapt at the contact.

She turned her attention to the basket, tubs, and blanket on the ground. "Don't we need to pack up?"

"Nah, no one will mess with it. We can gather it on our way back."

The sun had begun to lower in the sky, and with it, the temperature. Angela wore jeans and a short-sleeved blouse, but had forgotten a sweater in her flurry to get out the door. Goose bumps rising on her skin, she crossed her arms over her chest.

Simon shrugged out of his jacket and handed it to her. "Here."

"Oh, I can't take that. You'll be cold."

"I won't have a woman freezing on my watch."

When she still refused to take it, he looped it around her shoulders. Instantly, warmth—and a woodsy, rugged scent—enveloped her. "Thanks." Angela shoved her arms into Simon's jacket, which was nearly double her size, and rolled the sleeves so her hands weren't covered.

Simon led the way down to the lakeside path, and they started walking. "Up ahead is a tree so famous that it has its own hashtag."

"Really?" There were trees all around them, covering the path with their shade. The water to their right became more difficult to see thanks to the dense foliage. "Which tree?"

"You'll know it when you see it."

They'd only walked a minute or two when Simon stepped through a break in the vegetation and headed toward the water once more.

He was right. She did know the tree when she saw it. And not just because of the group of people crowding the beach, vying for the best place for a photo op or selfie.

With only six or seven main branches—most of them thin—the willow tree appeared to be nothing special in and of itself. But its position in the water, growing ten or fifteen feet from shore, and the fact that it listed dramatically to the right made it extraordinary.

"Inspiring, yeah? They say it started off as a fence post eighty or so years ago and was so determined to live, it grew into that. It's called 'That Wanaka Tree.'"

Angela couldn't tear her eyes away. Something about what he'd said resonated deep inside her. The vibration grew and grew, so much her hands began to shake.

She needed to move.

Turning to face Simon again, she asked the first thing that popped into her head. "So, is your office far from here?"

If Simon was surprised by the sudden question, he didn't show it. "I'm actually a freelance writer, so I telecommute and work for several newspapers, magazines, and websites. It allows me a lot of flexibility, especially when Benjamin and Ella don't have school."

"That's wonderful that you can be there for them like that. Unfortunately I have to work a lot, so my kids spend a lot of time at my mother-in-law's."

They left the clamor of photographers behind and moved back onto the dirt path adjacent to the lake.

"What do you do?"

"Before Wes died, I stayed home with the kids. Now I work as a receptionist in a realty office." Well, before she'd quit to come here. She still had no idea what she'd do when she returned. Unsettling thought.

"Do you like it?"

"Not really, but it's a paycheck."

"If you could do anything, what would it be?"

"I used to want to be a doctor."

"What happened? Decide it wasn't for you?"

How honest should she be with this guy she barely knew? But he'd opened up, and so could she. They were just two new friends getting to know each other, right? "My plans were interrupted. I got pregnant my sophomore year of college and then married Wes."

Even now, sixteen years later, Angela felt that old familiar sense of shame rise up in her. What would he think of her? She recalled how it had felt to tell her aunt and dad about Kylee. Heard her father's gruff reply saying not to contact him again.

Remembered the words her aunt had spoken: *"I'll take you to get an abortion right away."*

The fact she'd considered it.

And the warning her aunt had relayed to her: *"If you have this baby, all of your dreams will be just that—dreams. Becoming a mother right now will ruin any chance you have of achieving what you want in life."*

Simon burrowed his hands into the pockets of his jeans. "It's funny the curveballs life throws our way sometimes. As a boy, I dreamed of being a pro snowboarder, but I injured myself on holiday my last year of secondary school, and my chances of that disappeared. So I decided to attend university and met my wife in my first class."

"I'm sorry about your injury. That must have been difficult to accept."

He shrugged. "That's the awesome thing about life. We think we want one thing, and then something happens to show us the biggest blessing was maybe that we didn't get it."

20

Not even in her competitive running days of high school had so much ridden on one race.

Angela blew into her hands and shook them out, bouncing from foot to foot. It had been nearly ten years since she'd participated in a race of any sort—and the last merely a 5K Fun Run—but the *whoosh* of blood pounding in her ears and the excitement buzzing around her remained familiar.

A crowd of more than three hundred people had gathered on the grounds of a resort just outside of Arrowtown. Like most of them, Angela wore a white badge with a number pinned to her shirt. It was a breezy sixtysomething degrees out and she was a bit chilled, but there was no point in wearing a jacket today. Her movement would warm her up as soon as the marathon began.

"Hey." Eva reached Angela after maneuvering through the thick crowd, Marc and Kylee on her heels. As usual, she looked sleek and exotic, her hair tied back in a long braid, her lean body clothed in tight black runner's leggings and a purple racerback tank. "The line at the bathrooms is insane. We're lucky to have found our way back to you."

"No problem." Angela looked beyond Eva to Kylee, who kicked at a rock. Her shoulders hunched and she kept chewing her lip—the same thing Angela always did when nervous or unsure. "Hey, hon. Thanks for doing this with us."

When Angela had returned from her night out with Simon, she'd taken his advice and knocked on Kylee's door, asking if she wanted to go running with her the next morning.

To anyone else, her daughter's shrug and "Whatever" might have been discouraging. But to Angela, it had been an action full of promise.

Now Kylee glanced at Angela and nodded. For a moment Angela's eyes registered something akin to longing in Kylee's. Did she want to mend their relationship as badly as Angela did?

Marc gripped the back of Eva's shoulders and gave her a quick squeeze before letting go. "You ready for this?"

"Yep." Eva stiffened at the touch, and the smile erupting across her lips seemed forced somehow. Hmm. What was the dynamic between those two? Did Eva feel the same way as Angela about the possibility of starting a new relationship?

Angela had been tempted to change her mind about dating Simon when he'd walked her to her door and leaned in for a tentative kiss—proving his interest after all. She'd turned her head and his lips had grazed her cheek instead. With a quick goodbye, she'd hauled it inside, her heartbeat erratic.

What was wrong with her? This was ridiculous. She was thirty-six years old. If she wanted to kiss someone, she should just do it. It's not like she had to marry the guy. People dated casually all the time.

But Simon didn't seem the kind of guy a woman would date casually—or could. She'd be wise to keep her distance.

A horn sounded, and the crowd began to shift forward. "That's the signal to get to the starting line." Angela turned to Kylee again. "You still okay to stick with me?"

"Yeah." Kylee gnawed on her lip and played with the cuffs of her black running jacket.

A talkative one. But still, she was here. It was a start. Now if only Angela could manage not to mess it up again.

"You sure you don't mind Marc and I running the whole way?" Eva's brows knit together.

"Not at all. I know you guys want to push yourselves." They'd offered to come back after crossing the finish line and join Angela and Kylee, wherever they were, but Angela had said they'd be fine.

She really hoped that was true.

"If you're sure." Eva eyed Marc. He'd actually been against the idea—saying they should practice running as a team—but hadn't argued when Angela insisted.

In truth, she wanted time alone with Kylee. Maybe something could shake loose between them if they had to spend hours with only each other for company.

A man's voice came over the portable sound system. "Racers, on your mark. Get set. Go."

A loud blast sounded from a horn, and the competitors surged forward as the cheers of those on the sidelines—including Sherry, Zach, and Lilly—rang out. Angela and company were somewhere in the middle of the pack. It was a bit disconcerting to be pushed toward the starting line, like cattle being led to slaughter. Wasn't that a pleasant thought?

Beads of sweat formed on Angela's forehead, and they had nothing to do with the sun shining. She fisted and unfisted her hands, which dangled at her sides.

"Mom, chill out."

Angela peeked at Kylee, who watched her with a wary eye. "I'm fine." Like that tone would convince anyone.

"Just have fun. Isn't that what you tell me when I run?"

So some things did stick with her daughter after all. Maybe Angela hadn't totally failed. "Good advice."

The starting line came within view—only a few rows of competitors in front of them.

"So take it."

They stepped over the starting line and moved to the side for those who wanted to break into a run. Marc and Eva waved and took off, pacing themselves to run eight-and-a-half-minute miles.

Kylee and Angela settled into a fast walk. The marathon would swing past flora and fauna of all different kinds throughout the Queenstown Lakes region. It would take them by Lake Hayes and the Shotover River and into the more familiar areas of Lake Wakatipu and Queenstown, finally ending at the Recreation Ground in the heart of the city.

As they walked, the hills grew closer, so at one point they ran on a trail situated between a smaller mountainside and the lake. The relative silence between them was only broken by the biting of their shoes against gravel and other runners passing them.

Despite Angela's desire to ask Kylee how she was really doing, she kept her mouth shut, afraid to interrupt the peace of the moment.

"See, this isn't so bad, is it?"

Ten miles of walking later, Kylee's question split the air, and Angela's heart gave a happy thump. Who was this girl initiating conversation with her mom? "Not as bad as I thought, no."

In fact, instead of becoming tired and weighted down, like she'd anticipated, her limbs slowly became infused with more adrenaline. So this was what it felt like for her training to pay off. She still had a ways to go before being ready for the ultra-marathon, but she would take this victory, however minor.

Or maybe she just needed to acknowledge that it *wasn't* minor. Maybe it was okay to say it was huge—to her, at least.

Maybe it *was* okay to dream a little.

Angela flashed a conspiratorial smile at Kylee. "You want to try running a bit?"

The grin that came onto Kylee's face was answer enough. Together they picked up the speed. And ran. Gratitude welled up inside

Angela and overflowed her heart into her veins, and that kept her running even beyond what she thought she could do.

Her toes ached. She had to actively ignore a hot spot on her left foot rubbing against her shoe. Her knee started to throb, and she could feel her body temperature ratcheting up. Not wanting to be left behind, her nose began running as well. They had to stop to use the restroom more than Angela would have liked—yay for the aftereffects of having carried three babies.

And yet . . . she loved every moment.

Along the banks of Lake Wakatipu, they finally reached mile twenty-one, the place most marathon runners lost steam. Angela channeled the little blue fish from one of Lilly's favorite movies: *"Just keep running, just keep running . . ."*

"I know, Mom."

Oh. She must have started saying it aloud. "Sorry."

As they approached a water station at mile twenty-four, Angela decreased her speed, flinching at the blister that had surely formed beneath her sneaker thanks to the mixture of heat and moisture.

Still, the fire pumping in her blood was new and recognizable all at the same time. "That was amazing."

They both grabbed water and tossed it back as they walked. The cold liquid was like heaven. To their right, the bustle of the city reminded her how far they'd come across the wilderness.

"Mom?" The small voice caused her to look over at Kylee, who stared up at her, joy shining in her eyes for the first time in . . . well, a long time.

"Yes?" Angela nearly choked on the word.

"I know I haven't really acted like it, but . . . I'm glad you're doing these races for Dad."

The words were a punch to her gut—the reminder of the reason Angela was supposedly doing all of this. Why everyone assumed she was, anyway. If she were honest, she hadn't given Wes one thought this morning, nor the last several times she'd run. Instead, training had become more about reclaiming something of a past that had been stolen from her. About finding herself again.

But it should have been about Wes and her family—shouldn't it?

"Me too."

They passed a few stragglers who had paused on the side of the path to survey the lake.

"How did you know you loved him?"

Angela wanted to leap for joy and groan at the same time. Her daughter was finally talking to her, but why this subject?

It shouldn't have been so difficult to talk about Wes. In the last month since coming here, she'd had more memories from their life together pop up—many before anger had become the defining feature of their marriage. But she didn't want to unpack all of that. Those memories only served to remind her of what she'd lost even before Wes died.

Because despite her initial resistance, she'd eventually fallen for the amiable, stable Wes Jamison. Hard. She'd given him everything, and he'd stuck by her even when life hadn't turned out the way they'd planned.

But then . . . he'd changed, making her own sacrifices somehow feel less than.

"Mom?"

"I . . ." How much should she really tell her daughter about her relationship with Wes in those early years? "As you know, we started off as lab partners. Then we became friends. And then . . . more."

By the look on her daughter's face—furrowed brow, bitten lip, a frown—she didn't appear to be satisfied with Angela's answer. "So how will I know when I'm in love?"

Where had that question come from? Angela said the first thing that popped into her head. "Maybe praying about it would help."

A raised eyebrow. "Do you pray anymore, Mom?"

"Of course." *Liar.* Her conscience mocked her because yes, it had been awhile since she and God had been on speaking terms.

It wasn't like she blamed God for Wes's drowning. It had been Wes's choice to be there exploring that shipwreck in the first place, despite her begging him not to go.

But God required forgiveness, and she didn't know how to bear his disappointment in her at not being able to forgive her husband.

Oh wow.

Angela sped up once more until she full-on sprinted. Knees groaned, hips creaked, armpits chafed, but still she couldn't outrun the thought.

Now that it was out there—now that she'd admitted it to herself—it couldn't be stuffed back in the box.

"Mom, wait." Kylee caught up to her.

"Sorry." She slowed to a jog.

There was silence once more between them. In the distance, a cheering erupted. They were getting close to the finish line. Incredible. It had gone much more quickly than she'd expected.

"I think I might love Ethan."

Angela nearly tripped at the quiet words. Her attention zoomed in on Kylee, who stared straight ahead. Had Angela heard her right? Was that the name of the boy she'd seen her daughter wrapped around a week ago? And had she seen him since, despite Angela's directives? "Who is Ethan?" She tried to control the indictment in her voice, but no dice.

"Never mind." Kylee's face hardened. "I don't know why I thought I could talk to you about this stuff."

Then her daughter sped toward the finish line—and away from Angela.

As Angela followed, completing her first marathon ever, victory didn't taste as sweet as she thought it would.

Eva downed the last of her water and crumpled the paper cup in her fist. "I still can't believe we made such great time. Under four hours? It's unreal."

The Queenstown Recreation Ground, a large public gathering place inside the city, was playing host to the end of the marathon. Past the finish line, volunteers had set up tables displaying an assortment of water cups, fresh fruit, bagels, and other refreshments to help the competitors recover from the race.

"I can. You've been rocking it during training." Marc grabbed the cup from her and threw it into the garbage can along with his. They'd already eaten some of the food the organizers provided and then had waited with Sherry and the kids for a while afterward at the finish line for Angela and Kylee. But Marc was still thirsty, so they'd headed back this way. "Where's the hot chocolate when you need it?"

"Look, there's chocolate milk." Eva snagged one and tossed it to him.

With a quick flick, he twisted the cap and took a swig of the milk. "Not the same."

"There's always coffee." She pointed to a food truck serving artisan drinks made with fair trade beans.

He pretended to shudder. "I don't know how you can drink the stuff."

"Because it's delicious." She poked Marc in the ribs.

He snatched her finger with one hand. "Yeah, well, so is hot chocolate." He pulled her close so she was inches from his chest. "When was the last time you had it, anyway?"

Her joviality fled with his sudden nearness. Ever since her chat with Kimberly, she'd been purposeful about not spending too much time alone with Marc. But she couldn't help but feel drawn to him after four hours straight of running together, chatting about everything under the sun.

"Uh, I don't know. Not since I was a kid, I guess. But then I discovered I despise chocolate in all forms."

"Someday you should try it again." Marc released her hand. "If you want to, that is."

"Sure. Maybe." Eva inclined her head toward the finish line in the distance. "Angela and Kylee could be arriving at any moment. We'd better get back."

Eva spun on her heel and led the way toward her family, who huddled around Angela and Kylee. Oh man, she'd missed their arrival. "Hey, guys. You did it!"

Angela turned, and the frown etched across her face as she stood next to her daughter was in stark contrast to the success Angela should have felt. What was going through her mind?

Eva zeroed in on Kylee, whose eyes were downcast. "Nice work, girl." She pulled her into a hug.

"Thanks, Aunt Eva." Kylee stepped away and glared at Angela.

Sherry watched the two who had just finished the race, her eyes seeming to understand the undercurrents of the family dynamics much more than Eva did. "Why don't you go grab some food? There's a lot to choose from. Zach and Lilly can help you find the best snacks."

The youngest siblings nodded with enthusiasm and dragged Kylee off by the arm.

Sherry turned to Angela. "The kids want to do lunch at Isaac's. Does that sound good to you?"

"Actually, I'm completely toast. Would you mind if we just drove back to the house and had lunch there?"

"Not at all. Or we can pick up something quickly here if you prefer." Her mother-in-law turned her discerning eye on Eva and Marc. "What about you two?"

Marc had driven the racers into town this morning so they could catch the shuttle out to the racing line, and Eva had planned on riding back with him.

Eva shrugged. "Not sure. We might grab lunch and then come home."

"I've got something in mind." Marc winked.

Her cheeks felt warm.

Sherry chuckled, and she and Angela walked off in pursuit of the kids.

Walkers and joggers still crossed the finish line every few minutes, but the crowd had thinned considerably. Random cheers punctuated the backdrop of trees, mountains, and the ever-present lake.

Eva quirked an eyebrow at Marc. "So, what did you have in mind exactly?"

He pointed toward the lake. "I overheard some runners talking about cooling off in the lake after the race, and it gave me an idea."

"You do know that lake is super cold, right?"

His mischievous smile sent a thrill through her. "What do you think?" The breeze ruffled wisps of his normally gelled hair, and Eva had the sudden urge to run her fingers through it.

Remember why you're here, Eva.

"Sorry, I have no desire to drive back to the house in wet clothes." Plus, the thought of swimming alone with him . . . Yeah, that wouldn't be wise given the current train of her thoughts.

He cocked an eyebrow. "You chicken, Jamison?"

Her hands found her hips, and she shot him a saucy glare, edged with teasing. "I know you didn't just say that to me."

"Prove it."

"By swimming in a lake?"

"No. By jumping into it. Off a fifty-foot cliff." He grinned, likely remembering how she'd always been game to do crazy things with Brent.

But Brent wasn't here.

And that was the problem, wasn't it? Because she was. And so was his best friend.

She wanted to jump. And yet where would that lead? What did it really mean to do life without Brent?

A tear trickled down Eva's cheek.

Marc's face crumpled. "Oh man, Eva, I didn't mean to make you cry. Forget I said anything. Let's just—"

"No, it's fine. Let's do it." She wiped the tear away and straightened.

"Are you sure?"

"No. But . . ." Eva fiddled with the end of her braid. "I want to try." Did he understand her deeper meaning?

Did she? And would she regret expressing it?

His eyes never left hers as he reached for her hand.

She took it. Her heart picked up speed.

They walked together toward the car, then got in. Marc followed his GPS's directions for about ten minutes, then pulled off to the side of the road where several other vehicles were parked. "This is it."

After getting out, they found a short dirt path that cut through the brush and trees. The path led down to several cliffs overlooking the crystal-clear water where a group of men and women stood. One by one, they catapulted themselves off the edge, their jubilant yells echoing all the way down.

As Eva and Marc approached, she saw that plant life clung to the upper edge of the lake all around them, but no rocks blocked the way. Nothing would keep them from jumping.

Nothing but fear.

Marc let go of her hand for a moment and removed his shoes. She did the same. The sun had risen to the top of the sky and birds twittered in the trees above them. They'd had many moments like this since he'd arrived, enjoying the call of nature surrounding them. But this still felt different.

Because there was a lot at stake. A reverence in the quiet. An unspoken something that had shifted between them.

Inching to the edge of the cliff, Eva sat and dangled her legs over. Marc followed, and for a moment she allowed herself to forget about all of her hesitations. The guilt.

Even Brent.

She laid her head on Marc's shoulder, and he put his arm around her. Closing her eyes, Eva breathed in the scent of pine trees and peace. "Ready?"

His arm loosened around her, then dropped from her shoulders. Marc scooted back a bit so he faced her more fully. His fingers brushed some hair that had fallen from her braid behind her ear.

She shivered at his touch. So gentle.

"Are you?"

"Maybe." Oh boy. Those eyes, as chocolate as the drink he loved so much, observant, true. Eva averted her gaze. "I don't know how to do this."

But did she have to know right now? Or was it enough to simply take this small step toward the unknown? To fall and let an ocean of possibilities catch her?

Or a lake of them, anyway.

"Me either." Marc gently hooked a finger under her chin and brought her eyes to meet his once more. "But we can figure it out together."

Brent's face flashed through her mind. He'd said something similar once. When was it?

Heat flashed through her whole body. Why couldn't she remember? She'd never had trouble recalling a single thing about her time with Brent.

If she leapt, would she lose more than just a memory?

Oh goodness. No.

Backing away, she couldn't bring her voice to more than a whisper. "I'm sorry, Marc. I can't."

The rejection in his eyes almost hurt more than the pain of missing Brent that nettled her heart.

Eva hopped up, grabbed her shoes, and fled back to the main path, rocks and twigs stabbing her feet—a physical reminder of the agony threatening to shred her insides.

21

A lot could change in four months.

When she'd agreed to this crazy journey, Angela could not have pictured herself here, trekking a steep mountain trail outside of Wanaka, New Zealand, slightly winded but not anywhere close to stopping.

And she definitely would not have believed she'd be here with a man—one whom, despite her reservations, she'd grown to like more every time they'd hung out in the last two weeks since the marathon.

"Can you believe this view?" Simon's voice was partially lost in the wind blowing from the top of the mountain.

Countless peaks zigzagged across the skyline, creating a whole valley of triangles that split off in all directions. In the distance, the surface of Lake Wanaka glinted as if it held millions of tiny blue-white diamonds. From deep greens to browns and yellows, the vibrant landscape seemed the work of a masterful artist.

Nothing in a long time had made her feel quite so close to the Divine as this.

"It's . . ." There truly wasn't even a word for it.

"I know."

The ground beneath them flattened, and the searing in Angela's leg muscles lessened. As they walked along the saddle of the mountain, there wasn't another human in sight. Simon's broad shoulders carried a backpack with emergency supplies, and his muscular legs were tan from lots of time spent in the sun.

As they neared the peak of the mountain they'd been climbing for hours, Simon turned. "This last bit might be tough, but it's worth it."

"Thanks for the warning."

Simon led them up the last part of the trail toward the top. Angela's lungs screamed at her, and she focused on breathing, on inhaling the scent of rock and dirt and pine and—for a brief moment—freedom.

At last they made it to the peak, where the path evened out and came to a stop. They were rewarded for their labor with striking panoramic views unlike anything she'd ever seen. She thought the colors had been bright on their hike up, but nothing compared to the display in front of her. It was more vivid than she'd ever imagined.

And it was all imbued with a sense of triumph—hard work mixed with good fortune. Blessing.

When was the last time she'd actually felt blessed?

"Like I said. Worth it, eh?" Simon's voice broke into her thoughts, but it wasn't an unpleasant interruption.

Angela peeked at him as he stood at the edge of the mountain, gripping the straps of his backpack, chest pushed out as if welcoming the breeze that tickled their faces, basking in the warmth of the sun that played hide-and-seek with the puffy white clouds overhead. He'd mentioned his love of the outdoors numerous times in the last few weeks, and she finally understood—he was in his element.

And it was extremely attractive.

As if they were two magnets, Angela moved closer. She hadn't meant to spend so much time with him, but after the marathon she'd called him, desperate for his insights into what she should do about Kylee. His gentle advice to simply have patience with her daughter and be there in case she wanted to talk was sound, and Angela had appreciated the logic in it. And even though Kylee hadn't opened up any more about Ethan or what was going on in her heart, she hadn't completely retreated again like Angela expected. She'd even joined her mom and aunt for training most days. For now they were once again attempting a shaky truce.

That late-night advice session had turned into a get-together with Simon nearly every night, whether it was catching a movie at the local cinema, eating dinner beside the wharf in town, or taking a stroll along the lake. Simon and his children—who were wonderful, well-adjusted kids from what Angela could tell—had also spent time over at the Jamisons' rental house, and the kids got along surprisingly well. Those new friendships were likely the reason none of the kids were acting out in the stereotypical way when a parent started spending time with a "special friend."

But were they all getting too attached? Angela had tried to casually remind her kids that someday they'd have to leave the Kings behind, but Lilly's response last night had stuck with Angela: *"I know, Mommy. But what if we didn't?"*

Of course, that was a ridiculous notion. The end of March would come, and the Jamisons would depart. But sometimes Angela still indulged the foolishness for a moment or two. What if there could be more between her and Simon? Was it even possible for her to be in a relationship without losing herself, without having to sacrifice what she wanted? A selfish perspective, perhaps, but it still gave her pause. She definitely wouldn't rush into anything.

Not that Simon had pushed at all. In fact, since their first "date," he hadn't verbally hinted at wanting more than friendship. But the interest in his eyes was clear.

Even now his gaze turned from the great beauty surrounding them . . . to Angela.

Sudden self-consciousness overtook her. "What?"

"Nothing. Just enjoying the view." A smile curled on his lips.

"Yeah?" She couldn't help the grin that spread on her own.

"It just got infinitely better. You put nature to shame when you smile."

Angela fidgeted with the zipper on her jacket. "There hasn't been a lot to smile about . . . until now."

"I understand how it might feel like that. But look at all the amazing things in your life and what you've accomplished."

"And what exactly have I accomplished? One of my friends back home is a published author. Another a lawyer with a huge firm. Yet another homeschools, runs her own in-home business, and serves on practically every church committee. Providing for my children's basic needs doesn't seem that high on the list of note-worthy accomplishments."

"You can't compare yourself with everyone else. You've got to do the tasks you were given to complete—nothing more, nothing less. And from where I'm standing, I see a woman who has done so much more than provide the essentials for her kids. You love them so much it scares you. Love might not seem like an accomplishment, but it's lifeblood to us all."

The words thickened Angela's throat like a lot of things did these days. "Funny thing is, I never wanted kids."

"Why is that?"

She shrugged. "My father was a career military guy. Navy. My mom died from kidney disease when I was six, while my dad was serving on a ship. He came back for the funeral, then sent me to live with my aunt, who worked crazy hours and really didn't want me. But there was no other family willing or able to take me, and my dad didn't want to give up his prestigious post. The arrangement was only supposed to last a few years till he retired."

"And how long did it actually last?"

"Till I graduated high school. Then after I told him about being unmarried and pregnant, he wanted nothing to do with me. We haven't spoken since." She hurried on—wanting his understanding, not his pity. "Anyway, that's why I never wanted children. I didn't grow up in a real family, and I didn't think I would be a good mom."

"Clearly that's not the case."

Angela gave a small smile. "Kylee might not agree with you."

"Like I said, you can't base anything on what a teenager thinks." He nudged her. "And despite your fears, you chose to have kids anyway."

"I certainly didn't choose to get pregnant. The first time, at least." She kicked at a rock. "I nearly aborted Kylee." The thought stung the air, tainting the artistry around them.

He wasn't as quick to answer this time. "But you didn't."

"I know, but . . ." How could she explain? "The moment the nurse first placed her in my arms, I wept. With joy, yes, of course, but also with guilt and regret. Sometimes I just look at her and think, *What if?* What if I'd done it? What if she wasn't here anymore? And I'm so grateful I made the decision I did. Not that I condemn others who make a different one. I just can't imagine life without my baby girl. But sometimes I wonder . . ."

Simon's hand found hers. He held on to her palm and squeezed, infusing strength into her.

She swallowed. "I wonder if the reason we have so much tension between us is because she somehow knows I didn't start out wanting her. That I cried for months, wishing she wasn't inside of me. Praying that I'd wake up and find it all some sort of sick dream."

She'd admitted that to Wes once, about eight years into their marriage. He'd shrunk back as if she'd slapped him.

"You still blame me, don't you?"

"This isn't about you."

"No, it's about how you wanted to be a doctor and I derailed your plans by knocking you up."

"Don't say it like that." What had gotten into him? Wes never spoke in such a crass way. "I had a hand in it too."

"It's not like you loved me, Angela. You were lonely, I was there—"

"Wes, don't be ridiculous." Maybe she'd said yes to a date from her good friend at first because she'd craved connection, and he was clearly enamored with her, but now? He was her husband. The father of her children. They'd built a life together from nothing. A good life. He'd given her the stability and love she'd craved all her life, had satisfied the cry of her little-girl heart, which had been disregarded by her father. He'd stood by her when things were uncertain and rough. "Of course I loved you."

"Are you sure? Or have you always just settled for me because of the kids?"

"Hey." Another squeeze to her hand brought her back to the present. To Simon. "You and Kylee will be fine. She's a teenager. It doesn't matter what happened in the past. What matters is that you love her and would do anything for her. She knows that deep down, even if she won't admit it."

"I hope you're right."

22

This was going to be a disaster.

Groaning, Eva tossed the rose she was holding across the floor in the back room of Joanne's shop, where she sat surrounded by a variety of flower-filled buckets and tools, from shears to floral tape, bouquet pins, and ribbons.

Why in the world had she said yes to Joanne? Sure, the florist had sounded desperate when she'd called earlier this afternoon. Her husband had had an asthma attack—not major enough to be a life-and-death crisis, but urgent enough to warrant a visit to the hospital. The problem? Joanne had six bouquets to assemble for a wedding tomorrow. She'd gotten behind on a few other orders and had intended to stay up late arranging the bouquets, but now the emergency put her in danger of not getting to them in time.

She'd asked Eva if she'd mind arranging as many of the bouquets as possible until Joanne could join her. Eva had tried saying no, but "yes" had popped from her mouth anyway.

That was hours ago, and here Eva still sat, nothing complete.

Outside the window, the sun had already given up for the day, an action Eva wished she could emulate. A velvety sky stretched over the sleeping town of Wanaka, clouds obscuring the mountain peaks that were the town's constant companions.

Over the last month, Eva had tried to actively focus on moving forward, praying that one day her creative juices would flow again. But thanks to her near jump in the lake with Marc, her artist's spirit remained as stale as ever.

He'd flown home the next day, and they hadn't talked about the incident since. Instead, they'd simply reverted back to being friends and coworkers who chatted once a week about the business and the ultra-marathon training. Perhaps she'd misunderstood his intentions anyway.

And she was fine with that. Really.

But this bouquet disaster felt like she was being pushed to the brink of what she could handle. Eva had stared at these flowers for two hours, and despite Joanne's instructions to throw together something simple yet elegant, she couldn't find inspiration to save her life.

She should have just told Joanne the truth—admitted to herself the truth—that she couldn't do this anymore.

No. She couldn't fail this unknown bride. Eva's wedding had been perfect, down to the last detail, and every bride deserved that.

"Okay, Eva. You've got this." Maybe if she put the . . . No, that looked horrible. Or what about the . . . Ugh, rookie move!

Her phone interrupted her self-deprecating thoughts. Her caller ID said it was Marc. When they needed to talk, he'd taken to calling her around five or six o'clock in the morning when he first got up. She accepted the video chat. "Hi."

His face filled up her screen. "Hey there." He was surrounded by burgundy pillows, and a modern black headboard peeked from the edge of the picture. Was he calling her from bed instead of his normal spot on the balcony outside his apartment? Did he even have a shirt on?

Whew. Suddenly it felt far muggier in the plant-filled room.

"What are you up to?" His husky, early-morning baritone filled the previously quiet space.

How did someone manage to sound so kissable at five in the morning?

Get a grip, Eva. She wiped the thought from her mind, propping the phone on a chair so she could fiddle with the flowers and chat with him at the same time. "Filling in for Joanne. She had a family emergency and needed me to create a few bouquets for her."

"Yeah? How's it going?"

Eva held up her two empty hands. "Fantastic. Can't you tell?"

"I sense sarcasm."

"Unfortunately, yes. I shouldn't have agreed, but I wanted to help."

"Why shouldn't you have agreed?" Marc put his arm behind his head, accentuating his bicep. The edge of a white T-shirt made an appearance. So he was fully clothed after all.

Goodness. Her Catholic mother would cross herself three times if she were privy to Eva's thoughts. Of course, even when she'd been married to Brent, Mom acted like Eva's thoughts should be entirely too much like the Virgin Mary.

She couldn't help the grin that spread across her lips at the memory.

Marc's eyebrows shot up. "What's that smile all about?"

"Ah, nothing." Hopefully color wasn't as visible on the phone, because her cheeks felt like they were flaming. She cleared her throat. "And, um, to answer your question, I shouldn't have agreed, because I'm out of practice. I haven't done this since . . . well, for a long time."

"Why is that?" The quiet usually meant Marc was mulling. "I just assumed it was because you got busy with working at the heart center. But it's more, isn't it?"

Eva snatched a few Alaskan roses out of the nearest bucket. She had to throw something together, even if it wasn't very grand. "At first, maybe it was. But when Brent died, I lost the heart I had for my work." She'd expected awkwardness after their near-jump, but Marc still treated her the same, and she found herself responding to his care with openness of her own.

"Maybe this will be the push you need to start again."

"I'm doing a terrible job so far." She began stripping the flowers of foliage and carefully removed one thorn at a time.

"It looks nice to me."

She rolled her eyes and snorted. "And you know lots about floral arrangements how?"

"I never claimed to. Just said it looks nice to me."

"Well, thanks."

A few moments of silence passed while she worked. Then, "Eva, are we ever going to talk about what happened?"

The hesitation in his voice caused her to fumble the shears and look up at him. She swallowed, hard. A thousand different emotions played across his features, but there was love shining in his eyes.

Love?

No. That wasn't possible.

She'd always been a master at reading her own feelings, but at the moment, gaining a pulse on them seemed impossible—probably because they were jumbled and fell at opposite ends of the spectrum, waging a war for her heart.

"I'm not sure what to say." She wound floral tape around the roses and added some carnations and hydrangeas.

He sighed and rubbed his hand across his face. "I wish I was there to talk to you about this in person. I know it's hard over the phone. But I'm dying here."

Avoiding his gaze, Eva plunged some viburnum berries and paua shells willy-nilly into the emerging bouquet.

"Look, I understand you might need time, but can we at least get on the same p—"

"You know, Marc, I really should be going." He had been right at the lake. She *was* a chicken. "I've got to focus on these flowers."

His features hardened for a moment. "I care about you, Eva. As a friend. And more. There, I said it." The desire in his voice . . . Oh man, she was in trouble. "If you need time, I get it. I'll wait as long as you need me to. You're worth it to me. But if you don't feel the same way, please just let me know."

The problem was, she did.

But alongside those emotions, the pressing weight of guilt nearly crushed her.

Sure, she might like Marc. A lot.

But could she ever love him like she'd loved Brent?

Did she even want to?

Eva kept her fingers busy as her mind raced. "I really don't know how I feel. You're my friend, and I don't want to lose you. But . . ." She couldn't finish. What would she say?

After a few moments of silence, he sighed. "I guess I'll let you go then."

"Marc . . ."

"It's fine, Eva." He paused. "Good luck with the flowers."

After a hurried goodbye, she looked down at the bouquet in her hands—and her mouth fell open.

It was gorgeous. Like, magazine-worthy.

"Oh, Brent. I'm so sorry."

As if the flowers were on fire, she flung them across the room and allowed the sobs racking her body to come.

23

It was hard to believe the ultra-marathon was in six weeks.

Angela increased her speed as she and Eva ran the same loop they did multiple times a week. Her stamina and endurance had grown exponentially since arriving in New Zealand two months ago, though she was still far from the athlete she'd been in high school. Maybe she would never be that fast again, but that was all right.

She'd come to crave their daily training, whether it was a flat course around the lake like now or running the hills in more remote parts of the South Island. The high of completing a marathon had only served to boost Angela's addiction to the hours they spent on the trail. And other than a bit of flagging irritation in her right knee, her body had grown strong. Calluses had formed in the place of blisters, and Vaseline was her best friend against chafing whenever it became an issue.

In many ways, Angela had been reborn. Those moments when she ran, she felt more like herself than she had in years.

Eva and Angela passed a young couple standing next to the lake, the girl lifting a single red rose to her nose, the guy obviously trying to figure out a way to go in for a kiss. Then a couple with white hair and weathered skin strolled past them hand in hand. The woman laughed at something the man said, and ten years seemed to drop from her face.

"Brent always said people must have Valentine's Day on the

brain as soon as February begins." The words fell flat from Eva's lips.

"Oh, right, it's the first, huh?" Would Simon want to do something together for Valentine's? Her heart pitched at the thought.

"Let's go faster." Eva didn't wait for Angela to answer, just took off running at nearly breakneck speed past the older couple.

What in the world?

Angela hurried to keep pace. Eva had seemed quiet all weekend, hiding out in her room on Saturday, begging off of their planned hike yesterday, and finally emerging with bags under her eyes today. Sherry had mentioned Eva had stayed up late at the florist shop last Thursday helping out the owner, but that was four days ago. And something about Eva's rigid stance and droopy lips spoke of an ailment far beyond lack of sleep.

She had the urge to ask Eva what was wrong, but even after living under the same roof for two months, the sisters-in-law just weren't that close.

And whose fault is that?

Inwardly, Angela groaned. Eva had made several efforts to go deeper with Angela, but she hadn't been ready, hadn't known what to say. But now? Something in her cried out for bonding with the only woman other than Sherry who knew what it was like to have loved—and lost—a Jamison man.

Yes, indeed. This trip was doing weird things to her.

After a mile of dashing down the ambling path, Angela grabbed her sides as she decreased her speed. "Whew. I need to catch my breath. Sorry."

Her sister-in-law slowed to a walk, sighing. "No, I'm sorry. I didn't mean to go so fast."

"It's good for me, right?"

Eva lifted her arms over her head, the bottom of her ribs protruding when she breathed in. "It's easy to lose sight of why we're here sometimes."

The woman who had instigated this entire thing because of her husband—who had created a memorial out of her life—was losing sight of her purpose? Whoa.

Angela, on the other hand, had initially come for her children, and they'd seemed to thrive here. Even Kylee. But what about Angela herself? True, she felt she was in the process of changing, but as things shifted within her, she found more to explore. About her needs and desires. About her life with Wes. About his death.

Eva pulled the rubber band from her long hair and ran her hands through it, smoothing out the top before creating a messy bun piled on top of her head. "Angela, are you and Simon a thing?"

That's definitely not where she thought this conversation was headed. "No." Given how much time they spent together, it wasn't a ridiculous speculation. And there was no doubt they had chemistry. Angela felt it every time he was near, like the static shock kids knew would come after going down a plastic slide at the playground.

It wasn't just the physical attraction, though. He understood her soul. Oy, how cheesy did that sound?

"Oh. I just assumed."

"I think he'd like more, but it's just not practical." If nothing else, she could always fall back on that reason.

"Why not?"

"He lives here and I live in New York, for one. And I've got the kids to consider." Her children seemed to love Simon and his children, something she hadn't predicted. In fact, she'd expected Kylee to be suspicious about their relationship, but it hadn't happened. Maybe her daughter was too busy obsessing over her own relationship woes to be concerned about Angela's—though as far as Angela knew, she hadn't seen Ethan again since that day in the coffee café.

"So." Eva twisted her hands. "If you lived in the same place, and you didn't have the kids to think about . . . you'd date him?"

Where was she going with this? "I haven't really thought about it. But sure, I guess. Maybe." If she could ever let herself fall in love again.

Because, despite all odds, she had still loved Wes at the end—even if she couldn't forgive him for dying.

"You don't feel like it's too soon? Like you'd be disrespecting Wes's memory by giving your heart to someone else?" Eva's words might have sounded judgmental, but her tone did not. In fact, it sounded like . . . a plea.

Ah.

There was no denying the way Marc felt about Eva. It had been obvious whenever he looked her way. "Eva, are we still talking about me and Simon?"

Her sister-in-law bit her lip and shook her head.

Did she want Angela to ask more? Or would she freely share if willing? Angela didn't want to unwittingly push Eva away, not when they were finally opening up to each other.

They rounded a corner, and the house came within view. Zach and Lilly played on the dock under Sherry's watchful eye.

It made her feel better whenever Simon took her hand and squeezed in a friendly way, so Angela did the same to Eva.

Her sister-in-law stopped walking and gave her a full-on hug. Wetness spread against Angela's shoulder, and Eva inhaled a shaky sob.

A fondness for her sister-in-law filled Angela's chest. The woman certainly cried more than Angela did, and she had no clue what it was like to be a tired and stressed-out mom, but right now, in this moment, more drew them together than split them apart. Because they shared a mutual pain, an emptiness where there used to be a husband. That was a bond that could never be broken.

Wherever the wind took them after this, they would always be family.

Angela gave Eva one last squeeze and pulled back, swiping the mascara streaks from Eva's cheeks. "How about we wrangle some popcorn and see if we can convince Kylee to watch *You've Got Mail* or something equally obnoxious?"

Eva laughed, her voice hoarse. "That sounds really nice, actually."

And they walked into the house hand in hand, nothing really resolved, questions still lingering, but something having changed nonetheless.

24

"That was fun, Mommy." Lilly skipped through the front door and twirled. "When can we go again?"

Angela, Kylee, and Zach filed in after her. Kylee immediately fled upstairs without a word. She'd been sullen the entire drive home from the bowling alley near Queenstown, where they'd spent time with Simon and his kids. She'd been having a fun time at first, then suddenly turned white and retreated to the bathroom.

Zach pushed the glasses up the bridge of his nose. "You only got, like, ten points. In bowling, that's pretty bad."

"That doesn't matter, bud." Angela squeezed Lilly's shoulder. "I'm so glad you had fun, sweetie. Of course we can go again."

Sherry walked around the corner, drying her hands on a towel. "Did you all have a good time?"

Lilly charged Sherry and threw her arms around her middle. "Grandma! I got to bowl on the same team as Ella and we got a four-pound ball!"

"And how about you, Zach?"

"I creamed Benjamin." Zach struck a pose. "Then I victory danced like this." He wiggled his hips and whooped, pumping his fists in the air.

Angela rolled her eyes, laughing. "And then you were reprimanded for not being a good sport, weren't you?"

Her son shrugged. "Benjamin didn't care. He beat me once, so we'll see who wins best two outta three next time."

Next time. Angela ran her hands along the base of her neck, her teeth tugging on her bottom lip. How would her children feel when they had to leave New Zealand, likely never to see the Kings again?

How would she feel?

She refocused on Sherry, who watched her with inquisitive eyes. "What did you and Eva do while we were gone?"

"I visited with Fiona. I got back a bit ago." A frown stretched across her face. "I think Eva stayed in her room all evening. I'm worried about her."

Since Kylee had been training with them all week and Eva had retreated to her room most nights after the kids were in bed, Angela hadn't had much opportunity to engage Eva in conversation alone again after their talk several days ago. Maybe she should check on her. "I'll go see if she needs anything."

"That'd be great, dear." Sherry directed her attention to the two younger kids. "What do you say we raid the freezer for some ice cream before bed?"

A great chorus of cheers rose from Lilly and Zach, who took off running toward the kitchen.

Angela turned and padded up the stairs to the second floor. Eva's room was at the end of the hallway next to Lilly's. The air was a tad stuffier up here, but it was quieter and darker too. As she approached Eva's door, Angela halted at the sound of muffled crying.

It was coming from Kylee's room.

Angela raised her hand to knock on Kylee's door, then paused. What would her daughter want? Back at the bowling alley, when Kylee hadn't returned from the bathroom after half an hour, Angela had gone in search of her. The teen had finally emerged from the stall, her eyes red and puffy, and she wouldn't say anything to Angela except, "I'm fine, Mom."

Would an inquiry from Angela now be equally rebuffed?

She stepped away from Kylee's room, determined not to intrude on her privacy, but the sobs wrenched her heart in two. She remembered being a child, a preteen, and a teenager crying into her pillow, alone, wishing her aunt would find her, hold her, tell her it was going to be okay.

But no one ever came.

Angela's hand made a decision before her brain did. The knock seemed to resound in the hallway—or maybe that was Angela's heartbeat. *Please, don't let me mess this up.*

"Go away."

Angela ignored the mumbled words and eased open the door, stepped inside, and closed it behind her. She walked to the bed, where Kylee sprawled on her stomach in the semidark, her face mashed against the purple pillowcase. The calm of the lavender-and-cream room—with its lacy bedspread and curtains, pictures of peonies adorning the walls, and the soft glow of a bedside lamp—did not seem to permeate Kylee's gloom.

Easing herself down next to her daughter, Angela reached out a hand and stroked Kylee's back in gentle circles. Was it her imagination, or did her daughter's shoulders seem to melt into the bed at her mother's touch?

They stayed that way for a while, Kylee's sobs lessening. Angela found herself humming "Hush, Little Baby," the tune she used to sing to a very colicky infant fifteen years ago as she rocked and bounced, rocked and bounced, until her feet ached and her arms grew weary with the girl's weight.

Finally, her daughter rolled half over and stared up at Angela, pushing wetness away from the underside of her lids. Angela started to ask what was wrong, but a small voice inside urged her to be silent and continue humming. So she did.

Kylee shifted herself upright and nestled among her pillows

against her bed's headboard, hugging her knees to her chest. "Ethan was at the bowling alley. With another girl."

Angela held back a wince. Was Kylee about to let her have it for breaking her and Ethan up? What was the right reaction? Would her daughter respond with anger if Angela said she was better off without him? That he wasn't worthy of her?

Perhaps sympathy was the best alternative to those thoughts. "I'm sorry, hon."

Kylee picked at her cuticles, then chewed on her thumbnail, her eyes not meeting Angela's. "I guess he didn't really love me after all." Her lips trembled.

Oh, forget it. Angela couldn't stand by in silence and watch her daughter suffer, constantly afraid of saying the wrong thing. She reached for Kylee's hand, surprised when her daughter didn't pull away. "That's his loss, then."

"I just thought . . . I mean, he said such nice things." Another tear coursed down Kylee's cheek. "He told me I was beautiful and that I was special. I guess I'm pretty stupid for believing him, huh?"

"Considering the fact that you are both of those things— beautiful and special, that is—no, you're not stupid at all." Angela snatched a tissue off the side table and pressed it into her daughter's palm. "But the right boy will say those things and mean them. And you will never doubt that they're true."

"Was Dad the right boy for you, Mom?" The question sounded so small, and Kylee suddenly looked so very tender, huddled there on the purple bed, face glistening, voice scratchy, hair mussed.

Her daughter wasn't as young as Angela kept trying to keep her. She was becoming a woman, so maybe Angela needed to start talking to her like one. And that began with honesty. Some, anyway. "Yes. I loved your father, Kylee, and he loved me. We didn't have a perfect marriage, but I never doubted that he meant the sweet things he said."

Not every guy would have suggested they get married when he found out the girl he'd been dating for six months was pregnant. But Wes had. He'd done the honorable thing when he could have easily reacted just like her aunt and father had. Like a lot of other guys would have.

She hadn't thought much about that in a long time. In fact, Angela had been so focused on how he'd abandoned them in death that she'd nearly forgotten how he'd been there for her at the start of Kylee's life. He had been a principled and trustworthy man at heart. And yes, maybe he'd gotten caught up in the adventure of thrill seeking—a midlife crisis of sorts—but underneath he'd still loved his family. Even in her anger toward him, she couldn't deny that.

A tiny bit of warmth lit Angela's heart.

Kylee pressed her thumb against the tissue, wearing the soft fiber down until it tore. "Then why couldn't you tell me how you knew you loved him?" She ripped the tissue in half.

"It's complicated, Kylee." Angela couldn't seem to stop the old exasperation from coming through in her tone. Because honesty could only go so far. If she told her daughter the whole truth, Kylee might surmise the part about her unexpected conception—and Angela did not want her ever wondering for one second if she was wanted. She'd had enough grief and heartache in her short life.

Her daughter sniffed, and instead of anger, her shoulders sank as if in defeat. "Please, Mom. Tell me."

Angela rubbed her nose. "Please understand. It's difficult for me to talk about it."

"So you want me to be honest, but you don't have to be?" The tissue now lay in shreds, scattered on the bedspread. "That's not fair."

"There's just more to all of this than you know. More than I can tell you. I'm sorry, sweetie. I love you, but you're still just a kid. My kid. And I want—"

"I know you blame Dad for dying."

As soon as the words left Kylee's lips, she turned pale, her eyes wide. She chomped down on her lip.

Heat bloomed in Angela's cheeks. "What?" She could barely choke out the word. How could her daughter possibly know that?

"I read your diary." Kylee looked like she might cry again. "You were mad all the time, and one day when I was in your room borrowing some jewelry, I saw the diary on your bedside table, and I couldn't stop myself. I'm sorry. I just wanted to know what you were thinking."

She'd only written in her diary once since Wes died, and her daughter had read the words she'd slashed there? Angela wanted to feel enraged, to push away any other emotions, but what rose instead was great sorrow. Sorrow that she'd had to write the words at all. That her daughter had felt the need to snoop instead of simply asking Angela how she felt. Regret that she probably wouldn't have told the truth if Kylee *had* asked.

"Baby, those words were very raw. I haven't been great about . . . well, any of this. I've never done this before. I know you haven't either." She picked up the pieces of Kylee's tissue and tossed them in the garbage.

"So you aren't mad at Dad for dying?"

Honesty . . . or protection? Angela sighed. "To tell you the truth, sometimes I am."

"I was, too, at first."

Angela took her daughter's hand once more. "Really?" How could she not have known that? She and her daughter were more alike than she'd ever wanted to admit.

"Yeah, but Juliet helped me work through it at group."

"Well, it's something I'm working through too." She could finally say those words truthfully, even though she didn't know what the final result would be. How would she know when she was done "working"? "I don't want you to worry about it, though."

Kylee studied her for a moment. "Are we ever going to be okay again, Mom?"

"Someday, sweetie. I know we have a long way to go, but I'm willing to walk that path if you are. Together?"

Kylee's nod was so slight, Angela almost missed it. But when she saw it, she felt like doing a victory dance herself.

25

"My girlfriend is going to love this." A short twentysomething Kiwi man with a collared shirt buttoned to the top handed Eva his credit card while admiring the simple bouquet of calla lilies she'd arranged for him.

"I'm glad." Eva ran the credit card through Joanne's register, tapping her finger along the metal edge while it processed. She'd offered to watch the flower shop for an hour or two so Joanne could run out for a quick lunch with Graeme, who was feeling much better after his asthma attack over a week ago.

The register whirred as it spit out a receipt. Eva ripped it from the spool and handed it to the man along with his credit card. "Thank you for your business. And good luck with the proposal."

With a thank-you and a wave, the man left. The shop was quiet once more, only the hum of the hanging glass lights buzzing in the air. She tucked her hair behind her ear as she straightened a carnation spray here and a ribbon there. Eva hadn't been back to the shop since she'd created some of the most beautiful wedding bouquets of her career. Hadn't chatted with Marc since then either.

Because there was a profound awareness in her gut, and she wasn't ready to deal with it. If he saw her face or heard her voice, he might realize it too. So anything she'd needed to say to him, she'd texted.

At least some good had come from the strife. She and Angela had been on surprisingly close terms. Her sister-in-law had even gone out of her way to check on Eva last night after she'd spent most of the day curled up in bed.

The bell over the florist shop's door dinged, and Joanne walked in, followed closely by her husband. They held hands and she laughed at something he'd whispered in her ear.

When Joanne saw Eva, she beamed. "Thanks so much for letting us step out for a bit, love."

"You weren't even gone that long." Eva ducked into the back room to check her phone messages, giving Joanne and Graeme a moment of privacy. She only had one text from Angela confirming their plans for an early-evening hike.

Eva sent Angela the thumbs-up emoji and locked her phone, sticking it back into her purse and returning to the shop floor.

Joanne was now alone, humming and smiling from her perch on a ladder as she dusted a high shelf in the corner.

"You and your hubby are so cute together." With no customers to assist, Eva decided she'd get started on an order that had come in while Joanne was out.

She headed to the vase of purple larkspurs, which some said represented first love—appropriate for the small bouquet a man had ordered for a first date tonight. Twenty to thirty dainty blooms shaped like stars clustered around each stalk, creating an ivy-like trail of flowers along the stem, each increasing the beauty of the plant as a whole. Without this one or that, odd gaps would exist, and the flower would look incomplete.

Marc had been like one of those flowers in her life. A friend when she'd needed someone who understood her loss. A balm to her spirit. A partner who had made her quest doable.

And maybe . . . more.

If she could only get over her fear of the unknown.

The sigh that leaked through Eva's lips was far from voluntary.

Pausing, Joanne quirked an eyebrow and climbed from the ladder. "Something on your mind?"

Should she confide in Joanne? Eva hadn't even told Kim about her last real conversation with Marc, mostly because her best friend would probably just urge her to keep moving forward by "getting back out there." But Joanne was far more impartial. She'd met Marc a handful of times when he was in town, but never for more than a few minutes. And Joanne had experience in this department.

No way could Eva focus on an arrangement right now. She dropped the larkspur back into its water with a tiny plop. "I've never asked. What led you and Graeme to finally realize you were interested in being more than friends?"

The shop owner replaced the rag and furniture polish behind the front desk. "Now that's an interesting story."

"You don't have to tell me if you'd rather not."

"I don't mind, love. As I've mentioned, when I first moved to New Zealand, Graeme was my neighbor, and he was ten years older than me—so late thirties at the time. He'd never married, never had children, but we became quick friends and he offered to help me in the shop when he wasn't working, or watch my boys for me when I was. When the kids were older, he took them to play football at the park and camping in the mountains. He became a father figure to boys whose own father had abandoned them for a new family." Despite the words she spoke, Joanne's tone held no malice. She'd obviously dealt with her ex-husband's actions and moved on.

"Sounds like he was really there for you all." Eva's mind instantly flew to Marc. He was the same kind of man.

"He was." Joanne's hands played with the pearls at her throat. "After a few years, he confessed he had feelings for me that went deeper than friendship, but I was still so broken from my failed marriage. I know it's not the same as losing a spouse—that it's a different sort of grief—but it's grief all the same."

"Of course it is. So what happened?" This story was shaping up to be better than the Hallmark movies Kimberly had made Eva watch with her in the months after Brent died. She'd mindlessly sat through countless shows until one day she realized that seeing the love stories played out on the screen were too painful because she'd never have that again.

Now, though? Something like hope rested like a seed in her heart, waiting to push through the soil. Perhaps she only had to water it. And stories like Joanne's made it feel more possible that someday Eva might be able to tip the watering can. That a beautiful lavender larkspur of her own could grow.

Joanne considered Eva. "I told him I didn't plan to date anyone until my children were out of the house. And I didn't. Even though it eventually became very clear to me that I couldn't see my life without him. That I loved him."

"So how did you go from that to married?"

"I returned home from moving in Neil at university and found Graeme waiting on my front porch. When I approached, he got down on one knee and said, 'I've waited all these years, and dating at this point seems silly.' He held out a ring and proposed. And of course, I said yes."

Yep. Definitely better than a Hallmark movie. "What an amazing story."

"It is. But I could have been happy sooner if I'd only opened my heart when he'd first declared his interest. I used my children as an excuse not to take a leap toward loving again. Instead of months, I could have already had years of marriage to the man I love." Joanne batted away the single tear trailing down her cheek. "I try not to live with regret, but I struggle with it regarding this. Because my greatest sorrow isn't in the things I lost that I had no control over."

The shop owner peered into Eva's eyes, as if she could see that little seed of something inside. As if urging it on. "No, my biggest sorrow is more about the things I lost to fear."

26

When Simon said he had a surprise for her after dinner, she hadn't pictured this.

He'd made her keep her eyes closed as he tugged her gently from the rental house down to the pebbly beach along the lake. The younger kids had all giggled, clearly in on the secret, when Angela and Simon left them behind in the kitchen. Even Kylee had smiled at Angela, albeit sedately.

She hadn't known what to expect, but a two-person kayak, life vests, and double-bladed paddles were definitely not it. "Oh cool." Was Simon fooled by her fake enthusiasm?

She'd seen plenty of tour groups and single kayaks rolling by on the lake since she'd been here and not once had the urge to go. It's not as if she had anything against water sports—not ones that kept you on the surface, anyway. She was just more of a lay-on-the-beach-and-read kind of girl.

"I hear from reputable sources that you've never been kayaking." Simon kept hold of her hand even though she no longer needed his guidance down the beach. "I used to go all the time but haven't pulled it out this year. Someone's been keeping me busy." He winked.

"It's not my fault you find my company irresistible."

Listen to her, flirting. But around Simon, she couldn't help it. Getting to know him and his children over the last month had been . . . well, wonderful really. He'd encouraged her in regard to parenting and the upcoming ultra-marathon, and she'd told him her story: the good, the fears, the accusations, the unforgiveness, the broken dreams. All of it. They'd also laughed together and enjoyed each other's company—always toeing the line between friendship and something more. She sensed he was simply waiting for her to give a sign she was ready.

And in some moments she'd been almost tempted. But she was finally finding the real Angela again and couldn't allow a new relationship to jeopardize that.

"It's not just your company." Simon squeezed her fingers and turned his face downward toward hers. "It's you."

Whew. Yes. Temptation. She dropped his hand and gave him a light shove. "So you just felt like showing me this lovely hunk of wood?"

If Simon noticed her very obvious change of subject—and how could he not?—he didn't show it. "I thought maybe we could take this 'hunk of wood' for a sunset jaunt. I'd like to show you around New Zealand in a way you haven't seen it before. Might be a fun adventure."

Kayaking was fairly tame as far as adventure went. In the early days of Wes's adventuring after Roy died, he'd invited Angela along several times. Eva went with Brent, after all. But Angela had no desire to bungee jump, scuba dive, or hang glide—and she couldn't understand why he did either. He'd always mocked Brent's fool-hardy stunts before. What had changed? Why had his father's death made him so reckless?

Maybe if she'd said yes back then, she would understand now.

"Okay." The word wobbled out.

"Yeah?"

"Yeah." This time she infused extra strength into her voice. A confidence that came from knowing she'd regret saying no one more time.

And maybe hoping things could be different.

"Great." Simon picked up the smaller of the two life jackets and handed it to her, then put on the other. He hauled the kayak into the water along the dock.

After slipping on her life vest, she walked the dock, and with Simon's coaching, climbed into the front hole of the kayak, which had a closed deck. He handed her a paddle, then expertly climbed into the back, the boat rocking a bit with his addition. The water looked fairly calm tonight and a breeze blew down from the mountains, making Angela grateful that Simon had asked her to change into pants, a jacket, and closed-toe shoes before coming outside.

"Ready?" Simon's steady voice floated from behind.

"I think so."

"Here we go." He launched them and started paddling, his strokes strong and sure.

She joined, attempting to match his paddle movements. They didn't speak for several minutes as they drew the boat away from the shore. The house disappeared from view, as did Wanaka, and other than the occasional zooming boat or squawking bird, it was quiet out there on the water. As the sun dipped lower in the sky, it cast orange and pink shadows along the craggy cliffs lining the lake. Trees waved a quick hello and goodbye as Simon and Angela passed, whispering well wishes as a breeze rustled their branches. Reflections of the Southern Alps, their lacy white tips twinkling, appeared along the rippled face of the lake.

"What do you think?" Simon stopped paddling for a moment.

Angela followed suit, resting her paddle along the ridge of the kayak. "I don't think even you could conjure up adequate words to describe the beauty we're seeing."

"Agreed. I'm not that talented."

"You are talented." In fact, the piece he'd written about Eva and Angela and their quest to run the ultra-marathon for their husbands had nearly brought her to tears—not an easy feat, considering she hadn't cried in so long. "But there's something about this place that moves my spirit. And you're right. It's a different way to see New Zealand. Even though we've been here for two months, I haven't felt quite like this before."

"Look who's waxing poetic now." Simon's teasing tone made her wish she could turn around and see his eyes. Probably better that she couldn't. Surrounded by this much beauty and this much peace . . . yes. Definitely better.

Maybe it was time to return home. "Should we be heading back soon?"

"I'd planned to stop at a beach just a bit farther up the lake. What do you think?"

"I guess so." As long as she could get out and stretch, clear her head. "Will we be able to find our way back since it'll be dark soon?"

"Absolutely. I know this lake well. If you feel nervous, though, we can turn around right now."

"No. I trust you." And she did. If that wasn't evidence of some deeper change in her, nothing was.

They resumed paddling, and Simon pointed them toward a beach tucked away in a small cove surrounded by greenery. As they pulled closer, Simon climbed from the kayak and pushed the boat onto the shore, then helped Angela out.

They were alone on the beach. The sun had fully sunk behind the mountains, and stars popped along the upper reaches of the sky, which was layered with stripes of ever-deepening blues until it turned utterly black at the highest point above them.

Simon unclipped a yellow waterproofed bag from the kayak and snagged a blanket from inside. "I thought we could look at the stars for a bit."

"Great." Great? No, it wasn't. Sitting or lying on a blanket next to Simon was a very bad idea—especially if she was going to be honest about the fact she couldn't have a relationship with him. And he deserved to know.

She followed him to a spot not too far away, where he spread the blanket and sat, strong arms wrapped around his knees, one hand casually gripping the other. After a moment of hesitation, Angela lowered herself next to him. The blanket was smaller than it appeared, so she couldn't sit without their arms touching. Together they rested, watching the lake, listening to the birds warbling.

"If you look up, you can see Sirius." Simon lifted his finger. "It's the brightest star in the sky."

Angela had to crane her neck, leaning closer to him to follow his line of sight. "I see it."

"I don't want to scare you off, but I can't go another day without telling you . . . you're quickly becoming that in my life, Angela. My Sirius. My bright star."

Her eyes squeezed close. *Courage. I need courage to tell Simon the truth.*

"I can't be with you." The words tumbled over themselves, as ungraceful as Angela herself. "But it's not you, it's me. I'm the problem."

Silence.

She opened her eyes and twisted so she could look at Simon. Mistake. His eyebrows knit together, his deep eyes quizzical, mouth flattened, tiny wrinkles at the corners.

Angela hurried on. "I'm just not sure how to be in a new relationship with all of the unresolved feelings I still have about Wes and our marriage. Over the last several weeks, I've been slowly peeling away the layers of my life, and I've become aware that, like most moms, I often sacrifice what I want for my kids. I did that in my marriage too. In fact, before coming here, I hadn't thought about what I want, or what really brings me joy, in forever."

As he listened, Simon's hand found hers. His thumb rubbed circles in her palm, his touch light but oh so powerful.

Angela chewed her lip. "I know that sounds extremely selfish. But I truly do love my children and want them to have the world. And I've realized that if I'm constantly giving to them and nothing is filling *me* up, then what?" She released a breath. "I fear that I'll make the same mistakes with you—with anyone—and simply fall into a life again instead of purposely choosing it."

The breeze blew cold against her face. Angela's gaze found Simon's. He hadn't said a word during her confession. Now, though, she longed to know what he was thinking. "So?"

"Thank you for sharing that with me."

"Thank you for listening."

"Always." His brow furrowed. "You've been honest, and I need to be too. I know you say this isn't about me, but I can't help but think you might feel differently with another man. I never want you to feel trapped in our relationship, as if I'm asking you to be anyone other than yourself. I love the person you are, Angela Jamison— even the parts of you you haven't figured out yet."

He hadn't said the words "I love you," but he might as well have for the way his gaze stole her breath.

"That's not true. It really isn't you. You have been patient and kind and nonjudgmental. A true friend despite my wishy-washy emotions."

"And I will always be your friend, if that's what you need." He looked away from her for the first time since she'd started talking. "I want you to find the thing that fills you up. And I won't stand in your way while you do it."

Her heart screamed at her as she leaned against him. Had she just pushed away something that might bring her joy because of the fear it might be stolen instead?

27

Eva was just plain tired. Tired of the heartache—Valentine's Day had come and gone yesterday without fanfare.

Tired of the constant need for mental pep talks, of the inner questions.

Even tired of running.

But she and Angela were only halfway done with a twenty-two miler through hilly country populated by not much more than trees, rocks, and mosquitoes. Never had she been more grateful for bug spray as she was on this warm and cloudy day.

They'd slogged through their mileage as the dirt trail rose and fell, alternately running and walking through the tree cover—though only doing the latter momentarily to catch their breath or take a water or bathroom break.

In one month they had to do seven times this distance over the course of seven days. No matter how badly her body wanted to, stopping wasn't an option. They needed every second of training they could get.

As if Eva wasn't in enough of a funk on her own, Angela had also been less than chatty since she'd returned from her late-night kayak ride with Simon earlier this week. Seemingly lost in introspection, she'd barely spoken two words to Eva this morning.

All of that gave Eva ample opportunity to think about what

Joanne had said last week: *"My biggest sorrow is more about the things I lost to fear."* Even so, fear was a fierce adversary.

But the thought kept popping up as they ran, growing like the lichen attached to many of the large boulders and tree trunks they passed in the forest. Like a fungus, it clung to her heart, covering it, suffocating it, making it difficult to focus.

She desperately needed a distraction. "Is something going on?"

Angela's head snapped up. "What?"

"You've been quiet all week. And I've noticed you haven't spent any time with Simon lately. Everything okay?"

"Yes, I—" Angela slowed to a walk. "I guess that's not true. Something *is* going on, but I'm not sure talking about it is going to solve anything, considering I don't know how I feel about . . . it."

Sometimes her sister-in-law was her own worst enemy. "I find that verbally processing helps me."

In her case, Eva didn't need to verbally process. She knew what she should do about Marc. Even what she wanted to do. But she couldn't bring herself to actually do it. At this point it'd been over two weeks since they'd spoken about the incident at the cliff, and disturbing the normalcy they'd recultivated wasn't a palatable option—especially when she didn't know what Marc was thinking. He might have decided that pursuing someone with so much baggage wasn't worth it.

"It's just my relationship with Simon. I'm not sure if I've shot myself in the foot."

"I can so relate to that." Eva pulled a few protein bars from her backpack and tossed one to Angela. "Marc basically told me he wanted to date, and I couldn't give him a good reason not to."

"I've seen how you look at him. You obviously want to." Months ago Angela's tone might have seemed caustic, unfeeling. But Eva's sister-in-law was changing—or maybe it was Eva's perception of her that had shifted.

"You're right. I do. But I'm scared. Seems like you feel the same way about Simon." Angela didn't contradict her. Eva unwrapped her bar and took a bite. "Both of us have these amazing guys who want us despite all the pain we carry. Why do we push them away?"

Angela polished off her own bar and stuck the foil in her pocket. "Lots of reasons. I just don't know if any of them are right."

A breeze rustled the wrapper in Eva's hands before she finished eating and stuffed it away.

They started running again, both breathing steadily and focusing on the course ahead.

"Speaking of pushing people away . . . I know I've done that to you in the past, Eva. I'm really sorry about that."

Eva couldn't help the way her jaw dropped, but she shut it quickly so as not to get a mouthful of bugs as they jogged down the course. "Um, it's okay."

"No, it's not. I let my jealousy of you get in the way of our relationship."

Angela, jealous of *her*? "What do you mean?"

The leaves of the trees above stirred, as if leaning in to listen.

Her sister-in-law turned her head to acknowledge Eva. "I've always wished I had the freedom you do. I love my kids, but sometimes I wonder . . . how would life be if I could do what I wanted, without the pressure of others depending on me?"

Eva might have that freedom, but she didn't know what in the world to do with it. "And all this time I've wondered what life would have been like if Brent hadn't gotten so caught up in growing his business and having his adventures. He thought we had all the time in the world to start a family . . . and then we didn't."

Wait.

Was she actually . . . upset? With Brent?

No. They'd had a wonderful marriage, and he'd been a wonderful husband. Her Prince Charming, really.

Emotions spun through Eva, confusing her heart, bruising her mind. The only thing left to do was physically work out the pain. To run. Hard.

"Eva, hold on!"

But she couldn't slow down. Had to elude—

The upper half of Eva's body went flying, then snapped back toward the ground. At the same time, her elbow slammed into dirt and twigs, and her neck cracked to the side.

"Eva!" Angela crouched next to her. "Are you okay?"

It took a moment for her to feel the pain in her arm and hip, but when she did, a groan eked out. "I think so. What happened?" Now she knew why cartoon characters always had those stars whirling around their heads after a fall. The world tilted for a moment before it righted.

"You tripped over a large root sticking out of the ground."

"That wasn't too smart of me. I was a bit distracted, I guess."

"That's an understatement. Are you okay?"

"Physically? Yeah, I think so." Some blood welled from a scrape on her elbow. That would require a bandage but wasn't too bad. "Emotionally? Not sure on that front."

Then she stood—and yelled. Sinking back down, she clutched her right ankle.

Angela squatted again. "You're not okay."

"I must have twisted my ankle." This could not be happening— not a month before the biggest race, the biggest quest, of her life. "I'm sure I'll be fine." Because she had to be.

"Let me take a look. It might be broken."

"Do you know how to tell?"

Angela rolled up Eva's pant leg, her touch surprisingly gentle. The ankle was already starting to swell. "I was premed in college.

That was a long time ago, but I took a sports medicine class as an elective. I'd intended to work as a trainer on one of the university's teams my junior year."

Angela never really talked about that time in her life. All Eva knew was she and Wes decided to get married, she quit school, and they had Kylee soon after. She flinched as Angela's probing hit a tender spot.

"Does it hurt there?" Her sister-in-law pointed to the soft part of Eva's ankle.

"Yes."

"Any tingling or numbness?"

Eva considered the question. "No, I don't think so. Just pain when I try to move it or when you touch it."

Angela prodded the spot over Eva's anklebone. "How about here?"

"Not really."

Her sister-in-law sat back on her haunches. "Good. I don't think it's broken."

"That's a relief."

However, Angela's eyes did not convey the same sentiment. "It's probably a sprain. And if you tore a ligament, it could take six weeks to heal."

"But the race is in a month."

"I know."

No, no, no. She'd come too far—they'd come too far—not to be able to race now. "I'm sure it'll be fine tomorrow."

"I think you need to get a professional's opinion before you go making any plans."

But plans were already made. They couldn't change now. Too much was at stake.

"Knock, knock." Angela peeked into Eva's room, where her sister-in-law sat with pillows piled all around her, ankle wrapped with a bandage and elevated. She held up an ice pack. "Sherry asked me to deliver this."

"Thanks. Come on in." Eva tossed aside the fitness magazine she'd been reading. "Didn't realize it was time to ice it again."

Striding forward, Angela placed the pack on Eva's ankle. The one bright spot in all of this was that Angela's assessment had been correct—it was just a sprain, and a minor one at that. The doctor at the urgent care yesterday hadn't even recommended X-rays.

"How are you feeling?" Angela settled into a wooden rocking chair next to Eva's bed. Outside, the sun was about midway through its ascent into the sky, and it promised to be another beautiful day—one Eva would probably miss. Getting her upstairs last night had been difficult, but she'd been determined to sleep in her own bed, and until they secured some crutches for her, she wasn't going back down anytime soon.

"I've been better." Eva readjusted, wincing as the ice pack slid to the side.

"Here." Hopping up, Angela replaced the pack, securing it more firmly this time. She took her seat again. "Did you sleep well?"

"Not really." The darkened skin under Eva's eyes testified to the truth in her statement. "It was nice of the kids to bring me those." She pointed to the vase of yellow flowers on her side table, the only splash of color in the black, white, and gray room.

"Joanne helped Kylee pick them out."

"I figured." Eva turned to study the flowers. The vase held several stalks, each playing host to individual flowers, their petals open and alert, yet soft.

"What kind of flowers are those? I don't think I've ever seen them before."

"They're called gladioli, also known as the sword lily." Eva fixed her gaze on Angela, something determined in her eyes. "Did you know that every flower symbolizes something? The gladiolus denotes faithfulness. Honor. Strength of character. Remembrance."

She stumbled over the last word, as if trying not to cry.

"Joanne knows how much this race means to me. And I think by selecting these flowers, she's encouraging me to stay the course."

Who knew a small flower represented so much?

Eva shrugged. "Or maybe I'm reading too much into it. Either way, that's exactly what I'm going to do."

That was twice in the span of twenty-four hours that Eva had surprised her. The first time was yesterday. As Angela had helped her hop back to the house—teeth gritted, tears held at bay—she couldn't help but recognize a quality she'd never noticed in her sister-in-law before: tenacity. Eva had always struck her as wishy-washy, someone whose artistic spirit led her to jump from one thing to the next, never really thinking about the consequences, always living in the moment.

But the grit she'd shown while in pain, facing a potentially devastating setback head-on—there was something inspiring in it.

Still. "Didn't the doctor say you needed to stay off of it for a while? The race is in four weeks and if you can't train . . ."

"Yeah, but he also said sprains are unpredictable. The most minor of them don't take nearly as long to heal. That's what I'm choosing to hold on to."

Optimism had its place, but perhaps this wasn't it. "You could injure yourself worse if you try to run on it before it's totally healed. What did Marc say?"

"I haven't told him. Please don't mention it yet."

"Eva . . ." Angela tried—and failed—to keep her "mom tone" from emerging. "He's our teammate. We should be honest with him."

Being honest with Eva yesterday had felt better than Angela

had anticipated. Maybe the truth really did set you free. Except when it came to her talk with Simon nearly a week ago. Since her bluntness then, neither of them had called the other or scheduled a time to get together. But Angela couldn't in good conscience ask him to hang out, knowing how he felt about her and that there was no future between them. That would be cruel.

"I'll tell him. But I don't want him to try to talk me out of the race." Eva pounded a fist into the soft bed comforter. "I'm not giving up."

"But maybe giving up is exactly what we should do, Eva. There have been so many things against us, and while it's been an amazing experience to be here, perhaps running the race wasn't the reason we really came. Besides, we can't complete the ultra-marathon if your ankle hasn't healed."

Eva pulled her braid over her shoulder and stroked the end piece, a contemplative look on her face. "Perseverance, secret of all triumphs." The words were almost a whisper, a breath of a kiss as if from a ghost.

A shiver coursed through Angela. "What did you say?"

"It's just something Brent used to say. When it looked like his and Marc's business might go bankrupt. When he got the flu just before a huge meeting with an investor. When an impending storm threatened our honeymoon plans and we had to scramble for a plan B. I'm not sure where he first heard it—"

"It's a Victor Hugo quote. Wes used to say it too." It had been one of his favorite encouragements, especially in the early days of their marriage and parenthood. How had Angela forgotten?

After all the hard work she'd put in, why was Angela so willing to abandon ship—especially if Eva was still up for it? Sure, Angela had done the training, although sometimes begrudgingly. But had she ever really dug in her heels and told herself she would finish the race, no matter what?

That she would find a way to forgive Wes, no matter what?

That she would discover how not to just survive but to find true joy . . . no matter what?

Angela's gaze rested on the yellow flowers on Eva's bedside table, and she imagined herself as strong and honorable.

Faithful to her family.

To love.

To herself.

Angela inhaled softly. "If you're sure you can do this, then I'm with you." She reached across the bed and snatched Eva's hand. Her sister-in-law's eyes widened. "One hundred percent, I'm with you."

28

Even though she was in New Zealand in large part to train, having time away with her children was by far the greatest perk of this trip.

And Angela hadn't seen them this excited in a long time.

"Please follow us and we'll finish our tour at the Green Dragon, where you'll receive a complimentary Hobbit Southfarthing beverage." Their tour guide, Chrissy, led a group of twenty-five down the last leg of the Hobbiton Movie Set Tour—a surprise for Zach's birthday. The tour alone cost a decent amount, not to mention flights for Angela and all three kids to Auckland, but Eva had insisted on paying, and Angela couldn't refuse since it meant Zach got to visit the set of his favorite books turned movies.

It was just too bad Eva and Sherry couldn't join in the fun, but her sister-in-law's main priority was getting her ankle healed as quickly as possible. And there was no way their mother-in-law was going to leave her alone at the house to fend for herself.

"Mom, can you believe this?" Zach whispered for the thousandth time. His jaw had remained permanently locked in a position of awe as he darted from one side of the path to another among all the little hobbit holes. They were built into rolling hills, each one with grass for a roof and a squat, round wooden door. The doors displayed an assortment of earthy colors, from greens to reds, browns, yellows, and a few pops of a robin's egg blue. Stone chimneys only slightly taller than Angela piped out faint wisps of smoke. Most of the plants in the vicinity appeared to be short, sprawling greenery.

As the tour group slowly made its way through the rest of the quaint village, Angela gathered all the kids for a quick snapshot in front of one of the homes.

Kylee motioned to her. "Mom, you get in this one too."

Yes. Nowhere she'd rather be. Imagine if she'd said no to Eva's crazy scheme to come to New Zealand. Where would they all be today instead? Certainly not in a place that resonated with the glory of creation all around them, the brilliant sun warming her hair, the greens so vibrant they almost looked fake, the magic of newness clustered tight around them.

The only thing that could have made today better was if Simon and his kids were here.

Stop it, Angela.

But she couldn't help missing him, given she hadn't seen the Kings at all in the last few weeks. That was Angela's fault. She'd let Sherry take the kids over to hang out with Benjamin and Ella, but she hadn't joined them.

When she wasn't working with the kids on their schoolwork, she'd busied herself with preparing for the ultra-marathon—training sometimes twice a day, getting even more familiar with the general area where they assumed the race would be held, and contemplating the terrain. The preparation helped her feel slightly more in control of a situation that still felt so far beyond her abilities. No matter how hard they trained, this race would require everything she had and then some.

At least it provided a distraction from missing Simon.

Angela asked a woman nearby if she'd be willing to take a photo. When the woman agreed, Angela handed over her camera and hustled to join her children. She threw her arms around them, huddling her little chicks close. Lilly snuggled against her leg, Zach groaned good-naturedly, and Kylee squeezed her back. When the photos were snapped, it was almost difficult to let go.

Because it was only three weeks until the ultra-marathon. Which meant it was only about four and a half weeks until they returned to New York. To the cold weather. To forty-plus-hour weeks, if she resumed a similar schedule as before. To far less time spent with her children.

Lilly pointed to a pasture in the distance where several fluffs of white dotted the landscape. "Can we cuddle the sheep? Please, Mommy, please? The lady said we could."

"After the tour ends, all right, baby? Chrissy said we could even help bottle-feed the baby lambs. Would you like that?"

Her youngest daughter's face lit brighter than it did on Christmas morning—quite a feat. "Yes!"

She and Zach sped off after the tour guides, toward the only building in the vicinity that wasn't built into a hillside. On top sat a thatched roof and five or six chimney stacks. The many round windows and doorways, in addition to the pub's location next to a pond, made it look like something out of a storybook, a place where beefy men with swords might gather to drink from large wooden mugs of frothy beer and make merry.

"Thanks for bringing us here, Mom." Kylee walked the compacted dirt path next to Angela. "The kids are having a blast."

"You have Aunt Eva to thank for all of it." Angela considered her daughter: the way she seemed to walk more upright lately, her makeup simpler, her hair in fewer ponytails and more often down and curled around her shoulders. She'd called her younger siblings "kids"—and even though Angela would have put her oldest into that category a few months ago, she couldn't say the same now. "And how about you?"

Her daughter shrugged. "I mean, I'm not all crazy about this stuff like Zach is, but it's pretty cool." She peeked up at Angela. "And it's nice to have some family time away from everything else."

"I know I've spent a lot of time training lately." While the kids' schoolwork hadn't necessarily suffered because of the time she spent getting ready for the ultra-marathon—Sherry had helped fill in the gaps—today was one of the first times they'd done a trip purely for pleasure in . . . well, a long time. "I'm sorry for that."

"You don't have to be sorry. I already told you I think it's cool you're running this race for Dad."

Some members of their tour group wanted to stop for a photo op, so everyone paused to linger. Kylee leaned against a little picket fence in front of one of the hobbit homes.

Angela eyed Zach and Lilly, who hopped up and down stone steps a few yards away. Then she swung her gaze back to Kylee. A bush next to her exploded with a rainbow of flowers—violets, reds, yellows, indigos.

A rainbow . . . a promise.

And Angela had promised to walk the path toward healing with her daughter. Which meant speaking the truth. All of it. "I'm not sure I *am* doing it for him."

"What do you mean?"

"Initially I came for you guys. Because I knew you needed me to work toward healing. I couldn't seem to get out of the rut I'd fallen into after your dad died. And I was desperate enough to try anything."

"For what it's worth, it seems to be working."

"Yes." But what would happen when they went home? That was the question always burning in the back of her mind. How did she take what she'd learned—what she was still learning—and apply it to her life back home, where distractions and responsibilities would threaten to take over?

The group started moving again, and so did Kylee and Angela.

They passed a tree that was larger than the other plants nearby. It seemed like the kind with roots that ran deep: strong, its trunk branching off into hundreds of limbs, each one stretching toward the sky.

"Mom, what's life going to be like when we leave here?"

It was as if her daughter could read her mind. "I'll have to go back to work. Beyond that, I'm not sure."

"Are you going to work for Aunt Eva and Marc?"

"Maybe." When her sister-in-law had originally made the offer, Angela had written it off as typical Eva—not thinking ahead, not seriously considering the consequences beforehand. But perhaps she'd been wrong.

Whatever the case, it wasn't as if she'd be able to get a job doing something she really loved. Still, Simon's praise about providing for the kids and his perspective on finding a gift in the unexpected had penetrated her heart as she'd thought about his words over the last several weeks. There was something to be said for living a normal life, working a normal job, and providing for her family. Not every person had to live a huge dream to find contentment.

Whatever she ended up doing, she just wanted to go in with eyes open. With purpose.

"Didn't you want to be a doctor a long time ago? Maybe you should go back to school."

Her daughter remembered that? "I've considered it, but that would mean more time away from you guys. I want to be the best mom I can."

I also don't know if I want it anymore.

Whoa, what? Angela's first instinct was to erase the blasphemy from her mind—but instead, she mulled it over.

Why did the idea of being a doctor no longer seem like an unrealized pipe dream . . . and instead was more something she wouldn't want to spend time doing?

Then she recognized a knowing. A part of herself she hadn't listened to in a long time.

The other day when Eva had injured her ankle and Angela had assessed it, there had been no thrill in it. She was simply applying knowledge, just like she'd done every day in her office job.

However noble and worthy a pursuit, there was no added joy in the thought of becoming a physician.

Huh.

Kylee stopped walking and studied Angela. Her eyes softened. "We all know that you love us, okay? And that you'd do anything for us if we needed you to. But I think you can still be the best mom if you did something for yourself. Because, really, you following your dreams is only going to make us want to follow ours."

Before Angela could throw her arms around her daughter, Kylee skipped ahead into the Green Dragon Inn. Angela quickly followed, and they all ordered mugs of soda at a log table overlooking the pond.

Outside the window, the broad tree she'd seen earlier stood firm despite a sudden gust of wind—bending, but not breaking.

29

Today was going to either change everything—or be very, very awkward.

Maybe both.

Eva sat in a hard plastic chair just outside the airport coffee bar, squinting at the Arrivals screen. She should have checked the status of Marc's flight before heading over, but who knew that it would be delayed three times in the span of an hour? At long last, the screen indicated his flight had arrived. Now she just had to wait for him to emerge from the terminal and walk her way.

She stilled her bouncing knee and drained the rest of her latte. Maybe she should go back for a second hit. Liquid courage sounded good about now.

Because in the last two and a half weeks, life had delivered a swift kick of perspective. And today she was going to act on it. Eva only hoped it was the right decision, and that she wasn't too late.

Overhead, a pleasant-sounding Kiwi woman announced the boarding of a flight to Auckland, where Angela and the kids had been a few weekends ago. The house had been so quiet with them away, a reminder of what her life would be like when she returned to New York.

A text pinged on her phone, and she fumbled it in her attempt to pick it up quickly.

From Marc. Finally landed. Be off in a few.

Short and to the point—businesslike, just like all the other texts and conversations they'd had in the two months since he'd left and Eva had basically run scared. He'd only asked where they stood that one time on the phone, and she hadn't had the courage to bring it up again.

Because if she had to be honest with him, she'd have to tell him the intensity of her emotions, which only grew stronger every day.

But enough was enough. In eight days they were embarking on a journey that was bigger than all of them, and Eva would not allow romantic tension or drama to mar that experience.

I'm here outside the coffee bar.

Once she hit Send, Eva put down her phone and fiddled with the bundle sticking out of her purse. Had it been a horrible idea? She'd had to exhaust Joanne's contacts to find someone nearby with an early crop in order to get ahold of this particular flower—but it had to be the king protea. The cellophane encasing the single flower crinkled as she rubbed it between her fingers, admiring the white bloom. Once fully open, the triangular petals would burst from the center like a sun, creating a five- to ten-inch flower head that was as majestic as it was beautiful.

This was silly. What man wanted a woman to give him flowers?

"Hey, Eva."

Her head snapped up and she stood abruptly, knocking her purse to the navy-blue carpet at her feet. "Oh. Hi." The sudden movement sent a tiny twinge through her ankle, but thanks to kinesiology tape and as much rest as she could manage when training for an ultra-marathon, the pain had lessened considerably.

Marc looked rumpled and exhausted, though a full day of in-ternational travel would do that to anyone. But it was more than that.

The smile he gave her didn't show in his hazel eyes. Those seemed lax around the edges, as if weighed down by great sadness. He'd shaved his beard, but the five o'clock shadow gave him a slightly rugged appearance.

One bag resting on his shoulder and one roller suitcase at his feet, he advanced, then looked as if he might back up again. He stuck his hands in his jean pockets.

"How's your ankle?"

"Doing much better, thanks." She'd told him about her sprain a few days after the injury occurred, once she was certain she'd be okay. "I'm still grateful the sprain was so minor."

"Me too. Is everyone else at the house?" His gaze scanned the surrounding area, as if he'd rather be anywhere but here.

Only one way to tell how badly she'd botched things. Eva squatted, picking up her purse—and the flower. Rising, she took a deep breath. "Yeah. I wanted . . . well, a moment alone with you to . . ." Ugh, why was this so difficult?

Eva had memorized a whole speech—a laughable notion for her—but it flew out of her brain now. "I got this for you." She shoved the bloom at him.

"Um . . . thank you?"

Eva twisted her hands together. "It's a king protea. It has a lot of different meanings. Like daring. Transformation. Change." She swallowed. "And courage."

When he stepped close, she caught a hint of the pretzels he must have eaten on the plane, combined with the spicy scent that was all his. How did the man manage to smell so good after twenty-four hours in and out of airports?

He tilted his head, gripping the flower to his chest. "Okay."

The word wasn't dismissive—in fact, just the opposite. He'd invited her to finish explaining.

Eva closed the final gap between them. She lifted a trembling finger and touched the flower, whose petals had only recently separated from a tight bulb—anticipating. Preparing to bloom. "The others were already fully open, ready to be displayed and admired. But I felt like this one was a better representation of us." Her hand moved to his arm, and his eyes followed her actions, then swung back to her face. "Marc, I know I've pulled away. I'm sorry. I imagine that's been confusing to you."

"I figured I'd pushed you too hard. Or misinterpreted what you were feeling."

"You didn't." Hopefully the squeeze on his arm reassured him. "What I feel for you makes me nervous. And it makes me feel guilty, if I'm honest. Because I like you, Marc." Her gaze drifted back to the floor. "And I understand if it's too late to say that to you now, but . . ."

"Eva, look at me."

She did—and whew. How handsome he was.

"What I feel for you makes me feel the same way, you know. Brent was my best friend. I'd never try to replace him in your life, and yet, what if that's what he'd think I was doing? I mean, would he bless the thought of us together—or would he punch me in the throat?"

"First of all, I know you're not trying to replace him. He'd know that too. And second, Brent was never violent a day in his life."

"A man can do crazy things when he loves a woman like you, Eva Jamison."

Okay then. She swallowed. Hard. "Well, if you don't want to give this a shot after what I've put you through, I totally get it. But if you're open to exploring what this could be . . . then I am too."

"You don't have to tell me twice." Marc dropped the bag from his shoulder and set the flower on top of his luggage. "I'm all in. But how about we're both totally honest from here on out? No more pulling away, no more pretending. Just open communication about a situation neither of us saw coming, and that, if we admit it, is a little weird."

A light chuckle rose from her throat. "Deal."

"Good." He tenderly cupped her cheeks between his hands and brushed his thumb over her lower lip. "If it's okay with you, I'd really like nothing more than to kiss you right now."

Courage, Eva. Courage.

"It's more than okay with me."

And then his lips met hers in a gentle whisper that quickly grew into a shout.

30

In less than twenty-four hours, what had started as a dream more than six months ago would become reality.

Eva stepped out of the hotel elevator with Angela and Sherry into a lobby bustling with people from all walks of life. A mix of Spanish, German, English, Chinese, and other languages she didn't recognize swirled around her as the three women crossed the lobby. The energy buzzing in the air created a palpable presence.

They exited a side door of the rustic hotel, which was situated in a town near Wanaka. Kylee had volunteered to stay with the younger kids, who were asleep in their room, and Marc was finishing up some last-minute work on his computer. Sherry had suggested a walk to calm the women's last-minute nerves. Immediately following tomorrow's compulsory briefing and lunch, competitors would be bused to Camp 1, so this was Eva and Angela's last chance to decompress.

Emerging into the night, they followed a curving path through outdoor seating, past a hotel restaurant playing music and alongside one of the hotel's pools. Goose bumps attacked Eva's arms despite her thin jacket.

"You've both been rather quiet all evening. How are you feeling?" As Sherry strolled between them, she pulled her sweater tight across her middle.

What a question. Eva's lips twitched. "There are highs and lows for me. Incredible excitement mixed with tension. The question of whether we can do this. Whether my ankle will hold. Whether my mind or my body will want to give up first. Whether we'll let down everyone who pledged money to the heart center by not finishing."

And then there was the question of what happened after this was all over.

"You've put so much pressure on yourself, my dear. You both have." Sherry pointed to a short grassy hill that overlooked yet another gorgeous New Zealand lake. "How about we sit and talk for a bit?"

No one protested, so all three lowered themselves onto the grassy embankment.

"And how are you doing, Angela?"

At Sherry's question, Angela crossed her legs and picked at a blade of grass, pulling and twirling it in her fingers. "The nerves aren't exactly getting to me. But it's all becoming more real."

Angela had really upped her game in the last few weeks, training harder and longer than she had before. Did any of that have to do with Simon? Unlike Eva and Marc, Simon and Angela hadn't seemed to reconcile.

Eva ran her own fingers through the grass. "Yeah, it's one thing to think about it, even prepare for it, but to be on the cusp of it . . ."

As soon as her sister-in-law tossed one blade aside, she reached for another. "It reminds me of running in high school. There's this moment right before the horn sounds, when you're crouched in anticipation. Your muscles quiver; your breathing ratchets up a bit; your heart rate increases. But then it all gets oddly calm. That's how I feel right now."

"I sense that about you." Sherry reached for both of their hands. "You've both come such a long way, and I am proud of you—as proud as if you were my own flesh and blood." An uncharacteristic sniffle melded with a cough.

A lump formed in Eva's throat. "Whenever people talk about mothers-in-law being annoying or whatever, I feel extra grateful that I got you."

"Same here." Angela's soft answer filled the space between them.

"In many ways I feel like Naomi with two Ruths. Two women I am blessed and honored to call my own. My sons chose well."

Ugh, what was Sherry doing to her? Eva used her available hand to bat away the free-falling tears.

An owl hooted in the distance.

"Angela, I am proud of the way you have faced your grief head-on. I know from experience how difficult it is to be honest with ourselves after we've lost the man we love—especially when that love wasn't perfect. When he wasn't perfect. When we weren't perfect." Sherry's voice trembled, but she kept going, strong, bold in her praise. "And, Eva, you are coming into your own. Seeing you work at the flower shop has been such a joy for me. The world needs to see beauty, and you have so much inside of you bursting to get out."

Did this woman know the life she spoke? Eva had thought her days of floral design—and of actually enjoying it—were behind her, but something about this whole journey had reawakened that desire in her. And while she didn't understand it, maybe she didn't have to. Maybe it was enough to be thankful that there could be life beyond Brent, even if she couldn't quite see what that looked like right now.

And even though it hurt like nothing she'd ever felt to leave him in the past.

"Thank you, Sherry."

Clouds shifted in the dark sky, and moonlight spilled from above, shining a spotlight on the lake.

Angela shifted. "Yes, thank you. You've . . . Well, I don't remember much about my own mother. And you . . ." She paused, then cleared her throat. "You've been the best mom I could imagine."

"You girls have given me a new lease on life. Losing my husband and my sons . . . I wouldn't have made it through without you."

How was it possible to feel so much love and hope in the midst of tragedy?

Sherry released their hands, leaving a permanent imprint on Eva's fingers. "One more thing and I promise I'll let you two get some rest. Not that you need my blessing, but I wanted you to know that I heartily approve of the young men who are in your lives. I don't presume to know where things are with either one of you, but I feel it needs to be said. New love is difficult for a number of reasons, but there's nothing but beauty in it."

Did her mother-in-law know the doubt Eva sometimes still carried? "Thank you, Sherry. I definitely struggle with feeling like I'm betraying Brent by dating Marc."

"Not at all. Like I've told you before, my boy would want nothing but joy for you." Sherry's gaze swung to Angela. "And you, Angela."

At this, Angela grabbed for another hunk of grass. "I'm thankful to you for saying that, but I've decided I need to work through some things before I can see dating anyone. Maybe falling in love again just isn't in the cards for me. I don't need the distraction anyway." Was she trying to convince herself or Sherry and Eva?

"I'm sorry to hear that," Sherry said.

"Yeah, you and Simon seemed really great together." Would Eva's next question cause Angela to clam up? But who else in her life would ask the question if her sister-in-law didn't? "Are you sure it's not just your fear talking?"

Angela's set jaw flinched. "I . . . I suppose that could be part of the equation. Wes and I had our issues, and that makes me cautious about getting into another relationship. I didn't fully support his adventures, and things didn't end on a very positive note."

"Why didn't you support them?" Eva longed to understand, especially because Brent and his adventures had been so dear to her.

"They changed Wes."

"You never went along for any of them, did you?" She tried to keep her tone light, non-accusatory.

"He asked me to. Even tried to get me to go skydiving on our anniversary three years ago. But I always found a reason not to. Maybe I would have understood him better if I had. That's partly why I'm here, really. To try to understand. I'm still figuring it all out. But I'm trying. And I guess that's progress, right?"

"Most definitely, my dear." As always, Sherry's voice smoothed over the rough edges. "Progress is not measured by feet and inches, but by how much closer we come to understanding ourselves. And God."

Eva tugged off her shoes and buried her toes in the grass. The sudden cold made her feel more alive. "Agreed." And she did— although the part about God pricked her heart. Had she ever really tried to get close to the Divine? Not in a metaphysical sense, but the kind of oneness Sherry seemed to experience?

"Girls, if grief has taught me anything, it's that we don't know what's around the corner. It could be a dream come true. It could be heartache. And that's a scary place to be. But when you're worried about the future, just take the next step. Just do the next thing. And trust that God has something wonderful planned, even if our definition of wonderful might not be the same as his."

Instead of brushing off Sherry's beliefs as something Eva could never have, she settled into the idea of having faith in something bigger than herself. Bigger than Brent. Bigger than this race.

She'd have to think on it more.

Eva stared up at the sky as long white clouds slid over the moonlight once more. "Those are the perfect words to take into the race."

What came after this was anyone's guess. But for now, they'd just keep putting one foot in front of the other.

⌒

"Thank you for joining us this morning." A slight woman with a shock of red hair stood at the front of the hotel's ballroom, where all two hundred of the ultra-marathon participants had crammed into rows of chairs. Volunteers with bright orange T-shirts and name badges on lanyards lined the walls. The woman's Irish accent carried via microphone throughout the large room. "I'm Molly Purcell with Ultimate Race Adventures. Welcome to beautiful New Zealand."

The room burst into applause. From the corner of her eye, Angela glanced at Eva and Marc, who sat next to her. Their hands were casually entwined, and they smiled at each other.

Good for Eva. She deserved to be happy again.

And what about you?

No. She wouldn't think about Simon. Again. What was wrong with her? Five weeks of not speaking to him had nearly undone her, so she'd pressed into training with a new vigor and resolve.

Because she wasn't here for love. She'd come to regain control of her life, to reconnect with her kids, to process her emotions over Wes's death. And slowly that was happening. She couldn't allow herself to get off track.

"This morning we are going to review everything you need to know about the race. You should have received your bib and final instruction booklet upon check-in." Molly held up a packet. "This booklet contains everything from your race map to specific instructions for nightly camp check-ins and what to do in case of medical emergencies. It's basically your bible for the week. If you open to page three, you'll see the itinerary."

The soft flutter of paper filled the room.

"I know that most—if not all—of you have this memorized, but I'm required to go over it anyway, so bear with me. As you're aware, the seven-day race is broken into six stages, the first four of which consist of forty kilometers, or twenty-five miles, each. Stage 5 is known as the Long March and is just under eighty kilometers, or fifty miles, in total. This stage is formatted similar to the others, with checkpoints every ten kilometers, or six miles. You may stop and rest for as long as you like at these checkpoints, but you also may race throughout the night. Then Stage 6 is blessedly short, at only ten kilometers. And believe me, you're going to be incredibly happy that's the case."

Laughter echoed in the room.

Angela's fingers left sweaty smudges on the booklet's shiny pages as she stared at the numbers and listened to Molly drone on for what seemed like hours about other details, like the fact they'd have from 7:30 a.m. to 7:30 p.m. to complete each day's stage or face disqualification. A decent chunk of time was also spent discussing the risks and hazards of running in the New Zealand wilderness, and what to do in different types of emergencies. She forced her brain to spend its energy absorbing the minutiae instead of zeroing in on all the ways they could fail.

The eerie calm she'd felt the night before quickly began to fade.

"Each checkpoint will have water, though you will need to carry your own as well, and the overnight camps will have hot water available to make your meals."

Thank goodness Marc had been on hand to help them pack their final rucksacks. While Angela and Eva had done their best to track down all the necessary equipment, Marc was the one with camping and survivalist experience. He even knew which dried meals tasted best and would be most filling, and what would take up the least amount of space in their heavy backpacks.

Getting everything to fit had been a feat in itself, considering the backpacks contained a sleeping bag, extra clothing, sunscreen, toilet paper, eating utensils, a Swiss army knife, and a few other mandatory items, not to mention optional but nice-to-have items like a towel, camera, thermal underwear, and compression socks. Thankfully, they didn't have to pack tents, as those would be provided, assigned, and set up by race volunteers.

"Now I'd like to turn it over to our media coordinator, Fatima Anwar."

A pretty woman wearing a hijab stepped forward and took the offered microphone. "Thanks, Molly. And welcome to you all." Her British accent was upbeat. "I wanted to quickly review our media coverage of the event, and then we'll break for lunch. After that, you'll be bused out to the first campsite, where you can spend the afternoon and evening getting to know one another and preparing for the first leg of the race."

Was it nearly noon already? Angela checked the black sports watch she'd purchased for the race. Yes, many hours had already flown by since they'd gotten up, eaten breakfast, and checked out of the hotel. Their overnight suitcases would be transferred to a hotel in Wanaka for concluding ceremonies, and they'd brought their rucksacks with them to this meeting. In fact, volunteers were likely checking the bags at this very moment, ensuring participants had every item on the mandatory list and nothing forbidden that would offer a hidden advantage over other competitors.

Not many hours lay between them and the start of the race.

Angela's booklet creased in her strong and sudden grip.

Eva leaned over. "You okay?"

"I'm fine," Angela whispered. "Just ready to get this show on the road."

Fatima continued. "We will be livestreaming the event, posting hourly updates about race leaders and conditions, et cetera, on our website. Of course, we will also be uploading photos and videos of the event across social media platforms. Lastly . . ." The woman paused, scanning the room as if making sure competitors were still paying attention. "We will have a few reporters from various media outlets at the overnight checkpoints. They might ask you for a quote or a photo. If you'd rather not participate, that is completely fine. Just let them know and they'll move on to another victim."

Everyone chuckled.

"The volunteers will all be wearing orange shirts, and our media folks are in green."

Angela's eyes trailed along the wall, seeing pops of green here and there—and suddenly her mouth went dry.

Staring right at her, from a spot not too far away along the wall, stood Simon. The lime green of his shirt left no question as to why he was here. But why hadn't he told her?

A hot buzzing filled her ears, and Angela averted her eyes.

"All right, that's all I have for you. I believe I'm supposed to dismiss you for lunch, which is provided just next door. We will gather back here at one o'clock to begin the busing process. Thank you."

People rose all around Angela, some rushing for the door to be first in line for the food, but she remained firmly planted in her seat. It was very warm in here, even with the dissipating bodies. She fanned herself with the booklet.

Next to her, Eva and Marc stood.

Marc stretched. "Nothing makes me want to get this race started more than having to sit all morning."

Eva poked him in the arm. "Oh, come on. You're used to business meetings." She turned to Angela. "You ready for lunch?"

"You guys go ahead. I've got to hit the restroom first."

"We'll save you a seat."

Angela put her head into her hands, waiting for the noise in the room to grow quieter. Eventually it did. Gathering her courage, she peeked up again. Most everyone had gone, but one green-shirted man still leaned against the wall, arms crossed over his chest, head tilted, studying her.

She blew out a breath. "Hi." The word seemed to resound in the high-ceilinged room.

Simon pushed off the wall with his foot and walked toward her. He lowered himself into the seat next to her, careful to turn so their shoulders didn't touch. "Hi."

"So, you're here." She tried to inject enthusiasm into her voice, but it came out all wrong. Like an accusation. But he didn't have anything to be sorry for. It was all her.

Just like with Wes. It was all your fault then too.

Wait, what? That voice inside . . . it knew something she didn't. Or rather, something she hadn't acknowledged. But what?

Angela groaned.

"Yeah, I'm here." Simon's voice was soft. Softer than she deserved. "I've known for a few weeks that Ultimate Race Adventures wanted me to do an in-depth feature on the actual race—especially your and Eva's experience."

Wonderful. In-depth. That meant he'd have to interview them.

She'd been able to resist him by removing herself from the equation. But being with him every night, the thing her rebellious heart wanted more than anything at this moment . . . how could she remain aloof then? "I wish you'd told me." So she could have prepared—if that was even possible.

"I wasn't sure how. Or when."

She caught his shrug. His frown. "Because we stopped talking."

"Pretty much, yeah."

"I thought about calling or texting so many times, but I didn't want to hurt you any more than I feared I already had."

"I understand. And I would have said no to avoid making you uncomfortable by coming here, but this is my job and the offer was too good to pass up." He lifted his hand as if to place it on her shoulder, hesitated, then dropped it back into his lap. "But I don't want you to worry. I'll remain strictly professional the whole time."

"I know you will." *But will I be able to do the same?*

31

Here they were, once more, at the starting line of a race.

But this wasn't just any race. This was *the* race. The one that would hopefully give her the final peace she needed to move forward and into a new life. So why did Eva feel almost numb at the thought?

She stood between Marc and Angela, surrounded by other competitors at the starting line, where a twenty-foot red inflatable stretched in an arc across the path. Sherry and the kids—along with hundreds of onlookers—held encouraging signs on the other side of the rope dividing the course from the nonparticipants. Lilly danced to the rock music pumping from the speakers. Kylee shot Angela a grin and mouthed something to her. Zach waved his fists up and down, thumbs pressed to the sky. Seeing Brent's family there sent a pang through Eva, one she'd not felt so acutely for several weeks now.

But she wasn't a sobbing mess. How . . . unexpected.

The straps of Eva's rucksack settled snug against her shoulders, a water bottle attached to each one. Collapsible hiking poles were secured inside the top of her backpack, ready to be used when the trek got hilly. She'd made the overall load as light as possible but knew she'd feel the weight over time.

All three of them wore running tights that covered their legs completely, plus long-sleeved running shirts and waterproof jackets. The sun had barely meandered over the horizon, and light cloud cover blocked the full intensity of its rays. Though it didn't show today, rain was still a possibility along the course. The weather would be as varied as the terrain, with temperatures as hot as the upper eighties and possibly down into the forties in the mountains where part of the race would take them.

Essentially they had to be ready for anything.

Eva continued observing the crowd. Funny how loud it was now, with so many people milling about, and how quiet it would soon be, especially once the serious runners left them in the dust each day.

She'd finally come to peace with potentially being at the end of the pack, so long as they finished each day without being disqualified. The only way that would happen was if they didn't cross each individual finish line as a team, or if they didn't make it to each overnight checkpoint within the allotted time.

Despite the fact her sprain had healed, Eva would continue to wrap her ankle with kinesiology tape for the duration of the race.

All ducks were in a row—the ones they could anticipate and control, anyway.

"Hey." Marc's voice pulled her from her thoughts.

"Oh. Hi."

He leaned in, kissing her cheek. "Have I told you how pretty you look in the mornings?"

She ran her tongue along the inside of her bottom lip and smirked. "Marco Cinelli, you're a charmer."

"You're the only one other than my mother and aunts who can get away with calling me by my full name, you know."

"Good. I like that. Marco."

"Okay, now I'm stealing another kiss. This time a real one." He lifted an eyebrow. "You got a problem with that?"

"Your feisty side is coming out. I like that too." Eva laughed as he swooped in and kissed her, this time on the lips. It was quick but still stole her breath.

Beside Eva, Angela cleared her throat. "Please don't tell me you guys are going to subject me to this for one hundred and fifty-five miles. Because I already have extreme third-wheel syndrome."

Eva stage-whispered to Angela, "Don't tell Marc, but he's actually the third wheel."

A poke in her right side made her giggle. "I heard that."

"What?" She swung her head back to him, batting her eyes and widening them as if innocent.

"I should kiss that smirk right off your face. But I'll be considerate of Angela."

"Much appreciated."

Laughter burst from all three of them.

Just then an announcer welcomed them and started the countdown.

Holy cow, holy cow, holy cow. Eva's breaths came in a barrage of spurts. She grabbed Marc's and Angela's hands, crushing them with her own.

The crowd counted down from ten, and after they reached one, a buzzer sounded. A collective surge sent the group of competitors forward, some running, others jogging, including Eva and her team.

Soon the noise from the nonparticipants faded as Marc, Eva, and Angela moved deeper into the country—a desolate wilderness, from all appearances. She'd heard the volunteers talking about how today's trails would take them into the up-and-down landscape of the Nevis Valley, an area known for the early New Zealand gold mining rush. A ring of snow-tipped mountains created an inspiring backdrop. Swelling tussock grasslands dotted with boulders and dark gray-green shrubs seemed to go on for miles. Varying heights of yellow grass bent in response to the occasional breeze.

Supposedly several creeks trickled from the mountains to feed a twenty-five-mile river that flowed through the valley, but Eva didn't see them. Yet.

They came upon the first checkpoint sooner than it seemed they would, grabbing some water and hitting the trail again. One down, only three more to go today before they made it to the fifth and final one, where they'd camp—and then start all over tomorrow.

But for now, they were doing fine. When they walked, they chatted about anything and everything. When they jogged, silence reigned as they took in their surroundings and allowed the beauty to soak into the soles of their feet and travel to their hearts.

It wasn't easy by any means, but their training had prepared them. If they'd been running the entire time, it definitely would have been more challenging. But while tiring, the trails weren't impossible. It was shaping up to be a very pleasant first day. In many ways it felt like they were out on another of their long training runs.

No, this was not at all how she'd assumed she would feel today. What did that mean?

Of course, it was only going to get harder from here. Tomorrow was said to be the first of a few difficult days, with extremely narrow trails and sheer drops where they'd have to really focus on safety.

But her attention had to be on the here, the now. Today.

And today, gorgeous views greeted them with jots of history written into the scenery. The path meandered right next to a large waterwheel that towered over them, and several stone ruins hinted at the area's past.

Everywhere the earth burst with fabulous color.

Yes. Whatever she was or wasn't feeling, she was supposed to be here right now. She'd embrace the pleasant and conquer the challenges when they came. They were all part of the journey, right?

When they reached the fourth checkpoint—only six miles from the end for today and with four hours to spare—Angela asked for a fifteen-minute break to rest, so they all grabbed cups of water, thanked the volunteers sitting behind the table, and sat in the shade. As the sun had emerged and warmed everything up, they'd shed their jackets. Eva's ankle felt a bit sore, but she wasn't in any pain.

"Take a walk with me?" Marc crushed his paper cup in his hand and tossed it into the rubbish bin.

Eva did the same. "Haven't I been doing that all day?"

"Alone."

She looked at Angela, who had climbed onto a rock by herself, eyes closed, the breeze blowing wisps of hair across her face. "Okay, sure."

He took Eva's hand and led her off the trail marked with pink flags. They emerged onto a small bluff projecting from the hillside, and she finally caught a glimpse of the fabled river cutting through the valley in the distance.

Eva sat, and Marc settled behind her, pulling her close so she leaned back against his chest, his legs on either side of her, his arms nestling her in. His chin rested against her cheek. "How are you doing?"

The question ran deeper than the physical, she knew. "Okay." She paused, gathering her thoughts. "I expected to be overwhelmed. To cry a bunch today. To be thinking constantly about Brent and feeling sad."

"But you don't?"

"No." How could she explain? "I mean, I felt a lot of angst leading up to this. But it feels almost wrong not to be as heartsick today as I expected. Like I'm not doing Brent's memory justice somehow. I mean, he should be here with us, and he's not. Why isn't the thought of that completely breaking me apart?"

"Maybe it means you're finally moving forward."

As her eyes followed the path of the rushing water, Eva sighed. "And I know that's a good thing. It's what I want, ultimately. What

I need." She pulled his arms tighter around her. "I mean, I love this thing we have going."

"Me too."

Eva didn't want to push him away with her next words, but they'd agreed to be honest. "But while I want to move forward with you, I also don't want to leave Brent behind."

Marc waited a few moments before speaking, but she felt his warm breath caress her cheek. "I don't want to either, and you know I'd never ask you to. He was a huge part of our lives, and he always will be. It's not like people we lose are here one day and gone the next. Physically, yeah, but when it comes to our memories of them, how we carry them in our hearts—that defies time."

"I'm so glad you understand."

Eva turned her head slightly so she could look up at Marc. He read the thoughts in her mind and, meeting her halfway, lowered his lips to hers. Delicious warmth curled through her as she leaned into the kiss—and what might be her future.

32

Angela had never been more physically miserable in her life. Forget childbirth. At least that had been over in twelve hours.

But on day three of the ultra-marathon, her feet were run ragged. This morning, after a night of little sleep thanks to muscle soreness, she'd hardly been able to shove her swollen feet into her shoes, which she'd purchased one size bigger than normal based on the race organizers' suggestion.

Not only that, but crossing a small river a few miles back had resulted in damp shoes. With every hit against the path, excess cold water squelched between her toes.

Squish.

Squish.

Squish.

Also, there was the matter of food, which normally pepped Angela right up. But as much as she'd tried to enjoy them, the meals Marc had chosen left her stomach scraped raw with hunger given her inability to choke them down. It didn't seem to matter that they'd tested the meals beforehand. There was something different about eating them now, when all she wanted was a cheeseburger and some fries. At least she'd tolerated the quick lunch of beef jerky and dried fruit several hours ago.

Squish.

Squish.

Squish.

Yes, definitely not the most comfortable she'd ever been. And the emotions swirling through her shook her up and down almost like pregnancy hormones. What a ridiculous sight she had to be, getting angry over the smallest things and then elated moments later when nothing momentous had truly occurred.

Angela wiped her sticky forehead with the back of her hand and noticed her arms looked a bit pink. "I think I need more sunscreen."

Even though it had been quite blustery today as they crossed a gorgeous mountain range, the sun harassed them nearly wherever they went. The only relief had been a bit of mist and cloud cover as they reached the summit.

All she wanted at the moment was to crawl into a tent, drink a gallon of water, and down a pizza. Maybe two. Ooo, and chocolate cake. With a mountain of frosting.

And yes, she knew that sounded whiny, so she didn't say any of it out loud. Grin and bear it. That's how she'd been raised, and that's what she'd do.

"According to my watch, we're approaching the second-to-last checkpoint of the day." Marc's fancy Fitbit had helped them keep track of their time and distance.

"I'll just wait until then."

Go, go, go, Angela. You've got this. You have to have this. You can't chicken out now. Push through the pain. Just get it done. Get. It. Done.

They continued on, the trail twisting up and over rolling green and yellow hills. Thank goodness for the trekking poles Marc had suggested they take to help make the steep sections easier to climb. They were great for helping Angela navigate the rocky terrain and produce better balance and pacing.

At an "oomph," Angela glanced at her sister-in-law. Though Eva tried hiding it, the grimace on her face made it clear her ankle was bothering her.

"You okay?"

"Fine."

"I can check—"

"I said I'm fine," Eva snapped. A pause. "Sorry."

Apparently Angela wasn't the only one in a mood. "No worries."

They slogged on.

Squish.

Squish.

Squish.

Would it get better or worse from here? The first day had felt like a piece of cake for all of them, really. She'd felt such a high after running the last mile into camp. Stage 2 had been much more difficult—they'd woven through numerous wineries, past a gold mine in Bannockburn, across the Kawarau River, and up, up, up a grueling seven-mile tramp into the Pisa mountain range, ending the day at Snow Farm. Angela and her burning feet had never been more grateful to see a ring of tiny tents.

The only sign that Marc was struggling with anything came from his constant side-glances at Eva. It seemed like he had something on his mind but had no idea how to say it.

In a way, Angela could relate—except in her case, she didn't fully know what she wanted to express. It had been a fight every night at camp to force herself into her tent when all she really wanted to do was find Simon and kiss him senseless.

When had she become such a sap?

She was just tired and cranky, that's all. Her physical condition was robbing her of her ability to think clearly, and she refused to make stupid, emotional decisions that would affect her future.

The white tent of the checkpoint came into view. "Finally."

Eva's scowl turned into a grin. "Race you."

How the woman had energy for that, especially with a semi-hurting ankle, was a wonder to Angela. But the idea of cold water and an excuse to rest for a few minutes, maybe even remove her shoes and dry them out for a bit, beat out Angela's logic. "You're on."

They both shoved their trekking poles into Marc's hands and took off, leaving Marc to yell, "Thanks a lot," which made them laugh as they sprinted. The tent got closer, and when they reached it—Eva slightly ahead of Angela—they leaned over, hands on their knees, sweat dripping down their cheeks.

Marc jogged in a few seconds after them and whistled. "You ladies are killing it."

"Yes, they are."

Angela straightened as if lightning had struck her in the rear. Her eyes found the source of the comment. Simon sat in a chair behind the table that held the large cooler of water. A few other volunteers milled about in their orange shirts. He rose and shook hands with Marc.

"What are you doing here?" She hadn't meant the words to come out so abrupt. But this checkpoint was supposed to be a tiny refuge from the journey they'd been on. Once again, she wasn't prepared to handle an interaction with him, especially with her feet throbbing, her throat dry, and her emotions on the fritz.

Simon's eyes flashed with hurt—and something else. Determination? "I thought I could walk the last few miles with you all today. Observe you in action."

"Aren't all media personnel supposed to remain at camp?" Angela marched to the cooler and poured herself some water, spilling a bit thanks to the tremble in her hands.

"When you're writing a feature story for the race organization's magazine, you carry a bit more sway."

Angela looked to Eva for help. But Eva wasn't paying attention, and Angela didn't miss how she winced as she leaned into a stretch that involved her ankle.

Finally, Angela groaned. "Fine. But you can't distract us with a bunch of questions, all right?" Goodness. She sounded like an irritated Kylee. Simon was her friend, and he'd done nothing wrong. And this was his job—it wasn't like he'd purposefully arranged to hang around in order to bully her into a relationship. It was a difficult situation for both of them.

She stepped closer to him, lowered and softened her voice. "I'm sorry. Today has been kind of rough."

His shoulders relaxed. "I can imagine. But you've done, what? Seventy miles?"

"Sixty-nine. But who's counting?" Angela forced some levity into her voice.

"Right." Simon winked, and something fluttered to life in her stomach.

Uh-oh.

They all finished their water and took off walking again, Simon chatting with Marc about the experience so far. Since he couldn't very well write and walk at the same time, he used a digital recorder to tape the conversation. Marc oozed enthusiasm for the scenery and the opportunity to honor his two friends. Sometimes Angela forgot that Marc had originally planned to do this race with Brent and Wes—and then he'd gotten stuck with her and Eva instead. Not that he minded being with Eva, although Angela imagined it must feel strange to be out here with his best friend's wife.

Angela relaxed into the walk, commanding her heart rate to slow, her feet not to feel the rub, rub, rubbing of foot against wet sock, to embrace the pain as motivation. As remembrance.

Then Simon moved on to chatting with Eva, and Angela felt the adrenaline build in her veins, rushing, rushing, never stopping. Her heart seemed to throb to its own rhythm as Eva chattered, her thoughts a jumble of musings about why she was here and what she was feeling. What would it feel like to understand her own emotions?

Why was it so difficult to know her own heart? Angela had made progress, sure, but would she ever come to the point where she could be an open book emotionally—to herself and the world?

"Your turn, Ang." Simon dropped back to walk next to her.

Angela checked her watch. They had approximately one mile until the final checkpoint for the night. That meant she only had to spend fifteen, maybe twenty more minutes in Simon's presence for today. "Okay."

The path clung tight to the side of a curving hill, and the front pads of her feet smoldered against her shoes as they descended. But suddenly the passage straightened and plunged downward, large boulders on either side. A view of some lake overtook the entire horizon. From where she stood, she couldn't see the rest of the trail.

Simon clicked on the recorder once more. "How has the race been for you so far?"

Angela eyed the device in his hands and then focused on the roadway in front of her so she didn't stumble. "Look around us. It's amazing." That was the truth, even if her aching body and fuzzy brain couldn't allow her to fully appreciate it.

"What about the race itself? What emotions have you been feeling?"

"Pretty much the gamut. It's been a challenge."

Silence. "Anything more specific?"

The trail became steep, and she planted one foot in front of the other. "Who's asking? Simon the journalist or Simon my friend?" *Come on, Angela. He's just doing his job. Don't make it worse.* "I'm sor—"

"I didn't think Simon your friend existed anymore." He stuffed the recorder into his pocket. "Or that you acknowledged him, anyway."

Angela yelped as her right foot slipped. Thankfully she regained her footing quickly. "I thought you said you were going to keep things strictly professional." Her tone . . . ugh, so nasty.

Her stomach cramped with hollowness. She needed this to end. Now. But she couldn't leave Simon in the dust. Like a good teammate, she had to stay within fifty feet of Eva and Marc at all times.

At last the land leveled out, and in the distance she saw the Stage 3 overnight checkpoint and hundreds of tiny tents beyond it.

"You're right, I did." He blew out a breath, his tone exasperated. And who could blame him? He was dealing with the worst version of Angela at the moment. Still, he should know better. "But blast it all, Angela, I can't. Not with you. I know it's not fair to put this on you now, here, but at some point we need to talk."

A few yards ahead, Eva glanced back at Angela. She could probably hear every word.

This was so confusing—because Angela didn't have the answers. She didn't know how to be a friend to Simon when all she wanted was to throw herself into his embrace.

Oh, who cared about the rules? "No, we don't." Angela broke into a run.

She needed to get away. From Simon, from the pain of walking seventy-five miles in three days, from her pathetic excuses.

From Wes.

This was all his fault. All of it. If he'd only listened to her. If he hadn't been drawn in by Brent's adventures. If he'd seen the blessings in front of him—his wife, his children—and hadn't gone gallivanting around the country.

If he'd stayed, Angela wouldn't be here right now, racing like a rabid dog was nipping at her heels, Marc and Eva yelling at her to come back, the wind stinging her eyes.

She'd be back in New York with him, homeschooling her kids, attending church, talking with God, being with her friends, growing old with the man she'd given up everything for.

Angela's lungs burned as she blew past the checkpoint and

straight for the tent assigned to her. She dove inside, zipped the door shut, unhooked her backpack, and plopped onto the thin tented floor. Then she pulled her knees to her chest and raked in dry, ragged breaths.

$$\backsim$$

What had Angela been thinking?

Ignoring the spasm in her ankle, Eva stalked past tents 98, 99, and 100, until she finally arrived at 101. Her stomach still felt folded over on itself, as it had when she'd watched Angela barrel ahead of them and cross the Stage 3 finish line—alone.

She'd nearly disqualified them by crossing without her teammates. In fact, she had, but Marc and Simon had managed to smooth things over.

A quick peek into tent 101 showed it empty of all but Angela's gear. Where was she?

Even though Eva had gotten closer to Angela, she still had no clue what was really going through her sister-in-law's mind. Was she so hung up on Simon that she was willing to throw away this opportunity—for all of them?

"You looking for the gal who was in that tent?"

Eva turned to find a woman with a southern accent and blonde dreadlocks sitting outside tent 102 using a kit to treat blisters on her feet. "Yeah, actually. Do you know where she went?"

"That way." She pointed around the bend, down toward a wooded lake. "She looked real upset. I asked if she was all right and she kind of blew me off."

Of course she had. *Not nice, Eva. Something is clearly wrong.* "Thank you so much."

She weaved through the rows of one-person tents, all low to the ground and fairly plain. Each camp had been set up with small round tables with backless stools where participants could eat, play cards, and chat together during camp hours. The camp already burst with activity.

Eva took a trail with tall brush on either side that sloped downward. She shouldn't have raced Angela earlier—her ankle had throbbed ever since. Marc had noticed her limping a bit, but she'd shrugged it off as a blister. He didn't need to be concerned about anything except pacing them and making sure they reached their destinations on time each day. Of course, neither of them had thought to worry about Angela breaking one of the only rules that could get a team thrown out of the race.

Eva clenched her hands into fists. Upset or not, Angela needed to know how much she'd endangered their mission here today.

Gray and red rocks rose around Eva as she dropped toward the silver-blue water. She rounded the corner and found her sister-in-law leaning against a large boulder at the lake's edge. Upon Eva's approach, Angela didn't move.

Folding her arms across her chest, Eva waited. Was Angela going to apologize? Or did she even realize what she'd done? If they'd been forced to quit, they wouldn't have reached their goal of a million dollars raised. They'd have done all this training only to be disqualified. They'd have dishonored Brent's and Wes's memories.

That was unacceptable.

Out here, by the lake, they were isolated from the sounds of camp—the banging of pots, the white noise emanating from the propane stoves used for heating water, the din of good-spirited chatter after a long day of walking and running. The cadence of the lapping water and call of a few gulls superseded everything.

Angela retrieved a stone from the shore, studying the droplets of water that clung to it and danced in the waning sunlight. Her thumb smoothed over the stone, back and forth, back and forth. Then she reared back and tossed it a decent distance. The plunk broke the placid surface of the lake, sending ripples that almost reached them at the shore.

Finally, her sister-in-law spoke. "Are we kicked out?" Her lips settled into a grim line.

Was that all she had to say? "No. We got a thirty-minute delayed start penalty for tomorrow instead."

"Good." The word fell flat, giving Eva no indication of Angela's emotional state.

What else is new?

"Angela, why did you run ahead of us like that?"

"I had to get away."

"From Simon?"

"From all of it." Another stone flew from Angela's hand into the water. No attempt to skip it across the top. Just a hard toss and in it went.

A flurry of wind skated across the water's surface. Eva burrowed into her jacket. "Why?" There were so many questions contained in the word, but only one shook loose of Eva's heart. "Why don't you want to honor our husbands like I do?"

"Why should we honor them?" *Plop.* "They promised us forever, and then they left us."

Angela finally looked at Eva. Her stormy eyes sent a wave of sympathy down Eva's spine.

Eva squatted, picked up a stone, then stood and handed it to Angela, who took and pitched it. Over and over, Eva selected rocks and gave them to Angela to throw into the water. Finally, she dusted off the flecks of mud on her pants and leaned against the boulder next to Angela.

"Brent and Wes didn't choose to leave." She'd never once been angry at Brent for what was clearly an accident. But when tragedy struck, people often looked for someone to blame.

"Wes left before he died."

Surprise flickered through Eva. "Like, he moved out?"

As she scooped up another large pebble, Angela shook her head. "Emotionally. After Roy passed away. I told you, he changed. And he left me behind. I told him doing all the stupid stuff Brent did would end with him hurt, or worse. And he didn't listen to me."

Eva tried to ignore the instant defensiveness that rose inside her at the mention of Brent's "stupid stuff." She flexed her fingers. "Maybe he was more afraid of never really living than of dying."

Her sister-in-law's head whipped toward Eva, her eyes zeroing in on her like a hawk. "So you think his wife and children weren't enough *life* for him?"

"That's not what I—"

"No, really, Eva. What's the real meaning of living? Huh? And why did Wes get to be the judge of that? Why did Brent?"

"Don't bring Brent into this."

Angela's biting laugh echoed off the boulders. "He's already in this. He's the whole reason you're here. The whole reason both of us are." She paused. "You know, I never understood why you were so adamant about doing this race in the first place."

"I . . . I wanted to honor Brent."

"You say that, but for goodness' sake, you've already dedicated your life to his legacy. What about yours, Eva? Don't you want to do this for yourself? The whole rest of your life can't be about him . . . even if it was when he was alive."

"Excuse me? It wasn't like that."

"Wasn't it? Didn't *he* decide what adventures you took? Wasn't *he* the one who decided not to have kids yet, even though you wanted them? He wasn't perfect, Eva. He was just a man, but you've got him way up on a pedestal like some sort of god."

Eva flinched as if Angela had struck her with the rock in her hands. "How dare you talk about my husband like you knew him well. Like you know anything about our relationship."

Her sister-in-law rolled the rock between her fingers for a few moments before speaking. "That all came out much harsher than I intended. I'm sorry." A long exhale blew from her lips. "But even though my delivery stinks, I think maybe deep down you know that some of what I'm saying is true. It's okay to admit that you didn't have a perfect marriage. That Brent was flawed. And that you don't need to live your life as some sort of shrine to him."

Eva had never in her entire existence had the desire to hit someone—until now.

But not because Angela was totally off her rocker. And not because she'd been completely rude.

It was because she'd spoken a truth, at least in some small part, that Eva hadn't been able to admit to herself.

But Angela was wrong about one thing. "I did come here for Brent, yes. But I came here for myself too. To figure out if life could ever be colorful again."

Her sister-in-law took a step closer and ever so gently placed a rock into Eva's hand, curling Eva's fingers around it, securing it. She met Eva's eyes. "Then embrace that fully and stop acting like Brent is the only reason you're here."

Eva felt the cold solidity of the stone. "You're right." Her chest heaved as her fingers propelled the weight across the water.

33

Angela couldn't sleep.

She'd been trying for—she clicked on her watch light—nearly two hours. At first she'd blamed her insomnia on the sounds of other competitors talking, the picking of a guitar some volunteer must have busted out, the rustle and zipping of nearby tents. But for at least an hour now, all had been quiet except for distant birds squawking and crickets buzzing.

She sat up on her sleeping mat, and the air felt charged with static. Her body was certainly exhausted enough to fall into a deep sleep, but her mind wouldn't let it.

Sighing, she rubbed her eyes. She'd been too severe with Eva earlier this evening. Her sister-in-law had nearly wilted at her words, and Angela had done her best to salvage the situation. At least by the time she'd left, Eva hadn't seemed mad at Angela anymore. Just in deep, tortuous thought.

How was Angela so capable of diagnosing Eva's problems and yet she hadn't been able to ferret out why she couldn't quite forgive Wes?

What a hypocrite you are.

Ugh. No way she was going to go back to sleep right now. She needed air.

As quietly as possible, she slipped from her sleeping bag, and a cold draft hit her thinly covered thighs. She threw on her tennis shoes and jacket, grabbed her emergency communications device as a precautionary measure, then unzipped her tent and stepped through the flap, praying the sound wouldn't wake anyone. Thankfully, the full moon provided plenty of light for her to walk through camp without using her mini flashlight, but she clicked on the beam once she left the camp and headed for the lake. She selected a different path this time, one that wound around the entire lake, hugging the shore and flirting with the water's edge.

Angela inhaled the crisp night air, smelling the combined scent of the earthy dirt and pine. The beam of the flashlight reflected off a large spider web tangled in trees that seemed to lean together, creating an arch across the trail. She stepped over rocks as she made her way around the glittering lake on her right.

Up ahead, a faint bluish-green glow by the bank caught her eye, right at the base of a tree that grew next to the water. Angela switched off her light again and approached the gleam, which flickered as she drew nearer despite the stealth she'd attempted. An entire bush of undergrowth radiated flashes of light.

Glowworms.

She plopped herself onto a patch of dry dirt, mesmerized by this unexpected discovery.

A memory surfaced. Did she dare speak it out loud? To . . . Wes? It's not like he'd really hear her, but Eva had once said that talking to Brent made her feel better.

No one around to call her crazy. So why not?

"Remember that time we were walking on the beach after our third or fourth date, and we saw that bioluminescent algae glowing bright blue in the water?" Angela kept her voice soft as she grabbed a nearby twig and poked the dirt next to her feet. "I started spouting off all of these facts about why bioluminescence happens, and you laughed at me. And in that quiet way you had, you pulled me into your arms and said, 'All of that is good to know, but let's just enjoy it for now.'"

She swallowed at the recollection. "I guess even then you were more sentimental than I was. More about experiencing the moment." A knot in the twig rubbed against the upper padding of her middle finger as she pushed it through the soil and sand.

"And experience it we did." He'd kissed her for the first time, and she had felt it down to the tips of her toes and knew without a doubt she'd found her person.

Of course, she'd not told him that then. She'd been too practical, too sure that love took years to form, if it ever really did.

"That was the moment I fell in love with you."

Angela squinted at the glowing bush, looking for the individual glowworms, but because there were so many, all she could make out was the effect of them. "I know you think I settled for you, but that was never the case, Wes. I'm sorry I didn't make it clearer. Especially in those early years, you showed me in a thousand ways how much you cared." Made her coffee in the mornings. Brought her mint chocolate chip ice cream for no reason. It wasn't uncommon for her to come home from running errands to find a single red rose in a vase on the counter.

She pushed harder on the twig and it snapped, making her jump.

Angela closed her eyes, imagined her husband sitting on the bank next to her, squeezing her knee and encouraging her to go on. She inhaled deeply, almost able to also conjure a whiff of the Dove soap he'd used. "But then you changed, and I didn't feel like I fit into your life anymore. And maybe I should have changed, grown with you, come with you when you invited me along. But I didn't think I should have to."

Here came the part she hated. The root of the shame. The guilt. "After all, when I got pregnant, the life I'd always envisioned for myself was gone. And yes, I grew to love the life you and the kids gave me, but there was always a piece of me filled with regret, thinking I'd missed out. But at least we were in the same boat. We were a team, because you'd given up some dreams too. And then I felt like you jumped ship into this new life, pursuing a new dream *you* had, living a reckless life that endangered the one we'd built together. You and Brent became the team. You . . . you left me, just like my dad did."

While it felt good to say the words out loud, she'd already known she felt this way. There was more there, if she could just . . .

A thought lingered so close to the edge of her consciousness she nearly reached out and touched it. It brushed the fingertips of her mind.

She opened her eyes and looked around. Yes, she was alone, but she didn't feel alone. She could sense . . . maybe, God? It had been so long since that had happened—she'd almost forgotten what it was like.

And then full cognition fell into her grasp.

Was she really still upset with Wes for pursuing a new dream? After all, like Eva had pointed out, he'd tried to include her.

Or was the one she really was upset with . . . herself?

Could she speak the words out loud? *Yes.* Her spirit pressed the words from her lips. "Wes, I think I've blamed you for how my life turned out. Not the pregnancy, but the trouble in our marriage. The adventures. Your death. But the real problem is that over the years I . . . I forgot how to dream, and you somehow didn't. And I think I resented you for it."

The words flowed from the confines of her bruised heart, the one she'd kept tightly laced. Her gaze blurred as tears at long last dripped from her eyes, landing on her lips, the salty liquid seeping in. The weight of the moment both crushed her and made her feel lighter than ever.

All of that anger with Wes had really been fear masquerading.

Fear of disappointment. Fear of the unknown. Of banking her future on a dream that was never going to see her through.

Not only that, but all that bitterness she'd been clinging to had really been a defense mechanism. If she was mad at Wes, she didn't have to miss him, to really examine the great loss of him and what that meant for her heart. She didn't have to allow her volatile emotions to drown her.

Angela Jamison could keep on swimming with nothing holding her back.

But now she could clearly look back and see that she'd been dog-paddling at best, moving in circles, staying in the same place. Surviving. Only surviving, just like Juliet had said all those months ago.

And eventually, because of this race, because of being here, her defenses had slipped. But she wasn't drowning like she'd expected. Something—someone—was holding her up.

Thank you.

She sat there for a good long while, listening to the cadence of the night, soaking in the holiness of the moment. Finally, Angela rose and headed back to camp. And when she settled her head onto her pillow, this time her mind was as fatigued as the rest of her. She fell into a sleep that promised to be more restorative than any she'd experienced in a long, long time.

34

Angela's verbal beating on day three had nearly undone Eva. What misery would day four hold?

Eva walked side by side with Marc along the ridge of a mountain in one of the most beautiful landscapes she'd ever seen, but her heart still felt like the sorest muscle in her aching body right now.

The path before them was packed tight with dirt, boulders scattered on either side to form a solid trail, and it twisted to and fro along the mountains, rocky outcroppings towering over them and then falling away. Thankfully a good solid taping and some ice had helped her ankle feel better last night, but if she wasn't careful today, one wrong move could easily make her physical state in as much turmoil as her emotional one.

At the moment Angela hiked several feet behind them. She'd been subdued all morning and had barely spoken. If she felt guilty about the fact they'd started thirty minutes behind all others, giving them only eleven and a half hours to complete Stage 4, she didn't show it.

Above them, the sky seemed darker today, as if sensing Eva's mood—only glimpses of the sun among clouds, building and gathering in anticipation of what seemed like a storm. Grief was such a strange thing, much like the weather in New Zealand. She could be walking along enjoying the day and—*boom!* Sudden rain would wash away any plans she had for an activity outside.

Eva put one trekking pole—one foot—in front of the other and sighed.

"What's going on in that head of yours, Eva?" Marc asked. "You wouldn't talk to me last night. Will you now?"

Eva longed to take her fingers and smooth out the wrinkles marring his forehead, but her hands remained wrapped around her poles.

He kicked a small rock in his way. "Remember what we agreed to at the airport?"

No pulling away. Open communication. "Yes."

"So?"

She lowered her voice so her sister-in-law wouldn't overhear. "Last night Angela challenged my reasons for being here." She summarized the conversation. "And I've been thinking about it all night and all of today. I hate to admit it, but she's right. Brent wasn't perfect. And maybe I've been pretending he was. I did that when he was alive too."

"What do you mean?"

The emerald cliffs around them flattened out, and wild bushes, grasses, and other small plants scattered across the mountaintop.

"I admired him so much. He really did enthrall me and my artist's heart to no end. And instead of us forging a life together, I think I sort of did whatever he wanted. I was so wrapped up in him, in the exciting life he led, that it became what I wanted too. But there were a few things . . . I mean, it's my fault for not speaking up, I guess. But then again, it's also his fault for never asking."

Like having children. He thought they'd have time, but he'd been wrong. And his death had left her all alone.

"That's heavy stuff. How did you feel about what Angela said about living your life as a shrine to Brent?"

"I suppose she said it because I worked somewhere that was important to him and ran this race in part to honor him. But is that really so wrong?"

"No, but . . ." Marc spoke slowly, with deliberation. "Don't you think there's more to it than that?"

"Like what?"

"Look, I don't understand what it's like to lose a spouse. I would never presume to judge you. At all. I hope you know that."

"But . . ."

"Have you thought about what life looks like when we get home?"

"I've tried." Whew. It was getting warm, despite the clouds. "Constantly. But I can't quite imagine it."

"Not even in practical terms? For example, are you planning to go back to the heart center, or do flowers again? Will you clear out Brent's office at home and closet like you've mentioned you need to do? And will we . . ."

She studied him, the way his hands white-knuckled his poles. "Will we what?"

"Will we still be together? Or will you decide that you'll never be able to even try loving me because you can't love anyone the way you loved him?" He said it matter-of-factly, but his eyes oozed vulnerability.

What could she tell him when she didn't know the answers herself?

Up ahead, a vista jutted off the pathway, granting views of a plush valley below. When they reached it, Eva dropped her poles, grabbed Marc's hand, and dragged him off the trail. She peeked back and saw her sister-in-law lower herself onto a boulder facing the opposite direction several yards away. Thankfully she'd received the hint to give them their privacy.

Eva returned her gaze to the valley below. A river ran through, touching the plants along its bank, giving them life as it moved.

"Marc, I don't know what's going to happen after this. It's truly all I can do to get through this race." It was breaking her down piece by piece—her body, her mind, her spirit. She only prayed at the end of it she would somehow be built back up, a newer, better version of herself.

Marc squeezed her fingers. "I know, and I wasn't trying to push you into anything. Sorry if it felt like it."

"It just felt like you being honest, which I so appreciate. It's true I don't know what I'll do career-wise or what I'll do with my home. But I do know that I want to be with you, Marco Cinelli. I made that decision weeks ago, even before you came back to New Zealand. But I was afraid to tell you because . . . well, the unknown is frightening. And I have some of the same fears you do—like what if Brent was it for me? Still, I care about you so much and I want to see where this can go."

And he deserved to know just how much she cared. Here went nothing. "Do you remember that night we were video chatting and I was trying to create bouquets for a wedding? The first bouquets I'd created since Brent died?"

"Yes."

The man paid attention. She liked that. "When I hung up the phone, I was shocked to see a picture-perfect flower arrangement in my hands. One of the best I've ever done."

"Okay."

She wasn't making sense, was she? With her free hand, Eva rubbed the tip of her nose, her mouth moving to one side as she considered her next words. "Marc, there's only been one other time I was inspired to create in that way—without any thought to what I was doing, without believing I had it in me to do it. And that was the day I met Brent."

Silence. What was Marc thinking? Maybe she shouldn't have told him. Perhaps he'd be offended that she'd compared him to Brent.

Finally, he spoke. "So what does that mean?"

Courage. The whisper to her soul felt familiar, like a long-lost friend tapping on her door.

She studied Marc, but his eyes were unreadable. "It means I found my inspiration again. In you." And that was the truth of it. Because even if . . . But it was impossible, for her to love him, right? They'd only been dating a few weeks. "And I thought you should know."

"Thank you for telling me." He pulled her into his side and kissed the top of her head.

Together they watched the river rush and splash, bringing sustenance to the world around it by simply being itself, the distant roar of its victory in their ears.

"And I would love to take credit for inspiring you, Eva. But the truth is, I'm just a man. That inspiration came from somewhere inside of you."

∽

As Angela, Marc, and Eva trudged across the Stage 4 finish line, a gentle rain began to dot the dirt around them.

Marc whisked Eva under a nearby tree and turned to kiss her softly. Angela maneuvered around them, giving them the privacy now like she wished she'd been able to earlier. But with only fifty feet permitted between them, she could only do so much. Clearly, though, their talk had proven fruitful. Angela would ask Eva about it later tonight.

As for right now, she had another mission on her mind.

Angela needed to apologize to Simon, because he'd never done anything wrong to her. In fact, she'd wronged him, abandoning him without explanation last night on the trail. And that was inexcusable.

Feet numb and legs trembling, Angela lumbered through camp. This one was situated in an open meadow surrounded by a few hills and a small forest of trees on one side. The rain tat-tatted against the polyester tent roofs, and she shivered as the mild precipitation grew more urgent and the breeze chillier against her wet cheeks. Finally, she came to her tent, and though the urge to hunker down was strong, instead she tossed her rucksack inside, turned, and headed toward the media tent, pulling the hood of her jacket tighter around her face.

As she drew closer, she caught sight of Simon sitting underneath the cover of a blue pop-up canopy, his laptop on a table, fingers flying across the keyboard. Nearby, two female reporters Angela recognized from the social media coordinator's introduction sat across from each other chatting, coffee mugs curled in their hands. They both looked up at her approach, while Simon seemed oblivious. Unless he was ignoring her—in which case, she deserved it.

Angela stepped underneath the awning, crossing her arms over her chest to stay as warm as possible. What she wouldn't give to go huddle in her sleeping bag, but this was too important. She had to say her piece before her nerves failed her.

When Simon failed to look up, Angela tugged off her hood and cleared her throat.

His eyes rose at last, widening slightly when he saw her. "Be right back."

"All right."

He flipped the lid of his computer closed, picked it up, and hurried into a nearby tent that was much bigger than the competitors' tiny one-person tents.

A bead of water trailed from her hairline down the side of her face. Angela pushed it away and tried to smooth her hair as well, but the evidence of her soaking surely still remained.

Simon emerged from the tent with a blanket in hand, his laptop left behind. He'd thrown on a jacket and a white beanie that brought out the bronze in his skin tone.

How could the man look so attractive no matter what he wore?

"Here. You look cold." Simon held the blanket out to her. A month and a half ago, he would have wrapped it around her himself, but the time for such familiarities was likely past.

Again, she deserved it. But maybe she could at least give them both some closure by explaining herself.

"Thank you." Angela took the blanket, rough against her rather frozen fingertips, and unfolded it enough to drape around her shoulders. "Can we talk?"

With a nod, Simon motioned for her to lead the way.

It was then she noticed the rain had stopped nearly as quickly as it had begun, leaving everything a little damp. For privacy's sake, Angela walked to the outskirts of camp and found a worn log to sit on.

He lowered himself next to her and waited.

Angela pulled the blanket tighter, hiding her hands inside of it. "I wanted to apologize for my behavior on the racecourse yesterday." *Keep going, Angela.* "I ran off before we could really talk. What did you want to discuss?"

Simon folded and positioned his hands in front of his mouth as he leaned forward on the log. "That day on the beach, I was taken aback. Didn't know what to say. How to process the fact that you didn't see a future with me, when I clearly saw one with you."

From under the beanie, a stray piece of his hair lay curled against his forehead, making him somehow more vulnerable than she'd ever seen him.

He continued. "Despite all that, I was determined to give you your space. There were a lot of times I nearly broke down and called, texted. I let you go. But when I saw you here, I felt something. Six weeks later, there's still a spark between us, Angela. And I guess I wondered if you'd . . ."

"Changed my mind?"

Finally, he looked at her, lips not pursed as she would have thought, but screwed up to the side in concentration. "Yeah."

Angela's heart stuttered. "I don't deny we have a deep connection, Simon. Every day we were apart, I missed you."

"I missed you too."

"But still, I wasn't any closer to figuring out what really went wrong between me and Wes. How I could prevent the same thing from happening again. Last night I got a little closer." She recounted her epiphany—about how fear had been disguised as anger, how she'd blamed Wes for causing instability in her life, how she'd lost herself and her ability to dream because she'd been afraid.

How she'd sensed God stirring her heart toward forgiveness and bravery.

"And now?"

"Now? I guess I feel . . . almost ready. To dream again."

"With me?"

The hope in his voice crushed her—because she longed to have it too. "I think I need to start with finishing this race. It's a dream I have chosen to pursue, and if we can accomplish what we set out to do when the odds seemed so against us in the beginning . . . well, that will give me hope. That maybe other things will turn out okay too." Angela bit her lip at the implications.

She studied him. How she longed to trace the contours of his face with her fingers, draw him close, feel his lips on hers.

But one thing at a time.

"And then? When you've finished it?"

"I don't know. But . . . I'm hopeful. For the first time in a long time, I can see that maybe dreams don't have to end in disappointment."

35

The Long March was aptly named. The team was only on mile twenty of fifty. To Eva, running seemed like a distant memory since they'd mostly walked today.

Actually, *slogged* seemed a more appropriate term.

The fading light of day as they crested a hill was proof of their slower pace, but they could make it up by continuing on through the night if need be. Based on Marc's tightened features, Eva wasn't the only one concerned about their slower speed.

And it was mostly her fault. Okay, all her fault. Funny, since at the start of all this it had seemed like Angela would be the one to hold them up. But Eva's dumb ankle had given her a run for her money—no pun intended. Last night when she'd taken off her tape, she'd discovered her ankle swollen to nearly triple its size. Elevating and icing it as usual hadn't seemed to keep her from discomfort all night long. And this morning it had looked just as bad, if not worse.

Now Eva couldn't control a wince at the pain that ricocheted when she nearly tripped over a rock despite her death grip on her trekking poles.

"Whoa. You okay?" Marc steadied her, his brow knit together.

"Yeah. Fine."

"Eva." Angela stopped, so Eva and Marc were forced to as well. "Let me check your ankle."

"We can do it at the next checkpoint."

"That's not for another four miles." Marc squeezed her elbow. "It won't take her long."

Groaning, Eva lowered herself onto a large boulder. "All right. But quick. We're already behind." They were still in the mountains, and the terrain had grown quite rocky, not much plant life sprouting along the trail. Supposedly a valley with beech forest flats was coming up, but they had to fight their way to level ground first.

And then there was the sky. Ironic how it looked perfectly clear—in the opposite direction. They were headed right into a storm.

Angela squatted and rolled up Eva's pant leg, pushing and prodding with care, asking Eva questions and then going silent. "We need to get ice at the next checkpoint. In fact, I'd suggest resting there overnight."

Not what Eva wanted to hear. "I can keep going if I get a good icing."

"That's not how it works." Angela pushed down Eva's pant leg. "You've got to give your ankle adequate time to rest."

Eva read between Angela's words—that they never should have done this. When Eva got injured, she should have canceled the race.

But she never would have forgiven herself for the missed opportunity. And she knew that, despite the odds, Angela felt the same way. It had simply taken her sister-in-law longer to come around to the idea.

They may have started out doing this for their husbands and family, but somewhere along the way it had also become about them. About fighting for a new life that didn't have to end with the tragedy that had overtaken them. About finding joy in the journey.

But for them to find all of that, they had to finish. Quitting now would be like seeing a vibrant new vista on the horizon but never climbing to the zenith.

"How about we see how Eva is doing at the checkpoint and

decide then?" Marc eyed the sky. "I have a feeling the ankle is not going to be our only challenge tonight."

Just then a raindrop hit Eva's forehead. She nodded, then stood.

They started walking again in a light drizzle that soon became a torrential downpour. Eva drew her beanie down over her ears and tugged on a pair of black fleece gloves. The rain kept coming. Funny how the steady pounding that she would have considered rhythmic and soothing if she were inside her tent now felt like knives being driven through her skull.

When the trail turned upward once more, hiking grew more difficult, an extra force pushing against them like an invisible hand. They dug their poles into the ground, staking their claim, their right to finish this race. At some points it seemed her poles were the only things keeping her from tumbling backward.

The last vestiges of day tripped over the horizon.

"Time for light." Marc's words were nearly lost on the wind that howled through the tunnel of mountain walls sloping upward around them.

Eva pulled her rucksack from her shoulders, which were shaking from the cold. She unzipped the pocket where she'd placed her headlamp. As quickly as she could manage, she secured the lamp to her forehead, tightened the strap until it was snug, and flicked on the light.

As Marc and Angela's lights joined hers, more strongly illuminating the path before them, Eva was once again grateful for the benefits of teamwork. If she'd been alone out here, there was no way she'd still be going. She'd thought she was strong, that her motivation would keep her warm and moving forward even in the toughest trials, but today was proof yet again that for Eva to be happy, she needed strong people in her life.

Although Marc's words from yesterday had played on a loop in her brain: *"That inspiration came from somewhere inside of you."*

Was it true? In this moment it felt anything but.

As they continued up the trail toward the top of the hill, the dirt became mud. Her feet slipped a number of times, aggravating her ankle despite the secure tape. Finally, they crested the hill. Thick fog spread across the valley below, reminding her of how the clouds had looked on their plane flight coming into Queenstown nearly four months ago. If it wasn't for the reflective nature of the pink flags lining the trail, they'd have no hope of finding their way to camp.

The next two miles were slow going as the rain continued to soak not only them but the earth. How she longed to curl up under a few rocky ledges they passed, sheltered from the storm for just a few moments and resting her ankle. But when she brought up the idea to Marc and Angela, Marc frowned. "We can definitely stop if you need to. But do you think you'd be able to keep going after that?"

He didn't have to say the rest—that they had no guarantee it wouldn't rain all night long, and they still weren't halfway through the Long March. If they didn't make it to a decent stopping point tonight, there was a strong likelihood they'd not make it to the final Stage 5 checkpoint in time.

"You're right. Let's keep on then." Eva forced a brave smile that she couldn't feel. She rubbed her hands together and tried to ignore the trembles racking her body.

"Uh, guys." Angela pointed to the path ahead. It curved narrowly around the next mountainside. "That doesn't look good."

Eva squinted in the darkness, and her heart skittered at the sight of a washed-out road.

What? No, no, no.

Everything went numb inside Eva.

Marc jogged over, Eva and Angela following at a slower pace. When they arrived at the spot, Marc's tone was grave. "I think the rain caused a mudslide."

"Can that actually happen on an established trail like this?" Angela tilted her head as if examining the road more closely.

"Yeah. It's all about the pull of gravity on the slope, and something like a heavy storm can shift the rocks and debris just enough. The slope's probably been moving a little every year, and the rain might have been the push it needed to fall."

"What do we do?" Despair rose in Eva's throat and threatened to cut off her air supply.

Marc indicated a ledge behind them. "Looks like you're going to get to rest after all."

"No. We can't stop." Her voice sounded like a toddler whining for ice cream. But this was so much more important than dessert.

This was everything.

"Come on, Eva. Let's at least get out of the rain." Marc held out his hand, and she took it begrudgingly.

The ground beneath the ledge was dry. Eva settled on the cold dirt between Angela and Marc. "Do you think they'll come looking for us and realize the road washed out?" Eva threaded her fingers together and covered her mouth, breathing warmth into them. Breathing hope into them. Trying, at least.

Despite her gloves, her hands remained stiff with cold.

"Not unless we use our emergency communications device or miss our checkpoint tomorrow night. It's too bad our personal locator beacons don't have two-way radios. At this point I don't really see much choice other than activating one."

"But that would cause the organizers undue panic," Eva said. Also, activating a beacon would take any power they had out of their hands. They'd be stuck waiting here until the emergency response team was able to reach them, and in this weather, who knew how long that might be? Waiting around when they were already behind might lead to disqualification. "There has to be another way."

Angela's foot tapped against the soft earth as she hugged her knees to her chest.

"Let me think for a minute," Marc said.

How could her teammates be so calm about all of this? Especially Angela, who'd uprooted her kids to be here. Quit her job. Invested everything in this training.

Finally, Angela spoke. "What if we could go up and around it? Do you think there's a safe way to do that?"

Marc pressed on his chin. "Possibly." He stood up and studied the cliffside above the ledge. "It looks like maybe the mudslide wasn't a big one, and that terrain up there appears safe. I could go check it out." He returned to Eva's side.

The idea of Marc putting himself in danger so they could finish this race made her stomach roll. "I don't know . . ."

"It's either that or turn on our beacon. We could try hiking back to the last checkpoint to find out if there's another option, but since we were the last group through, that checkpoint has probably been packed up and cleared already. In which case we'd have wasted time and energy."

Eva snatched his hand and leaned against him. He smelled of dirt and his deodorant, which gave off hints of coconut and fig. "What's the likelihood that you get hurt doing this?" She'd never forgive herself if that happened.

Pressing a kiss to Eva's forehead, he squeezed her fingers. "I wouldn't say super likely, especially since the rain is clearing up for now."

She'd been too distracted to notice, but he was right. A mist hung in the air, but the rain had mostly stopped. "What do you think, Angela?"

Her sister-in-law pursed her lips and stared outside. "I say if Marc doesn't want to chance it, I will. We didn't come all this way to quit now, right?"

When had Angela's commitment to finishing this race risen above Eva's?

Marc eased Eva upright, then stood. "That settles it. I'm going. It shouldn't take me long."

"Be careful." Eva grabbed his hand and tugged him back down, kissing him quickly on the lips. She wouldn't feel okay about this decision until they were all on the other side of that mudslide.

"I will."

Eva felt the promise in Marc's gaze down to the tips of her toes.

He slid from view, and Eva could hear the scrape of his boots against the earth above them as he climbed. Five minutes passed, then ten, fifteen, and all the while her palms sweated inside her gloves.

"This was a mistake. He could be hurt."

"He's probably fine, Eva. Sit and calm down."

But even Angela's best mom voice couldn't get Eva's inner child under control. "What if he's not? And what if he is, but there's truly no way out except to wait on a rescue team? Angela, we've flown around the world. We've secured pledges from some really well-to-do people, and that money can be used to help a lot of people with heart disease. Simon is writing a story about us. What if nothing comes of it all?"

"Eva, we've both fought hard to be here. You've got the ankle to prove it. My feet are shot. And we both know we pretty much lost our minds fifty miles ago. Probably before that." Angela chuckled despite her clear exhaustion. "But we are *not* giving up. Even if Marc comes back and tells us there's no way up and around, we will not quit. We will see this through. We will have our happy ending. Our dream will come true. Accepting less is just . . . well, unacceptable."

Whoa. Angela wasn't just surviving anymore. She was fighting back.

"Okay."

The word was meager, but Eva's agreement wasn't. She just didn't have the energy to say more.

They huddled together against the cold for another ten minutes. Waiting, waiting. *Come on, Marc. Where are you?*

"Hey."

At Marc's greeting, Eva and Angela scrambled out from under the ledge and looked up. He stood above them, outlined against the sky dotted with stars breaking through the receding clouds.

Angela spoke first. "So? Did you find a path?"

"I did, but it'll obviously require off-roading." He turned his focus to Eva. "You going to be able to manage that, Eva?"

"Yes." She had to. The road here had been too long—literally and figuratively. And what was the alternative? To go back? To stay here, stuck in between the mountaintop and the valley, never knowing which place she'd end up?

"All right, then. Who wants to go first?"

36

They'd be lucky if Eva's ankle survived the day.

Angela downed a gulp of instant coffee as sunlight broke over the mountain. She sat cross-legged on a vista not far from the midway checkpoint they'd finally reached at two in the morning after crossing the ridgeline above the mudslide. With careful steps, Marc had led them to the other side. They'd rested awhile and then, despite Angela and Marc's protests on Eva's ankle's behalf, had continued on until the next checkpoint, where her sister-in-law had secured some ice.

With no tents to stay in, they'd clustered together in their sleeping bags for a few hours.

Now, with the dregs of lukewarm coffee dribbling down her throat, Angela warred within herself, torn between the desire to finish this race strong and to see that Eva didn't cause herself any sort of permanent damage in getting there.

"What should we do, God?" The question had been resonating in her spirit all night, but this was the first time she'd expressed it outwardly. A tiny thrill ran up her spine at the idea of reconnecting with the Lord. Kylee had been right—she'd been avoiding anything spiritual for a while—but now her spirit felt freer than it had in a long time. There was still much healing to be done, but her former methods hadn't been working. Maybe this could.

A breeze brushed across her cheeks, a gentle stroke that rustled her hair and the collar of her jacket, spilling in her soul a joy that told her she wasn't alone. That maybe she never really had been.

"Beautiful, isn't it?"

Angela turned to find Marc standing just a bit behind her, hands in the pockets of his red hoodie. Weariness edged his eyes, and his hair lay flat—the same hat head she probably had after wearing her beanie for so many hours over the last few days.

"It is, despite the chill." All the fog from last night had cleared, leaving a crisp view of the landscape, but a nip remained in the air. She pointed to the highest of the mountains, brushed with snow. "I keep thinking we are going to end up there somehow. But the road is always unpredictable."

That used to scare her. It still did sometimes. But this experience was opening up her mind. She never would have thought that off-roading like they had last night would have turned out okay. But it had.

Sherry's words from their last night together floated to her mind: *"But when you're worried about the future . . . trust that God has something wonderful planned, even if our definition of 'wonderful' might not be the same as his."*

Angela still wasn't sure how her husband's death could be categorized as "wonderful" in any universe. But then again, she was slowly finding herself for the first time in decades. And that might not have happened if she hadn't loved and lost Wes.

Marc squatted, his left forearm flung across his left knee, his hands looped together. "Everything about this journey is unpredictable."

"Like falling in love with Eva?" The words were out before she had a chance to consider them, but she didn't doubt their truth.

Marc lifted an eyebrow. "Like falling in love with Simon?"

His words both squeezed her insides and lit them on fire. "You fight dirty."

"You started it."

Look at them—friends together on a journey, linked indelibly by tragedy. And yet both had found more than they'd ever bargained for.

Marc cleared his throat. "It's strange, isn't it? I keep thinking it's a dream. Like I'll wake up and Brent won't really be gone. Like I won't have to shoulder the business alone anymore. Like I'll have my best friend back. But then, there's Eva. And if Brent were here again, I'd be . . . and of course she'd choose him. As she should."

Angela touched his arm. "But Brent really *is* gone."

"I know. And as you said . . . I've fallen in love with his wife."

His rough voice tore at Angela's sympathies. "You're a good man, Marc. Brent would be glad to know Eva is being taken care of so well."

"That's not just me. You've been a big part of it too. Not only have you become a true sister to her, but I haven't worried about her ankle as much knowing you're looking after it. You're calm and levelheaded, and I know I can trust you to tell us if we need to stop, even if you don't want to." He paused. "I heard you were going to go to med school once upon a time."

Maybe Eva had told him that. "Yes, but I'm not sure that's what I want to do anymore."

"What do you want to do?"

"I don't really know."

"Well, whatever you do, I know Wes would want you to be happy, Angela." Marc sat and stretched his legs in front of him. "He lived to make you and those kids happy. I think that's why he took to extreme sports so well."

"Now, that I don't understand, Marc. He said it made him come alive, which to me meant that we weren't enough for him." Sure, Angela had made her peace with Wes, but she still didn't have the answer to that crucial question.

And she'd come to terms with the fact that she never would.

Marc fixed her with a serious gaze. "He and I talked about it once, how there's something about challenging the odds, placing yourself firmly in the grip of the Divine. We know full well that anything could take us from this life at any moment. Cancer. A heart attack. A car accident. Wes didn't see doing extreme sports as putting himself needlessly in harm's way. He saw it as living fearlessly. And in those moments, when he was suspended in the air or exploring the depths or racing down a mountain, that communion with the spiritual was something that filled him up, overflowing his heart. And then he was able to bring that joy home to you and the kids. I think it made him feel like a better husband and father, because he had more to give you."

Had Wes felt empty before he'd started his adventures? Now that she looked back, she could see how he'd whistled more once he began to have those experiences with Brent. Laughed more. Spent more time playing with the kids. Tried to plan date nights with Angela.

But she'd been too worried, too angry, too negative to see those things then. All she could see was him living a dream when she was stuck in the monotony of life. Abandonment instead of an invitation.

"Why wouldn't he have just told me that?"

"Maybe he didn't know how."

And maybe she wouldn't have listened. Hadn't been ready to. But now . . . now she was.

Her soul whispered a silent thank-you for an answer she'd never expected to receive.

᳀

Pure grit was going to carry her through today.

Eva rolled up her sleeping bag and secured it to her rucksack, then surveyed the surrounding land in the light of day. Everything looked wet, and the darkened sky in the distance promised an encore of last night's performance. Frigid ground let off the smell of loamy earth fresh after a rain.

She spotted Marc peeling off from where he sat with Angela to talk to the two male checkpoint workers. Eva approached her sister-in-law. "You guys about ready to head out?"

"I am. Marc just wanted to ask about the latest weather update first. How's your ankle?"

"Still puffy, but the ice, pain relievers, and rest made a bit of a difference." So far this morning it had proven painful to walk on it only if the terrain was angled, and supposedly they'd be blessed with a fairly flat landscape today.

Marc joined them. "They say there's another storm headed our way sometime this afternoon or evening."

"In that case, let's go." Eva hoisted her sack onto her shoulders. The added weight didn't do her ankle any favors, but what choice did she have at this point? She just needed to keep going and embrace the pain.

But the thought didn't hold the same appeal it had months ago.

They set off after Marc spent five minutes double-checking her resolve to continue on. She didn't really mind him taking care of her—he wasn't patronizing, just concerned. The walk was slow going as they headed down from the mountain and into a valley, thankfully still fast enough to reach the end of Stage 5 on time tonight if they were able to keep up this pace.

Marc regaled them with tales of his adventures with Brent and Wes, and Angela surprisingly didn't seem to mind. In fact, she actually asked questions and laughed at some of their antics. Thinking about how much her sister-in-law had changed—how much they'd both changed—during the course of the last six months was almost enough to distract Eva from the pain radiating from her ankle and working its way up her leg.

Almost.

Every now and then Eva would suck in a breath without realizing it, the discomfort hissing through her teeth.

And she wasn't the only one in pain. Her teammates both had their issues. Angela's feet were so bad she'd lost a toenail sometime in the last day or two, and Marc's eyes revealed his pure exhaustion— mental and physical.

They rested far more often than they should have, but what choice did Eva have? She had to give her ankle a break or she'd never make it.

Thankfully, the terrain had finally smoothed out, circling back to long stretches of farmland. Sheep grazed along the rolling hills and even up on the mountainsides, and packs of alpacas roamed near the thick wooden-slatted fences. Their humming sounded like a mixture of cows mooing and sheep bleating. Every time they passed a sheltered stack of hay bales, Eva was reminded they neared civilization.

Tomorrow they'd only have the last six miles to complete. Then they would arrive in Wanaka weary but triumphant.

And then . . . well, she didn't know exactly what would happen. But she was determined that life wouldn't be gray anymore. She'd find the color even if she had to root it out.

To create inspiration, not just look for it.

And having Marc and Angela's family in her life would certainly play a big role in that.

Eva just needed to stay focused. In those moments when her ankle sent fire bolts up her leg and into her hip, she pushed her teeth together as hard as possible, flexing her jaw and narrowing her gaze at some point on the horizon.

It was in one of those moments that she caught the first flash of lightning. "Did you guys see that?"

"Yeah." How was it possible for one word to hold so much dread? But Marc's did.

They plodded on, and finally, the storm met them. By Marc's

calculations, they only had three miles left to go for the day, and a little over an hour to arrive at the final Stage 5 checkpoint.

They weren't going to make it.

The realization struck Eva as the first raindrop slid down her face. The rumble of thunder drowned out the grinding of their shoes against tiny pebbles. Eva imagined herself in a movie—this would be the moment when music would start playing, something both upbeat and ominous. The audience watching would be scared for her, worried she'd buckle under the pressure, breathless with the anticipation of wondering if she would give up and let the elements destroy her resolve, or rise up and fight against them.

And maybe for a moment she'd be tempted to sit down right there in the middle of the path and cry from the agony ripping through her ankle, allowing the fear to take over. But then she'd keep going, because that's what heroes did. They kept on even when everything in them wanted to give up.

Brent had been her hero. And now she had to be her own.

But life wasn't like the movies. This she realized when she felt a new popping in her ankle and then tumbled down, her poles failing to keep her upright, her knee striking a rock, hands landing in mud that lined the outside of the trail.

"Eva!" Marc ran to her side, flinging his poles and pack off in the process.

Lightning burned a trail across the sky above them.

Eva squeezed her eyes shut, waiting to disappear, waiting to awaken from this nightmare. She felt gentle hands lifting her upright until she sat with her legs in front of her. Felt smaller hands probe her ankle. Heard a soft groan from Angela's lips.

"How bad is it?" She managed to open her eyes.

"I think we're done, Eva." Angela rocked back on her behind, arms resting on her knees as rain streaked her face and the wind pulled wisps of hair from her ponytail.

Eva opened her mouth to protest, but instead leaned back against Marc, who was propping her up. The next words would be the hardest she would ever say—but maybe she could be a different sort of hero today. "I might be done. But you guys should go on without me."

"What? We can't. We're a team, remember?"

"Actually . . . you can. Don't you remember the rules? If one team member is injured during the race, the rest of the team can finish as individuals." Eva bit the inside of her cheek until she tasted blood. "So I want you guys to go. If you leave now, you should make it to the final checkpoint in time." Even though the idea burned, it was worse to consider none of them completing the race.

But instead of filling with hope, Angela's eyes narrowed. "We aren't leaving you."

"I can stay with her, Angela." Marc squeezed Eva with his knees. "You go on. Finish this thing for all of us."

Angela looked between them, indecision warring in her features. Then she shook her head, tight. "We all finish, or none of us do."

"Ang . . ."

"We wouldn't be here without you, Eva. Without your dream for us." Hands moved to Angela's hips. "And I am *not* leaving you behind."

"But I don't know if I can put any pressure on my foot."

"Then we will carry you."

She couldn't let her sister-in-law sacrifice her chance to finish. "I—"

"Nope. No arguments allowed. You in?"

Eva studied Angela and knew her odds of winning. "Fine. Let's do this."

37

They were going to get across that finish line on time. Angela wasn't taking no for an answer.

She repositioned Eva's arm across her shoulders, supporting her weight. Eva hopped on her left foot, a renewed sense of vigor and determination infused in her. Over the last two miles, Marc had carried her on his back and Angela lugged her own pack plus Eva's—an awkward feat, to say the least.

Marc would have continued carrying her except his back had started to hurt. Unfortunately, they only had twenty minutes left until their time would run out for the day.

The rain had alternately spit and poured buckets on them, making every step a slick one despite the trekking pole Eva used with her free hand.

Angela focused on watching the path, keeping Eva supported by holding her around the waist with one arm and grasping the hand thrown over her shoulders with the other. They hadn't done much talking, saving their breaths for the grunts that expelled from their lungs with every jerk of their steps.

She tried desperately to ignore the way every joint felt taut and achy, especially her hips and bothersome knee. And then there was the burning where her toenail used to be . . .

Marc glanced down at his watch, his lips drawn into a straight line.

Eva hopped over a small rock, nearly tripping Angela in the process. "How are we doing on time?"

"Twelve minutes left. Maybe a quarter mile."

"Let's pick up the pace." Eva inclined her head toward Angela, a question in her bloodshot eyes.

Was the strain too much for her? The mother in Angela wanted to make Eva stop and rest—but the newly awakened competitor knew they'd all regret it if they didn't give every last ounce of sweat and pain to the effort. "Okay." Angela increased their speed, and it worked for a minute or two, but Eva soon stumbled, and they both ended up on the ground.

Eva pushed the heels of her hands against her forehead. "We tried. Now you guys run. Finish."

Hadn't Eva heard Angela the first time? "Marc, I need your help." She maneuvered so Eva was behind her. "Put her onto my back, will you?"

"You can put her on mine again."

"Yeah, I'm too big for you."

"Are you kidding?" Angela huffed. "You're a tiny twig of a woman and I'm . . . well, not. Marc's back is shot, and we don't have time to argue. Get on my back so we can finish."

Despite her grumbling, Eva got onto Angela's back with Marc's assistance. Then Marc helped Angela stand and gathered all three rucksacks. They set off at a jog, Eva's knees tucked against Angela's waist and under her arms.

Every step felt like running on a trampoline, sinking and then springing from the soil, but thankfully the trail was more imbedded gravel and less dirt and mud.

Angela's lungs heaved air, and Eva's prayers and encouragements bounced in and out of her ear. Lightning bolts of pain shot through every muscle in her straining body.

"Three minutes," Marc yelled just as the bright white of the final checkpoint came into view.

"Oh, thank goodness." This dream wasn't over after all. She'd finally get to see one through to the end. Well, there was still tomorrow—but if they could make twenty-five miles today, they could certainly make the last six.

"One minute. Let's go."

The flat farmland opened up into a wide valley, mountains and rock arcing above them, and the team crossed the final checkpoint with ten seconds to spare.

Angela put Eva down, and her sister-in-law grabbed her up in an embrace. How could tomorrow possibly feel better than this?

A woman with a green shirt and poncho ran toward them, a clipboard in hand. "The Jamison and Cinelli team, I presume?" Behind her, the campsite looked the same as always—except it was nearly deserted. Where was everyone?

Angela nodded.

"Good, we've been waiting. We need all competitors to get to their assigned tents immediately."

Angela helped Eva stand. "My sister-in-law needs a medic to examine her ankle."

The older woman's face looked like stretched canvas over bones. "That's fine, but the two of you"—she pointed to Marc and Angela— "will need to head to your tents."

"Is everything all right?" They'd never been confined to their tents before.

"Just a precaution for now. We simply need everyone accounted for." The woman waved at two men under the medic's tent and they came jogging over. "Please examine Ms. Jamison's ankle and then escort her to her tent."

Eva turned to Angela, her brow furrowed. "Ang . . ."

"I'll figure out what's going on. You take care of that ankle."

When the men tried to help Eva, she leaned toward Marc, who helped her hop to the medic tent.

While the authoritative woman cast a wary eye at her, Angela grabbed her bag and took off for tent 101, then stopped and looked back. The woman had left. Angela tiptoed toward the media tent, where she spied Simon chatting quietly with a short blonde reporter.

He spotted her and came over. "Hey. I was worried about you."

"Yeah, Eva's ankle gave out, so we were a bit delayed."

"Sorry to hear that."

"We almost didn't make it. But we did." Instead of joining in with her enthusiasm, though, Simon's eyebrows knit together. "Wait, what's wrong?"

Simon glanced around. "They don't want anyone panicking, but there's a bad storm about to blow through here. It's freakish, actually. Unusual at this time of year."

Angela smoothed her wet hair away from her forehead. "Really? Because we just came through one. Several, in fact." Studying the now nearly cloudless sky—when had it stopped raining?—she had a hard time believing the ominous weather report to be true.

"There's about to be round two, and it might be bad enough to flood the area for tomorrow's race."

"So what does that mean?"

"That they might have to evacuate you all."

His words took a moment to sink in. "Evacuate? What about the last stage?"

"The race would be over. Normally they'd just reroute you, but since there're only six miles left, there aren't many options that wouldn't be affected by the storm. So they'd just take you all back to Wanaka by bus and determine winners based on results as of today."

They wouldn't get to finish. "No. This can't be happening." Not when she'd finally decided to pursue something again, had put her whole heart into it. Had made peace with Wes. With God. Thanked him for giving her a new dream.

Thought that there might be some hope for a future with Simon . . . once she finished this race.

"Angela? I know this is disappointing, but you look really pale." Simon ran the tips of his fingers down her upper arms. "Are you all right?"

"I . . ." She shook her head. "I'd say this is unbelievable, but why not believe it? Things don't change, Simon. Not for me."

It sounded like a pity party, but it wasn't. It was just the cold, hard truth.

For Angela Jamison, dreaming was just an exercise in the futile.

38

"You asleep?"

Eva shifted in her sleeping bag and propped herself up on an elbow as Marc stuck his head inside her tent. "No. Get in here before you're soaked." Despite a brief break in the weather, it had now been raining for an hour at least. Night had fallen, but her electric lantern splashed the tent with a soft glow.

Marc ducked in and zipped her tent flap shut. "I wanted to bring you some dinner." He held up an MRE pouch. "Unfortunately, I had to use cold water, so I'm sure it's not the tastiest sweet and sour chicken I've ever made. Still, I figured it'd be more filling than beef jerky."

"Thank you." Given the condition of her ankle and the tight quarters, Eva struggled to maneuver to a sitting position without kicking Marc. Once she had the MRE and a fork in hand, he moved on to the sleeping bag next to her. Warmth radiated off of him as she plunged the fork into the bag. Bits of chicken, rice, and pineapple clung to the utensil as she shoved it into her mouth. "Mmm, gourmet."

He laughed. "I thought so."

She chewed, swallowed, hardly tasting any of it. "What time is it?"

"Nine." He leaned back on his hands. "I hope you don't mind me sneaking in here. I was worried about you."

"I'm fine." Well, her ankle looked like a blimp on steroids, but she'd taken as much medicine as the medics thought advisable, so she could hardly feel it. "What's going on with the race? I heard you and Angela talking outside my tent earlier but couldn't make out all the details."

"Weather delay. They aren't sure if we'll be able to start right away in the morning." He frowned. "Actually, they aren't sure we'll be starting at all."

Eva set the empty MRE pouch aside. "What? Why?"

He explained about the possible flood conditions and the alternate plan. "I don't think they'll know anything until the morning, so it's best if we get all rested up as if we're going." Marc glanced at her, wariness in his eyes. "But . . ."

"But what?"

"Part of me wonders if this is a blessing in disguise. You're pretty hurt, Eva, and I don't want to see you any worse off."

"I want to finish."

Marc sat upright again. "But earlier you said—"

"I know, but that was more about not wanting Angela to feel like I held her back. Now we're so close to the end." She reached for his hand, squeezed. "I got this."

He pulled her hand to his lips, kissing her palm lightly. "I know you do." Even in the low light, his eyes seemed to trace the contours of her face. He reached up and did the same with his fingers. "But I can't help but worry."

"You don't have to worry about me."

"I know I don't have to. It's my privilege to."

She was struck with the realization that it was more than concern radiating in his eyes. "You take very good care of me."

He sighed. In the distance, above the din of the rain, rose the gentle call of an owl. "I don't think I ever told you this, but Brent . . . he asked me one time . . ." His voice cracked with emotion, and his

Adam's apple bobbed. "He told me that if anything ever happened to him, I was the one he wanted watching out for you."

"Ah, so I was an obligation then?" She teased, not sure how to process that piece of information.

Marc pinned her with a look that was anything but teasing. "You have never been an obligation to me a day in your life, Eva Jamison. But . . ." His fingertips still lingered on her cheeks as he searched her eyes for something. Some sort of permission. "I just . . . I hope Brent would bless this. I think he would. Still, I sometimes feel like the worst friend in the world. He asked me to watch out for you, and I ended up falling in love with you instead."

In love . . . All breath fled her lungs.

How was it possible to feel both heartache and joy in the same moment? To comprehend that without Brent, she and Marc wouldn't even know each other? That without his death, this love never would have existed?

Did she love Marc too?

Why bother asking? She knew with every fiber of her being that she did.

Eva placed her hand on Marc's chest, felt his heart beating as rapidly as her own. Her lips longed to profess the words back to him, but she couldn't. Not yet. What held her back?

All she knew was she did feel it, despite her fears, and she wanted to show him, even if she didn't have the strength to tell him yet. Eva fisted his jacket in her hand and pulled him closer, meeting his surprised lips with her own. It took a moment, but he kissed her back, and soon he'd wrapped his arms around her waist. She looped her arms around his shoulders, intensifying the kiss.

His lips slowly moved to her earlobe, and a heady feeling buzzed inside her. It felt both new and familiar, and she longed for a deeper connection.

"I love you, too, Brent."

The words split the air, dousing the flame of passion between them as Marc jerked back from her like he'd been burned.

Her hand flew to her mouth, trembling. "Marc. I'm so sorry. I don't know . . ."

Other than his ragged breaths, silence filled the tent. The rain beat out a morbid rhythm above them, beside them, all around them.

"I don't know why I said that. I didn't mean . . ."

"Are you sure?" Marc asked, torment in his tone. "Were you imagining him when you kissed me?"

She hadn't. Right? "I . . ."

"It's my fault, Eva. I pushed you. You aren't ready."

"You didn't push me. I kissed you first, remember?" And how right it had felt. So why had Brent's name found its way out of her mouth? Tears streamed down her cheeks.

Marc groaned. "I love you, Eva. But I was an idiot to think you could ever be mine. You'll always be Brent's. Maybe that's how it should be. Either way, I can't compete with a ghost."

Before she could say another word, he unzipped the tent. When he looked back at her, the light from the moon allowed her to see the pain flickering through his eyes.

"Marc, wait. I do love you. I do."

"Even if that's true, I'm not sure love is enough to make this work between us." He slipped from the tent.

Eva tried to stand, but pain shot through her ankle at the movement. She grunted and side-crawled to the edge of the tent, sending a prayer heavenward. *Help me fix this.* A loud whimper burst from her lips as she attempted to restrain her tears. She ducked her head outside, but Marc was nowhere to be seen. He must have fled into his own tent.

"Eva?" Angela climbed out from her tent. "What's wrong?"

Eva couldn't answer, just buried her face in her hands and cried, her shoulders shuddering.

"Come on. You're getting all wet." Angela lugged Eva back to her bed, then stroked her hair while Eva cried some more.

Whether they got to finish the race or not, now she just couldn't see a scenario where this ended well.

When her tears were spent, Eva glanced up at her sister-in-law, saw the hardened lines around her eyes and mouth, and wondered what demons Angela was battling even while she listened to Eva fight her own.

39

The next morning, despite the utter agony her body was in, Angela headed out to find Simon. Maybe he'd give her the 4–1–1 on their situation.

Rain still tumbled from above and slicked off Angela's rain poncho onto the muddy ground. The once-azure sky had grayed and purpled. It would have been a beautiful mixture if it didn't mean the demise of a dream.

On her way to the media tent, the only competitors she saw out and about were huddled together under a pop-up canopy, their breath releasing in puffs as they spoke in low tones made unintelligible to Angela's ears by the rain.

So far there was no sign of Marc or Eva, though after last night's events, Angela expected both to stay tucked away—Marc to lick his wounds and Eva to continue despairing. Angela had done her best to console her sister-in-law, and when Eva had finally fallen into a fitful sleep, Angela had snuck back to her own tent and attempted the same.

But every time her eyes closed, she'd seen a future she wasn't all that excited about. Yes, she and Marc had just spoken yesterday about setting her up with a position at company headquarters when she returned. Only forty hours a week and good pay and benefits. But once again, she was falling, not choosing. Circumstances were dictating her life instead of Angela being in control of her destiny. And yes, she could still try to go after what she wanted—if she could ever truly figure out what that was.

But at what point did a person admit defeat?

Still, maybe Simon could offer her an inkling of hope—something small to cling to.

"Ang!"

Turning, she caught sight of him striding toward her from a copse of trees, his clothing rumpled, a dusting of stubble along his jaw. There was something appealing about a man who looked like he'd just rolled out of bed . . .

She shook herself. "I was just looking for you."

"In that case, take a walk with me?"

Did she really want to walk more than absolutely necessary right now? But she wouldn't want him to get in trouble for giving her insider information, so they needed to speak privately. "Where?"

Placing his hand on the small of her back, he led her toward a little trail traversing up a hill that overlooked the campsite. Ugh.

Just a few more steps, Angela. Then you can sit again.

Once they'd walked in silence for several torturous minutes, she spoke up. "So what's going on with the race?"

"It's still not looking good. Just wait a moment and I'll tell you more."

Suddenly the trail ended and the trees fell away. They were at the top of the bluff, where a small overhang sat tucked into the side of the hill, almost like a cave but not quite. Simon indicated that she was to climb under first, so she did. He crawled in after her.

"So it's not looking promising?"

"I believe they're going to give it another few hours and then call it if the rain doesn't let up."

Angela nodded, resigned. What more could she say?

Simon moved closer to her, their shoulders almost touching.

"Last night you said things don't change for you." From the corner of her eye, she saw him turn his head so he could see her. "What did you mean?"

So he hadn't just pulled her up here to talk about the race.

She bit her lip, considering how to begin. "As a child, I had high hopes for my life. Big dreams, you know? I wanted to be someone important, like my aunt. To have a career that helped people, and yes, that also provided for all my financial needs so I didn't need to be dependent on anyone else. Life and my own mistakes derailed those dreams, though God still gave me something amazing. And I settled into those blessings and, in a way, I embraced them. Then Wes died."

She paused. "And once again I was given a life I hadn't asked for. It took me awhile to dream again. But here I am, once again disappointed. I'm so tired of the constant ups and downs, always feeling kneed in the gut just when I think things are finally going to go the way I'd hoped." Angela shrugged. "But maybe I simply need to be content with what I have and stop asking for more."

"But what's life without dreams?"

"Why dream when you know all you'll get is let down?" Angela sighed, pulling her knees into her chest. "I'm choosing to be logical. A realist."

"Logic isn't a bad thing, but a lot of things can't be explained by it. If you stay rooted in your limited world, only among things you understand, you're going to miss out on a lot." He pulled Angela's hand into his, running his fingers over the ridges of her knuckles. His touch brought a shiver down her spine, as did his words. "Life is about dreaming, even if those dreams never come to fruition. God is the planter of dreams, and in his timing, he will make those dreams grow. But we have to keep watering them, keep hoping, even when life throws things at us we don't expect."

Angela shook her head. "I don't know how. Everything's so

jumbled. All I do know is when I want something—really want it—it doesn't happen. What am I supposed to do with that?"

For a moment Simon considered her. "Angela, what *do* you really want out of life? And I don't mean what things do you want to do, or what relationships do you want to improve, or what job do you want to have. What's that underlying thing you want out of life?"

Her eyes slid back to the rain-sodden trees beyond the cave, their leaves dancing, never doing the same move twice. How could she sum it all up in a few mere words?

"I used to think it was stability. That's what I really grew up valuing, because I didn't have it. And I thought I had to achieve it on my own. Thought I could achieve it by becoming a doctor. Then I married Wes, and he provided it for a while. Until he didn't. Now, though? I think I just want to find a balance between dreaming and being content with where I am. Not settling, but also recognizing when I don't have control over a situation—and finding peace in that."

Yes, yes, yes. Her soul leapt at the words.

Simon squeezed her fingers. "You're there, I think. Look at how you've already broken free of the past. So things don't look the way you thought they would, eh? You're still here, and a different woman at that."

She had changed, hadn't she? But there was so much growth that needed to happen before she was fully transformed.

"I want to keep changing." Angela wiped away the moisture dripping from her eyes. "I'm so afraid of getting stuck again, though."

"You don't have to do it alone, you know. Let God help you." Simon leaned in and kissed her forehead. "Let me help you."

Angela closed her eyes. If only. Even if she could bring herself to try again with a new relationship, Simon lived halfway around the world—and that seemed to set them up for the biggest disappointment of all. "I . . ."

"It doesn't have to be a big decision right now, eh? Finish this race if possible, then go home, settle back in, write me, call." Simon smoothed her hair back. "We'll suss it out from there."

She didn't know whether it was possible to work things out, but right now hope nestled in. "I can't believe you aren't running the other direction."

The incredulous look that passed over his face would have been comical if it didn't sear her in the gut. "Not even close."

He leaned toward her—and she finally gave in to her impulse to hook her arms around his neck and pull him near.

Then Simon surprised her by kissing her cheek where the tears had been. "Not." Then the other cheek. "Even." Finally, he pulled his face back just slightly so their noses touched. "Close."

He stayed there, watching her, waiting. For what?

Oh.

For her.

He was giving her a choice.

Angela wound her fingers into Simon's hair, shut her eyes, and allowed him to kiss her. It was soft and sweet—a gentle pressing of their souls together as she lifted a prayer for the strength to dream again.

The kiss ended, and Simon nudged her, pointing outside the cave. "Look. The rain. It's stopped."

40

When Angela came to Eva's tent around 10 a.m. and told her the race was back on, Eva slumped against her pillow.

Her sister-in-law was clearly excited, and something else—the worry lines around her eyes had relaxed, and a smile took up a large portion of her face. Peace. That was it. She looked at peace.

Would Eva ever feel that way again?

"That's great." It was the expected response, right? She should be as thrilled as Angela. More, in fact, considering this whole thing had been her idea.

But the thought of facing Marc after last night's debacle . . . Ugh.

"Eva?" Angela crawled into the tent. "You seem a million miles away. What's going on?"

"My ankle. It hurts." That and everything else—her heart most of all.

Angela helped Eva unzip her sleeping bag and pulled the cover aside. A blast of cold air hit Eva's whole body as Angela examined her ankle. "It's pretty bad today. Do you really want to do this?"

"Yes." Maybe everything would be better if she could just finish this race. It's what she'd told herself when she'd dreamed of it months ago, and she couldn't give up now when the potential payoff was so close. Whatever was happening with Marc, she couldn't let herself down.

It would take the very last shred of resolve she had. But what else could she do?

Eva bit back a yelp as Angela worked on placing fresh tape on her ankle. "Didn't you mention that Simon could get me some crutches or something?"

"Yes." Angela finished taping and started helping Eva on with her shoes. "And hopefully they'll help more than the trekking poles since you can actually place your full weight on them."

Eva worked up the courage to ask the question she'd been mulling all morning. "How's Marc?"

"I haven't seen much of him, but he'll be okay. You guys will get past this."

"How? He thinks I haven't moved on." She loved Marc. But she loved Brent, too, and she always would. Could she ever reconcile the two?

"I've come to hate that phrase. *Move on*. As if we leave our husbands behind and the people we were before." Angela patted Eva's leg. "But all of it becomes part of us, right? I don't think we ever move on. Like Sherry said, we just keep moving. One step at a time. And eventually the hurt isn't so bad. The past doesn't hold us back from our future. Yes, there will always be moments that trigger us, when we feel like the pain might drown us again. But I'm hoping those moments become fewer and further between the more time that elapses."

"I hope so too. Although I never want to forget Brent and what he meant to me."

"You won't. You just might not feel completely gutted whenever you think of him. And you can't compare your grief with other people's. No one can tell you when you're ready for a new relationship. And it's okay if you're not there quite yet."

That's the thing. She wanted to be ready, at long last. But did her slipup last night mean she wasn't?

From outside, three short whistle blasts sounded. Angela squeezed Eva's hand. "We've only got thirty minutes. Let's get you up and about."

Eva got dressed, used the restroom, and wolfed down a slab of beef jerky. The crutches Simon secured had seen better days, but at least neither of her teammates would have to carry her for miles. By the time they reached the starting line, other teams had already begun to cross it, taking off with their packs held high on their backs, itching for a win.

Eva's eyes landed on Marc for the first time since last night. He stood chatting with Simon, looking as handsome as ever. Her heart swelled with love and heartbreak when he turned and looked at her, then swung his gaze promptly away.

Her sister-in-law was wrong. They'd never get past this.

Angela spoke first. "All right, should we head off?" The sky was still darker than most days had been, but streaks of sun had begun to break through the clouds.

Marc jerked his head. "Yep." The terse statement didn't bode well.

Simon snapped a photo of them all on his phone. "I'll be waiting at the finish line."

"Tell Sherry if it gets too late, she and the kids don't have to stay." Angela seemed suddenly shy around Simon. Had they mended things between them? If they could, maybe it wasn't such a stretch to think she and Marc might be able to as well.

But Angela hadn't called Simon by her dead husband's name while kissing him and professing her love, so . . .

A headache started to form behind Eva's temples, and her armpits already felt the pressure of leaning on the crutches. "Let's do this."

Simon whispered something in Angela's ear, then pressed a kiss to her lips.

A blush engulfing her cheeks, Angela turned to face Eva and Marc. "Ready?"

"Ready." Marc grabbed Eva's rucksack from the ground before she could protest and started walking.

Eva and Angela followed, a slow and painful process. Navigating the road was tricky, what with the gravel and sporadic shrubbery, but the hilly course started to open up to a view of something big. As they reached the edge of a bluff, Eva gasped. "Lake Wanaka?"

Angela looked to Marc for confirmation, who nodded. "The path around the lake has always been really flat and free of debris. That's good news."

Finally.

They descended and reached the lake's edge. The familiarity of it welcomed them and gave Eva an extra surge of energy despite her pain and exhaustion. They were almost there. Almost back home. Well, not home, but back to the place that had become a refuge to her these many months. They'd have to return to their actual homes soon. And how would that feel?

How would it be to return to a world surrounded by Brent's things, his memories? Should she finally donate his clothing? Pack away his wall of awards, his computer and files, and convert his office into a guest room? If what Angela said was true, then moving on didn't mean she had to get rid of any trace of him. But then, how could she ever be sure she had continued to move forward?

Stop it, Eva. She didn't have to know all of that yet. All she had to do today was focus on the race.

Finish line. Finish line. Finish line.

But eventually her thoughts slipped out of their singular chant and back to the ache in her heart. Even if Marc hadn't been walking slightly in front of her, Eva couldn't help but watch him, almost begging him with her eyes to look her way. But he never did; he just remained fixated on the road ahead. If he asked her a question about how she was doing, he looked at her ankle—that was it.

They walked mostly in silence, except for the slow and steady crunch of her crutches against the ground and the lapping of the water against the shore. The tall reeds waved in the breeze, and the leaves of the overhanging trees had begun to change to a golden hue.

Autumn was coming, and nothing could stop it. The seasons marched on. Life did too.

And where did that leave Eva?

They took frequent breaks, drinking water and sitting by the lakeside munching on their energy bars. Marc ambled to the lakefront below and hunkered down on a rock within view. Eva longed to follow him, but given the condition of her ankle—to say nothing of the condition of her spirit—it simply wasn't possible.

Angela was the only bright spot in the day, cheering her on and carrying her when the crutches had her underarms feeling raw and then numb. Despite the daunting day, something about her sister-in-law seemed lighter. Eva would ask about it later, but for now, her own emotions nearly crushed her with their weight.

At long last, the sound of a crowd's cheers reached their ears. Marc checked his watch and declared they were a half mile away.

Pressing on, every muscle aching, they finally came within view of the finish line on the edge of Wanaka. Among the din she could make out Angela's children's voices screaming, "Mom! Aunt Eva! Marc!" Her eyes scanned the crowd and she saw her nieces and nephew, along with Sherry, holding a large neon-pink sign, jumping up and down. Eva pointed them out to Angela, whose eyes filled with tears.

When they were a few feet away, Eva tossed aside the crutches. Marc and Angela came on either side of her and wrapped their arms around her back as she slid her arms around their shoulders. She leaned into Marc, relishing the closeness that she might never know again. Together, they moved while she hopped—one, two, three—across the finish line.

As soon as they were over the line, Marc's hand dropped and he lurched aside while the children surged forward, tackling them.

"Mom! I lost a tooth while you were gone!" Lilly shouted.

"You finished with exactly one hour and six minutes to spare." Oh, Zach.

"So proud of you guys!" Kylee squeezed Angela tight.

Sherry came alongside Eva. "Looks like you've had quite a time. But you did it. My boys would be so proud of you."

"Thank you. I hope so." As Eva clasped her mother-in-law's hand, her eyes scanned the crowd and caught Marc melting away.

One painful step at a time, they'd made it here. Done what they'd set out to do. Her legs could barely hold her upright, but somehow she still stood.

At the same moment, the sisters-in-law turned to each other and threw themselves into each other's embrace.

"Thank you, Eva." Angela's jagged whisper doused the noise around them. "Thank you for inviting me on this journey. I haven't felt this way in a very long time. Maybe never."

Eva's throat filled with cotton. "Thank *you*. I couldn't have done it without you."

And even though she still had no clue what lay ahead, Eva clutched Angela tight and allowed herself to rejoice in a job well done.

Maybe now life could finally bloom again.

41

SIX WEEKS LATER

Angela's fingers hovered over the mouse for the briefest of moments before she sent a prayer heavenward and clicked.

Friend Request sent.

"Whew." She exited out of Facebook and closed her web browser, sitting back in her desk chair. Even though her office door remained shut, her feet could pick up the vibration of the Latin music Danica used to teach the Pilates class next door. The eucalyptus smell had snuck down the hall from the main entryway of No Frills Fitness and pervaded her small little corner of Marc and Eva's gym, where she was now an administrative assistant.

A knock sounded on her door, and she straightened when Marc poked his head in. "Hey, boss."

In his hands he held a magazine. "You're still here, huh?"

"Just about to head out." She'd stayed late to pop on social media and do the thing she'd been dreading for weeks. Now the ball was in her father's court. If he wanted her and the kids in his life, he'd respond, even though he hadn't returned her three attempted phone calls. And if he didn't, she'd done all she could to forgive him for the past and move forward.

"Wondered if you'd seen this yet." Marc slid a copy of the *Worldwide Runners* quarterly magazine onto her desk.

A majestic photo of the mountains of New Zealand and the man who'd won the ultra-marathon graced the cover. Angela ran her thumb over the glossy finish. "Hard to believe it's been six weeks."

Marc flew home the next day, and after spending a final week recuperating in the Wanaka lake house, the rest of them had returned home. Angela had started her new job right away, and the kids had gone back to school for the last few months of the semester. On a normal day she was home in time to make dinner and spend the evening helping the kids with homework. And on Fridays she'd started attending group at Philip's Place with the kids. What a difference that had made.

Regarding everything else, she was still praying about what came next. If anything.

When Marc didn't answer, Angela peeked up at him. He'd leaned against the wall, thumbs in the pockets of his slacks, staring at the magazine.

She flipped it open to the table of contents, found the story she sought, and turned the thin pages to page fifty-two. Her eyes skimmed the photos of her, Marc, and Eva throughout the race, as well as the title, "A Hard-Fought Journey," finally turning her gaze to the byline.

Simon King.

Angela couldn't stop her finger from stroking the two precious words. Clearing her throat, she closed the magazine. "Mind if I keep this to read later?"

"I already read it. It's all yours." He paused. "It was a good article."

"I have no doubt." Angela studied him. "You okay?" From what Eva had told her in their few-and-far-between interactions of late, she and Marc kept all communications strictly business related and in the form of emails since returning to New York.

"I guess, considering." Shoving both of his hands all the way into his pockets, Marc frowned. "How's Eva?"

That was a loaded question. Her sister-in-law had come over only a handful of times since returning home. She'd pretended everything was fine, but when Angela tried to pull her aside to press the issue, Eva would suddenly remember a boutique sale or a dentist appointment she'd forgotten about. Every time she'd raced from Angela's home like her yoga pants were on fire.

Angela rubbed her nose. "I don't think she's doing all that well." She'd tried to stay out of the whole thing, especially since Marc was now her boss and she didn't want to stick her nose where it didn't belong. Still, after all they'd been through . . . "Have you tried talking to her about what happened between you two?"

"No." Marc stared up at the ceiling above Angela's desk where one of the tiles hung slightly askew. "I can't win. If I have to convince her to give us another shot, then I'll always wonder if she's really ready. And I feel like the worst cad in the world to even want that, you know, because of Brent. And if I just leave it be . . ." His voice sputtered.

"You feel like you might never recover from the hole in your heart?"

She knew a little something about that. Despite her agreement to call Simon once she was home, she hadn't—and not from lack of wanting to. But she still had a few things left to settle with God before she could. Even then, a fear of the unknown threatened her happiness, and she couldn't seem to shake it.

Marc didn't acknowledge her statement, checking his watch instead. "I've got a dinner meeting I need to get to. Give those kids a hug for me tonight, all right?"

"You got it."

After Marc left, Angela gathered her things, turned off her computer, and headed home, thinking of Simon and trying not to think about him at the same time all throughout the subway ride to Queens. When she finally made it to the house, she unlocked the door and smelled Italian spices. Was Kylee cooking? Sure enough,

Angela walked into the kitchen and saw her oldest standing at the stove mixing spaghetti sauce. Zach and Lilly sat at the kitchen table doing their homework.

Angela planted a kiss on her two youngest children's heads and squeezed Kylee around the shoulders. "Yum, that smells amazing."

Kylee's red cheeks gave away her pleasure at the compliment. "Grandma taught me her secret recipe." She lifted a wooden spatula to her lips and tasted the red sauce. "Doesn't taste quite right yet, though."

"Let me try." Angela leaned over while Kylee spooned some into her mouth. Hot, but the salt and garlic popped on her tongue. "Mmm, that's just about perfect. Maybe try adding a bit more sugar to balance out the saltiness."

Kylee mixed in a teaspoon. "So Coach Miller stopped me in the hall today."

Angela grabbed a bag from the fridge, pulled open the top, and dumped the lettuce into a bowl. "About what?" From the counter she snagged a carton of grape tomatoes and started washing them.

Her daughter tasted the sauce again, then nodded, satisfied. "She wanted to know if you had any interest in assistant coaching cross-country in the fall."

The carton slipped from Angela's hands, and a few tomatoes escaped down the drain. "What do you mean?" She dug in the drain for the lost tomatoes.

"I guess Coach Bailey is going on maternity leave and no other teachers have applied for the job. It wouldn't be full-time, just after school and on weekends during meets and stuff. And just for next season, unless Coach Bailey decides not to come back after having her baby."

Wetness covered Angela's hands. She looked down to see she'd crushed a few tomatoes and the slimy insides had oozed out. "But I don't have a degree. I'm not a teacher."

"I told her that, but she said something about a temporary

certificate that was easy enough to get." Kylee shrugged. "I dunno. Sounds like the perfect fit for you, honestly."

Angela didn't emulate her daughter's confidence, although she really liked the idea of inspiring kids in the same way her coach had encouraged her once upon a time. Flicking on the faucet, she washed the tomato yuck away. "You think so?"

"Duh, Mom. You love running. And you love teaching. Win-win. And like, if you enjoy it, you could go back to school and get a teaching degree and become a permanent coach somewhere."

How had she really never considered that option before? Like tea, the idea steeped, becoming fuller and more delightfully tasty the more she thought about it. She'd been praying for direction—could this be her answer?

"You don't have to decide right now. Just give Coach a call. One step at a time, right?"

Angela stared at Kylee, amazed. "How did I manage to raise such a wise daughter?"

Kylee hip-bumped her. "It was a fluke, Mom. A total fluke."

42

It should have felt different.

Eva stared at her bedroom ceiling. The smooth eggshell color started to morph into a subtle gray, the moving sun outside the window changing the boring hue ever so slightly.

Rolling over, she pulled the comforter tighter across her shoulders. Nearly two months after she'd returned home from New Zealand, and she was right back where she'd started. She'd traveled halfway around the world to find herself here once more, drowning in a bed built for two.

Her phone buzzed, but she ignored it. Probably Kimberly again. Her friend had left her a message a few days ago. Apparently the florist for the Carlton wedding had gone bankrupt and Kimberly was desperate for a replacement. And since she'd wanted Eva in the first place, couldn't her bestie fill in?

Eva hadn't even been able to return the call and say a polite no. Because she couldn't admit the truth to Kim—that Eva was broken. That all her efforts to make life colorful again, to find happiness, had been useless.

An hour later, someone knocked on the door. Eva sat up, rubbing her ankle. The race had taken a toll on it, but now it only ached occasionally.

Whoever was at the door could come back later. Or not. It didn't matter.

Her phone rang again. "Argh." She grabbed it off the side table, glancing at the caller ID. Angela. "Hello?"

"Are you home?"

"Yeah."

"I'm here. Can you answer the door? Or do I need to break it down?"

Eva held in a groan. "I'll be right there." She hung up and climbed from bed. After a quick glance in the mirror, she shrugged. Angela could deal with her pajamas, greasy hair, and lack of makeup. Making her way to the door, she swung it open to find Angela holding a large white paper bag.

Her sister-in-law breezed past her. "I brought dinner."

"How did you know I didn't have plans?"

Angela looked her up and down and quirked an eyebrow before turning on her heel and heading toward the kitchen.

Sighing, Eva closed the door and followed her. Her sister-in-law removed several white containers from the bag. The aroma of mandarin chicken and sweet and sour sauce met Eva's nose.

The last time she'd had Chinese was in the tent with Marc. Before she'd ruined everything.

"Thanks." Eva opened one and found tiny broccoli trees mixed with juicy beef. She pulled a few plates from her cabinet and two forks from the drawer.

Angela scooped some rice and chicken onto one of the plates, and Eva did the same. Once Eva snagged a few water bottles from the fridge, they sat at the table across from each other.

Angela stabbed some chicken with her fork. "So. How are things?"

"Fabulous." She hated the sarcastic tone she spewed. But this was why she'd avoided much contact with others. She wasn't pleasant to be around anymore, and she was tired of trying to put on a front and act like everything was okay.

"Come on." Tapping the fork against the ceramic plate, Angela tilted her head. "Talk to me. Please."

"There's nothing to say." Eva shoveled some rice into her mouth.

"Is this about Marc? Because he's pretty miserable without you too."

He was? The thought shouldn't make her happy. It didn't, exactly. But it was nice to know he missed her. She shook her head. "It's more than that."

After a few moments, Angela broke the silence. "Well?"

"I feel worse off than I did before the race. How is that possible?"

"How did you expect to feel?"

"Less confused, that's for sure." Eva moved some food around on her plate but didn't lift anything to her lips. "I truly don't know where to go from here. I can't even figure out what to do with my days, so I watch television and work out and cook and shop. But nothing brings true pleasure, nothing feels right—not returning to the heart center, not creating flower arrangements again, and definitely not working the business with Marc." Eva paused. "And before you ask, I've talked with my counselor and we both agree I'm not depressed. Just stuck."

"I know how that feels, believe me." After a few moments of thoughtful chewing, Angela continued. "In a way, New Zealand was about healing, yes, but also about discovering happiness again. For both of us. But maybe happiness is this illusive thing that's really dependent on circumstances—something we can't find and control, much as we want to."

The words niggled something in the back of Eva's mind. "That reminds me of a conversation I had months ago with Sherry."

"What did she say?"

Eva put herself back there, under the starry New Zealand sky. "I'm trying to remember the exact words, but basically that happiness and joy aren't the same thing, and that joy is found in trusting

God, even when life is at its worst." Eva bit her lip. "The problem is, I don't know *how* to trust God."

"It's not easy after what we've been through. Brent's death took something from you, just like Wes's death took something from me. But I've started believing our loss can still be used for good."

"How?"

"Instead of letting grief overshadow our lives, we can let it transform us."

What a thought. "I want that. I really do. But . . . how?"

"Like Sherry and Kylee and every other person we love has been telling us: one step at a time. Maybe grief isn't a process to get through, in the sense of doing certain things and getting to check them off a grieving to-do list." Angela smiled. "Maybe it's more like our journey through New Zealand. Lots of ups and downs, winding roads and beautiful forests, flat land and mountainous regions filled with mudslides and floods that take us unawares. It was really difficult in some moments, but every challenge moved us closer to our goal."

"But what's my goal now?"

"Sorry, sis, only you can answer that. And I have to do the same for myself. I *can* tell you that my goal in life used to be mere survival, but what I really needed was to learn to experience the grief and realize it was okay to mourn, for life not to be perfect, for life to surprise me sometimes." She fisted her napkin. "I'm still learning that in a way. Still trying to find a way forward in a few situations."

"I'd like to know that all of this suffering hasn't been wasted."

"Me too." Angela tilted her head. "I know in the past you said that Brent was your muse, and now that he's not here, you've hidden your creative self away. But what if the ultimate muse is really God, and he's got this amazingly full and creative life waiting for you, if only you'll step back into it? Is it possible to allow all the pain and the beauty of life to inspire you? To allow God to inspire you—not just to create, but to live?"

"Wow. I . . ."

"I know, it's a lot. I didn't mean to barrage you with my thoughts." Angela polished off her food and stood to collect the dishes, then headed to the sink and set down the plates.

"Thanks for coming over, Ang." Eva joined her at the sink and threw her arms around her sister-in-law's shoulders. "You've given me a lot to think about."

"I'm here for you. Just remember that." Angela looked at her pointedly. "And I think Marc would be, too, if you'd let him."

After Angela left, Eva sat down on the couch ready to flick on the TV. Her brain hurt from all they'd discussed. But as her finger hovered over the remote, an idea formed.

Eva huffed. No. She had to find a new goal. She couldn't take one more failure.

But what had Angela said? *Is it possible to allow all the pain and the beauty of life to inspire you?* Maybe she'd been looking at it all wrong.

Eva got up and walked to her window. In the distance she could make out the treetops of Prospect Park. A haze covered the skyline of New York City, and buildings jutted against the horizon, creating an intricate puzzle. So different from the mountains of New Zealand, though no less beautiful.

Her life now . . . it was beautiful too. Different from her life with Brent, yes. But still beautiful, because God could use her sorrows to deepen her strength, to draw her closer to himself—maybe even someday to help others going through something similar.

But it would only happen if she allowed *him* to fill her well of creativity. Not to look to others to do it. Not even to herself alone.

Her fingers tingled. It was time. To try. Even if she failed.

She picked up her phone, opened a text, typed a message, and hit Send.

43

She was more than three years late in accepting Wes's invitation.

But better late than never.

Angela sat like a sardine lined up with eleven other people, six in each row. Eva and a man she'd never met before today were strapped together directly in front of Angela and the instructor she'd been paired with—John or something like that. She'd been too nervous during the brief instructional video and waiver signing to pay much attention to his name.

For such a tiny plane, its engine roared outside as it took them higher and higher into the air, heading for ten thousand feet, if the video could be believed.

The video had also said she didn't have anything to worry about. That the instructor would take care of everything—telling her when to jump, pulling the parachute, landing. He'd even placed goggles on Angela and banded their harnesses together a few minutes ago.

Her spine tingled. Why had she decided this was the best way to spend the second anniversary of Wes's and Brent's deaths?

"We're getting close." John's voice rattled in her ear—or maybe the rattling came from the sliding door that would soon roll up vertically to reveal an exit. "Your bucket list will have one less item after today."

Bucket list? Sure, let him think that.

But no matter how much her hands shook at what was coming, a deeper peace settled in her spirit. This was where she was supposed to be today. And with the way Eva had grinned at Angela's suggestion, she knew her sister-in-law felt the same way.

The pilot made an announcement that they were close to the drop zone. Angela's insides cramped, and she fiddled with the zipper on her orange-and-blue jumpsuit that made her look like a prison inmate.

"Here we go."

Angela gave John a wobbly thumbs-up in reply.

Eva's instructor opened the rolling plane door, and a breeze attacked them all, whipping across Angela's forehead and cheeks. Then Eva and her instructor crouched by the door, waiting for a big red light to turn green.

Glancing at Angela, Eva mouthed, "Are you okay?" Other than her concern for Angela, her excitement was clear. This wasn't her first time doing this, since she'd gone with Brent before. Still, the fact that she could bring herself to do this now, without Brent, on today of all days, was proof of how far her sister-in-law had come.

Angela nodded at Eva's question. She was as okay as one could be when about to leap from a flying airplane.

And then, before Angela could blink, the light turned green and Eva and her instructor disappeared from view.

Angela's breath left her. Could she do this?

Lord, help.

Then, again a peace came, one she didn't understand.

John nudged her forward, and she crouched on the edge of the plane, anticipating the free fall to come. Her heart galloped.

"One."

What am I doing?

"Two."

I can't, I can't, I can't.

Yes, I can, I can, I can.

"Three."

With a gentle push from John, Angela grimaced and stepped off the ledge.

Her own shriek filled her ears as she rocketed toward the earth. She'd expected a sensation like a roller coaster, when the bottom falls out beneath you, but it wasn't like that. Instead, the wind blew against her—and she discovered there was nothing like being cradled by invisible air.

That's when her screams turned to laughter.

Angela lifted her arms like a bird and flew. She floated.

And yes, she fell. But there was joy in the fall.

Because in those forty-five seconds before her instructor pulled the parachute, she learned what Wes had meant about living fearlessly.

Stability was overrated.

Trusting God to catch you . . . that's what life was really about.

44

There was nowhere Angela would rather be than running in her neighborhood next to Kylee on this lovely Saturday afternoon at the end of May. Lilly and Zach were sleeping over at Eva's, so Angela and her oldest had plans for a fun night in.

Their shoes pounded pavement. "Coach is so excited you said yes, Mom."

"I'm excited too." Becoming a nonteacher assistant coach would require a few summer courses, and Angela would need to re-up her first aid certification, but all of it had been surprisingly easy to arrange once she'd decided to take Kylee's advice and give coaching a try. The extra bit of pay would be nice, and she'd get to spend time with Kylee during her junior year that she wouldn't have gotten otherwise. Marc had been great about offering flexible hours, too, during cross-country season.

And who knew where it all might lead.

"Liam and Erin have teased me about getting special treatment from you, but I said they didn't know you very well."

"Hey!"

Kylee twisted out of the way as Angela tried to pinch her.

Months ago she never could have imagined life could look like this. "By the way, I've been meaning to ask if you wanted to invite Liam over for dinner soon."

"You'd be okay with that?"

"I'm not quite sure you're old enough to date yet. But you'll be sixteen next month . . . and I trust you." Angela's heart still seized at the thought of her daughter dating, but the last part was true. Despite the fiasco with the boy in New Zealand, Kylee had shown herself lately to be a responsible girl who was quickly becoming a woman. And Angela couldn't wait to see how her daughter took on the world and changed it for the better.

Kylee wiped a drop of sweat from her forehead before it hit her eye. "Thanks, Mom. Speaking of dating . . . have you talked to Simon?"

"You know I haven't." Angela looked both ways and crossed a semi-busy intersection, Kylee beside her. "He lives in New Zealand, honey. And for all I know, he's already seeing someone else."

Ever since her talk with Eva about happiness, joy, and transformation at the beginning of the month, she'd been working up the courage to call Simon. But she'd allowed fear and excuses to keep her from it. How easy it was to fall back into old patterns.

"Mom. He's totally not dating anyone else because he's crazy about you. And how will you know unless you try? Take the risk. Call him."

"*What I really needed was to learn to experience the grief and realize it was okay to mourn, for life not to be perfect, for life to surprise me sometimes.*" Her own words floated back to her and took on a new meaning. Because like it or not, she'd dreamed of a life with Simon—and if it never came to be, she *would* mourn. Pretending the pain didn't exist wouldn't change that. And if that's what it came to, she'd embrace the grief and ask God to help her shoulder it.

And who knew? Maybe life would indeed surprise her. "All right. I will."

"Right when we get home?"

"Fine, you win. Right when we get home."

"Good." A breeze whistled through the trees as they turned down a quieter street. "Mom, remember back in New Zealand when I asked you how you knew you loved Dad?"

"Yes."

"Are you ready to tell me now?"

Was she? Would the truth tear apart the relationship they'd finally built? Angela prayed not—but whatever Kylee's reaction, a solid relationship had truth as a foundation. "Okay."

So as they zigged and zagged around garbage cans, barking dogs chained to their yards, and sprinklers spraying across the sidewalk, Angela delved into her and Wes's love story. Kylee asked questions, laughed, and listened, from Angela's explanation of the awkward beginning to their first kiss.

And then they reached the culminating moment, the turning point that had changed everything—Kylee herself.

"I already knew you guys got married because you were pregnant with me."

"What?" Angela and Wes had been so careful never to mention that fact in front of their children.

"Duh, Mom. I can do math." Kylee bit her lip. "But what I want to know, I guess, is . . . did you regret it?"

Angela's chest burned, and not from the exertion of jogging. "I used to think so. Not having you—I love you and can't imagine my life without you. But getting married because we were pregnant . . . I used to regret that, I think."

"Why?" Kylee's face seemed purely inquisitive, not devastated as Angela had anticipated.

"I think I saw marriage and motherhood as cages I was forced into. I didn't see that I had another option." Angela put one foot in front of the other. "But there *were* other choices—I could have had an abortion or placed you for adoption. For a long time I didn't recognize that I'd actually made a choice."

"So what made you decide to keep me and marry Dad?"

"From that first ultrasound, I knew you were alive and that you belonged with me. And I loved your dad. It might not have been my plan, but that day I married him, I got what I'd always craved: a family. Funny, because becoming a doctor and continuing down my predetermined course would have likely led to a lonely life, like the one my aunt had."

Kylee grew quiet for several minutes. They turned the last corner before reaching their house, and she stopped. "Thanks for telling me, Mom. That reveals so much to me about who you are and who Dad was." She folded herself into Angela's embrace.

"Oh, sweet girl." Angela kissed the top of her daughter's head and thanked God for a gift she'd never asked for, but had needed all the same.

They headed toward home. When they were a few houses away, Kylee turned to Angela. "So, remember those good vibes we just shared, okay, Mom? And don't be too mad at me." Then she raced toward the house.

What in the world?

Angela followed fast, approaching the front door—and halted so suddenly she nearly tripped.

There on the stoop, Kylee embraced a man and quickly scooted inside.

The man rotated to face Angela, and her heart skittered to a stop. Simon King was as handsome as ever in a plaid button-up rolled to his elbows and jeans, blue TOMS on his feet. And he still took her breath away.

She continued up the walkway, their eyes connected the whole time, until she joined him on the top step. His grin brought with him all the sunshine and laughter she remembered from her time in New Zealand. Because despite all the rain, the brilliance was most memorable.

"What are you doing here?" The question came out weak, choked.

"Eh, I was in the neighborhood."

She pushed his shoulder slightly. "You're about nine thousand miles from home and you just happened to be in my neighborhood?"

His silly grin sobered, and the corners of his eyes creased as he studied her. "I'm sorry I showed up unannounced—though I did have a little help knowing when to arrive and whether my visit might be welcomed."

"Kylee?"

"And Eva. Hope you don't mind. But I couldn't stand not knowing anymore."

Angela gulped. "Knowing what?"

"If you're as mad about me as I am you." He ran his knuckles together. How adorably nervous of him. "I never thought I'd love anyone again, but then you came into my life. You're more than just a story to me, Angela Jamison. You're *the* story. A page-turner. The only problem is that I've reached the end of the manuscript, and I'm desperate to know the ending. But if you don't know it yet, that's all right. I'll wait till you're sure."

He loved her. After all she'd done, after the pain she'd caused him, he still loved her. He'd come all this way to show her how much and was willing to give her space to thrive if she needed it.

He'd so not been part of her plans—but then again, the best things in her life hadn't either.

She pushed past the lump in her throat to speak. "I still don't know how things will work between us since we live in completely different corners of the world, but I can't ignore it anymore." Time for the full truth, whatever the cost. "As much as it scares me, I love you too."

Placing his hands around her waist, Simon tugged her close. "That's the best news I've had all day. All year, really." He leaned in and kissed the tip of her nose. "And about that long distance . . . well, I can write anywhere in the world. So if you're willing to give this thing a go despite the risk—"

"Let me stop you right there." Angela threw her arms around his shoulders and waited until their gazes met again. "Simon King, you are one hundred percent worth the risk."

And to prove it, she pulled him in for a kiss he'd never forget.

45

Diving back into life wasn't easy, but it was necessary.

And Eva couldn't be more grateful for the opportunity.

She carried the last of her bouquet-filled vases and set them on one of twenty or so round tables filling the elegant Manhattan penthouse where the Carlton wedding would take place in a matter of hours. A mixture of lovely scents drifted from the kitchen, and the chatter of people permeated the space that would soon hold two hundred of the most elite socialites in the country. All around Eva, Kimberly's assistants and vendors bustled, arranging everything from ivory tablecloths and crystal goblets to sound equipment and exquisite centerpieces, which featured large hurricane vases and candles.

Once Eva added her flower arrangements, they'd be complete.

Her hands and back ached from several long days bent over flowers and greenery as she'd worked to ensure that each bouquet and centerpiece was perfect. But satisfaction flowed through her as she examined each bloom in the natural light that cascaded through the windows on every side of the room, creating a 360-degree view of the city she loved.

"Eva, hey!"

She turned to find Kimberly walking toward her, four-inch heels snapping against the oak floors. "Kim, everything looks gorgeous."

Kimberly looked at the clusters of flowers. "Especially those. You nailed them, girl."

The bouquets—featuring an understated mixture of astilbe, lily of the valley, astrantia, sweet peas, and jasmine—were made to appear simple but elegant, though the effort put into the effect was more than anyone but Eva would know. And the bridal bouquet also included a sprig of myrtle, a symbol of love and hope.

She'd chosen well, hadn't she?

When the bride had given Eva artistic license, she'd nearly panicked. At first she'd worried about inspiration, especially with such a quick turnaround, but an internal whisper had told her what she needed to do.

Where she needed to go.

And even though the visit to the East Side Garden had been difficult, it had also brought a comfort she hadn't expected. Sitting on that bench where Brent had proposed, leaning on a God who understood grief and had promised to hold her through all of it, she finally was able to let go of the dreams she'd held so tightly to and move forward into the unknown.

Not that she'd ever be "over" Brent and all they'd lost, because that was not how it worked. And it didn't mean the hard days wouldn't come, because they did. But when they did, she wasn't alone. And she knew she'd survive.

"It felt good to create again."

"I'm so glad you said yes."

Someone waved to Kimberly.

"Duty calls. Do you need help getting all of this set up? I can ask Roberto to assist you."

"Maybe. I'll let you know."

"Fab. Still on for brunch tomorrow?"

"Absolutely."

Kimberly squeezed her arm and then flitted off to do her thing.

Eva got to work placing the centerpieces on the tables, adjusting ribbons, and fluffing baby's breath so each arrangement was flawless. When she finished, she sighed at the beauty of the venue. It had been lovely before, but now, with the decor and flowers set, it had become the perfect blend of classy and modern.

Soon a bride would have her happy ending.

Something pinched in Eva's gut. Being here, in this romantic setting, made her long for Marc.

Whoa. The realization struck her.

Her first thought hadn't been about Brent.

What did that mean?

Straightening, she grabbed her purse and headed off to find Kimberly, walking past the long oak and stained glass bar into the kitchen, where she'd seen her friend disappear a few moments before. Here the smell of everything from steak to lobster, fresh tomatoes to spices like garlic and onion became more powerful. The catering staff was beginning to arrive, and the chef and her sous chefs worked on some sort of bisque and gave direction to the staff for plating salads.

Kimberly chatted with a squat woman arranging gourmet cupcakes on a large spiral stand.

Eva approached them, and Kimberly introduced her to the baker, Elyse.

"She seriously makes the best cakes and desserts I have ever tasted in my life. Not only that, but she sells gourmet hot chocolate at her shop just up the road. It's to die for. I know you hate chocolate, but even you would love it." Kimberly went on chatting with Elyse as Eva said goodbye and slipped from the room, pain wrenching her chest.

Hot chocolate. Even the mere mention of it made her think of him.

Angela had said Marc was just as miserable as she was. The

thought had spurred Eva to almost contact him several times during the last month. But she didn't want to start something again that her heart wasn't ready to see through. Not again. She couldn't do that to him.

You're ready now.

She nearly stopped in her tracks. The whisper had come from somewhere deep in her soul.

And she knew it to be true.

As she headed down the elevator from the penthouse, Eva whipped out her phone and searched Google Maps. She copied an address into a fresh text message, along with the words, Meet me in fifteen?

The elevator doors opened on the bottom floor, and she stepped out as a return message dinged.

Okay.

A brief response, but that was all right. He was coming.

Nerves flitted through her, but she felt the rightness in it all. She walked past the doorman and made her way to Elyse's little bakery, open for another hour today.

Eva entered and waited in line. The bakery was adorably French in décor, and crowded to boot, but when she caught a glimpse of the baked goods lining the display case, she could understand why. Brownies, gorgeous cakes, and unique cookies were only the beginning. The neatly arranged case also exhibited an array of high-end pastries, some of which Eva couldn't identify without the small placard in front of them.

But she hadn't come here for any of those.

When it was her turn, she ordered a drink, then found a seat once served. Finally, she took a tentative sip.

Blech.

Still as awful as ever.

Oh no. This just wouldn't do.

After checking the time, she hurried to the cashier and asked him to surprise her. A peach tea was delivered into her hands, and when she sat down and tasted it, flavor exploded on her tongue.

And color . . . at last it burst all around her. Eva couldn't help the tear that fell from her eye.

Just as she swiped it away, Marc slipped into the chair next to her. "Hi." He folded his hands together on top of the table.

She breathed in the sight of him. He'd let his beard grow back and was once again dressed in pressed slacks and a button-up shirt. Eva had gotten so used to seeing him rumpled and unshaven—so casual—like he'd been during the ultra-marathon. Of course, she liked this too.

She just liked him.

Loved him.

So tell him. Right.

"Hi." Eva set down her cup. "Thanks for coming."

Marc watched her, intense emotions playing across his features. What was he thinking? "How are you, Eva?"

"I ordered a hot chocolate." Smooth as always. Oy.

Surprise and questions mixed in his eyes. "I thought you hated it."

"Actually, I do. I thought I could make myself like it, and I tried, but nope."

"Okay."

She was totally blundering this. "But then I got a peach tea. And I found it refreshing and delightful."

"Uh, good for you?" Now he was just plain bewildered. "Why am I here, Eva?"

"All right, so I had this whole speech prepared—well, I kind of came up with it in the last like two minutes. But anyway, I was hoping I could tell you that my tastes have changed, that I like both hot chocolate and coffee, that I don't have to choose one over the other. That they can both be part of my life and I'm only sorry I didn't see it sooner. But then I hated the hot chocolate, and my analogy was ruined." She closed the chasm between them and reached out her hand, touching his.

His gaze roamed her face. Finally, his eyes met hers completely. "There's nothing worse than a ruined analogy."

"I know, right?"

"So, for the sake of argument, let's say your analogy had worked out—and you hadn't completely despised the best drink that ever existed. What would we really be talking about?"

"I think you know the answer to that. At least, I hope you do."

A full-on grin split his face, and he scooted her chair closer to his, the legs scraping against the tile floor. "And if you *had* liked the hot chocolate, does that mean I might have persuaded you to one day even love it?" He tucked a strand of her hair behind her ear and watched her with those eyes that saw so much, then retook her hands in his own.

"If I had in fact liked it, I would say that there would be no persuasion needed." Eva leaned in, bringing her lips to linger just in front of his. "That the finer qualities of hot chocolate had me head over heels from the first sip."

Then her lips met his, and Eva Jamison knew without a doubt that a brand-new adventure awaited her if she just kept moving forward.

One step at a time.

Acknowledgments

As I sit down to write this page of thank-yous, I've just sent off the final proofs for *The Joy of Falling*. I am nearly in tears thinking about how much emotion, time, and energy I've put into this story.

But it's not just me who has worked hard on it or had an influence on what it has become. I'm so grateful for all of the wonderful people who have stuck by me and helped to give this little story its wings.

Thanks first to my readers. All of you are the reason I write. If even one of you feels hope after reading my stories, then my work has been totally and completely worth it.

Joanne Nicholls: Thanks for participating in the contest to name Simon King. It was so fun creating a character with your name!

Lisa Davis: Your insight into grief and the counseling process were so incredibly helpful. Thank you for pouring into other people and giving hope to those who need it most (including ME).

Ruth Douthitt: Besides being an amazing friend, you are such an inspiring person. Thanks for sharing your running expertise with me.

Kara Isaac: You totally rock for reading an early draft of this book and helping me make the New Zealand and running information as authentic as possible. You saved me from many a gaffe. Any mistakes are totally mine.

My Panera Ladies (Tina, Sara, Liz, Ruth, and Jen): Where would I be without you?? Sometimes our writing nights are the only thing that keeps me sane in an industry that can feel very lonely. Your encouragement means the world!

GLAM Girls (Melissa, Gabe, Alena): Thanks for talking me off cliffs and brainstorming with me and encouraging me and all the things you do exactly when I need them most. Love you ladies with all my heart.

Liz Johnson: For all of those Elevate-and-Panera writing dates, movies, texts, emails, and hugs, thank you. You're an answer to my prayers too.

Rachelle Gardner: So glad we get to do this together. Thank you for your consistently amazing advice and support of my work.

Kimberly Carlton: It was so wonderful getting to meet you in person at long last. Our visit confirmed what I already knew to be true: you are AWESOME! This book wouldn't be what it is without your insightful questions and gentle prodding. Thanks so much.

My team at HCCP Fiction (Kerri, Paul, Allison, Amanda, Becky, Matt, Laura, and Kristen): What a privilege it is to work with you all. I'm grateful every day that I am so blessed.

My family, especially Dad, Kristin, and Nancy: I literally couldn't do this without you. The way you love me and my kiddos gives me the time and ability to spill my stories onto a page, and I'm so thankful.

My boys: I am so proud to watch the young men you're growing into and the way you love others and God. Being your mommy is my best job!

Mike: You are a steady rock I can lean on, and you always have my back. I love you and this crazy life we share.

And God: The fact you can take the greatest grief of my life and turn it into *this* is still so incredible to me. Thank you for allowing me to share the joy you've brought into my life despite the pain I've experienced. You gave me the words when I had none that were adequate. Please use them to deliver hope to those who need it.

Discussion Questions

1. Are you a runner? Would you have felt more like Eva (excited) or Angela (hesitant) at the prospect of completing an ultra-marathon? Why?

2. What was your favorite part of the story (e.g., favorite character, scene, plot point, etc.)?

3. Did you relate more to Eva or Angela? Why?

4. C. S. Lewis said, "Grief is like a long valley, a winding valley where any bend may reveal a totally new landscape." What do you think this quote means? How do you see it relating to Angela and Eva's journey?

5. Eva loves to consider the meaning or symbolism of different flowers. If you were to choose a flower to represent your own love story (or your favorite kind of love story), which would you pick?
   - Pink carnation: "I will never forget you."
   - Lavender: Devotion
   - Peony: Shame, bashfulness, anger
   - Pansy: Thoughtfulness and remembrance
   - Daffodil: New beginnings
   - Rue: Regret

6. Was Eva and Marc's hesitation to date each other

understandable? Did they handle the strangeness of the situation well?

7. In your opinion, what is the difference between happiness and joy (if one exists)?

8. At one point, Angela says, "Like most moms, I often sacrifice what I want for my kids. I did that in my marriage too. In fact, before coming here, I hadn't thought about what I want, or what really brings me joy, in forever." Can you relate to this statement (either for yourself or someone you're close to)? Why do you think this happens, and what can moms do to avoid it? Or should they simply embrace it as part of motherhood?

9. What was the most romantic gesture in the book?

10. Can joy come from heartache? Why or why not?

Brought together across time by a love
of story, three women in England fight to
defy expectations, dream new dreams,
and welcome love into their lives.

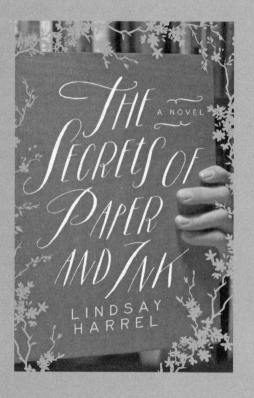

THOMAS NELSON
Since 1798

Read more from Lindsay Harrel!

Two Sisters, One Heart
Transplant, and a Bucket List

About the Author

Lindsay Harrel is a lifelong book nerd who lives in Arizona with her young family and two golden retrievers in serious need of training. She's held a variety of writing and editing jobs over the years and now juggles stay-at-home mommyhood with writing novels. When she's not writing or chasing after her children, Lindsay enjoys making a fool of herself at Zumba, curling up with anything by Jane Austen, and savoring sour candy one piece at a time.

Connect with her at LindsayHarrel.com
Facebook: LindsayHarrel
Instagram: lindsayharrelauthor
Twitter: @LindsayHarrel